Danica Winters is a m
author who writes books ...
to drive emotion through suspense and occasio...,
touch of magic. When she's not working, she can be
found in the wilds of Montana, testing her patience while
she tries to hone her skills at various crafts—quilting,
pottery and painting are not her areas of expertise. She
believes the cup is neither half-full nor half-empty, but
it better be filled with wine. Visit her website at
authordanicawinters.com

Justine Davis lives on Puget Sound in Washington State,
watching big ships and the occasional submarine go by
and sharing the neighbourhood with assorted wildlife,
including a pair of bald eagles, deer, a bear or two, and a
tailless raccoon. In the few hours when she's not planning,
plotting or writing her next book, her favourite things are
photography, knitting her way through a huge yarn stash
and driving her restored 1967 Corvette Roadster—top
down, of course. Connect with Justine on her website,
justinedavis.com, at X @justine_d_davis or on Facebook
justinedaredavis

Discover more at millsandboon.co.uk

MYSTERY ON THE RANGE

DANICA WINTERS

COLTON IN THE WILD

JUSTINE DAVIS

MILLS & BOON

First Published in Great Britain 2025
by Mills & Boon, an imprint of HarperCollins*Publishers* Ltd
1 London Bridge Street, London, SE1 9GF

www.harpercollins.co.uk

HarperCollins*Publishers*
Macken House, 39/40 Mayor Street Upper,
Dublin 1, D01 C9W8, Ireland

Mystery on the Range © 2025 Danica Winters
Colton in the Wild © 2025 Harlequin Enterprises ULC

Special thanks and acknowledgement are given to Justine Davis for her contribution to *The Coltons of Alaska* series.

ISBN: 978-0-263-39720-8

0725

This book contains FSC™ certified paper and other controlled sources to ensure responsible forest management.

For more information visit: www.harpercollins.co.uk/green

Printed and Bound in the UK using 100% Renewable Electricity at CPI Group (UK) Ltd, Croydon, CR0 4YY

MYSTERY ON THE RANGE

DANICA WINTERS

For all of those who have never fit in,
lean into what makes you different.

It is what makes you awesomely you,
and it is likely your greatest strength.

Prologue

The man's screams pierced the evening air. The wails of pain and terror echoed across the glacial moraines of the park and crashed down on her, making the hairs on Jamie Trapper's arms rise.

She'd never heard a sound like it before, but she held no doubts that it was the call of a dying man.

She hadn't brought a gun, and she knew her best friend Matt Goldstock hadn't, either, but she instinctively looked to his hip as he stopped ahead of her on the dirt trail leading to Avalanche Lake.

"What in the world was that?" Matt asked, turning toward her.

Matt was a good man, but not well versed in the ways of the wilderness, especially not an area rife with dangerous predators—both of the four- and two-legged varieties.

"That means we need to run." She cinched her backpack tighter and took off in a full sprint toward the sound as the man cried out again.

She found strength in the fact he was still making the strong, haunting sound. If he was fighting, he was still alive.

Her footfalls crunched in the gravel of the trail as she

moved as fast as her body would allow. She hadn't moved this quickly since...*that night*. She couldn't think about that now. No. She shook the thoughts of John away.

There was a strange, animalistic scream in the dusk and the man's cry followed, but it was muted, warbling. They were locked in battle. Man versus beast.

If she had to guess, beast was winning.

She sent out a silent bid for the man to persevere and push through, to summon the power and animalistic nature within him to come out on top—or at least continue to survive.

She pushed herself harder.

Matt brushed by her and she tried to keep pace. Her lungs ached as she pushed up the mountain as the elevation grew exponentially. She'd spent too many days in the flatlands rodeoing and it was catching up with her.

It angered her she couldn't catch Matt, but she wasn't about to tell him to slow down when a man's life hung in the balance.

Matt's foot slipped in the gravel and he grabbed an exposed root to steady himself.

"Are you okay?" she asked between heavy breaths as she caught up.

He nodded but he was gasping for breath. "Go."

She drove forward. Pushing over the crest of the gain in the trail, something flashed across the path in front of her. In the thin light, all she saw was a dark mass that she could identify as animal and nothing more.

Ahead of her, amid torn-up dirt and a smattering of blood, was a man.

His clothes were ripped, and blood gushed from his forehead and down his face. "Matt!" She screamed. "Matt! Get help!"

She unclicked her pack and dropped it to the ground beside the man, pulling out her emergency medical kit.

There was so much blood on his face and clothing that it looked as if he had bathed in red. Even his khaki hiking pants were nearly covered. It appeared as if the animal had mostly attacked his upper body, head and neck area, but without pulling back his shirt, she couldn't be sure.

Matt moved beside her. "Let me do this." He gave her a knowing look as he pressed his fingers against the man's neck and checked his vital signs. "Don't worry, he's still alive. For now."

She hadn't noticed how badly her hands were shaking until he motioned toward them. That was new. She'd been so good in emergencies until Wyoming.

Until Wyoming.

It was humbling how a person's entire existence could change when a solitary haunting moment was consumed by tragedy.

Chapter One

Being stalked by a mountain lion was like a failing relationship: a person rarely saw the deathblow coming. And man, oh man, had Pierce missed the signs that his breakup was imminent.

Even though it had been six months since his ex, Haven Andrus, had called off their engagement, he was still fielding calls about what was supposed to have been their wedding date this week. He laid the phone down, just having acknowledged the latest unprovoked attack via text message from his great-aunt Kim who had, for some unknown reason, decided it was a great idea to reach out with condolences.

He hadn't needed the reminder that today was supposed to be his rehearsal dinner.

Yes, he was glad his cousin had set a reminder in her mother's phone—but it would have been even better if she had remembered to delete the stupid thing. It would have saved Pierce the salt in the wound.

As if saying a clipped "Thanks" didn't make it clear enough that Pierce didn't want to delve into the emotions and pain that filled this week, his phone pinged again with another message from his aunt. This time he ignored it.

He couldn't handle chatting. Emotions weren't his strong suit, and his aunt was far too much like all the women in their family—they just wanted to pick apart anything and everything that involved feelings until all that was left on the ground were bones.

Though today was supposed to be his day off from work as a ranger at Glacier National Park, he'd picked up a shift for his friend Vince Sanford. The worst part was that Vince had taken the days off to be his best man. He had offered to take Pierce anywhere he wanted for the week, but the last thing Pierce had needed was to have more free time to think.

He needed to run a chainsaw and pick up logs until his fingers were raw and torn beneath the fingertips of his gloves and sweat pooled at the base of his throat. Better, he needed to pound at the earth with a pickax and shovel— to tear and gnaw at the dirt like it was the feelings that he needed to turn to dust and bury.

Yes, work would keep him busy and be the catharsis he needed so desperately—especially at Glacier. This summer they were expecting to host at least three million visitors. Those kinds of numbers brought big-city problems to the backcountry of Montana. To cap it off, many tourists expected the amenities of cities but were instead faced with narrow winding roads, the realities of winter weather in summer months, predatory animals, elevation sickness and the unpredictability of nature. Usually, that meant he had all kinds of shenanigans to deal with.

At least as a federal employee he had a lot of freedom in his job. Today, he was running the southern boundary of the park near Apgar. Last week, he'd been working up north near Polebridge. He wished he was back there; up north there were fewer people and the residents who lived there year-round were some of the quirkiest around. His favorite townie was a woman named Poppy, who had a two-hundred-pound gray wolf named Luna she walked through the center of the one-laned town every day. Sometimes Luna even wore a little bone in her hair.

There was a rumor Poppy had found Luna in an abandoned wolf's den after the mother wolf had been hit by a tourist's car. Luna had been the only cub that had survived. There was also another take on the tale that she had stolen the pup from a wolf den. The latest he'd heard was far less entertaining: Poppy had merely bought the pup from a dealer near Missoula.

He liked to think Poppy had been doing something philanthropic—even if it was something he could write her a ticket for doing. In a small town, where he needed folks to be his friend and allies, it often worked to his advantage to turn a blind eye. Luna was happy and well-kept, and Poppy loved her immensely and didn't put humans or the wolf in any situation where either could be hurt. So, if she had saved the wolf pup from starvation, he was okay with how things had turned out. Plus, it was nice seeing the pair.

He drove around the long, snaking line of cars that was barely moving as the tourists poured out of the gates near West Glacier. He gave Lloyd, his favorite gatekeeper and park employee, a wave as he drove through the entry gates and made his way inside the park.

Apgar was just closing for the day and the doors to the markets were half shut and waiting for the last straggling customers to leave. Soon the bells on the doors would stop constantly dinging with the comings and goings of the visitors purchasing little mountain goat magnets, Sasquatch playing cards and T-shirts with *Glacier* printed across the backs.

Oh, and he couldn't forget the bear spray. Everyone would drop forty dollars on a can of bear spray that they would throw away at the end of their trip. Several local kids had learned they could hit the garbage cans both outside the airport and inside the park, when the maintenance crews weren't around, to find unused bear sprays they could re-sell outside the gates of the park for twenty bucks. They made a killer profit, from what he could tell—they always had a line.

He couldn't begrudge their hustle. If the local kids wanted to benefit from the constant barrage of guests, kudos to them. If anything, he just wished that they'd had bear spray to sell when he'd been a kid so he could have run the same hustle. It really was brilliant.

His phone pinged several times with a series of messages as he neared the main ranger's headquarters. The build-ing was new—well at least by the park's standards, hav-ing been built in the early 2000s—and it had been kept in the style of the other chestnut-brown-painted log buildings that adorned the village. Its windows were framed in white, which it gave it a quaint charm. In fact, it was so charming and in line with the other buildings of the town that no one ever noticed it was tucked back behind the shops—they'd hidden it perfectly in plain sight.

As he pulled into his designated parking spot, his phone pinged. He glanced at the message.

There had been an attack. Any and all available rangers were to report. Normally, as a National Park Service Spe-cial Agent, he would just handle matters affiliated with law enforcement, but according to the GPS on his computer in his truck, he was the nearest available responder.

According to Dispatch, the animal attack had happened close to Avalanche Lake. From the GPS coordinates they'd sent him, it was about two miles up the trail. Little was known except the man attacked had been alone at the time of the event and, at the time of the call, was still alive. The hikers who had found him were with him now and awaiting help.

He typed a quick message to Dispatch, letting them know he was taking the call and advising them to notify Two Bear Air that they would need an airlift for the victim to Logan Medical Health Center in Kalispell.

He pulled out of his spot at headquarters and sped through the town, turning on his lights and sirens. He weaved between cars and made his way down the road toward Avalanche Lake. It normally took thirty minutes to get there for the average driver, but he could do it in fifteen.

Without a doubt, he would beat the life-flight helicopter. He would have to sprint up the mountain to reach the victim and get him stabilized and ready for flight before their arrival.

As he raced down the road, he did a mental checklist, going through all the items in his kit, and what he would do when he arrived. If the man was as bad off as Pierce assumed, he would be lucky to be alive. Big cats loved to go after the neck, and they normally attacked from behind. If it was a bear attack, it was probably a grizzly that had gotten a hold of him. In which case, it was good there were other people with him as the animal was likely to come back and finish the kill.

Either way, the man was likely bleeding profusely and

would need a high level of care. He would have to get it under control before he could make any moves.

It took fourteen minutes and forty-two seconds to arrive on scene. It was a personal best. When he pulled up to the trailhead, there was nowhere to park, but he pulled to a stop blocking the main gate. The visitors to the park could work around him.

He grabbed his medic's bag and rushed out onto the trail. As he jogged up the winding trail, his boots clacked on the wooden boards until he hit the dirt. The trail was a beautiful one, and normally he enjoyed taking his out-of-state friends on the well-groomed path to the crystal-blue lake fed by waterfalls. Yet today he barely noticed the pines as he ran through them and past the babbling creek.

He checked his phone. Two Bear was still on the ground and wouldn't be taking off for at least twenty more minutes as they were waiting on their flight crew. They wouldn't be on scene for another forty-five minutes, at least.

If the victim was down where Pierce assumed he was, there wasn't a location where the helicopter could land. They would have to run lines to him, and they would have to airlift the man out.

It would be a tricky save.

Nothing about this call was going to be easy.

As he twisted through the first mile or so, his lungs started to fight. It wasn't a huge elevation gain, but running with gear was tough. His thighs and calves burned. He just needed to get past the initial pain. It was unusual, but he loved that feeling, that pull from his body telling him to stop and yield to the ache. It was powerful to keep going, to take control and refuse to quit.

Rounding a corner, he nearly ran into a couple who were

Mystery on the Range

wide-eyed with shock. The woman put her hands up in panic. "There's a man…" She pointed in the opposite direction. "That way…"

"He's not doing good." The man, who was wearing high-end hiking clothes, finished her sentence.

"But he's still alive?" Pierce asked.

The man nodded.

"How much farther?" he asked.

"Quarter mile," the man said as he and the woman he was with stepped to the side of the dirt trail to let him by.

He nodded as he ran past them. "Thanks," he said, trying to hide the fact that he was winded by his run.

The woman had been terrified by what she had witnessed, so much so that she and the man she was with had left the scene. That in and of itself was strange. Most people stayed to witness the turmoil unfolding, classic rubbernecking. Bystanders were common and, in situations like these in the woods, they could even be extremely helpful.

Checking his breathing, Pierce sped up. If the man was only another quarter of a mile or so ahead, he wasn't as far in as the GPS coordinates he'd been given, and he was grateful.

The smell of the attack hit him first; it was strong with the ripped earth, decaying pine needles and the metallic scent of blood.

He hated that smell.

The last time he'd come across a scene like this had been on a call to an unwitnessed death by Logan Pass, where a woman had taken her own life at the base of a tree overlooking a glacial moraine. It was a memory that regularly haunted his thoughts.

Pierce turned the corner and came into a small opening.

Blood was splattered over the bunchgrass and smeared on the ponderosa pine nearest him. It was far worse than the woman's self-inflicted gunshot wound. There were masses of overturned dirt where there must have been a fight for survival.

It looked like a murder scene. From the volume of blood around the space, he found it hard to believe the man was still alive.

Moving carefully through the area, he came over the small hill and found a man with his back to him, staring down at the ground. He was wearing a Western-styled, red-plaid shirt and Wrangler jeans. Odd clothing for hiking, but he'd seen stranger. The man didn't seem to hear him as he approached.

Crouching beside the victim was a blond woman.

Pierce slowed down and tried to catch his breath. He didn't want to bring any additional stress to the situation. He had to be calm, cool and collected.

"Hey, guys," he said, trying to catch his breath. "My name is Pierce Hauser. I'm a ranger here at Glacier Park. I'm here to help."

The woman squatting beside the cowboy turned and looked up at him with vibrant blue eyes and gave him an appreciative nod of welcome.

The cowboy turned. "Glad to see ya." His face was stoic. If Pierce had to guess, the guy had seen trauma before. "We did what we could to try and stop the bleeding. He's doin' better now, but his pulse is getting' darn slow." He motioned toward the crouching woman.

From where he was standing, all he could see was the man's bloodied leather hiking boots. One of the boots was off and lying next to his socked foot in the middle of the trail. The cowboy stepped out of the way. The victim came fully into view.

Pierce walked over, trying not to stare at the woman who was wiping some of the blood from the man's face with a wet bandana. She was cooing soft words to the man, telling him he was going to be all right. Pierce appreciated her attempts to mollify the victim, but she had to know just as well as he did that with this amount of blood loss death was a real possibility.

The woman looked up at him with those striking eyes. Her eyes were the same crystal blue color as Avalanche Lake. Yet they looked far more haunted thanks to the scene around them. "His blood pressure is low. If we don't get him out of here soon, I don't think he's going to make it."

He nodded. "A helicopter is on the way. They'll be here soon. It looks like you have done a fantastic job getting him stabilized. What's your name?"

"Jamie... Jamie Trapper."

"Jamie, do you mind if I get in there and take his pulse?"

He motioned for him to take her position and she stood up and moved away from the man. As she stepped back, she exhaled with what he took to be relief.

He could understand the feeling, he knew it only too well.

The man's face was beyond recognition. There were lacerations across his nose and cheek, and he may have lost his left eye. It was hard to tell due to the swelling around the socket and all that was damaged.

Jamie had done a nice job cleaning up the excess blood and dabbing at the wounds, but they were still seeping blood. The fact that there was seepage was good—dead men didn't bleed.

"Does anybody know his name?" He squatted down beside the man and took his sluggish pulse, realizing he was dangerously bradycardic. "Has he been conscious at all since anybody arrived on scene?"

"We don't know his name. And, he hasn't woken up. Sorry. I tried to get him to come to, but we got nothing." Jamie shook her head, her blond hair falling loose from behind her ear where she had tucked it. She pushed it back, her action almost angry, like her hair had done something wrong by breaking free in such a moment.

They had placed a polyester belt around the man's thigh and wrapped it tight with a stick. The tourniquet was high and perfectly placed on the femoral artery. The woman had known what she was doing. Farther down the man's leg was a large gash in his jeans. They were nearly black with blood. He pulled the fabric back, exposing four smooth lacerations on the man's thigh.

Just below the lacerations was a bite mark. Two large canines, not far apart. From the looks of it, a mountain lion had been behind the attack.

He sucked in a breath. This event was about to become a major problem. Not only was the news of this attack going to be blasted across the papers, but they were going to have to deal with the fallout. Every action he took, or didn't take, was going to come under scrutiny. His butt was going to be on the line.

Plus, they were about to have a wave of panic throughout the park.

Cats rarely attacked people, but when they did, they didn't do it just once. When they started attacking humans, it meant they were desperate, and desperation only meant heightened danger.

Chapter Two

Jamie stared at the blood on her hands as she stood beside the creek before bending down to wash them. It was hardly the first time her hands had been covered in blood, but the last time she had promised herself she'd never be in that kind of situation again. That was what she got for saying *never*.

However, there was no way she and Matt could have ignored the man lying in the trail. It hadn't taken long for the helicopter to drop the line to the ranger and airlift the injured man out. And, as soon as he was gone, and the helicopter's thumping blades grew faint in the distance, it was almost as if nothing had happened. Silence returned. There was simply the sounds of forest animals and the babbling water. The only evidence of chaos was the blood.

She'd spent so many days on the rodeo circuit across the US that she'd seen all kinds of injuries—everything from goring to men crushed under trailers.

The last time she'd seen an injury this bad had been when her former boyfriend had gotten pinned under a bull six months ago. She could still smell the arena dirt in the air. When she'd gone to sleep that night, the collective sound of the crowd's gasp had haunted her dreams. That horrible night, she had moved over that fence and run to his side before the bull had even been pushed back to the pens by the clowns, but she hadn't cared.

The only thing she had thought about at that moment was John.

She'd known the moment the bull had landed on him what the outcome would be. The gray Brahman was one of the largest bulls she had ever seen, well over a ton. Even though John was wearing all the protective gear, there was little it could do to protect a man from that kind of impact to the head.

He had died instantly, but she had held him in her arms until the paramedics had forced her to let him go.

She'd tried to remain on the rodeo circuit. It was what John would have wanted her to do, but she had lost her taste for it after he'd gotten killed. Whenever Matt went out, all she could think about was John. Matt had been John's best friend, too.

Matt was married to a woman named Sally, out of Juneau, and they rarely saw each other, but he was faithful, and Jamie loved him for his loyalty. Ever since John's death, Jamie had been traveling with Matt, and he'd supported her when she'd told him she wanted to go back to Montana and to her family's ranch after her father and brother had been found dead.

Thankfully, her brother Cameron had welcomed her with open arms. He had put her up in the main house and even given her and Matt jobs with the horses and cattle. She appreciated all he'd done for her when he could have just as easily told her to pound sand after she had been away from the ranch for so long. He had even gone as far as to give her a cut of the property even though she hadn't been named in their father's will. Leonard had always been the kind of man who'd valued a son over a daughter, so when she had heard she and her sister had been left out, she hadn't really been surprised.

She also hadn't been heartbroken when she'd heard about her father's death or surprised by the circumstances that surrounded it.

"Are you okay?" A man's voice pulled her from her thoughts.

She had no idea how long she had been standing at the side of the creek looking from her fingers to the bubbling blue water as it rushed down the purple rocks and splashed and pooled in the holes and eddies created by hundreds of years of floods and droughts.

She turned to see the ranger standing behind her. His dark hair was closely cropped, and his ranger's uniform was unmarred. She glanced down at her own clothing. Her T-shirt was covered in the stranger's blood, as were the knees of her jeans. He probably wondered why she was hiking in jeans, but he could wonder all he wanted. At least she had swapped out her Tony Lamas for a pair of hiking boots. Few things could get her out of her cowboy boots.

"Jamie?" he asked, reaching over and touching her arm.

She jerked away from his hand. "Sorry," she said, instantly regretting her action. "You're fine touching me... I... You just caught me off guard." She reached over and touched his arm, but he frowned at her fingers and she let them drift off his brown shirt and her hand fell to her side.

"Are you doing okay?" he repeated.

He looked over at the place where the man had been lying. There was a flat spot in the shape of a coffin where the board had pressed into the dirt.

"I'm fine. This just brought up some things I thought I had dealt with, that's all."

"Ah, I see." He nodded. "This kind of thing has a way of doing that. When I first became a special agent, I didn't realize one of my primary jobs would be working as a paramedic."

"Is it really?" She'd had no idea.

He pinched his lips like he hated the idea but had resigned himself to his reality. "Yeah. More often than not, I'm the first responder. This time, unfortunately, it was you. However, you did an excellent job and everything that I could've done. You should be proud of yourself. You saved that man's life."

"Did you find out what his name was?" she asked.

"His ID said Anthony Lewis."

She glanced up at the sky where the blue helicopter had disappeared. Matt was sitting down on a large pine, tapping away on the Garmin GPS and messaging device, probably letting Sally know he was at least safe.

"You and I both know that Anthony isn't out of the woods. He may not survive the flight, let alone the day. He lost a lot of blood. I've seen people die from less."

His eyes softened, like he wanted to ask her about what she had seen, but he held back and she was grateful that he did. Thinking about John was hard enough. She couldn't even imagine talking about him at that moment. She wasn't the type to cry and especially not in front of a handsome stranger with a badge.

"I have, too, but I'm optimistic for him because of you," he said, his voice supplicating.

She knew he was desperately trying to make her feel better and bring some solace to her, and though her emotions were still in turmoil, she decided to let him in. "Thank you, Ranger Hauser. Or is it 'Special Agent'?" she asked, glancing at his nameplate on his chest. She couldn't help but notice his well-defined pecs just under the surface of his brown shirt.

"Call me Pierce."

She gave a slight nod, but her cheeks warmed and she didn't know precisely why.

She would be lying if she said she hadn't noticed his muscular chest before, when he had been holding Anthony's body steady as it was lifted in the air by the helo crew. His arms were just as good. He worked out, but he wasn't entirely perfectly chiseled—he did have a little paunch that she would call one step away from a dad bod and admittedly made her even more attracted.

As she realized what she was thinking, right on the heels of John's memory, she snapped herself back to reality. She had no business thinking about the park ranger this way. He was a stranger who had been brought into her life by a tragedy; he would disappear in a few moments only to become a memory and a shadow in a story she would tell around campfires to come.

"I just wish there was something more I could do to help." She didn't know where her statement emanated from, but the moment it escaped her lips, she knew it was the truth. She felt so impotent standing there, not knowing if the man would live or die and likely never going to find out one way or the other.

Anthony had disappeared into the air and from her life. Beyond this moment in the woods, they had no other connections unless she continued to help—at least until they got word on his status.

"Is that your boyfriend over there?" he asked, motioning toward Matt.

She laughed aloud, almost snorting. "He's my best friend. His name is Matt. He's a bull rider and he is probably on the Garmin with his wife right now."

"Oh, glad to hear."

His last words fell flat and sat in the silence between them for a long awkward moment. "He was the one who really saved Anthony—if he makes it." She pulled at the back of her neck nervously. "Do you know what exactly attacked him?"

Pierce looked around like an animal was going to jump out of the woods at the mere mention of one. "I've been searching the ground for prints. Based on the wounds and the tracks I've found, I'm sure it was a mountain lion. Looks like just one. Probably a tom. They are looking for their own territories this time of year. Maybe he ran into it, but that is unlikely."

"So, what does that mean? Do you think the cat was stalking him?"

"I'm going to have to do some tracking to find out." He sighed. "And we'll have to find this cat. He needs to be taken care of."

"You're going to kill him?"

Pierce cringed. "I'd like to say no. If we can trap the cat and get him into a zoo somewhere, then maybe we can save him. Otherwise, his future may well hang in the balance. There are a few circumstances that could get the cat off the hook, though, if we could prove it wasn't really at fault—rather that it was human error that brought on the attack."

"*If* we find him or if we can prove the cat isn't at fault?"

Pierce put his hands up. "Wait… *We?*" he asked. "I can't

possibly take you with me while I'm tracking down a potentially dangerous animal which has already attacked one
person and is more likely to attack another."

Matt stuffed the Garmin in his pocket and sauntered over
toward them. "Sally is freaking out," he said, his words
slow in true Matt fashion. He didn't seem to notice that he
was interrupting, not even when Jamie shot him a look.

He wasn't always on top of things, but he had gotten
more than his fair share of concussions while riding bulls.
It was starting to show and was one of the reasons she had
wanted him to join her in getting off the circuit for a while.
He'd been great at the ranch for the last few months. Maybe
she could even get Sally to come down, eventually.

"I'm sure she is," Jamie said. "She isn't going to like
what we are about to do, either."

Ranger Hauser jerked as he looked over at her. "Don't
you even think about it."

She waved him off. "You can let us help you willingly,
or we can just follow behind you like little lost hikers. You
pick."

He grumbled something under his breath. "You do know
I have the power to arrest you, right?"

She smiled, knowing full well that she had won the battle. "You can't say you really want to be out in the woods
alone with a rogue mountain lion on the loose. Besides,
we can send Matt to the trailhead to let people know to
turn around."

That elicited a smile, and it made him even more rak-
ishly handsome. "There is a ranger on the way to close the
trail, but it would be good to have Matt head down and herd
tourists back who may have started up the trail."

"See, we are already proving invaluable." She sent him

her best smile and she wasn't sure, but she could have almost sworn that a red hue rose in his cheeks.

Matt looked over at Jamie and gave her a wink. "Just make sure my ass doesn't get chewed up by a mountain lion while I'm hiking alone, okay?"

She laughed. "You got it. Just call us when you get down to the trailhead. The good news is that you are probably going to run into tourists soon."

Matt nodded. "Fine, boss." He glanced over at Ranger Hauser. "Don't let her get hurt. She is good people."

Pierce smirked. "I have a feeling that when it comes to her and me, I'm the one who is in greater danger—and not from the mountain lion. This lady seems like hell on wheels."

Chapter Three

Pierce couldn't believe he had agreed to let Jamie tag along with him, and yet he had known without a doubt she was going to follow him one way or another. When it came to hardheaded women, he'd learned a long time ago that it was best to just let them do their thing. Some battles just weren't worth the fight.

If they came back without incident, he wouldn't even have to explain himself to his patrol captain. If push came to shove and Patrol Captain Reynolds met Jamie, he would see the futility he had faced as well.

He looked back at the blond woman and tried to control his smile. He'd be lying to himself if he tried to say he didn't like women like her. Sure, they drove him to distraction. His mother and sister were the same way, but they kept life interesting. If anything, they'd set him up to need women like them in his life—if a woman were a pushover, he wouldn't have known what to do with her.

"Did you see something?" she asked, looking at him and then down to the ground in fear.

As she did, he realized that as much as she was putting on a brave front in coming out here to help him hunt down a big cat, she was truly terrified. He couldn't blame her. For all they knew, the mountain lion had been watching them take care of Anthony the entire time. That was a lion's way—watching over their kill or returning to it to feed later.

There were studies that showed that in Yellowstone Park, the cats would have several caches and when wolves bothered them, they would lead them to one of the caches to get them off their trail. It worked wonderfully for the cats and the wolves got a free meal.

He had to admit, he didn't want to have a pack of wolves roll up on him and Jamie, either.

There was a break in the underbrush ahead of them and in the soft soil was a paw print. He pointed at it. "We are on the right trail."

She nodded, but she had a grim expression that made him wonder why she had wanted to come along with him. She could have left and gone back to her car with her buddy Matt and disappeared into the park never to be seen again. Yet she had chosen to remain—clearly, against her better judgment. She didn't want to be here.

He wanted to ask her outright, but he had a feeling that if he did, she wasn't about to give him a genuine answer. If she was staying to find the cat, that made her a bit of an adrenaline junkie—and while she'd said she and her friend were rodeo people, from the look on her face, the junkie angle didn't sit right. If she was staying to find out about Anthony, she could have just gotten Pierce's phone number, or he could have gotten hers. Then again, maybe she didn't want to give it out. Or, maybe, just maybe, she wanted to stay with him.

He chuckled at the thought.

If she didn't want to exchange numbers, she certainly

hadn't stayed out here just to be around him. Besides, he wasn't that good-looking. At best, his sister had always told him he was a Costco four—cute, but not that cute.

Regardless of the reasons for her staying with him, Pierce was glad for the company. Usually, he was out here in the woods working by himself. If he were around people, they would be guests who would treat him like a tour guide and badger him with questions about the park. He spent his time reciting facts he'd been telling people over and over for the last seven years he'd been working there.

He enjoyed teaching, but he'd come here for the animals, they were far more manageable and usually better company—with Jamie being the one exception.

"How long have you been doing rodeo?"

"*Doing* rodeo?" she repeated, laughing and making him realize how ridiculous he sounded.

He looked back at her, opened his mouth and started to apologize, but before he could, she continued. "I barrel race on the circuit. I've been doing it since I was old enough to walk. My dad started me on the back of sheep in the local fairs and I've been going ever since."

"Is there a rodeo around here? I'd love to come to watch you. You must be good."

She walked past him, following the cat tracks as he slowed down. "I'm okay. I retired recently. Now I'm working for my brother's ranch, the West Glacier Cattle Ranch."

"I've heard of it."

She raised a brow as she glanced over her shoulder at him. "Oh?"

There were few from the area who hadn't after last summer's homicides. "I'm sorry for your losses."

"I appreciate that, but we weren't close." She studied him

and he gave her a look that spoke of his knowing of her father's misguided actions. "So, I'm sure you understand."

He could tell the subject made her uncomfortable by the way she sped up as she walked. He hurried to keep pace. "You wouldn't believe the number of deaths I deal with around here. There are far too many people who come here for things besides vacation, if you know what I mean." He changed the subject. "Sometimes I feel like I'm just a coroner. It seems like we always have people missing in the park. If I was smarter, I would have become a tour guide and taught people about bears or something."

She slowed down and waited for him to catch up. "You like animals?"

He shrugged. "They are better than the tourists. They don't really cause problems."

She pointed toward the direction they had come from where they had airlifted Anthony out. "Until they do."

"True." He nodded. "You can hardly blame them, since we are in their territory."

She glanced around, like she was suddenly aware of what they were doing and where they found themselves.

"Don't worry," he said, motioning toward the bear spray and gun on his utility belt on his hip. "You are safe with me. I deal with the wildlife in this park almost as much as the dead. In fact, they are the ones that usually tend to find the creatures first. They are the harbingers."

"What about the grizzly bears in the park? I always heard they were a major problem even with spray?"

"Besides wandering through the hotel or hiking trails, they really don't cause problems. They are predictable. They are looking for easy meals. As long as we keep the food and garbage locked up, they aren't too much of an issue."

"So, people become the easy meal?" she asked.

He pinched his lips but shrugged. "I hate to admit it, but pretty much. That, and when people leave coolers in the back of their trucks unattended."

She laughed. "You do realize that you just equated dead bodies as being the same as coolers."

"It's all the same to grizzly bears." He pointed to the ground. "And big cats."

She shook her head.

"Sorry," he said, "when you've been at this as long as I have, you forget that other people don't have the same jadedness. I forgot I'm not normal."

She smiled at him, shooting him an almost flirtatious look from under her lashes. "I'm good with abnormal."

Was it flirtation? No.

He couldn't have read her expression right. Not in the context of what they were talking about. She couldn't have been as warped as him. Most people didn't find the topic of dead bodies and predation a source for bonding. He had to be mistaken.

He moved past her as he tried to control himself and his overthinking. Clearly, he should have taken the week off, like Vince had told him. Maybe he shouldn't have gone back to work.

If he had told his ex-fiancée about the dead bodies, she would have flipped out. She hated that kind of talk. The only thing she'd ever wanted to talk about was the pretty things in the park, the flowers and the plants and the cool hiking trails that—oddly enough—she never actually wanted to hike.

In the end, Haven had left him. He hadn't been enough for her. When it came down to it, Pierce wasn't sure he was enough for any woman, and he wasn't sure he was ready to put his heart on the line again.

He paused for a moment, watching as Jamie moved up the game trail ahead of him. Her jeans hugged her curves, showing her strong hips. The muscles of her thighs pressed against the fabric, and he could see exactly why her horse must have responded to her touch. She was probably a dang good racer.

She stopped about a hundred yards up the trail, her face obscured by a large branch as she turned back to him. "Pierce!" She said his name with an edge of panic.

He rushed up the hillside. "What is it?"

"There's… I think you need to see this." She pointed to the side of the trail and a large patch of bushes.

He moved fast until he found himself at her side. She motioned to the game trail in front of them. There lay a piece of tattered and sun-bleached cotton fabric. At one point, he guessed the cloth might have been black but now it was a light gray striped with darker gray where it had been folded on the ground.

Bending down, he picked it up, expecting to stuff it in his back pocket to throw it away in his garbage bag in his pickup later. However, as he lifted the fabric, it unraveled and from within the decaying cotton a bony appendage rolled out and dropped onto the ground.

It took him a long moment to realize what he was looking at thanks to the drying and mummified flesh and blackened toenail—it was a human's big toe inside of what had once been a sock.

He dropped the sock onto the ground. He continued up the trail toward Avalanche Lake and, not far off the main trail, lay a pair of men's hiking pants. They bulged in the area that would have been the right knee with what he assumed were bones. To the left and sticking out from beneath a wild azalea was a mandible, the teeth exposed with two large golden crowns on the back molars.

Beside the mandible was a human skull—or what was left of it, thanks to what appeared to be a gunshot wound on the left side of the man's head.

"Oh…" Jamie said, letting out a gasp.

"Don't touch anything," Pierce said, putting his hand up and stopping her from moving forward and disturbing anything further. "I'm not sure, but I think we found out why our mountain lion was around… He was still hungry after finding what looks like a possible homicide."

Chapter Four

Jamie had never been afraid of being alone, in the woods or of the dark, yet now that she was alone and standing in the dark and listening to the haunting sounds of an owl hooting in the distance, her skin prickled. A bird lifted from the pine limb beside her and made the branch crack, making her jump and cry out with surprise.

If Matt had seen her acting as she was, she would have been embarrassed. She glanced over toward the spotlights up on the hill where Pierce and his team had set up a makeshift crime scene around the remains while they waited for the coroner to arrive.

Another park ranger had arrived, someone he'd called Stephanie. She felt rather envious of the woman with her long brunette hair and even longer legs. The worst part of the woman was the penetrating gaze she had given Pierce when she had come to his aid. Anyone on the planet could have seen how much the woman cared about him. Heck, they could have felt it in the air—her desire was palpable.

They must have been together. If they weren't, Stephanie was definitely on the hunt.

Maybe she was the real cougar that Jamie needed to worry about—not that Stephanie had looked that old. In fact, and even more dishearteningly, Jamie had to guess she was at least a couple of years older than the woman. Even if she wasn't, she wasn't the type to tear down another woman for something outside of her control—if anything, with age came wisdom and really expensive Botox.

Jamie laughed at the thought.

If Pierce was the kind of guy to keep a stable of women, then she didn't need to think about him in the way she was thinking about him. Heck, as it was, she didn't need to be thinking about him. Period. He was nothing more than a park ranger passing in the night, literally.

They were simply two strangers meeting at a strange and macabre moment in time. A moment that was going to stick with her for the rest of her life but was likely nothing more than a Tuesday for him. This kind of thing, this level of stress and traumatic event, had probably made him like a crab in a pot of water: The trauma kept turning up the heat until the water boiled, and he was cooked.

She wondered if in some ways she had been the same way when it came to the rodeo circuit. It wasn't until John had died that she had realized she had grown accustomed to things no one else would have considered normal, or right.

Jamie feared the day she dealt with death with apathy. At least she still held hope.

The wind picked up and blew through the trees in the bowl of the mountain, making a whistling sound. It kicked up the waves on the lake and they crashed harder and harder against the rocky shoreline. The sound was cathartic, and it pulled her away from the thoughts of death, which surrounded her. In the moment, with the sparkling stars and unfaltering constellations, she was reminded of how insignificant she was in the world.

She walked to the edge of the lake and put her hand in the icy water, opening and closing her fingers until her bones ached from the cold and she was forced to pull out. There was a smooth log on the well-trodden lake edge, and she sat down as she opened and closed her fist, trying to warm her chilled fingertips as she reveled in the pinpricking pain of her skin.

"Jamie?" Pierce's voice pulled her from her meditation, and she turned abruptly.

He was standing there with his arms crossed over his chest. "I'm sorry, I didn't mean to surprise you."

She moved to stand up, but he subtly waved for her to stay put and he sauntered toward her. The full moon illuminated his V-shaped body from behind and she tried not to stare. He was so handsome in the twilight, and she loved the way the shadows caressed the chiseled edges of his jaw. It made her want to trace the lines of the darkness until it swallowed them both.

"You look upset," he said, sitting down beside her on the log. His body pressed against hers and the warmth radiated through her, making her realize that even though it was summer, she was still cold. "Are you doing okay?"

She looked at his hand on his knees. Even they were beautiful with his sun-darkened skin and well-kept fingernails. There was a small bit of what appeared to be dirt under the nail of his pointer finger. As he noticed her staring at the tiny imperfection, he lifted the finger and pulled her from her inspection.

"I'm doing okay." And the only thing that was upsetting her was how badly she wanted to graze her fingers against him. "Have you gotten any word on how Lewis is doing?"

She tried to pull the subject away from herself and back to the real reason she had stayed there.

"I haven't heard anything real recent, but that is usually a good thing." He glanced down at his watch. "I would guess he is either out of surgery or coming out of surgery soon. As soon as I hear anything, I promise I will tell you."

She nudged her knee playfully against his, the action almost out of place, and as she did, she felt the heat rise in her cheeks. She was glad it was dark and her face rested in the shadows.

Surprisingly, he didn't jerk away from her flirty touch. His reaction, or lack of one, made her question exactly how she felt.

"Did you find anything out about the body?" she asked, avoiding questions she didn't want to explore within herself.

He shook his head. "We found quite a number of bones, but no concrete source of identification for the remains."

"But do you have an idea of who they could belong to?"

He shrugged, and she didn't know how she should read his reaction but she knew enough that she should not continue to press.

"There are some missing folks in the area and some cold cases from throughout the years in the park I may have to look into," he continued, seemingly oblivious to her anxiety when it came to him.

"Do you think you can pull DNA?"

He nodded. "Sure, but that kind of thing is going to take a while. Often, we can get more information from our files and then put together enough pieces to get an identity and a probable cause of death long before we get answers back from the lab."

"Seriously?" she asked, shocked. She'd had no idea that

tests took that long. "My cousin did an ancestry thing, and it only took a couple of weeks to get back."

"They aren't sending their samples in to a governmentally funded crime lab." He chuckled. "That being said, if we have a high-profile case that is getting a lot of media attention, we can usually get our tests put through quite a bit faster."

She nodded. "I'm not surprised."

"Yeah, it's amazing what a little negative press can cause."

Jamie opened her mouth and closed it as she thought about the blood on her hands and the implications it wrought.

He put his hand on her knee and looked her in the eyes. "Don't worry about it. This will all be fine." His voice was calm and as deep as she imagined his soul to be. "And, as far as Matt is concerned, he is in good hands as well. Neither of your names will be released to the press if you wish. However, I would like to honor you both with a citizen's merit award for springing into action in a moment of need."

Her blood pressure rose, thanks to his hand on her leg, and his words sounded as though they were being spoken from the other side of water.

"No."

His eyebrows quirked up. "Oh. Okay." He sounded a little hurt at her abruptness.

She put her hand on his as he tried to move his hand away. "No, not like that. Thank you for offering to give me an award, but I don't deserve anything. I just did what anyone would have done."

"What about Matt?"

"No. He wouldn't want something like that, either."

"You said he wasn't your boyfriend, but..." He glanced down at her ring finger.

"He's not, and I'm not married." She tried to control the heat rising within her. "My boyfriend was a bull rider and Matt's best friend. We all rode on the circuit together."

"So, you do have a boyfriend." He moved to pull his hand away, but she gripped him tighter.

"*Did*. He died." She spoke matter-of-factly. For the first time since he had passed, she didn't feel the lump in her throat when she said the words and she felt guilty at the lack of reaction.

She tried to tell herself it had been long enough that it was okay to have finally accepted that he was gone and she was ready to move on.

Pierce's fingers moved around hers and, as they did, she questioned if she was ready after all.

"I'm so sorry for your loss." He dropped his head. "I know what it's like to lose someone you thought you'd have in your life forever."

She and John had never promised forever of one another, but that was splitting hairs as they had certainly been together long enough to have gone the direction of marriage and children. "I'm sorry for yours," she said. "Do you want to tell me about it?"

He shook his head and pulled his hand away. "Not even a little." He stood up. "We need to start heading back. I'll get you back to your friend."

She'd never felt more rejected. Now she understood how he must have felt about her abruptness, and she questioned why she had ever chosen to stay behind.

Chapter Five

Pierce couldn't stop thinking about Jamie. She was like a ghost in the corners of his mind and, no matter how hard he tried to focus on his work, she kept popping up along the edges of his thoughts and pushing her way into the center of his attention. She was something else.

A few years ago, Vince had asked him about his ideal woman. They had been three sheets to the wind during their conversation, but he could remember telling his friend he didn't care what the woman looked like, but he wanted a woman who wasn't afraid to get her hands dirty—in fact, he wanted a woman who would walk in off the street and be unafraid to become a hero.

It hadn't been a street, rather it had been a trail, but Jamie was unquestionably a hero.

He thought of her admission about her deceased boyfriend. She had been quiet on the hike back to the parking lot. Under different circumstances, he would have loved to have made that hike with her up to Avalanche Lake—it was one of his favorites. Though it wasn't quite as good as a hike few tourists knew about and even fewer took thanks to the healthy population of grizzly bears and wolves in the area. The Hidden Lake Trail.

Since he had seen her drive away with her guy friend, he had wished he had asked for her phone number. It would have been so easy, and he could have told her it was for any number of reasons, any of which would have seemed legitimate given the circumstances. Yet, his thoughts of where he should have been that week, and what he was supposed to be doing, had kept sprinting through his mind.

If only he had seized the chance to tell her the truth about himself and opened up, as she had. But he had never been the type to want to wear his heart on his sleeve. To do so was to risk being hurt again, and he had already been hurt enough for one lifetime.

He glanced over at the black-velvet box with Haven's engagement ring, which rested on top of the dresser his mother had given him as a child. Haven had hated everything in his house and especially the dresser—she'd said it was outdated thanks to its oak finish and brass handles—and, as soon as she'd moved out, he'd let the house sit almost empty except for his bed and that dresser for weeks.

It seemed somehow fitting that both things she had hated the most now sat together beside him. Though he was arguably the thing she now hated the most.

And that was exactly how he had fallen down the rabbit hole and missed his chance with Jamie—barbed memories of hate.

When Haven had left him, she had taken everything of value—including every shred of his heart. At least, he had believed so, until he'd seen Jamie on the mountain.

Between trying to control his staring and handling the mayhem he'd been presented with on the trail, he'd slipped into wondering if his attraction was lust or if it was driven by a more primal and dark force: the bloodied canine teeth of spite.

It was another of the many reasons he'd held back. It wasn't fair to Jamie or to him to flirt and shoot his shot when he was going after her for all the wrong reasons. If he started dating again, he didn't want to have Haven haunting his thoughts. That would be a major *if.* Dating sounded just about as fun as staring down a rabid grizzly bear on a narrow trail.

Actually, he'd rather run the odds on the grizzly bear.

He chuckled as he slipped on his utility belt and made sure it sat comfortably over his Kevlar vest and on his hips. It was bit of overkill to some to wear a bulletproof vest in the woods, but he'd learned a long time ago that it was best to prepare for the worst and hope for the best. And in this place, if it wasn't the environment or the animals that killed a person, there may be a person next in line who was happy and willing to do the job.

It was sad that nothing really surprised him anymore and he'd reached a point in life that death was just that... death. The end. Nothing more and nothing less.

There were things worse than death.

He knew.

He pulled his belt tight, so much so that it pinched his skin and reminded him of physical pain, taking away some of the edge of the emotional.

Since the loss of Haven, he'd sat on the edge of madness. He'd suffocated on the breakup. Wheezed around the memories of their laughter while he'd tried to fall asleep at night. He'd had to replace his pillow from smashing his fists into it too many times while trying to find comfort that he'd never seemed to find—until last night, when he'd finally found some solace in thoughts of Jamie.

He needed to see her again. Sometime.

As badly as he yearned to see her again, he wasn't under any misconceptions about attraction and lust. He knew exactly where it led—straight to heartbreak and loss, and he couldn't go through that kind of agony ever again. He was barely alive, even if he was breathing.

For now, he needed to focus on finding the mountain lion.

He checked his phone after locking his door and walked out to his work truck. Lewis was out of surgery and was in the rehab unit. He'd lost an eye, had received several units of blood and hundreds of stitches, but he was on the road to recovery. According to the nurse, he wasn't in a hurry to go hiking any time soon.

He couldn't blame the guy.

Big cats were one of the animals in this park that kept his head on a swivel. They were notorious for coming up from behind. Most people were afraid of the bears, but at least they were somewhat predictable, and a person could see them coming. This cat was going to come back to its cache, and it wasn't going to be happy about them removing the remains.

The good news was that it was likely to move on and disappear into the wilds once it found the body gone, but he would have to keep an eye on the trail for a few weeks to make sure visitors to the park were safe when traveling through the area.

He sighed as he found comfort in the predictability of his job. Maybe he would become one of those old rangers who lived in the single-room cabins, who went to bed at seven every night and got up at four every morning, and who focused their every waking hour on the constant barrage of blurring faces of tourists who came through the park's gates. They were as invisible to the tourists as the tourists were to them—just one more attraction for visitors to consume while on their vacation.

There was an ethereal beauty in their loneliness, and an element of altruism.

Yet, it was lonely nonetheless.

He wasn't sure he wanted to be lonely forever, or if it was fear that kept him tethered to his resolve to stick to promises of never dating until his memories of Haven dissipated.

In an effort to avoid the whirlpool of thoughts of loneliness and philosophy, he turned on the radio and tried to find solace in the guitar riffs of Tool. He tapped his fingers on the steering wheel as he navigated the empty road up to the Avalanche Lake trailhead. He'd slept far too few hours, but at least he'd slept more than the folks he'd tasked with holding the scene overnight. They would be glad to see the whites of his eyes this morning.

Stephanie was already at the trailhead when he arrived. She was smiling and her dark brunette hair was pulled into a tight French braid that landed halfway down her back. Most guys who worked at the park thought she was hot, and he couldn't deny she was pretty, but he didn't really care. She was good at her job and they got along great. Beyond that, everything else about her was just a benefit.

He pulled up to a stop beside her truck and rolled down his window. She walked over, flipped her braid over her shoulder and shot him a wide, almost too-warm smile. "Good morning, Pierce. You ready for a little of me in your life?"

He wasn't sure exactly what in the heck she meant by that statement, and he definitely wasn't sure how to respond without getting it all kinds of wrong.

"I'm ready for a hot cup of coffee and some good news, if that counts." He tried to avoid her verbal bullet.

"The good news is that you get me all day, if you want me. Second, we found more evidence this morning. We've already done the proper collection and cataloging. I have a bunch of pictures in my phone, if you want to take a look. We left everything in situ up there for you." She motioned in the direction of the back of her pickup.

"What did you find? Any further evidence as to the manner of death?"

"We found a speed loader for what looks to be a .45-caliber revolver."

"Did you find the gun?"

She shook her head. "No luck yet, but I called in a friend with dogs. Hoping maybe they can help us find exactly where the guy was killed and maybe there, we can pick up the gun."

He appreciated how she was on top of matters. "Send me a picture of the speed loader and its location in relation to the body. I don't need you today, you can go ahead and head home. I bet you're exhausted after being on scene all night." He tipped his head in appreciation and acknowledgment.

She glanced down at her watch. "Yeah, not gonna lie, I'm spent and the tourons will be showing up any minute now. They opened the gates thirty minutes ago. I'd rather not get stuck in a bear jam on my way back to my cabin. If you need anything…" She paused. "I'll be sleeping." She laughed.

"It will wait." He smiled. "Don't worry about a thing. As

for the 'tourons,' they are called tourists. We've had meetings, don't let the captain hear you calling them that—I don't want to have to sit in on another hour-long meeting about feelings."

"I'll stop calling them that when tourists stop acting like morons. Until that day, they are tourons in my book." She nodded, tapping the hood of his pickup with her hand in a goodbye. She smiled and waved as she turned away.

As she did, a white pickup pulled up on the other side of Stephanie's truck.

A blond woman in a cowboy hat turned to face him. *Jamie.*

His breath caught in his throat.

What was she doing here?

A broad smile lit his face, and he could feel it in his eyes. He tried to control himself and play it cool, but he couldn't control the tightening in his core.

Stephanie stepped over to his passenger's-side window and motioned for him to roll it down, her smile matching his. "I'll keep my ringer on. If you get done early, stop by. I'll have a pot of coffee on for you and a warm spot in my bed—if you're down." She spun on her heel and got into her truck before he even realized what she had implied.

He opened and closed his mouth, and his smile quaked into a look of shock. He had no idea what had just happened. Not really.

Stephanie was nice. He liked her. Most men would have given a foot and a couple of other body parts for what she had just offered him, but he wasn't interested in anything of the sort. He wasn't even sure if he wanted to think about another woman in bed yet.

As she backed up and pulled out, barely missing the front bumper of a rental car speeding down the road in the process, he found himself thinking of the ideas of feast or famine.

He stared down at his fingers on the steering wheel. There was a bit of dirt under the index finger on his right hand. He picked at it, wiping it free. It was stupid, he knew, but he normally got manicures. It was the one biweekly appointment he refused to give up. Tiffany would have his head if he came in with blood and gore under his nails.

Jamie tapped on his window and her facial features were tight.

He rolled down the window. He wasn't exactly sure what had happened to bring her back to this place this morning, but he was glad to see her. "Hi. Something I can do for you?"

"That's Stephanie, right?" She nudged her chin in the direction that Steph had just disappeared.

He nodded. "I thought I introduced you last night?" At the time, in the dark, he had thought nothing of it. Yet, last night he had introduced them together in a group of ten different responders and in the midst of conflict and elements of chaos. It was just a throwaway action that he hadn't thought about since. But now, in the light of day, there was some tension he hadn't expected, and he wasn't sure if it was coming from himself or the way Jamie had spoken her name.

"You did. I just didn't realize…" Her words tapered off like the thin flame of a freshly lit candle.

He wanted to tell her that there was nothing between him and Stephanie, but he wasn't sure if that was what she was talking about. If it wasn't, he certainly didn't want to bring it up. And, if it *was*, he didn't want to lie. Stephanie had come on to him, and regardless of the state of his feelings, he had never been one to deceive.

Chapter Six

How was it that when Jamie finally wanted to think about stepping back into the dating world, she picked a man who was inundated with women a thousand times prettier than her and gravitating in the man's circle? She wouldn't stand a chance.

Now, standing beside Pierce's pickup, she couldn't recall what she had been thinking this morning when she had woken up on the ranch and gotten in her truck and headed to the park. How could she think it was a good idea to come to this spot and try to reconnect with Pierce? It was only a shot in the dark that he would even be there again in the morning—she wasn't sure she was going to run into him again, let alone watch him carousing with a known threat of a woman.

She couldn't stand up to Stephanie, who was the perfect specimen of woman. Her breasts were perky and exactly the same size. Jamie's left one was slightly smaller than the right and when she looked in the mirror and flexed like she was throwing the lasso, the left lifted three inches higher. It looked almost grotesque. She couldn't even imagine what a man saw when she was on top and working away with him beneath. There her breasts would be, two little oranges moving around like marionettes on two independent puppeteers' strings.

It was a wonder anyone could even concentrate on the task at hand.

Perfect Stephanie probably didn't have the same issue.

She'd have perfect, well-placed tits. The kind that bounced like perfect little butter balls when she jogged and giggled with her gorgeous hair flouncing around her smiling face like she was an actress in some insipid commercial for minty fresh gum.

Ugh.

She really wanted to hate the woman. Yet she was enough of a feminist and proponent for other women to just be jealous and leave it there. Stephanie was probably as nice as she was *perfect*. Weren't they *always*?

There was something about the pretty ones with the ugly souls that somehow kept them from attaining true beauty. Then again, maybe it was her resentment of Stephanie that was assigning her with some benevolent *more*-ness.

She had to hope that her resentment was blind and, for once, it wasn't just love that cast the curtain of virtue.

Just because she wanted to like Stephanie didn't mean she was a good woman, just like all elders were not necessarily good people deserving of reverence and respect. Bad people came in all ages, genders, cultures and communities.

Only time would out.

That was, if she stuck around.

As she stared into Pierce's face, that was a topic of debate within herself. He was an incredibly handsome man, but she could look into his eyes and tell that he was lost. She couldn't explain exactly why, but there was a look within them that spoke of his being adrift in the sea of his thoughts and feelings. Feelings of what, she didn't know. However, she held out hope that there was a spark of desire for her.

"I'm surprised you're here. Did you lose something last night?" He ducked down and looked up the mountain toward the trailhead. "If you did, I can probably get you back up there to see if we can find it." He ran his hand over the back of his neck, nervously.

The only thing she had lost was her damned mind. Jamie couldn't tell him that she had only come back because she had wanted to talk to him again and that what had happened last night had kept her from getting any real sleep. She wasn't the kind of woman to let anything go half finished and apparently that extended to big cat attacks and dead bodies.

She tried to think fast. "I think I left my gloves up there, on the log where we were sitting. You know?"

"I don't remember you wearing any."

She felt her cheeks warm, but she had already started the lie and now she had to keep it going. "I… I took them off before you sat down. I think they fell off the log or something. I don't know. I was just going to run back up there if the trail was open and try to find them."

He nodded, appraising her features carefully, as though he were looking for something she wasn't saying. She glanced away before he could find his answer. "I'll go up with you. I need to check on my crew. The new investigation team is up there and looking for more evidence. I'm the lead investigator, so my boots need to be on the ground."

She nodded. "That sounds good. We can split up wherever you need. I don't want to be in your way." *I just want to get to know you more.*

Yet that wasn't the entire truth, either. Being that close

to the bleeding man had brought up so many memories about John. When she'd tried to sleep, images of her former boyfriend's face and the blood dripping from the corners of his mouth as he'd tried to speak had interwoven with the stranger's bloodied expression of fear as she'd tried to staunch the bleeding where the cat's teeth had penetrated his cheek.

She couldn't be alone, and she hadn't wanted to turn to Matt or anyone at the ranch. Matt had his own burdens to bear with John's death and she didn't want to appear any weaker than she already did when it came to her brother and their ranch hands—she had to appear strong. They were the Trappers, after all.

It was her and her remaining siblings jobs to repair the damage her father had wrought upon their name.

Pierce stepped out of his pickup.

Even though it was June, in Montana that still meant it was chilly in the mornings and she noticed he was wearing a thin coat over his uniform. Even through it, she could make out the V-shape of his torso that she could recall from his silhouette in the moonlight. He was built like a man who not only hiked but also lifted small trees and carried them around on his shoulders for fun in his free time.

Maybe he was the man behind the Brawny paper towel commercials. She giggled at the thought.

"Do I have something on my face?" he asked, running his hands over his chin self-consciously.

Though it was a tad bit evil, she dabbed at a spot by her mouth. "Yes, you have something. Right…there…" She reached over and touched his face where she had just been touching her own. There was a strange charge between them, and she soaked it in like rays of the sun after a long, dark winter.

His gaze drifted up from her fingers toward her eyes, but she dropped her hand and turned away. "Got it." She cleared her throat as if such an action could also straighten up her feelings. "Let's go."

He grabbed something out of the back of his pickup and slipped on a hiking pack as she walked over to her truck and grabbed her own. Hers was filled with only a few essentials: a knife, water, items to make a fire and bear spray in an outside and reachable pocket. The last thing she wanted to do was run into the cat who was probably still haunting the area.

She didn't know much about mountain lions, but she couldn't imagine an animal like that going to the work of attacking a human in an effort to protect its cache only to run off—even if people were in the area. The Avalanche Lake trail was always busy during the summer months.

There was a rental car parked in the lot and two older hikers were putting on hats inside. She wanted to warn them, but instead she simply pulled the straps on her pack tighter. If Pierce didn't think they needed to close the trail, she had to trust his judgment. The last thing she would want was some stranger coming up to her and freaking her out if she was about to go into the woods on a long hike that made her halfway nervous as it was, thanks to the many signs and brochures already warning about the animals in the area.

Yes, it wasn't as if they hadn't already been told.

She looked over at Pierce, who had started to head toward the trail. Hurrying, she caught up, her pack shuffling and making a rubbing sound on her polyester coat as she moved.

For the first half mile, they moved quickly, and he loudly hummed a song she didn't recognize. The second time he started the same song, she realized it was just something he did so that they didn't surprise animals along the trails, and she appreciated the simple action. She'd heard about people wearing bells along the trails, but in her family, they had always been a joke—simply called dinner bells.

Now, after last night, she kind of wished she was wearing one. Though she wasn't sure they would work on a big cat or if the noise would only let the cat know exactly where to find them.

She was freaking herself out and she moved in closer toward Pierce, who was leading the way. As she did, he once again looked back at her, checking to make sure she was safe. He smiled as he hummed. "You are doing great. How's the pace for you?"

"Good." She motioned toward the wooden pathway. "Flat is easy. It's when we start gaining elevation that it gets fun."

His smile widened and he moved so she could hike beside him in the widening trail. "I've done some backcountry hiking in this park where we gain a thousand feet elevation in less than a half mile. It gets wild. You have to use trekking poles and lines."

"I'm one for a good adventure, but that is not my kind of hiking. In fact, I wouldn't even call that hiking anymore—that is straight mountaineering. That's impressive."

"What's impressive were the women who were doing it in the 1800s in those huge skirts." He motioned around his legs like he was wearing a Victorian skirt. "There are pictures of women wearing them on the tops of the mountains after having hiked up in them and high-heeled shoes."

"How would they see where they were stepping?" she asked, imagining the logistics of the women who had undertaken such feats.

He shrugged. "You would know more about that than I would."

She thought she was tough, running headstrong horses at high speed. Yet, she wasn't sure she had anything on women who were willing to blindly stride up treacherous, nearly vertical mountainsides in a time in which women were expected to do little more in high society than be window decorations in their husband's affairs.

As they moved up the mountain, he showed her flowers—a yellow glacier lily that had just popped up and come into bloom and a three-petaled white flower called a trillium near a small spring. He pointed out dozens of mushrooms and plants and she found solace in his voice and passion for nature. He was so handsome as he spoke about what he loved as he hiked up the mountain toward their destination, she could tell why he had chosen to become a ranger—the job fit him.

He moved *with* the swollen, exposed roots and tearing, jagged rocks like they weren't problems to be overcome but opportunities to stretch and move his body. He flourished in the journey and the experience that nature provided.

She hadn't noticed it last night, but it made sense given everything that had been taking place.

Pierce bent down, his backpack shifting slightly as he motioned toward a small, needled bush on the side of the trail. "This is a yew bush," he said, smiling back at her. "It was used by Native Americans in their healing ceremonies. Modern pharmaceutical companies ended up studying it, and using the compounds found in it to make cancer-fighting drugs."

She loved how smart he was and, as he let go of the plant and it bobbed beside his leg as he stood up, she stared at his round, muscular thighs. He was even more handsome with every passing second. There wasn't a thing about him that wasn't *perfect*.

He was so out of her league. All she had going for her was an infamous family name and a ranch in disrepair while he had the world endlessly at his fingertips.

Continuing, they moved up the trail and Jamie could tell from the length of his steps that he was slowing down to make sure she was able to keep up with him. They stepped off the trail where she had helped Anthony. She had expected to see blood staining the ground where he had lain, but aside from a small patch on a yellowed, decaying leaf and upturned dirt, there was little to indicate the chaos that had taken place—even the coffin-shaped impression had disappeared over night.

In the distance, she could start to make out the sounds of the team working on the recovery of the remains and as they rounded a corner, a man in a red coat came into view. As the man looked up and noticed them, he gave them a two-fingered wave.

"That's David Slayton. He is a member of our Avalanche and Search and Rescue Teams as well."

She nodded, waving back at the good-looking and thin man waving down at them from up on the mountain.

"He and Stephanie used to be an item."

The hair on the back of her neck raised slightly. "Is that right?" She didn't want to be annoyed at the mere mention of the woman's name, but she couldn't help herself. "What happened there?"

He shrugged. "She has a tendency to jump around between men. It's one of the many reasons I would never date her."

It was like he was making a point of reassuring her, but she wasn't exactly sure why unless he was feeling the same pull and attraction that she was feeling toward him.

For the first time since she had seen him this morning, she felt as though she really had a chance at something more than just a simple friendship. While she wasn't exactly sure what she wanted from Pierce, she was grateful to be close to him and back in his circle and away from the ranch. For at least the next few hours, she could escape from the memories of the past that always seemed to sweep her up and carry her away to the gaping maw of endless pain.

Chapter Seven

David walked down the game trail and met them halfway. He had an excited expression on his face, and he stopped sideways on the trail, motioning for Pierce to follow. "Good morning, Special Agent Hauser." He dipped his head toward Jamie. "Ms. Trapper. Glad to see you back today." He shot Pierce a questioning look.

"Morning," Pierce said. "We touched base with Stephanie at the trailhead. She said you found a speed loader. Anything else of note? Any more sign of the cat?"

"We haven't seen the cat. I have a call out to the K-9 unit out of Kalispell. They will be here any time. They aren't used for treeing cats, but we can get a team for that if you want to mitigate the problem."

Pierce shook his head. "Nah. The cat was just doing what a cat naturally does, I don't think it is going to continue posing problems if it hasn't attacked anyone else. I'm expecting with us working here for a few more days, we may push it out. Let's see how this goes."

David nodded. "Didn't you hear? Patrol Captain Reynolds called before you arrived. He wants us to be out of here by the end of the day."

"What? You have to be kidding me. That makes absolutely no sense. With the dogs coming in? We haven't even finished collecting evidence. He must have lost his mind."

"He said he was worried about the missing hiker in Spring Valley." David shrugged and motioned vaguely in the direction of that area.

The hiker had been missing for a year and they had long ago given up looking for the man's remains, so it made no sense that when they had an active case his boss would suddenly want to focus on a cold case.

"Why would he be worried about that guy?"

David shrugged. "I think he said something about the fact that we have enough to ID this vic and anything else was just sugar on top."

Clearly, his boss needed to retire if he didn't actually want to do an investigation. They were law enforcement officials. Sure, they didn't work in Chicago or New York City, but that didn't mean that causes of deaths didn't need to be solved. Just because this case was a little more challenging than normal and would require a greater degree of effort, time and money didn't mean that they shouldn't pull out the stops. Just identifying the individual was hardly enough.

He opened his mouth to speak but he bit his tongue. Speaking his mind and sharing his concerns with David and Jamie wasn't appropriate. They didn't need to know or hear about interoffice politics or what could possibly turn into infighting. He was a professional. When he got a chance to speak with the patrol captain, Eliot Reynolds, he would clarify a few things—and make sure what he was hearing was accurate before jumping to conclusions. There was no sense sending his blood pressure out of control over what could possibly be a poorly translated conversation.

"If you don't mind, David, I'm going to go ahead and give the patrol captain a call."

David nodded. "That's probably a great idea. In the meantime, I'll make sure the night crew finishes up our paperwork and then morning crew is briefed for the day."

He gave the man an appreciative nod as he dialed Eliot's number. Jamie was leaning against a tree not far from him down the narrow trail. She was looking into the distance, pensively. She was probably thinking about how inept this investigation was. At least, she would be if she had ever been around any kind of investigation before. He hoped not. That way she didn't have any kind of barometer, and there was a chance he'd still appear somewhat in control and maybe even a little bit cool.

His call went to voicemail, and he hung up. He'd call him back later.

Jamie walked over, and she brushed her hand against his lower back as she carefully stepped around him on the narrow trail. "If your boss is on you about the time, then we need to get to work."

David looked at him with a quirk of the brow, questioning if they were really going to allow her to participate in the search. It wasn't conventional, but if the patrol captain was breathing down their necks and really wasn't interested in anything besides identifying their victim and not looking at this death at anything besides a suicide, then they were no longer dealing with a potential crime scene.

Whether he agreed or not, thanks to his boss wanting to sweep this death under the rug, the rules had now effectively changed.

Jamie walked up the trail and broke off up to the right and into the woods. "Wait!" he called after her.

She stopped.

David could think what he wanted. They wouldn't be on this mountain if it hadn't been for Jamie—she was the one who had found the hiker and saved his life, and then she had also found the remains. If anything, she had proven her merit and deserved to be here. In the future, if she was interested, he would have to talk to her about joining the volunteer search and rescue team he was involved with in Flathead County. She would be a perfect addition to the unit.

He hurried toward her. "Do you have bear spray?"

She nodded and pointed at the can in her pack.

"Perfect. If you're out here by yourself, I want you protected. Just make sure you're upwind if you use the spray, or you will be as incapacitated as the animal you're trying to stop."

"I can't say that I really want to be out here by myself," she said, her voice barely above a whisper. "I mean, I can... I'd just rather have you with me." She glanced over at David.

Her candor surprised him. *Was she trying to rescue him?*

He couldn't help the smile that graced his lips. "You don't have to. I need to still get a hold of the patrol captain and get some answers, but I have a feeling that I'm going to get answers I don't want."

She nodded. "In situations like that, I have found it can be better to feign ignorance. If a problem arises with your boss, just blame it on me. Tell him I was pushy or something. It's easier to ask for forgiveness—and I don't mind being your fall guy."

He laughed. "I'm not that kind of person, but I appreciate your willingness to fall on the sword. There're other work-arounds to this, though."

She chewed on the corner of her lip like she was thinking. "Do you guys ever work with local cops?"

He nodded. "Sometimes, if things require extra hands, we call in locals to create a joint task force."

She had a mischievous look on her face and her eyes sparkled. "My brother just got married to a detective. Her name is Emily Monahan. She could help—this is right up her alley. She's great."

"I like your thinking." It was a great idea, but he didn't know how he was going to make it happen. Under normal circumstances, he would have to get Reynolds's sign-off on a task force. "I'm just hoping we can find something today that makes it impossible for Reynolds to take us off this. Or, enough that if he gets his way, we can find the answers we need to pull together the events that led to this person's death—even if it was accidental or something else. This person's family deserves answers."

They searched in silence. The sound of the creek grew quieter as he moved farther up the mountain and away from the initial area they had found the person's jaw. They dropped over the top of the ridge and into the next ravine. The brush grew thick and clawing. Even if there were ten bodies in here, the only way they would find them is if they fell on the top of their hiking boots.

"Jamie?" he called to her.

"Yeah?"

"Let's start working our way back." He stepped out of the bushes. As he did, he saw the eyes. The big, black, cat eyes.

The mountain lion crouched low to the ground as it stalked him.

He grabbed his Glock, unholstering it.

He didn't want to shoot the cat.

"Hey!" he yelled, pointing the gun at the mountain lion's chest. "Hey, cat! Get back!" He lunged toward the animal without thinking.

The animal jumped up, and spun on its feet. The cat's tail whipped as it turned and started to run in the other direction. The lion turned and looked back at him one more time until it disappeared into a thicket of bushes.

Jamie moved behind him. "Is it gone?"

He nodded. "Stay close."

She was holding the bear spray in front of her body. Her hands were shaking, hard.

He slipped his gun back in its holster, putting his hand on his belt in an effort to control his own. He didn't want to let her see that he, too, was scared.

He motioned to the canister. "It's going to be okay. The cat won't be back. They are pretty skittish." She lowered the can to her side. Reaching over, he took hold of her free hand. "You're okay."

She nodded, but he could feel how tense she was, and he could understand her fear.

He held her hand as he walked with her to a small opening. "Here," he said, motioning for her to sit down. "Let's take a second. Regroup."

She didn't say a word as she allowed him to help her to sit. He reluctantly let go of her hand as she settled onto the ground. He sat down beside her, hugging his knees to his chest.

He scanned the area around them for the beady eyes of the animal that had been stalking them. He had only been half telling the truth. There was no way to know if the cat had left or not. It could have still been watching, for all he knew, but he wasn't about to tell her that the mountain lion could have still been on the hunt.

For now, all he could do was try to control the narrative and help her believe that they were going to be okay.

She was staring in the distance the cat had disappeared.

"You okay?" he asked.

She didn't move for a long moment, but finally she turned to look at him. "That cat was even bigger than I remembered. I can't believe Anthony survived. He fought so hard."

Reaching down, his fingers brushed against something hard that, at first, he thought was a rock. But as he ran his finger over the surface of the object, he realized it was pitted. Looking down to where his hand rested. He pulled his arm back.

Where his fingers had been lay a rib bone.

He stood up.

It was undeniably a human rib, as it was sharply curved and narrow. It had chew marks on it from where an animal, likely of the rodent kind, had feasted.

Not far to his left lay a tattered leather wallet. He reached down and picked it up. Inside was a man's driver's license. He recognized the face and the name: Clyde Donovan.

"Wow." He let out a long exhale.

He had thought getting stalked by the mountain lion was going to be the most dramatic thing to happen to him today. He was wrong. This was going to cause problems.

"Whose wallet is it? Do you recognize them?" she asked, sounding concerned.

"Yes…yes, I do. It's the mayor who went missing over a year ago. A man who had his fair share of enemies."

Chapter Eight

The ranger headquarters was situated in a dark brown log cabin set behind a café and shop in the small town of Apgar just inside the gates of Glacier. Jamie had driven by the place dozens of times throughout the years and had never noticed its presence, let alone realized its function.

A woman was typing away in the far corner, not bothering to look up as they walked in. She had headphones on and seemed hyperfocused on whatever it was she was working on. Aside from her, it appeared as though no one else was there. For this late in the evening, it made sense.

There were a few dozen desks, most empty aside from stacks of papers and files waiting to be handled. A few had pictures of families, one playing football in matching red-and-blue uniforms. Her family wouldn't have been caught dead doing anything of the sort, but it made her smile.

When her father had been alive, they had all been expected to help out around the ranch. There were always jobs to do. She'd been in charge of the barn and the horses. She had cleaned more stables and dragged more pastures than she cared to think about. Yet, that was how she had fallen in love with horses and had turned that love into barrel racing. She was always outside with her horses.

Her favorite horse growing up had been a well-bred Appaloosa named Fancy Face. The horse had been hers since before she had even started to walk. In fact, before her death, her mother had taken pictures of Jamie in a diaper riding on the back of Fancy Face. There was some discussion that her first real words were the horse's name.

She'd had her until her senior year of high school. One day she had come out and Fancy had passed. There had been no warning, and it had been quick, but the hole her passing had left in Jamie's life had been almost as immense and impossible to fill as the loss of her mother.

"A penny for your thoughts?" Pierce asked, giving her a pensive look.

A thousand dollars wouldn't buy them from her at the moment. "Oh, I was just noticing the pictures around your office. And I'm surprised this is all the rangers that work at the park." She motioned around the room. In total, there had to be no more than twenty-five desks and an office at the end of the room with a door that read "Patrol Captain Reynolds" on the glass.

He looked around as if he suddenly noticed how small the room really was. "Oh, yeah." He sighed. "There are a variety of different types of park rangers within Glacier and all federally owned parks. This office is just for the law enforcement side of things here. We don't have many on staff. The Feds don't like to give us too much money."

She was a long way from shocked. "Do you think that your captain will still want to you to back off this case now that we have a possible ID?"

He shrugged. "I couldn't believe he wanted me to in the first place." He spoke in barely a whisper as he glanced toward the man's office. "I've worked with him a long time. This is a first."

The subject made him uncomfortable, but she couldn't understand the captain's thinking at all. She pulled out her phone. Her fingers trembled as she looked at her contacts list and she considered texting her sister-in-law, Detective Emily Monahan, and telling her who and what they had found in proximity to the person's remains.

Emily would sink her teeth into this man's death and run. The investigation would be so different in her hands. Yet, perhaps Jamie was jumping the gun.

She pushed her phone back into her pocket. "Let's see how this meeting goes. He does know I'm coming with you, doesn't he? I don't want it to be a surprise."

He nodded. "I told him you made the discovery. He wanted to ask you some questions."

"I don't know what I could possibly help him with." She thought about Emily again. She always talked about suspects and people she brought in for questioning when she was investigating crimes. One of her favorite idioms was "A fish that keeps its mouth shut rarely gets hooked."

For some reason, it felt important in this moment.

"He can be a little intimidating, but don't fall for his façade. He is actually a pretty nice guy—most of the time."

She didn't want to point out that ever since she'd met Pierce, his boss had seemed far from nice—if anything, he seemed to be running on the fine line between honorable and wrong. In fact, she could even argue whether the way he was acting was legal or ethical.

"I'll try to trust your judgment."

He sent her a crooked half grin. "I have been wrong when it comes to people before, so feel free to use your own. I'll have to tell you about what I was supposed to be doing this week sometime." There was an edge of pain in his voice that made her want to ask him right now. But before she could ask, he turned away and strode toward his commander's door.

The knock reverberated through the nearly empty space. Finally, the woman in the corner looked up and seemed to notice them. She had a long scar over the bridge of her nose.

Though Jamie wasn't entirely sure, she could have sworn she smelled the sharp odor of fear in the air.

The woman started to open her mouth but slammed her lips shut and then stared back at her computer. Pierce didn't seem to notice as he tapped his knuckles on the glass of Reynolds' door.

"Come in." The man's voice was thin and raspy, like that of someone who'd smoked most of his life and lived in the bar for the remainder. Or maybe he just struggled to breathe.

She followed Pierce inside, keeping her gaze on the floor until he motioned for her to take the seat to the right while he took the gray cloth chair to the left.

Jamie sat down. In front of her was a man in a large black wheelchair. The device had all-terrain wheels. He had a joystick to control direction, and as she looked at him, Reynolds gave her a wave. "Good afternoon."

She tried to not act surprised. Pierce hadn't mentioned the man used a mobility aid.

"Nice to meet you…" She paused, unsure of exactly how to address the man. She glanced at Pierce for guidance.

Before he could speak, the captain spoke. "You can call me Eliot."

And just like that, she felt like a jerk for thinking ill of him.

"Nice to meet you, Eliot. I'm Jamie Trapper."

Eliot tipped his head. "So I've heard. Your reputation as a lifesaver precedes you. Thank you for the work you did in helping the man on the trail. I hear he is recovering well from the attack."

"I did what I thought was right." Her thoughts moved to this morning and how close they had come to becoming victims of attacks themselves. "Did Pierce tell you about our run-in with the mountain lion today?"

Eliot's gaze moved to Pierce. "What is she talking about?"

He nodded. "With the new findings, I forgot to tell you we had a minor bluff charge. The cat took off. I think the animal is just trying to protect its food caches, nothing more."

"Did it look unhealthy?" Eliot asked. "Do you think there is something we need to be concerned about as far as guests are concerned?"

"I keep saying I don't think so, but I've just been proven wrong," Pierce conceded. "I hate to make promises or assurances about things I can't guarantee. If anything, the only thing I can say with any degree of certainty is that if there are other bodies out there, or other caches that this animal has and a hiker crosses its path—this animal will attack."

A stone dropped in her stomach, but she didn't know exactly why. Perhaps it was the fact she hadn't even considered that there would be more dead bodies out there. In fact, there was nothing to say that the rib and the wallet weren't from a second body that had nothing to do with the remains she had initially located.

In fact, they could be dealing with a serial killer.

She was glad she was seated as her knees weakened at the thought.

If there was a serial killer dropping bodies in the park, and if they were watching the news of them locating the remains, did that mean she and Pierce would be placed in the sights of the killer? They could very well become the next targets. If they were taken out of the picture, they couldn't testify about their findings in a court of law. It would weaken any case a prosecutor would have—certainly not make or break it, but if a person was desperate to keep themselves from going to prison...

The thought made the hair rise on her arms.

It was true; no good deed went unpunished.

No, she was getting ahead of herself.

Eliot pulled something up on his computer screen. "We have been making headlines—already. This is what I was afraid of. In light of the new findings, I think it's important that we keep the cat under control and this new charge under wraps. Fair?"

It seemed wrong that he was asking them to hide the fact there was a dangerous animal on the loose but, given that there may have been a far more dangerous human out there, helped to keep her concern in proportion.

"What do you want to make of the mayor?" Pierce asked, his voice taking on a steely edge.

Something about Eliot shifted and he grew nervous, his gaze moved quickly around the room. "I hate this is in our laps."

"I think we should call in the locals—get a task force together. Detective Emily Monahan is Jamie's sister-in-law."

Eliot's face paled and he opened his mouth to speak but he closed it and took a moment before starting again. "I was hoping we could get away from this entire incident. It looks like that is going to be an impossibility."

"Is that why you told David you wanted us to work on the other missing person case?"

Eliot answered with a tiny nod. "So much for wishful thinking. There will be no minimizing this. As such, I need you to get going. Call in the task force. We have an ID. I had David run the remains to the state crime lab in Missoula. They are expediting their tests. I'm hoping we can at least find out if we have two victims or one within the next couple of days."

"Did you notify the mayor's family of the findings?"

"Don't worry about that until we have absolutely no doubt it's him. We don't want to make mistakes, given his family ties." Eliot gave Pierce a sharp look. "For now, you just handle pulling together the team. Vince can help when he comes back from vacation tomorrow. You guys need to find the gun. And, if this was a homicide, we need to find out who pulled the trigger."

Chapter Nine

Jamie was quiet as they walked out of headquarters and to his pickup.

"Want to go with me?" Pierce asked, looking over at Jamie.

Her face was tight and there was a look of hurt and confusion in her eyes. "That's fine. We can leave my pickup here."

It had been a strange meeting with his boss, but at least he had finally gotten somewhere with the man and received the approvals he'd wanted and needed to move forward. Yet, it still sat foul with him that Reynolds would have wanted to pull him off the death if they hadn't found the possible identity of the man—and learned it was the missing mayor.

And why hadn't he wanted him to do the death notification? Usually that fell to the highest-ranking officer, which was Pierce, to tell the family of the victim. He didn't see Reynolds handling it himself, he wasn't the type. That meant he must have been handing it off to David or someone else. Or, maybe he was just waiting until they had absolute confirmation on the ID.

If that was the case, he could understand. He wouldn't want to cause the family undue grief and heartbreak only to later learn that the remains they had located were, in fact, not Clyde's.

Yet he hadn't been wanting to give the notification in that moment.

He walked to the passenger side of the pickup and opened the door for Jamie. He waited for her to step up inside before closing the door and making the way over to his seat and getting inside. She turned to him as he clicked his seat belt into place. "What aren't you telling me about yourself?"

He was taken aback by her abruptness. "What? What do you mean? Are you upset with me?"

She shook her head. "I'm not mad." She softened her tone but he could tell she was forcing herself to remain calm. "Why would Eliot treat you with kid gloves? It was like he was worried about your feelings. Is there something going on with you that you aren't telling me? You said something earlier..."

For the first time today, he wished he was back dealing with the dead. "Are you hungry?"

"Are you just trying to avoid my question?" The anger returned to her voice.

He reached over and put his hand over hers, hoping she wouldn't pull away. When she didn't, he sent her a soft smile. "I promise I *will* tell you everything. I just need a minute."

She let out a long exhale and it made him want to tell her everything about Haven now. He looked at his watch and, as he did, he realized exactly what day it was, and his heart sank.

He needed the minute more than ever.

"I'll cook. I have steaks at my place. You okay with that?

I'm a pretty good cook. When we are done, I can bring you back and you can grab your pickup, or whatever you'd like. I'm sure you want to get back to it."

She nodded but remained quiet.

He hadn't meant to hurt her feelings or make her shut down. If anything, he'd wanted things to go in exactly the opposite direction. She was an incredible woman, and he had enjoyed every second he had spent with her—which was strange, given what they had been doing together.

It didn't take long for them to leave the gates of the park. He lived outside the park, near Hungry Horse Reservoir, with a place right along the edge of the lake. His mother and father had left him the house when they had passed away. When Haven had been living with him, she had taken most of his parents' things out and put them in the garage, replacing them with kitschy knickknacks and *Live Laugh Love* signs throughout the place.

When she'd moved out, she'd taken everything with her that was even remotely tied to her. Instead of buying anything new, with the exception of a 65-inch television from Costco, he'd gone out to the garage, pulled in all of his parents' old furnishings and put them back in the house. The pièce de résistance was his parents' old green-velvet couch complete with dark green fleur-de-lis that had been handed down from his mother's parents.

It was like stepping back in time, and it even carried the faint smell of his childhood. He couldn't quite put his finger on the scent, but if forced to explain, he would have said it was fryer grease mixed with his father's aftershave and his mother's at-home perm kits.

His thoughts moved to Jamie's family. All he really knew about the Trappers was what had been in the local newspaper, and he knew well enough to realize only half of what he read was true—and sometimes not even that much when it came to them making sure they had a good story. The truth was often obscured by perspective and battle lines.

"How many siblings do you have? You said your brother was married to Emily— What is his name?"

She looked surprised that he had suddenly broken the silence between them. He shouldn't have brought up her family when he was avoiding his own past, but maybe it would make it easier for him to explain things and not come off soft or like some loser.

He could tell she wasn't the kind of woman who wanted a guy in her life who was a pushover. She had dated a bull rider and her best friend was a bull rider. Her family was a ranching family. She could control a thousand-pound horse with her thighs. There was no way she would want a man like him in her life if he told her the truth.

"I had two brothers. My oldest brother died, I'm sure you heard about it, with my father. For a long time, the local police thought it was a murder-suicide. It was a whole thing. My other brother, Cameron, runs the ranch now. And then I have a sister who is younger than I am, who is running around Hollywood somewhere. Last time I saw her, she was in a commercial for yogurt." She laughed. "That was actually kind of cool."

"Do you talk to her?"

She shook her head. "I'm not even sure she knows my father's gone. And even if she did, I don't think she would care. My father was the epitome of misogyny. If I hadn't left home, I'm pretty sure he would have tried to have sold me off to the highest bidder to get me married and out of his hair."

He'd known her father'd had a reputation as a piece of work, but he'd not known the degree to which she'd suffered. Some of her hardness and also her capability and adaptability made sense. "It's no wonder you're so strong. I'm sorry you've had to go through everything you've had to go through."

She closed her eyes as she ran her fingertips over her temple. "I wish I would have gone to college. I always did well in school. However, that really wasn't an option for me. My father refused to help me with financial aid, and I couldn't afford to do it on my own even with some of the scholarships I received. I think that was the moment I really decided that I was going to leave the ranch and never come back."

And yet here she was. He couldn't imagine everything she was feeling in having returned to the one place she'd sworn she would never return. The more he learned about her, the more he wanted to take her in his arms and rescue her. However, he wasn't sure that that was what she was looking for; if anything, it seemed as though she was looking to find answers about herself.

"There's a pretty good community college here in Kalispell. What would you go back to school for?" he asked.

"I love animals, so I spent a lot of time thinking about veterinary medicine. However, after John's accident and now this, I don't know if I want to deal with trauma."

The rawness of her statement made him hurt for her. He could certainly understand her feelings. "I know how hard it is to compartmentalize."

"Compartmentalizing is what got me to where I am today."

Road noise sat between them like static on an old television, heavy and tense.

Maybe he wasn't as soft as he thought he was. Or maybe he had gotten her wrong. Perhaps, she was softer than he realized.

His old cabin sat at the end of the gravel road, tucked back in the timber. Hungry Horse Reservoir sat at the edge of his property, and he had a long dock that stretched out into the lake. As they drove up and parked, a white-tailed buck that was grazing on a bush near the cabin's front window lifted his head. He switched his tail, annoyed that they would interrupt his feeding.

"That's Gregory Peck. He was born on the property about six years ago. The doe who had him had lived here for ten years before that." He smiled at the thought. "It's funny how you get connected to the animals, even the wild ones. My parents had named the doe Fauna. She was around for a long time. My mom really enjoyed watching her. Some years she'd even have twins."

"My mom was like that on the ranch, too. We had a herd of elk that would always come down from the mountains during the fall. There was one cow that my mom had rescued when it was a calf and got stuck in our fence. After that, this elk would always come up to the front door in the mornings and bed down while my mom had her morning coffee."

He could tell from the tone in her voice that she missed her mom just as much as he missed his own. It amazed him that they had both been through so much loss and yet they were both relatively young. It made him wonder how much more life would deal him—good and bad. It also made him wonder how much a single person could withstand before they lost themselves.

"Gregory Peck probably won't run when we go to the

front door, just so you know. However, he doesn't know you, so he may, so don't be alarmed."

Some of the heaviness that had seemed to weigh on her dissipated as she opened the truck door and stepped out. The deer switched his tail again, but didn't bother to move. He looked at Jamie and then at Pierce, and then the deer put his head back down and started grazing on the bush once again.

Gregory Peck was the closest thing Pierce had to a dog, so he was glad that he had his deer's approval. It was silly, but he took it as a sign. Deer were extremely skittish creatures, and if he didn't feel the need to run from Jamie then Pierce could definitely tell her his truth without fear that she would turn against him.

They moved quietly inside and Pierce closed the door behind them.

"So, his name is Gregory Peck. Does that mean that you are a fan of classic movies?"

"Yes, *To Kill a Mockingbird* is one of my favorites and his best role." He smiled. "I'm a huge fan of classic movies and books. I'm a big reader. Around here, as I'm sure you know, technology is an amenity sometimes and electricity can be hit or miss in the winter. Books are always available and there's nothing better than sitting in front of a wood-burning stove and reading at night before you go to bed."

She tilted her head as she looked at him, appraisingly, and he was struck by how beautiful she truly was, inside and out. Those eyes had a way of just stopping him in his tracks. "You have got to be kidding. I used to get made fun of all the time on the rodeo circuit because I was the big nerd who would sit at the trailers and read while everybody else went to the bars and wanted to get rowdy."

"You can't tell me you didn't get rowdy once in a while. I thought we weren't lying to one another." He laughed, the sound coming from his core, and it felt good. It was the kind of laugh that he hadn't experienced in a long time, and he hadn't realized how much he had missed it until now.

Her eyes sparkled. It was stupid that he noticed such a thing, but they really did. Maybe it was the light, or maybe it was their being with one another, but it was like something in the way she looked at him had awakened.

Or maybe that was wishful thinking.

"Oh, I can be rowdy. You know what they say about barrel racers…"

"What is that?"

"It's always said in rodeo that the barrel racers are the wildest bunch out there. There's nothing we won't do— and I can honestly say that that's normally true. Some of the girls I raced with were balls-to-the-wall, all the time. They were a lot of fun, but you can only keep up that level of energy for so long."

"If you could, would you want to go back to rodeoing again?" he asked, careful not to bring up the accident and any pain it may cause.

She shook her head. "I tried to stick with it, I did. I just got…*old.*"

"You're far from old." He led her toward the kitchen as they spoke.

"Old doesn't have anything to do with age—not there, and not even in life. You know?"

He did. He knew only too well. "I hear you and I know how you are feeling." He walked to the sink, washed his hands, and then moved to the fridge and took out the package of steaks.

"Do you need help?" she asked.

"No, you sit down. I have some wine or beer, if you'd like. I may even have some iced tea. What would you like?" He stepped around the kitchen island, pulled out the oak swivel chair and motioned for her to take a seat.

She smiled at him as she sat down. "I'll take a beer. I'm pretty low maintenance."

He grabbed a Yellow Jacket out of the fridge and popped open the can and handed it to her. "I hope you like Banquets."

She took a swig. "Perfect. These are Matt's favorites, so I've learned to like them, too. The last time we were in Casper, my buddies ended up building an entire pyramid out of these damned things. It was awesome until some idiot, a bronc rider, decided to take a dive into it. He ended up cutting his arm and needing forty-five stitches. It really was a cool pyramid. We were going to send pictures into Coors and ask them to be our sponsors." She laughed.

"There's no way they could have turned you down if you had a performance like that." He smirked. "You never told me how you did on the circuit. You must have been pretty good. How many years were you doing it?"

She played with the tab on the can, making a thrumming sound as she let it go. "I was number three on the WPRA list of best barrel racers, and my total winnings my last year were well over a hundred and twenty thousand. I'd like to say it was me, but really, I had a fantastic gelding who was doing all the hard work. He was voted horse of the year."

"What is his name?"

"His working name is MacGyver Moonflash, but I just call him Mac. He is fun to watch—he's fast and agile. His lines are pure art."

"Do you still have him?"

She nodded. "Yeah, but I think it's a disservice to him. I think he could have still had a couple of good years running the circuit. I feel guilty. He loved his job. I've been thinking about selling him, but he is my best friend."

"Is he happy at the ranch?"

She tapped on the can. "I think so. I've been using him to work. Not so much barrel racing, but I do let him cut cattle. Well, we've been working on it. It's a new skill for him, but he definitely has it in his blood. He is taking to it naturally. You should see his pivot."

"Anytime you want to bring me out to the ranch, I'm game," he said, taking spices out of the cabinet over the stove and prepping the steaks for the grill. "And, for the record, I think Mac is probably just fine with you on the ranch. If you wanted, you could probably hire him out to stud and make a good living."

"I've talked to Matt about that."

He felt a wiggle of jealousy, though he knew it was senseless. Just because she was friends with Matt didn't mean there was anything or would be anything between them—and he wasn't in a position in which he was to worry about her; they were only friends. However, he wasn't the kind of friend she told him Matt was; he did want more.

He felt ridiculous for being jealous at a time like this. It was out of character for him, but maybe with everything that had happened over the last year, he had changed. Maybe that *life* thing had affected him more than he cared to admit.

"Are you going to stay around here, or do you think you are just going to stay at the ranch until you are back on your feet?"

She took a long drink of her beer and sat it back down on the counter with a thud. "Asking me my plans is like asking what the clouds will do next. I am the first person to admit that I can be a bit flighty."

Did that mean if he got close to her that she would leave him just like Haven had?

Now he wasn't so sure he wanted to open up to her and tell her what had happened. If he did, he would only make himself vulnerable and more apt to be hurt. He didn't need any more pain in his life—and neither did Jamie. They'd both had more than their fair share, not just in the last few years, but in their lives. It seemed as though both of their lives had been filled with incredible losses.

It was a wonder she had even agreed to come back to his house with him, that she had trusted him enough to be alone like this. Perhaps that was a good sign, one that indicated she wasn't going to run away. Yet he'd always followed the adage that when a person told you who they were, it was best to believe them.

It made him wonder how he would have explained himself—reclusive, jaded, unwilling to open up. If that were all true, was it really fair of him to have invited her back to his place and hope for a more romantic evening? Then he realized, if that were true, he wouldn't have invited her there, at all.

Perhaps what a person said about themselves was far harsher and more self-deprecating than was justified or accurate.

He knew only too well that he was his own worst critic. Actually, that may have been Haven right up until she'd left—she had loved to point out all his faults and to use them against him.

"You went somewhere." Jamie stood up and walked over to him as he stared out the window and toward the lake. She put her hand on his lower back and the action and warmth was so soft and unexpected that he tensed for a moment before relaxing.

When he did, Jamie's face softened. "Are you okay?" she continued.

He nodded and turned to her. She kept her hand on his back and, as he moved, she wrapped her other arm around him as well. Her touch made his pulse race.

He wiped off his hands and then reached up and pushed a strand of hair from her face. "Do you have any idea how beautiful you are?" He smiled at her as he looked into her eyes.

"Thank you." Jamie grinned but didn't look away coquettishly as some women would have done. She was so strong. "I have to tell you, from the first time I saw you on the mountain, I have been imagining what a moment like this with you would feel like."

He leaned down and his lips found hers. As his tongue grazed her bottom lip, he pulled her harder against his body. He slid his hand down her back and the other to the base of her head and slipped his fingers into her soft, thick hair.

Her breath caught as he took their kiss deeper, more fervent and wanting. He had wanted her, too. She had come out of nowhere and barreled into his life like hell on wheels and he loved her for it, he needed her—he needed her to bring him back to reality and to show him how it felt to be whole again.

She leaned away and looked at him. Her eyes were heavy with desire, and he couldn't help himself and he kissed her again, faster and hungrier.

Her fingernails dug into his skin as she kissed him hard.
He didn't know who was in control and he didn't care.

She tasted like beer and want.

She let go of him and put her hand to his face.

As her thumb caressed his scruff, he broke their kiss.
His body needed a moment for him to gain control. She
was so sexy. He wanted her so badly.

"You...you are perfect." His voice was raspy and heavy
with desire.

She laughed and looked away as she gently pulled free
of his arms. Jamie licked his kiss from her lips, the action
so unexpectedly sensual that he found himself wanting to
pull her into his arms and kiss her again.

How dare she remove his kiss from her skin? He wanted
to be there, to remind her of him for as long as he could...

At least until he told her the truth.

The truth... The thought pulled him to dinner. To why
they'd come here and what he had promised her. He needed
to be honest. Then, if he was, she could make an informed
decision between staying or going. He wouldn't begrudge
her if she decided his baggage was too heavy and his life
was too much for her to want to even dip her toes into.

He turned to the counter and pulled out two potatoes
and, cleaning and poking them, threw them into the microwave. He started it with a few pushes of the buttons
and it hummed to life, filling the space between them with
much-needed sound—and something besides his intrusive
and damning thoughts.

Jamie took a long drink of beer and she closed her eyes
like she was trying to capture the flavor on her tongue
forever.

"The beer isn't that good," he teased, grabbing some

crackers out of the cupboard and sitting them on the counter in front of her for a snack.

"I wasn't thinking about beer. I was thinking about how glad I am to be here, and to be with you. And I'm trying to hold back my desire to tell you all the ways I'm not perfect—and trust me, there's a long list."

He smiled. "I'm so glad you are here, too. And as far as you being perfect, you may not be what you consider *perfect*, but some things are best in the eye of the beholder."

"Then you may need glasses." She giggled and the sound was so endearing and sweet that it made his chest tighten.

"If anyone in this room is imperfect, it is me," he said, grabbing a package of frozen corn kernels out of the freezer, pouring them into a pot with water and putting them on the stove, setting them to simmer.

"So far, I haven't seen anything that would give me any inclination to worry," she said with a smile.

Pierce gave an internal groan, but there was no doubt that his moment had come—he had to tell her the truth. "I have a past and I've made so many mistakes." He considered grabbing a beer but stopped himself in case she told him she wanted to leave and he had to give her a ride back to her truck. He didn't want to have any reason to keep her from leaving him and this place if what he told her disgusted her.

"Oh?" she asked, pulling a paper towel off the roll sitting in the middle of the counter with a tearing sound. "Have you bedded a thousand women? Should I call you Don Juan? Or do you have so many dating apps that your phone has run out of storage space from all your pictures and videos?" She gave him a cute look from under her brows as she sat back down on the chair and waited for the heavy blow of his admission to fall.

It was as if Jamie knew he was going to drop some kind of ax.

He hated that it had to be to the neck of their new relationship. "I'm not a fan of Lord Byron nor his Don Juan," he said with a laugh. "I'm a long way from a womanizer. In fact, for the last four years, I've only had one woman in my life. Her name was Haven—and today was supposed to be our wedding day."

There was a long deathly silence—the only sound was the hum. That damned hum.

He waited for Jamie to say something, but he didn't know exactly what he wished she would say or do. He didn't want pity. Heck, he didn't want to talk about the fact he should have been standing in a tuxedo in front of a church in Missoula, nearly at this moment. He didn't want to tell her he was still paying off the trip to London and through the UK. A trip he was supposed to now either take or eat the cost of—either way, he was paying for two tickets.

Mostly, he didn't want to tell her how badly losing everything that was supposed to be his past, present and future had broken him. Until now and meeting Jamie, he wasn't sure why he'd kept working so hard and pushing. It would have been so easy to just succumb to his desire to run away to Mexico and live on a beach.

Jamie reached over and took his hand with hers. "Is she still alive?"

Of all the ways he thought she was going to go with his admission, this had been the last one—and yet, he should have guessed. "She is." He nodded as he laced his fingers through Jamie's and gave her a look of apology for her loss. "But she's with another man—my half brother, Dylan."

She looked at him like he was on some '90s midday soap opera.

He definitely felt as though that is what his life had become. The torrid relationship had split his family down the middle. "After my mother passed when I was a teenager, my father remarried when I was a freshman in high school. I liked his wife, but her son Dylan and I never really got along."

"Ever?"

"We are the same age. Our birthdays are a day apart. One year, our parents tried to do a joint family party and it ended up with him and me in a fistfight—he started it. I am not one for that kind of violence. I ended up breaking these two teeth," he said, pointing to his front incisors. "He said my mother dying was the best thing that ever happened to me. I was lucky to have a stepmother like his mom. She was more than my father deserved."

"So, he literally asked for the fight?"

He nodded. "I didn't throw the first punch." He sighed, running his tongue over the smoothness of his crowns on his front teeth. "We never spoke again. Haven was our go-between while we were planning the wedding and all the events around it. His two kids were supposed to be our flower girls."

"Is he married?"

"He is now going through a divorce." He cringed at the truth of his dysfunctional family continued to unfold. "This is why I hate talking about all of this."

She lifted their entwined hands and her warm breath caressed his fingers. Jamie dropped her forehead to their hands and paused for a moment before looking up at him. "You don't have to worry about me judging you for your family's actions. Regardless of what happened between you and this woman, you didn't push her into the arms of your stepbrother. She is an adult and made her choices. She, alone, is responsible for them."

"Some bridges are too far for respectful people and respectful families, and I understand that. Your family has a name in this community."

"My father ruined that name. You and I both know that. And regardless of what people think of my family, that has no relevance on my relationships. I will date whomever I want to date. I've spent enough of my time oppressed by my father and by the rules of society. I don't want anyone or any stupid unspoken standards running my life."

He pulled her to the edge of her chair and she wrapped her legs around him. The microwave beeped loudly and she turned and started to speak, but he took her by the chin. "No. Now you don't get to let a microwave dictate what we do, either."

He took her lips in a loving kiss. She really was everything he had been looking for; he'd always wanted a woman who would stop at nothing to get what she wanted and would say exactly what she was thinking and feeling. He appreciated directness—even though he knew it could be a double-edged sword.

Her hands moved to the edge of his shirt and he leaned into her, only too happy to oblige her bidding. She was everything in his world that mattered and the reason he wanted to breathe.

She pulled the fabric free of the confinement of his jeans and the cool air rushed over the warm skin of his abs, chilling him and making goose bumps rise. He took her face in his hands and looked into her eyes, trying to thank her and tell her all the things that he could not say—all the things he was feeling and couldn't even put into words in his soul.

Her fingers skimmed over the muscles on his stomach and she dug her nails into his skin just hard enough to make temporary, delicious marks. She must have known how much he loved the edges of pain. "As much as I want you," she whispered, breaking their kiss but allowing their lips to graze as she spoke, "I don't think we should take things to the bedroom tonight. Not tonight. Not *this* night. I'll stay at your place tonight, but we can't sleep together. I don't want our first night together to be tainted by memories."

She could no longer argue; she was his definition of perfection.

Chapter Ten

Jamie had spent the night staring at the ceiling in Pierce's bedroom. The ride back to her pickup had been cordial but not chatty, and she had been grateful. Things between them weren't awkward, but they weren't what they had been the night before and, when she'd walked into the ranch house, she was grateful to take off her cowboy boots, sit down on the leather couch and turn on the television.

There were the sounds of someone in the kitchen and the smell of hot coffee, but she didn't say anything in hopes that whoever was up and moving hadn't heard her try to sneak into the ranch house this morning. She didn't want to answer any questions—no matter who asked.

The news was depressing and it cast a shroud on her thoughts and memories of her time with Pierce. His kiss had been so...so *powerful*.

It wasn't like anything she'd experienced before.

She had thought she had known passion and want, but what she felt with Pierce was so different.

It was so strange and unexpected that she wasn't sure it could be real. Perhaps it was just the ice breaking on her heart and the feeling of it starting to beat again. After everything he had told her last night, it had been no wonder he had been hesitant in bringing her into his life and in wanting to tell her the truth about his life and his past. From an objective point of view, he was a walking red flag.

And yet it wasn't his fault. He wasn't behind the horrible things that had happened in his life. She'd told herself she wouldn't judge him and to do so would have been victim-blaming at its worst.

With everything that had happened to him, though, she had to be concerned whether he was healed enough to move forward and find love again—especially with her.

In fact, she had to ask the same of herself.

If Pierce was the man she thought he was, he was probably asking himself that exact question. She was as broken as he was—two hearts that were as busted as theirs had no business moving as quickly as they were.

They needed to step back and take a moment to assess whether what they were feeling was real or if they were merely connected through kindred experiences and communal pain.

Matt came walking out of the kitchen carrying two cups of coffee. He sat it on the table next to her and then plopped down in the chair beside the couch. "Long night?"

"Can you tell?" She picked up the mug and took a sip of the hot creamy coffee. "Thank you for this, I needed it."

"You look like you went through it, and not in the best way." Matt leaned back. "If you want, I can make some breakfast. If you're trying to work off a hangover, there's nothing like a couple of eggs."

She shook her head. "Not a hangover, just a confusing night." She wasn't sure she wanted to tell Matt where she had been or with whom—she didn't want him to think she was sullying John's memory for even a second or moving on too quickly.

Besides, things with Pierce were in the very early stages. After their quiet drive home this morning, it was quite possible that they were through. Maybe he'd spent his night as she had, second-guessing his actions and wondering why he had made the choice to kiss her.

"You wanna talk to me about it?"

She sighed.

"Got it." Matt clicked back the recliner.

Jamie appreciated Matt's ability to read her and work around her tender areas. Maybe he would be fine with her dating again and it was just she who wasn't entirely ready to put words to whatever was happening in her life.

"I talked to your brother and Emily last night. Sounds like she is amped about rolling out on the investigation. She isn't up yet, though." Matt glanced down at his watch. "I think she has to head in soon."

She hadn't thought about it, but Pierce likely had a very long day ahead if he was heading the joint task force and leading the investigation. He would have to pull in resources from around the area and orchestrate well-organized searches of the complete death scene as well as take a deep dive into the mayor's life and disappearance. And that was just to start.

The thought of what it would take to command the unit was impressive, to say nothing about the volume of information they would pull together as a cohesive unit.

She didn't envy the work he had to do today. Organizing people was a nightmare. She would always prefer animals to people.

Emily walked down the hallway, adjusting her belt.

Looking up, she spotted them. "You pour some coffee for me?"

"I'll grab you one," Matt said, putting down his recliner and going to the kitchen.

Emily sat down next to Jamie on the couch and grabbed her hiking books and started to put them on. "So, I was talking to your friend, Ranger Hauser. It sounds like he was interested in continuing the search of the mountain for more evidence. I'm going to run up there. If you are looking for a way to help, you are welcome to join."

"Is Pierce going to be up there with you?" she asked before she thought about what she was saying or how she must have sounded to Emily.

Her sister-in-law looked at her with a quirk of the brow.

Jamie looked away before Emily could see any tells on her face. She was a good detective, and probably good enough that even without looking at her, she had an idea of exactly what was happening. Jamie didn't need to give her any more information.

"I don't think he is hiking up to the mountain today. He is going to be incident command." Emily tied her boots and stood up. "Why don't you go ahead and ride with me up there? You can tell me about everything you know and catch me up."

Matt walked out of the kitchen carrying a to-go cup of coffee for Emily as Jamie stood up. She wasn't sure if she should stay or go, but there was nothing around here that Matt couldn't handle—he could handle feeding the horses and work with the ranch hands to check on the cattle.

As for going, things with Pierce had ended so quietly this morning. She pulled out her phone and looked to see if he had texted her—there was nothing. At minimum, she would have expected a "Thanks for last night" or "Have a good day." She wasn't about to be the one to reach out first. She wasn't thirsty.

If he hadn't texted, maybe she had been right about him regretting everything—or maybe she was just being neurotic and overthinking. It wasn't like he owed her anything and, even if they never spoke again, they had shared some amazing time together.

His kiss...

That had been one of the best kisses of her life. It was the only kiss she could even recall. When his lips had moved over hers, she had forgotten the world around her. Her hair had curtained her view of the world and there was only him and his kiss.

If she could, she wanted to see if she had the same feeling of weightless euphoria that she'd had before. If she did, then he and the relationship were something worth delving into, but more than likely, he had just been hurting.

She was his soft landing, a safe woman to keep from thinking about where he should have been and who he should have been with. Part of her wanted to see this woman. Yet, if Jamie never heard about her again, that would be entirely fine as well.

One thing was certain, she wasn't going to compete with a memory—and she wasn't going to make him compete with a ghost.

To bring her to his home, a home he may have shared with that woman, bothered her. Then again, the house hadn't looked like it had been worked over by a woman. If anything, it had looked as if a second-hand store had been giving furniture away and he'd taken what was left over at the end of the day.

She laughed at the thought. Maybe she wasn't so upset, after all.

Matt touched her shoulder. "You all right?"

She nodded. "I'm gonna run back up to Glacier and the investigation. Emily wants my help."

Matt looked over to her and she gave him a reaffirming nod.

She patted his hand. "Don't worry, man. I need to get out of the house and get my mind off things. This will be good for me. Would you mind tending to the animals for me? Make sure Mac is fed?"

"No problem. When I'm done, I may run into Kalispell and pick up some things at the store. I'll see you later."

"Sounds good. You know where the keys are for the ranch trucks." She motioned toward the board where all the keys were hung. "And, hey, thanks for the coffee."

He smiled widely. "Not a prob."

She followed Emily outside and to her blacked-out SUV. It was an undercover rig and it was badass. Jamie hadn't had the chance to ride in it before and she had a niggle of nerves as she stepped up to the door. It wasn't every day that she got into a cop car. As long as she got out, sans handcuffs, she would be fine.

As they drove toward the park, she told Emily about everything that had happened—from her rescue of Anthony to the cat's bluff charge.

"That's impressive. You've been through the wringer. I'm glad Ranger Hauser seems to have taken you under his wing," she said. "I don't know him very well, but it seems like he has taken to you. Yes?"

Oh, here came the twenty questions from the detective. She hadn't wanted to open up to Matt, and she'd known him far better than Emily, but Emily also hadn't been close to John. That wasn't to say she wouldn't judge her, but she had a feeling Emily had probably heard just about everything. Her talking about her emotions wasn't going to throw her sister-in-law for a loop.

"He has been good to work with. He's let me help, which has been cool."

Emily nodded, but she could see her looking over at her. "You know that isn't an everyday thing, right?"

"Yes." She didn't want to elaborate.

Emily smiled knowingly. And just like that, Jamie knew she had been caught.

"Is that where you were last night?"

There was no avoiding the conversation now. "Yes. It was supposed to be his wedding day. Nothing happened."

Emily's foot slipped on the gas pedal and the SUV lurched slightly. "His *wedding* day?"

"Exactly. He's a walking red flag."

Emily grumbled something unintelligible, but she could tell that Jamie was as bothered by the idea as she was.

"It was a bad breakup and not his fault. It's been a while since they have been together."

Emily's jaw unclenched, but only slightly.

"His family has about as much drama as ours."

Emily pulled to the side of the road after they passed through the front gates of the park. "Look, if you don't want to see Pierce ever again, I will take you back to the ranch right now. There is nothing here that requires your presence. I asked you here, admittedly, to try and get you to move things forward with him. After what you told me, maybe I screwed up."

It felt like an impasse—a choice between what could be and the end of complicated.

Jamie picked at her thumbnail. "I don't know if I *will* see him, but if I do, I don't mind. Just because he has a past doesn't mean I have any room to judge him. I have a past of my own. Most dudes would consider me a red flag, too."

Emily shook her head. "I highly doubt that—at least not when it comes to your past. They would probably judge you more for being a barrel racer. You know." Emily laughed.

Jamie stuck her tongue out at Emily and chuckled.

Emily pulled back onto the road and out into the line of traffic heading into the park. "You do what you think is right for you. If you think you are ready, don't let anything or anyone stand in your way."

"I appreciate that, sister."

Emily smiled. "You don't know how much that means to me. I was hoping we would get there someday. I wasn't sure how things would go with your family—or with you and your sister. Your brother said you were good people."

"I am," she said, tipping her head with grace. "I can't speak for my sister though."

"One step at a time. Considering your brother and I have only been together a year, I'd say things have come a long way in a short time."

"I think that just goes to prove how wrong we can be about people. Life and relationships are so complicated."

Emily nodded as she drove. "You don't have to tell me about that, I'm only too familiar. I don't know how much your brother has told you about how we got together, but it's a good whisky story."

The white incident command trailer was parked at the now-closed trailhead and a ranger was posted there to turn away any tourists who thought it a good idea to bypass the signs and enter at their own risk. As they parked, a woman in a burgundy Patagonia jacket, khaki shorts and a fanny pack with bear spray and two water bottles was standing in front of the man. She was leaning on two black trekking poles as though she was going to be hiking to the North Pole and not a well-kept and traveled trail.

Jamie could tell, based on the woman's scowling face, that she wasn't impressed that she was being turned away from the trailhead. The woman reached into her fanny pack and was drawing out her wallet, but the ranger was waving her off from what appeared to be a bribe.

There was a sign to the right of the ranger warning of the dangerous mountain lion and the recent interactions with humans, but apparently this woman must have thought something like that didn't apply to her. It was always this type of disconnect and apathy that created dangerous situations.

Regardless, Jamie was glad that they had decided to close the trail. If only they had taken it seriously earlier. At least no one else had really gotten hurt.

As Emily parked, she turned one last time to Jamie. "I'm going to leave this car open. If you don't want to stay around Pierce, or if the investigation becomes too much, you're welcome to find respite here."

Jamie nodded appreciatively. She said nothing as she got out, hoping that there would be no need for her to even think about running away or hiding. She could work with Pierce on the investigation without taking things to the next level in their relationship. They had no relationship, when it came right down to it. They were merely friends, and perhaps friends who kissed—maybe just that one time, last night.

It was amazing, but they both needed time before jumping any deeper.

Thinking about him, as though the simple act was some cosmic magnet, Pierce stepped out of the trailer and immediately looked in her direction. He smiled as he saw her. She smiled back, but it wavered on her lips as she thought about all the reasons they shouldn't be together.

A Black man stepped out of the trailer behind Pierce and tapped him on the shoulder, and he turned away. The man was wearing a ranger's uniform, but she hadn't seen him before. The two men were talking animatedly, and she could hear Pierce say something about Reynolds.

There was something about the way Pierce said the name that told her there were things the two men were unpacking when it came to their boss—and that relationship.

"We'll continue this later," Pierce said under his breath to the man as he turned to face them. "Hi, ladies. Jamie, I'm glad you came out—I wasn't sure you would."

So, he had felt the coolness between them this morning, as well. At least she wasn't alone in her assumptions.

"Hey, Vince," Emily said, sending a small two-fingered wave.

Jamie wasn't sure why she was surprised; of course Emily would know the rangers from the area. This probably wasn't the first time they'd worked together. Jamie was the newcomer here, not these folks.

"This is my sister-in-law Jamie," Emily said, introducing her. She noticed her gaze moving over to Pierce, but he seemed to look everywhere but at Emily, as if he could guess they had been talking. "She is considering joining my search and rescue unit."

Jamie tried not to act surprised.

Vince nodded as he walked over and extended his hand in greeting. "I'm a bit of a hugger," he said as she shook his hand and he pulled her into a gentle one-armed hug, their hands still clasped. "It's okay, you don't have to fake anything with me. Pierce already told me he has a thing for you. Just so you know, he is an awesome guy," he whispered, stepping back and sending her a wink.

Regardless of how much Vince liked him, when she stepped back, Pierce didn't seem to be able to meet her eye. Apparently, after last night, the best she could hope for in his life was an ancillary, accidental smile and promises of awkwardness.

Chapter Eleven

Pierce wanted to curl up under a rock and disappear.

He had made a major misstep in bringing Jamie to his house last night and there was no justification for his mistake. Of course, she would want nothing to do with him after that. The only surprise was that she'd come back to help with the investigation. However, according to Emily, she was thinking about joining SAR and her being there had nothing to do with him and more to do with her.

He could understand her desire to see this case through to the end. He regularly had to help with situations and disturbances within the park—especially partner and family member assaults in which he issued tickets or warnings but was then forced to leave the scene without really knowing what would come of his interceding.

In most cases, he had a feeling all he had done was make things worse. When women were victims of narcissistic abuse and domestic violence, a ranger or police officer coming in and writing tickets for the abuser's behavior would only escalate the danger.

At least for Jamie, she didn't have to worry about the violence continuing or worsening—well, hopefully. He hadn't heard from the medical examiner yet. If it was found that the mayor had died from anything more than a self-inflicted gunshot wound, then perhaps they did need to worry.

An ache rose in his gut.

He needed to make that call this morning. The results should be in today.

Vince motioned for him to step into the incident command trailer.

"Yeah?" he said, walking in and closing the door behind himself.

Emily and Jamie were standing outside. According to Emily, they were waiting for several other members of the SAR team. He was glad they were finally running at full capacity with the support of Reynolds. Even though everything was going the way it should, he had a sinking feeling he couldn't quite explain—and he didn't think it was entirely to do with the tension with Jamie.

Vince plopped down on the desk chair and it squeaked loudly under his weight. "Look, you and I both know Donovan was an ass. He had a reputation as a playboy and any one of his many girlfriends—or their husbands—could have been behind his death."

"You know how this goes. Everyone dies. It is just up to us to figure out the circumstances, not the justification or the righteousness. If we started to question if deaths were fair, we wouldn't be able to do this job."

Vince huffed a laugh. "That's no lie. All I'm saying is that maybe Cap was right in not pulling out all the stops for this one."

"He didn't know the ID when he was calling us off," he pointed out.

Vince raised a brow. "Oh?" He reached for an open bag of jerky and grabbed a piece. He pulled at the meat like he was some kind of scavenging bird. "You do know that Mayor Donovan was sleeping with Reynolds's wife?"

Pierce stopped. Vince had to be messing with him. "How do you know that? Is that just gossip or do you know something?"

Vince shrugged. "It was word on the street. Also, according to what I heard, the mayor's wife, Carey, was sleeping with any seemingly high-brow official she could get into bed. She was a social climber and would stop at nothing to succeed—even if that meant spreading her legs. I think she also wanted justice for Donovan's indiscretions—an eye-for-an-eye kind of thing."

"I only knew he had filed for a divorce, I didn't know anything about his wife. Or, their *situation*."

Vince nodded. "It gets better. What she couldn't get done with sexual favors, she gossiped about. She was notorious for running smear campaigns. She was one of the most toxic people I've ever met, and I gotta say Donovan would have been lucky to be rid of her."

"Was their divorce finalized when he went missing?"

Vince shoved the rest of the piece of jerky in his mouth and pulled open the laptop on the counter. He opened up the NCIC, or the Information Center, and typed Donovan's name. There was the complete list of everywhere he had ever lived, every phone number he'd been assigned, his social security number, and every single relative and relationship that could be used to track a person down.

The database was impressive, and as they dug around, they located Carey's information with a few simple clicks. According to what they found, the divorce had never gone through. However, she *had* filed a death certificate as she had an affidavit declaring he was suicidal and therefore he could be assumed dead.

That was interesting.

The marital property was still in probate and no ruling had yet been made. There was no information about the upcoming court appearance, but if there had been a filing, there would be a definitive date.

If there were any filings made now that they had found the body, and if there was any indication this was a homicide, they could file an injunction to stop the proceedings.

They needed answers, and fast.

There was no definitive proof that Carey was behind Donovan's death or disappearance, and it was very possible that her affidavit was correct, but there was something in Pierce's gut that told him there was more to this than Clyde just going to the woods and offing himself.

"Clyde was stepping out on his marriage, too. Do you know anything more about that?" he asked Vince.

Vince shrugged. "I only knew about Nicole, Reynolds's wife, for sure—Reynolds let it slip once. I can ask around at the courthouse, I have friends over there, but you might be best off just asking his dad, Judge Donovan. Or, you could talk to Emily. She worked in the same building and rubbed shoulders with the guy, I bet."

He nodded, but as he thought about talking to Emily his mind instantly moved to Jamie.

Maybe having her here wasn't a good thing. Everything he did seemed to make him think of her—she had become a distraction. That wasn't fair of him, and he had a feeling her being there or twenty miles away was irrelevant. He would be thinking about her regardless of her location.

Things between them had gone sideways because of him.

She hadn't done anything wrong—in fact, she had been right and the sensible one. He had apologized, but there was really no coming back from the major mistake he had made. Or maybe the fact that she was here and *wanted to* be here, meant that he had some room for redeemability.

"Don't worry about her." Vince smiled.

"Huh?"

"I can see you're thinking about Jamie," Vince teased. "Just do what you do best and be your charming self. She wants you, man." Vince stood up and cuffed him playfully on the shoulder. "Just maybe not on what was supposed to be your wedding night. Dude, that was amateur hour. At least, you shouldn't have told her."

"Just because you hide things from the women you date doesn't mean I do."

"Clearly, you've been out of the dating game for a while," Vince said with a tired laugh. "If you started telling every-one the truth, dating would go nowhere. You have to play the game a little bit, man."

Pierce had no game. That was a fact. Plain and simple, he didn't want to have game. He just wanted to find a good woman who respected him and didn't leave his heart shred-ded in the dirt.

If Jamie would give him another chance, maybe they could take things as they came and keep trying. They had so much in common and when he saw her, just like today, every part of his body lit up. It was like she was a sunbeam in the darkest of winter days.

"The closest thing I have to game is watching college football," he joked, stepping to the door. "If you manage to pull anything else about Donovan, let me know."

"Actually," Vince said, rubbing the back of his neck

nervously, "I want to tell you before it comes out any other way…"

"Did you date Emily or something?"

"Not Emily…" Vince gave him the guiltiest look he had ever seen him give. "Around the time Donovan went missing, his wife and I might have been having a *thing*."

He stopped with his hand on the door handle. Vince was his best friend and the man who was supposed to have been the best man at his wedding. He knew his buddy had a habit of bedding just about any woman who would take him, but this was a new low.

Pierce turned back to Vince and looked him square in the face. "You had better hope that the medical examiner comes back with a report that says there is no way this was a homicide. If they don't, you know you will be off this investigation…and will instead be put on the top of our list of suspects."

Chapter Twelve

Pierce came out of the incident command trailer a different man than when he had walked in. Even his gait had changed. When he stepped out, he was on a mission, and he charged toward Jamie, took her by the arm and led her to his truck. "You're coming with me."

She looked over her shoulder in Emily's direction, who sent her a look of concern. Jamie shook her head and mouthed, *It's okay.* Emily frowned, but she gave her a nod and motioned for her to call.

It was strange, but the way Pierce had just taken control of her and the situation was a kind of a turn-on. She liked that he didn't ask questions or want to dance around the issues anymore. Whether or not he wanted to talk about what had happened, he wanted her with him.

He walked her to his truck and opened the door. "We have to run some errands. Get in."

She could tell it wasn't a suggestion and she stepped up and settled in. As he got in and they headed out, she wanted to ask him what had happened inside that little white trailer, but based on his scowl, she wasn't sure she wanted to roll the dice. He looked as though he was jonesing for a fight.

After a few minutes of driving, Pierce picked up his phone and dialed. "Dr. Lee? Hey, yeah."

She couldn't really make out the words, just the baritone of the man's voice on the other end of the line.

Pierce asked a series of questions, but she didn't really track what the conversation was about besides the status of the remains and that he must have been on the phone with someone from the crime lab. From what she could make out, they weren't going to drive all the way to Missoula to see the remains again, but the doctor would be sending all the findings via email.

As they spoke, Pierce's expression darkened, and his frown deepened so much that it shaded his eyes and made them appear almost black. The effect was almost frightening.

He sped down the highway as he listened to the doctor. It wasn't until they were near to the city of Kalispell that he finally hung up the phone. The sun was breaking through the morning clouds and the fog was rolling off the yellow canola fields as they sped through Evergreen and to the city.

She opened and closed her mouth, not sure what exactly to ask without overstepping her place. "Where are we going?"

He looked at her as though he had nearly forgotten that she was in the truck with him. It took him a long moment before he spoke. "I was hoping we could just go get some breakfast and I could talk to you about last night and set things right, but thanks to that call, our day is going to have to take a different turn."

"We don't need to talk about last night. We are fine." Her voice was thin, but she meant what she said, and she hoped he knew she was being authentic. "I want to get to know more about you, but let's take things one step at a time."

He smiled widely as he looked over at her and the darkness in his eyes mostly disappeared. "You have no idea how glad I am to hear you say that. I was so worried. I thought I'd screwed everything up last night. And this morning… I just didn't know what to say or do to make things right."

She reached over and extended her hand. "It's all good. I don't get things right most of the time. Let's just stick together."

He nodded and slipped his hand in hers and gave it a squeeze. "You really are an amazing woman. We'll take things as they come." While he had meant the words in the best way, a lump formed in his gut.

Anytime he had ever taken things as they came, and allowed fate to take control of his life, things had a way of going a whole lot of sideways.

He sent Emily a quick text message to let her know Dr. Lee was sending them his findings and to expect them in the next hour. With that, the rush he had been feeling abated. He was tempted to find and question the women in Donavan's life, but as things stood, they hadn't even delivered the official death notification.

"Are you hungry?" he asked.

Jamie giggled.

"What?" he asked, looking over at her with a smile.

"I should have guessed that taking things as they come would mean taking me to breakfast. You are such a dude sometimes." She tilted her head back slightly as she laughed.

THE SOUND WAS light and heady, and it was so clear and clean that it made the knot in his gut dissipate.

That sound, her, this, and the lightness—this was what he had needed, what they had *both* needed.

"Until we get the answers we need from Dr. Lee, namely a positive identification on the remains, there's not a whole lot more we can do. So let me take you to breakfast. I want to learn more about you. On my end, I want you to learn more about me. Then if you decide you don't want to have anything to do with me, it has nothing to do with my past and it has everything to do with me. At least you can make an informed decision." He tried to give her his best charming smile.

She giggled again. "You're really rolling the dice, you know that, right?"

He pulled his truck into a parking spot in front of Bojangles, a greasy spoon if there ever was one. The restaurant hadn't really changed since he was a kid. His parents had always brought him here on Sunday mornings after church. There was the same tired train set that ran around the crown molding of the ceiling.

The place always smelled like maple syrup and bacon, and this morning as they walked in, it had the heavy scent of burnt coffee. And a waitress motioned for them to take a seat wherever they liked. Pierce picked a faded and cracked-vinyl turquoise-colored booth by the front window where he could watch his pickup.

The waitress hurried over and, without asking, flipped over the mugs that sat on the table, and poured them two fresh cups of coffee. The woman was wearing blue jeans and a pink shirt with the name of the restaurant on it. Its plainness seemed perfectly in line with the rest of the restaurant. He actually liked it for exactly what it was—lacking any pretense.

"The menus are there on the end of the table," the wait-ress said, motioning to them. "Is there anything else I can get you to drink besides your coffee? The woman had ob-viously been doing this job for so long that she didn't even need to pause to think. Everything she seemed to do and say was on autopilot.

Pierce was almost envious. It would have been nice to have a job where everything was routine and fairly predict-able. Plus, there was an honesty with her work. There was no vagueness or delving into the underbelly of human na-ture. She just came to work, did her job, and went home. Perhaps that was what he resented the most. There was no leaving his job at the door. It was his entire identity, just as barrel racing was Jamie's.

Walking away from that must have been so hard on her. He couldn't imagine how lost she must have felt choosing to leave that lifestyle. And from what he had gathered, she hadn't looked forward to coming back to the ranch.

He watched as she took a sip of coffee. He considered delving right into the topic of her loss, not only of her fi-ancé but of herself. Maybe their relationship could help her find new meaning in her life.

Then again, he didn't want to start a relationship on a cornerstone like that. That was a recipe for codependency, and it sounded so unhealthy. She needed to know and be comfortable in her own skin before adding him to her circle.

"You said you're helping your brother with the ranch. Is that what you plan on doing for the foreseeable future?"

Jamie shrugged. "I don't know what I want to do. I've actually been thinking about working with kids and horses. Doing some kind of equine therapy, or after-school pro-gram. But at the same time, I think that would be better when my life is more settled." She took another drink of her coffee.

He stayed quiet, and could tell from the look on her face that there was something more she wanted to say.

"Really, I'd like to go back to barrel racing. However, it just doesn't make sense. And I just don't know how to reconcile all the things I'm thinking about into a marketable career. I mean you and I talked about even studding Mac, but he's still a good horse and doing that kind of makes it sound like he's ready for retirement." She studied her fingers.

"And if he's ready for retirement, then you are, too?" He put his hand on her arm, trying to comfort her.

"Exactly." She put her hand on top of his and squeezed his fingers. "I'm too young and should just be *done*. I know I made the choice to walk away, but now that I'm in Montana and things are starting to calm down and I'm feeling better, I don't think I did it for the right reasons."

There was something in the way she spoke that sounded like healing. He loved it. It made him feel free to explore his feelings with her, and yet what she was saying was a little bit terrifying. If she wanted to run away and follow the rodeo circuit, she wasn't ready to settle down and he wasn't sure that he wanted a long-distance relationship. However, he wasn't sure he really wanted to have a settle-down-style relationship anyway.

If nothing else, they could just be hot messes together.

And perhaps he was wrong about the codependency thing, maybe healing together wasn't such a bad thing. Humans were always growing and changing, life wasn't static. If people waited for things to be perfect and unmarred, no one would ever be ready for relationship or friendship or to take things to the next level. Life was never flawless.

Now he was the one overthinking things. It struck him as a little bit funny that this morning had started out with him telling her that they would take things as they came, and yet he was sitting there lashing himself with *what-ifs* and *why-nots* and *can'ts*.

The waitress rushed back over with a notepad in hand, ready to take their order. "You guys know what you're havin'?"

Neither of them had glanced at the menu, but when he looked to Jamie, she nodded. "I'll just get three pancakes, please."

"I'll do the same, with a side of bacon and two over-medium eggs."

"You got it, hun." The waitress jotted down their order and shoved the pen behind her ear. "It should be coming right up. Charlie's on the grill today, he's real quick." She looked around the restaurant, which was only about half full of what looked like regulars, mostly retirees who were off this time of the morning. "You should see it in here on the weekends during tourist season. It's a madhouse. I swear, there are times where I'd be better off just handing plates through the crowds to get them to the right tables. Ya know?"

"I work up in the park, I know all about the tourist season and how crazy things can get."

The waitress smiled at him, looking at his uniform and then down at the gun on his utility belt. "I assumed as much. I heard all about that bunch of bones you found up there yesterday. Sounds like you guys got your hands on the mayor. That true?"

His jaw dropped, but he tried to control his shock. He hadn't told anyone about what they had found, or whom. He had no idea how word had gotten out not only through West Glacier, but all the way into Kalispell and into a tiny little diner in the middle of town. Kalispell was a city. That meant everybody knew what was going on in the park— potentially even Mayor Donovan's family.

If they had heard it through gossip, that would have been a horrible way to find out about their loved one's passing. It would look horrible for his department and the task force. His reputation was on the line for this case, and to have it blasted all over the Bojangles' pipeline was a problem.

"Right now, we can't really make any statements," Jamie said, taking the reins. "But we sure are looking forward to having a little breakfast. I appreciate you getting that order in." She sent the waitress an overly sweet smile that didn't leave room for further question.

As the waitress spun on her heel and hurried toward the kitchen, he leaned closer to her over the table. "Thank you."

She tipped her head in acknowledgment. "You need to work on your poker face."

"That right there is why I'm not much of a gambler. Don't take me to Vegas."

She smiled. "You know that there's other things to do in Vegas besides gambling?"

"If you mean the Little White Wedding Chapel, I've heard of it."

Her face pinkened. "That, and there are a ton of shows. I was down there for the NFR. We stayed at the South Point. You should try their spa. Oh my goodness, it's incredible— better than the Bellagio's."

He stared at her for a long moment and it struck him as

such a strange juxtaposition of things—here they were in a run-down diner in the middle of a nowhere town talking about which spa was the best in the best and most expensive cities in America. He smirked.

"What?" She caught his gaze, playfully. "Would you get married at the Little White Wedding Chapel?"

He thought about the big wedding he was supposed to have had with hundreds of guests and all the pomp and circumstance that had been associated with the event. "Truth be told, I'd prefer it to the grandeur. With the right person, it's not about the event or all the *stuff*. For me, it was always about spending time with the people I love and celebrating the promises of forever." There was a sourness in his voice that he couldn't hide.

"So, you were going to have a big wedding?" She took a drink of coffee.

He nodded.

"Yeah, not my style, either. I'd do it at the ranch or in a chapel in Vegas—maybe even at the park, sans the mountain lion."

There was that laugh again. The one that cleared all the pain from his thoughts and the cobwebs from his soul. He would do anything to keep her making that sound—even if that meant they kept talking about weddings…a subject he had thought he'd never want to discuss again.

"You faced it down like a champ," he teased.

"You know, of all the things I would do with my life, I never thought having a mountain lion try and attack me would be on the list."

"True, but look at the bar stories you can tell now. You are a queen." He chuckled.

"I was a queen before," she teased, puffing up in her

vinyl seat proudly. "I mean have you seen all this? I'm almost buff. I only get a little winded going uphill while hiking." She laughed loudly.

Yes, he loved that sound and maybe, if he was being honest with himself, he loved her, too. She was something special.

The waitress came over, carrying a stack of plates. "Here you go, guys. Syrup is there by the menus." She placed the plates down in front of them and motioned toward the three jars of syrup in the little carrying tray. The syrups were always the same—apricot, berry-something and maple.

As they settled in and smeared the little globes of butter over their pancakes, Jamie did a happy dance in her booth seat. He liked seeing her happy. It made him happy, too.

A few moments later, the waitress returned and refilled their mugs with piping hot coffee.

His phone pinged with a text message as she walked away. The email had shown up from the medical examiner. Unlocking his phone, he pulled up the encrypted document. There was a myriad of reports. He clicked through the osteology report and the anthropologist's findings.

According to their reports, it was concluded that the remains they had found on the mountain were, in fact, of a single person.

Thanks to the ID and the dental records they had pulled from the local dentist's office, they could safely presume that this individual was Clyde Donovan.

He had a positive identification.

As for the cause and manner of death, it was determined to be a gunshot wound to the left temporal lobe. From what they'd learned about Clyde, he was a right-handed individual. Therefore, based on this, the medical examiner had ruled the death as suspicious and yet to be determined. In short, this meant the ball was in his court.

Pierce stabbed the egg's yolk and let the yellow ooze out. There was nothing like reading a medical examiner's report over breakfast.

From the findings, it was likely that they had been correct in their initial assumption—they were dealing with a homicide.

Chapter Thirteen

Jamie was relieved everything had turned around between her and Pierce. Things could start fresh. Well, as fresh as it could get when they were dealing with death on their doorsteps.

Pierce's phone rang as they got into his pickup outside the diner. He looked over at her as he buckled up. "Vince was supposed to be my best man. He is a pretty good dude. A little screwed up sometimes when it comes to women and relationships, but I'm definitely not one who should be judging."

He answered and put the phone call on Speaker as he buckled up. "Hey Vince, what's up?"

"Hey, man, I saw the email." His voice sounded tired and drawn, like he was worried.

"Oh, good."

"You alone?" Vince asked.

Pierce glanced at her. "Actually, I'm sitting here with Jamie, you are on speakerphone. How come?"

There was a long pause. "You know that thing we were talking about earlier?"

"Uh-huh, why?" Pierce frowned.

"Can you please not tell anyone about that? I don't want

that getting out, given what they seem to think. You know what I mean?"

Pierce's frown deepened. "I do. I'll keep it under my hat as long as I can. In the meantime, I suggest you find something that keeps us from having to go there—got it?"

Jamie had no idea what they were talking about, but she felt like an interloper in their conversation, and she pointed toward the door, silently asking if she should step outside so they could take their conversation privately. Pierce shook his head.

"I just don't need anything to get out."

"We'll talk about this later. In the meantime, I'm going to go notify Clyde's family and wife about his death. I think, given the circumstances, I may have Emily meet me there. Is she there with you?"

"Yeah."

"Can you tell her to meet me there in thirty?"

"You got it, boss."

"The dogs on site?" he asked.

"Yeah, we are looking for the exact location where Clyde died. I think we are getting pretty close. Looks like he was near a large pine. I'll send you pictures of the scene."

"Great. Make sure you mark everything. Don't do anything without a sheriff's deputy working with you. We want to cover our bases in case this thing blows up, okay?"

Vince let out a nervous exhale. "Yeah. I hear you. Anything else?"

"Just be smart. Redundancy is better than absence of information."

"Yeah. I'll let you know how our search goes. Pictures will be coming your way as soon as we get everything narrowed down and the scene buttoned up. Talk to you later, bud."

"Later." Pierce clicked off the call. He stared out the windshield for a long time as though he wasn't sure what or how he should broach the awkwardness that had just planted itself between them. "So."

She waited, but he said nothing. "So." She lifted a brow. "You don't have to tell me the secret. Obviously, your friend doesn't want something to be talked about. I understand the need for secrets and boundaries in your line of work. If you want to tell me, cool, but don't feel forced."

He pinched his lips as he nodded plaintively. "He doesn't, but I could use an ear on how to deal with this thing."

Her heart leapt at the idea of him turning to her to be his sounding board. "Oh?"

"Whatever I share with you, it stays between us. I know it's probably not fair of me to ask you, but is that okay?"

She tried to control her excitement as she nodded. "Absolutely. I know how to keep a secret."

He started the engine of the truck and squeezed the steering wheel like he was fighting within himself whether he should talk to her about it or not. "Vince is more connected to this case than I would like. I don't want to pull him from the investigation just yet, as it would raise a lot of questions. Yet, if it comes out that he has anything to do with the death—it could cost me my career."

She didn't know the right thing to say, but what had been excitement was now only sourness in her stomach. "You are playing a dangerous game."

"Oh, you don't need to tell me. I love Vince—he and I have been friends for a long time—but he can do stupid things. However, when push comes to shove, he's always had my back and stood in my defense."

She smoothed her hair behind her ear as she tried to think.

"Hear me out," he continued. "Last year, I had a tourist file a complaint about a ticket I wrote. They had made it sound like they were saints and were helping an injured animal. While they were actually hazing a bear and trying to get a good picture for Instagram. Vince had watched the incident. If it hadn't been for him, and his statement, they would have gotten off and I would have been put on administrative leave for at least a week while Reynolds did a full investigation. The whole deal was incredibly stupid."

"I'm sure Vince is a great colleague and friend," she said.

"I know what you're going to say," he said, putting his hand up. "But I don't want to pull the rip cord and hand over the information just yet."

"Okay, but you know that you *should.*"

He tilted his head back against the headrest. "I have to trust him on this. He said he didn't have anything to do with the guy's disappearance. I can't imagine that he would have had a role in the guy's death. Vince is my best friend, not a murderer."

She loved how loyal he was to his friend, even if she could tell he was lying to himself. She wasn't involved in law enforcement, but even she was aware that anyone could kill if they were faced with the right set of circumstances.

Regardless of what she thought, now was her opportunity to be as good a friend to him as he was to Vince and stand beside him while he needed support. "Look, if you think he is trustworthy and you are willing to stake your reputation and career on him, then that says something. But I think we need to move fast. We need to find out who would have wanted this guy dead."

"Exactly what I was thinking," Pierce said, looking over at her and sending her a relieved smile. "Clyde was known for being a narcissist."

"Well, he was a politician—doesn't that go hand in hand?"

He laughed. "I can't say I know any of them personally, but I'd have to assume you're probably right. They seem like the type." He put the truck in gear. "And I have to say, while I never enjoy giving death notices, this one should be interesting."

"Oh?" she asked as he pulled out of the parking space and got onto the main road.

"Clyde and his wife were in the process of a divorce. He had filed the paperwork, but nothing had been finalized when he had gone missing."

That *was* interesting. She'd always heard in situations like this, it was always the spouse who was investigated and suspected first. "When he went missing, was she questioned?"

He turned down a side road, leading them through downtown Kalispell, which consisted of a collection of charming Old West–style brick buildings with cloth awnings. "I'm sure, but I haven't talked to Emily about it."

"I went to school with a bunch of the Donovans. You know it's a pretty big name around the valley."

He raised a brow.

"Their family homesteaded the area in the late 1800s. They still have a bunch of cattle ranches and farms that stretch down south into the Flathead Indian Reservation and north almost all the way to the Canadian border."

"So, they are well-heeled?"

She nodded. "But that probably isn't a huge surprise. It takes money to get into politics here...well, *anywhere*." She looked at the courthouse, which sat in the middle of a wye in the road in the center of town. It was an oddly out-of-place building and obnoxious in the way it forced everyone to move around it and pay homage to its grandeur. "His father was the district court judge. In fact, I think he still is, but I don't know for sure. I haven't looked it up since I've been back to see if he was reelected."

It struck her as incredibly odd that a mayor, who was also the son of a district court judge, had gone missing and no one had taken the fall. She would have thought heads would have rolled. Maybe things had changed while she had been away, but she thought small-town justice—or warped vengeance—would never fail.

"Maybe that is where we should start," Pierce said excitedly, slamming on the brakes and turning the truck hard to the right. "Has anyone ever told you how beautiful and smart you are?" He smiled broadly at her.

"What?" she asked, grateful for the compliment but confused by his sudden shift.

"We have to do the death notifications, but there are no rules about who we have to notify first. Given the circumstances at the time of his disappearance, I think it is understandable if we talk to his father first." He sent her a smile. "While we are there, and if he wishes, we could ask him a few questions. Then we can meet up with Emily at the wife's."

Jamie loved this side of Pierce. He was filled with hope

and excitement for the future. It was strange and exhilarating, and it struck her that in his own right, while looking for justice, he had become a predator.

Chapter Fourteen

Pierce stared at the No Firearms sign on the glass of the courthouse's front door as he held it open for Jamie. The courthouse hadn't changed since the last time Pierce had been there to get his wedding license nearly a year ago. It still carried the heavy scent of stress, anxiety and fear in the air.

When he'd first come here, he couldn't understand why they had put the justice of the peace in a place like this— where so many people's real-life nightmares were exposed to the air and the public and set out to be judged not only by strangers, but also potentially by the media. A shiver moved down his spine as he thought of all the trials and convictions that had been wrought within these walls. He also thought of all those who had been guilty of horrific crimes and yet had walked free.

Maybe, given how his marriage license thing had turned out, as well as what they were here to look into, the justice of the peace being in such a place did make sense.

He gave a dark laugh.

If he wasn't careful, this darkness could easily turn bitter.

In the center of the courthouse was a round mahogany desk that was about waist high. It was decorated with carved filigrees and swirls, similar to the cast-iron banisters on the stairs leading upstairs to the courtrooms and offices. Behind the desk sat a security guard and he waved them down as they approached. "Hey, guys, how's it going?" He looked at Pierce's badge and his nameplate. "How can I help you today, Ranger Hauser?"

"We don't have an appointment, but I am here to speak to District Court Judge Donovan. Do you know if he's in his chambers, or in trial today?"

The guard glanced to his computer, but from where Pierce was standing, he could not see what the man was looking at, exactly. "I think his trial was delayed today. And it looks like he's in his chambers. Let me see if he's available. First, do you mind telling me what this is in regard to?"

When it came to meeting with a judge, it wasn't easy getting behind those doors regardless of whether he carried a badge or not. They were busy, and their time was precious. However, he had a feeling he held the golden ticket—he just had to be careful how much he told the security guard. Then again, even the waitress knew about who they had found in the woods. By now, it was a wonder that this guy wasn't telling Pierce about why he was there and just ringing him through. Maybe that was why he had waved him down instead of assuming he'd known where he was going.

"We are here regarding Donovan's son. We need to ask him a few questions. Time is of the essence." He kept his face unreadable.

Even if the gossip mill had run rampant, he wasn't going to feed it any more than was necessary.

The guard stared at him for a second too long, giving it away that he did, in fact, already know exactly why they

were there and what they had found. It made Pierce wonder if there actually had been a newspaper article or something about what they'd discovered.

As the man turned to his computer and typed, it dawned
on Pierce how everyone seemed to know everything—social media.

It wasn't that he was a Luddite; he used social media,
too. It was just that he didn't use social media to get his
news or to hear gossip. He used it to find funny pictures
to send to Vince and his friends, but that was about the
extent. In total, he probably spent twenty minutes a day
watching stupid videos.

However, this guy, who sat behind a desk and waited for
people to enter the courthouse each day, probably had a lot
of free time. It was no wonder he knew what was going on.

"Judge Donovan said he will see you now. He will meet
you outside his chambers." The guard stood up. Standing,
he maybe pushed five feet, and Pierce couldn't help but notice that his gun didn't have a magazine racked and ready.
"He is on the third floor, second door on your left. You can
go in through the courtroom and his office is to the right.
You will see when you get there. If you get lost, I can help."

"Thanks," Jamie said, smiling graciously, but Pierce noticed her gaze slip to the man's soup sandwich of a gun.

The way the man had his gun, if there was an emergency, the best thing he could do with the unloaded gun
was throw it at the threat. As they turned away, Pierce tried
to tell himself that maybe the guy had just taken the No
Firearms sign to include him as well—sort of.

Jamie's boots clicked loudly on the marble floors of the
foyer as they made their way to the stairs. The place carried
the air of the 1800s in a way he couldn't quite put his fin-

ger on; perhaps it was the Western-style frescos of storming bison and cowboys carrying lever-action rifles on the domed ceiling overhead.

As they moved up the steps, he felt as if he should have been wearing something black with tails and carrying a monocle in his breast pocket. There was even a faint smell of pipe smoke, or maybe the scent was just in his imagination.

Jamie slid her hand on the black cast-iron banister as she moved up the stairs. "I forgot how cool this place was. It is beautiful."

He was surprised how differently they were experiencing this moment.

"Then again, it is a bit haunting—you know?" she asked, sending a look back at him over her shoulder.

"It's not my favorite place to be."

She caught his gaze, and her enjoyment seemed to falter. "Oh, I bet you are here a lot for work, huh?"

"Actually, no. I work for the federal government—this is all for state stuff."

"Oh, right." She turned back. "I should have known that."

He moved up to her side. "I try to stay out of courthouses—federal or otherwise." He grazed her hand with the back of his, trying to send her a tiny gesture to help her feel better. "There's a lot about your work and ranching that I don't know. Don't beat yourself up about it."

She smiled at him, a grateful softness in her eyes. Dammit if that look didn't make him melt. If she had asked him for the moon at that moment, he would have done anything to give it to her.

She grazed her fingers over his as she ascended the last

few steps to the third floor. "You've got this. Good luck."
She winked.

This was one thing he wasn't sure about—he probably
had a better chance lassoing the moon than prying information out of a man who made a living keeping secrets.

Emily hadn't sent him anything about the missing person's case, as they had only just confirmed the man's
identity. Maybe he should have waited to read up about
everything and all the statements that had been made about
the man in the past. However, this *was* just supposed to be
a notification.

Even if Pierce was there to question the judge about his
son's disappearance or life, he had a feeling that a judge
wasn't the kind of person who was just going to open up
and spill precious details.

He took a deep breath, preparing himself for whatever
he was going to face when he entered the second door on
the left. It was silly, but he was nervous. He had spent quite
a few days in court, having been subpoenaed on a myriad
of cases in which prosecutors had called him in after he
had been involved during the initial arrests. It was one part
of his job that he always despised. Maybe it was the lawyer thing. He'd yet to have met one that he could stomach.

He'd never liked a person whose loyalty was available
for purchase.

There was a solid wooden door with Lady Justice carved
into its surface. He pulled open the heavy door with its
glossy brass handle and waited for Jamie to step through.
Pierce was hit with the strong aroma of fear mixed with
industrial disinfectant and floor wax.

The courtroom was larger than he would have expected,
but much the same as every other he had been in within

this state—it had the same austere 1800's feel, thanks to its oak floors and whitewashed walls. It had leaded-glass windows that were opaque enough to let light in but obscure the views in and out. It was a disorienting space of professionalism and practicality.

Sitting in the middle of the empty courtroom, on the prosecution's side, was a gray-haired man. He was wearing a dark blue suit. He had his back to them, and he was tapping away on his cell phone, preoccupied with work.

As Pierce neared the man, he noticed that there was a hole worn in the seam of the right shoulder thanks to wear. The man turned with the sounds of the footfalls on the oak floor. "Ranger Hauser?" he asked, looking at Jamie and then to him.

"Yes, that's me. Judge Donovan?" he asked.

The man stood, stepped out from the bench seat and extended his hand to Jamie. "You are?"

"Jamie. Trapper," she said, taking the man's hand gently.

He cupped her hand and gave it a welcoming shake before doing the same with Pierce. He slapped him on the shoulder and motioned for him to sit down. "It's great to meet you, Ranger. I was wondering when I would get the knock on my door."

"I'm sorry we didn't get here sooner—before the rumors."

The judge sat down on the bench. He patted the seat beside him, the action strangely informal in what was an incredibly formal and stuffy room. Jamie sat down on the bench behind the judge, motioning with her chin for him to sit where the man had offered.

He slid into the seat, but he was so uncomfortable that

he would have almost preferred to be sitting in the defendant's chair in active court.

"You know the thing about rumors…" the judge said, staring up at the bench. "They are often true, but they never hold up in court. It's not until we are slapped in the face with evidentiary support that we can assign legitimacy. In this case, I was sincerely hoping that the rumors were wrong."

Pierce didn't know what to say, but he had a feeling this man wasn't looking for a response.

The judge pressed a finger in the space between his brows, like he was staving off a headache. "That boy of mine was always hard to track. When he wasn't off chasing women, he was chasing ideas. Neither tended to be good for him."

He wanted to tell the judge that everyone knew men who were like that—they were typically the type A kinds with egos too big for their hats. Vince came to mind.

"When he married *that* woman, I tried to warn him off." He sighed. "He listened just about as well as he did when he was a teenager. I told him she was one of those things I wasn't going to be able to bail him out of—and that divorce was going to be expensive."

At least Pierce's assumptions of Carey had been right— she had a reputation as a woman who was not well received in the Donovan family or in the community.

"She was a terrible woman before she met him. I'd seen her in my courtroom before they met. She had a penchant for stealing identities for financial gain and then, and worse, embezzling funds from her father's business. Luckily, she had a good defense attorney, and she was just pretty enough to get the pity vote from jurors. If she hadn't, she would have still been sitting in prison—I would have seen to it. Instead, she got married to my son."

Pierce tried to control his shock. He could even imagine being in this father's position. He thought he'd had a family with some drama—this was another level entirely. However, it did increase the likelihood of Carey having played a role in Clyde's death tenfold.

"Even though she was found innocent, you do believe she was guilty of fraud?" Pierce asked.

The judge made a face and shrugged, and Pierce knew it was the closest thing he was going to get to a real answer from the judge. Anything else would constitute potential defamation if the man wasn't careful.

He was smart, but Pierce wouldn't say he was lucky.

His gaze moved to the hole in the man's suit. The guy had spent a lot of time in that suit, and probably others just like it. He'd likely spent more hours in that suit than he had with his own son when Clyde had been growing up. Maybe that was why Clyde had become the man he had—and why Clyde had chosen to become a mayor.

Maybe he had thought that in becoming a city official, he would finally get his father's much-coveted and hard-to-obtain attention.

Pierce didn't know whom he pitied more—the father or the son and the living or the dead.

Chapter Fifteen

The judge's deep-set and heavily bagged eyes would haunt Jamie for years to come; she held no doubt. The man had to have seen so many horrors in his line of business, but from his vacant expression, she could tell that he was struggling to remain composed. It was as if he was teetering on the edge of falling apart.

She had never had a child, but she could only imagine the pain and anguish that came with the undeniable knowledge that a parent was to never see them alive again. A parent was not supposed to outlive their child. That wasn't the natural order of things. It broke her heart to even think about it.

If the judge wanted to talk about his son or the impact his loss had on his family, he was free to do that, but she didn't feel as if it was her place to start the conversation. This interview, or notification rather, was Pierce's job.

Pierce stood up and extended his hand to the judge. "If you need anything, or if you can think of anything else that could be helpful in our investigation into your son's death, please don't hesitate to reach out. I'm working with Detective Monahan on the investigation, so you are free to call her or myself."

The judge shook his hand graciously. "I appreciate you

coming here and telling me face-to-face. This has been a long time coming, but news I expected. Don't let this bother you. My son had his demons and it's just unfortunate that he couldn't get the help he needed in time to stop this outcome."

"We are sorry for your loss," Pierce said solemnly.

"I know it's probably too early for you to tell me for sure, but as a professional courtesy, can you please tell me whether or not this was a homicide?" the judge asked.

With all their talking, Jamie hadn't realized until now that they had not actually spoken about what had really happened to Clyde—or actually told the man his son was dead. It was just *known*. The closest thing Pierce had said was in his sympathies. Of course, the judge would have more questions.

"As you know, I can't make any official statements yet, but based on the medical examiner's findings and what we witnessed initially, your son died from a bullet wound to the left temporal lobe."

The judge raised his left hand and pointed his finger at his temple like he was holding a gun. "My son wasn't left-handed, and we are Catholic. We're strong believers that if we committed suicide we would be forever damned to purgatory. I know since his marriage that he hasn't been as devout as he was as a kid, but I know they talked about having children raised in the church as well. I don't see this being a self-inflicted wound."

"We were working off the same assumptions. I didn't know when we arrived today if you were going to be willing to talk to us a little bit more about this situation surrounding his disappearance, and the initial missing persons reports that were filed. If you are, we'd be happy to hear more about what happened and how you found out he had disappeared."

The judge closed his eyes and leaned back in the bench, the wood cracking under his weight as he shifted. The sound echoed around the empty room, almost reminiscent of a small-caliber gunshot.

"I couldn't tell you the exact date when he truly disappeared. However, his wife reported his disappearance on July 24 two years ago. Based on the cell phone records, he had been receiving phone calls. However, one week prior to that, he had made no phone calls and sent no texts. There had also been no financial transactions made with his credit cards during that time frame."

"What did his wife have to say about that?" Pierce asked.

"From the records, I was able to ascertain that she thought he had just ghosted her. They were going through the initial stages of divorce. He had filed, and they were supposed to sit down for a mediation, but he didn't arrive to the meeting. That was when she notified officials, and he was found to be missing."

Jamie had a hard time remaining quiet. Everything in her screamed that Clyde's wife had killed her husband. The timing was just too perfect for her not to have had some role in the man's disappearance. Even if Carey hadn't been the one to pull the trigger, Jamie thought she was behind the man's death. However, she wasn't in a position where she could say a word. Besides, she had a feeling that everyone in this room felt the same way she did. And just as the judge had started their conversation, it was one thing to suspect something to be the truth and another to prove it.

"At that time," the judge continued, "it was the Flathead county sheriff's department that was conducting the search.

They found his cell phone at his home, and so they really had no known last location beyond that which Carey had provided them. I tried to fund a search, and I posted a reward for information leading to his recovery, but nothing ever came from my efforts. I even had billboards, but the only phone calls I ever received were from some teenagers who thought it was funny to call."

"It's hard to perform a search when there's no information. I sympathize with both the sheriff's department and with you and your family. It's a really tough situation." Pierce leaned against the bench and crossed his arms over his chest.

"Yeah, but now I can move on. I'm grateful for that. We have confirmation that he is at least gone. I don't have to question whether he's going to walk in my door. Half of the agony is not knowing. Now our family can grieve and start looking for answers about how this happened and who was behind it." The judge stood up. "I have no doubts that you will do everything in your power to find justice for my son. Whatever resources you need from the county, let me know and I will try to make them happen."

Jamie was absolutely positive that the man was telling the truth, and they could have asked for anything and have gotten it. It wasn't until this moment that she realized how powerful Judge Donovan truly was. In a way, it frightened her.

The judge offered her his hand as they said their goodbyes and he walked them to the doors leading out of the courtroom. There had been many rodeos in which she had felt as though she was out of her league, but she had never felt more out of place than she had during the death notification. Yet she was glad she had witnessed it for Pierce. It helped her understand what he had to go through.

Life and death were so normal. Yet, faced with it like this, it was so visceral and real. It tore at her heart.

She didn't know how Pierce could do that kind of thing every day.

This moment with a father facing his son's loss put her life's tragedy in a new perspective. And while John's death was no less impactful, she was ready to let go of the tragedy as an event and moment in time that would forever define her. She couldn't allow John's death to forge her into someone she didn't quite want to become. She had to let go of what had happened and move on with her life.

Death was a constant and life needed to be lived at its fullest by those death had left behind.

She couldn't fear it and she couldn't keep reliving loss and being stuck in the moment. It would take so much strength, but she had to come back to herself.

If Pierce could find the strength to walk families through these times, she could have the fortitude to walk through it with him by her side.

As they neared Pierce's truck, there was a ping on his cell phone. He helped her up into her seat and then read the text as he walked around to his side of the truck and got in. He was frowning as he threw the device onto the dashboard.

"You did great with the judge in there." She didn't know if she should address the look on his face or just wait for it to disappear naturally.

"Yeah, Judge Donovan was helpful. Definitely backed up what Vince had said and filled in a lot of the holes." Pierce seemed to relax slightly, but his gaze flitted to the phone as he started the truck. "I think we need to make our next stop be the wife's. I have a feeling it may not go nearly as smoothly."

The phone buzzed on the dashboard again, sounding like an angry bee.

"Is everything okay?" she asked, motioning toward the offending device.

He grumbled something under his breath. "It's Reynolds. He wants you and me to come over to his place for dinner tonight to discuss the case. I told him we have too much going on to do a dinner, but he didn't budge." He grabbed the phone and shoved it into the cupholder in the console between the seats by the computer.

"Why wouldn't he just meet you at headquarters?"

"To be honest, I think he needs his wife's care in the evenings. After his car accident, he had the option to re-tire, but he came back while he was still recovering, and he's been doing a great job. Sometimes, though, we have to move around protocols and normal procedures to make sure he gets what he needs to be cared for appropriately. That's way more important than policies, but in this case… I'd rather be questioning people and sending him an email or jumping on the phone."

"How did his accident happen?" Jamie asked.

"It happened early in the fall a couple of years ago. He was just leaving the park—and he doesn't remember what happened. But, from the accident report and the recreated scene, Highway Patrol assumed that he must have swerved to avoid hitting an animal or something in the road and he ended up rolling his vehicle. He was thrown through the windshield. There is major injury to the C4, 5 and 6 as well as lower in his vertebral column. I saw the X-ray once of his back, and it looked like an S when they brought him into the ER." He gave her a wide-eyed expression.

"It sounds like he is incredibly lucky he even survived. How did he not have a major TBI? Was he a different man—you know, *cognitively*—after the accident?"

Pierce nodded. "Yes and no. I don't think that he had a TBI, surprisingly. It must have been how he hit, but most of the impact was his back and spine. They found him at the base of a tree, so there's some conjecture that he actually hit the tree, which might have saved him from dying instantly. Who knows?"

Pierce pulled out onto the road.

They made their way back through the center of downtown Kalispell and toward the older residential side of the town leading north.

"One thing is certain," Pierce continued, "he had a new perspective on life, and he poured himself into work as soon as he was out of the hospital."

That surprised her. If she had been in his situation and could not have gone back to work and spent her life behind a desk, she would have chosen to spend the rest of her days experiencing all the things life had to offer. She would travel the world and see all the horse arenas she had yet to visit. Then again, she assumed it had to be hard for Reynolds to travel. Her grandfather had been in a wheelchair for the last five years of his life, and though many things had been adapted to make life easier for those who needed mobility aids, there was still a long way to go to making things truly manageable—even airplanes.

"I bet his wife is glad he survived. And I'm sure he's grateful that she is there by his side. Do you think that's why he chose to stay here and just devote himself to Glacier?"

"I don't know what it is about this town, but before the accident, there was talk that Reynolds and his wife were on the rocks. If anything, I think that it saved their marriage. The things that they both had to learn to rely on each other."

She was surprised. "I thought when things like that happened, it tore people apart, I didn't realize that it could go the other way. That actually kind of helps restore my faith in humanity."

He chuckled, turning down a road in front of one of the local high schools. The place was deserted, except for a black sweatshirt that was hanging on the fence, forgotten by a child. There was something deeply sad about it.

"I don't know much about their relationship now, but Reynolds tries to be in control of things at the office. I don't always agree with his decisions, but I think that's the nature of a boss." He laughed.

A block ahead of them, a blacked-out Suburban was parked on the side of the road. She recognized it as Emily's work vehicle. She must have been waiting for them— or, rather, Pierce.

She glanced over at Pierce. He was staring at the house at the end of the cul-de-sac. It was a millennial-gray house, with two fake cedar trees in gray plastic barrels at the end of the driveway. It had white windows and white doors with thin black accents, and it looked like every other house on the block. It almost looked like it had been cut out of any advertisement for any construction company in any state in America.

It was a nice house; it just wasn't anything special. From what she had learned about Donovan's wife, gossip queen who was likely a Black Widow, the blandness seemed to fit.

It struck her how she had never met this woman, and

only knew her through reputation and what she had learned in passing, and yet she already despised her. That was almost a gift, for someone to leave that kind of social trail.

Jamie tried to tell herself that she needed to give the woman a fair shot, but the evil part of her chuckled exactly where she wanted to place the shot. Her father would have said center mass, or two to the chest and one to the head.

Yeah, that wasn't going to help the situation.

"When we get up here, I think it's best if you stay in the truck while I question Carey." Pierce motioned toward the witch's gingerbread house.

"I think that's fair. I'll be here when you get back." She held back the desire to mention the fact that he probably shouldn't leave behind a gun.

After spending the morning with Clyde's father and seeing the pain in his eyes, this woman was just lucky Jamie didn't believe in vigilante justice.

Chapter Sixteen

Pierce was looking forward to this death notification just about as much as he would have looked forward to jumping into a pit of rattlesnakes. He had met Carey Donovan once before at a Mule Deer Foundation banquet she had been at with Clyde.

She'd been wearing a skintight leopard-print dress that was two sizes too small on her large frame. She had to have been at least six feet tall, but probably more. Her boobs had been the talk of the night, as they had been precariously close to absolutely falling out of the top of the dress.

She had been hanging on to an investment banker out of California all night; the guy had been bidding on a private hunt on a ten-thousand-acre ranch in eastern Montana. If he remembered correctly, the guy had ended up walking away with the prize for close to forty thousand dollars. He couldn't imagine paying that kind of money for a stinky mule deer, no matter how big it was. The word around the bar later had been that the out-of-stater had also walked out with her. Something told Pierce he hadn't had to pay quite as much for that leopard-print dress to hit the floor.

He parked behind Emily and walked up to her window, leaving Jamie behind in his truck. Jamie had seemed only too happy to wait. He couldn't blame her. There was not a single part of him that wanted to do this, either.

He tapped on Emily's window and it slowly rolled down.

"How's it going?" he asked as Emily came into view.

She shrugged. "I've had better days, but it is what it is. I've seen some motion in the house, so I think that our girl is home. Given what we know about her, I think it may be better if you're the one to do the talking, she may respond better to a male."

He wasn't sure if he actually agreed with that logic, but he could understand Emily's line of thinking. "Well, let's get this over with. Do you know what you want to ask her? This may be our only shot before she lawyers up."

"Knowing this woman, she might have that done before we even make it to the door."

Pierce chuckled as he opened Emily's door for her and waited for her to step out. "Let's just see how this goes."

There wasn't even the sound of birds as they made their way up to the front door. It was almost like there was a calm before the storm.

He tried to find some thread of hope within himself that he was wrong in his assumptions about how this would all go. Then again, it was better to plan for the worst than hope for the best.

There was a camera doorbell and he pushed the button. A woman's voice came over the speaker. "Can I help you?" Her voice was shrill and flecked with a Valley Girl accent.

Emily stepped closer. "Hi, I'm Detective Monahan with the Flathead County Sheriff's Office. I was hoping to talk to you today. Can you please step outside?"

The woman gave an audible groan, as if they were interrupting her day. "I'm working. Can this wait?"

What kind of person told a police officer on their front porch to come back later, when it was more convenient for them?

Pierce could feel annoyance start to simmer in his belly. He normally wasn't an angry man, but this woman put him on edge. In an effort to control his temper, he clenched his jaw.

"Mrs. Donovan, this will not wait. You need to come to the door and speak with us. I'm sure your boss will understand."

There was a long pause, like the woman was trying to decide whether she would do as she was told or if she would continue to press her luck. While they had no probable cause to file for a search warrant yet, if she kept up this kind of behavior, it wouldn't take much to compile enough evidence to get the laws on their side—and it would stand up in court.

"I'll be down in five minutes. I need to put on my makeup."

Of course she did.

"We will be here," Emily said, sounding as annoyed as he felt.

There was an audible click on the other end of the line.

He leaned against the house and crossed his arms over his chest beside Emily as they waited. Emily was working away on her phone, but he couldn't see what she was working on. Jamie waved at him from the truck, and he gave her an acknowledging tip of the head to let her know everything was going to be okay.

Jamie glanced away and he took the chance to really look at her and the way the sun streamed through the windshield and caught the gold in her hair. Her locks lay loose around her shoulders, and she was running her fingers lazily through the strands. She closed her eyes, smiling and tilting her face up into the rays. She was so beautiful.

The front door of the house burst open. The tall woman stood there in too small jeans and a sage-colored crop top. She had eyelashes glued on that were so long and cheap-looking that they almost looked like black moths stuck on her eyelids. "What do you want?"

Emily stepped forward and put her foot just inside the door frame so the woman couldn't close the door. "Do you mind if we step inside so we can talk, Mrs. Donovan?"

The woman scowled. "Fine. Whatever." She motioned toward the small living room. It was painted pale gray and had two matching linen-gray couches at its center and a television mounted on the wall above a white fireplace. On the wall, near the front window, was a *Live Laugh Love* sign like Haven used to have.

She walked in, flopped down on the couch and motioned for them to sit opposite. "So, are you guys going to tell me what was so urgent, or are you gonna just waste my time all day?"

Everything about Carey was abrasive. He couldn't understand how she had ever even gotten married in the first place. There had to be some attribute of her that was positive. He looked at her face, trying to ignore the sneer on her lips. In the conventional sense, she was pretty with her dark brunette hair and green eyes.

Even when a woman was good-looking, with a personality like hers, it didn't matter. Ugly was ugly. It was the soul that made a woman beautiful.

Maybe Clyde just had the same ugly soul. Pierce and the former mayor had never really spent much time together, but what little they had, they hadn't clicked. Clyde was the kind of guy who landed somewhere in the gray area when it came to legal matters. And there were always rumblings about his willingness to get his business dealings handled.

In fact, an entire strip mall had been purchased and turned into housing for the homeless because of Clyde. In theory, it was commendable, and philanthropic. However, it was later found out that Clyde had ended up making three million dollars on the deal thanks to the suppliers who'd not only remodeled the shopping center but also from the companies that had supplied the warming shelter with everything it needed.

He was definitely a man who could have been bought. And with that, it made him think of Carey's leopard dress. Maybe that was exactly what had brought these two people together into marriage.

If Clyde's wife hadn't killed him, there would be a long list of people who could have also been suspects. They could potentially spend years looking into the nefarious deeds of this man. However, Pierce had a feeling that Judge Donovan was never going to agree that was what had happened. If they didn't find answers and the person behind this, not only would the judge start to handle this himself, but Pierce and Emily would probably be out of jobs. The judge was a shark.

Emily cleared her throat. "As I stated outside, I am Detective Emily Monahan, and this is my colleague, Ranger Pierce Hauser. We are here today to let you know that we found your husband's remains. And he is deceased."

Carey's face didn't move. She didn't even blink. "Where did you find him?"

It struck him how this woman was the only person they

had run into all day who had not heard about their find-ings. In this small town, there was no way someone hadn't already called her.

Perhaps that was why there was such a lack of emotive response. That, or she really was *that* cold. Even though they were going through a divorce, he would have thought there would have been some kind of sadness or even relief to know for sure what had happened to Clyde.

Then again, if she had something to do with his disap-pearance and death, this is exactly the kind of response he would expect.

"We located him high up on a mountain near Avalanche Lake, in the park." Emily tented her fingers between her knees. "It does appear as though he died from a gunshot wound, and at this point we are looking for the weapon used. Do you know if your husband owned any guns?"

Carey frowned, and he noticed the deep wrinkles be-tween her eyes. "First of all, he and I were on the outs. I'm sure you guys know that already if you were standing at my door. It wasn't a secret. And I also want to make it clear that I didn't have anything to do with his disappearance. I've already been down this road. Everyone wanted to question me when he first went missing and I'm tired of that crap."

Emily sat back on the couch, like she was trying to stay out of the line of fire.

"I'm sure that you've been through the ringer with your husband's disappearance." Pierce took the reins. "We don't think that you had anything to do with this," he lied. "We just are trying to accumulate as much information as we can to bring closure to his family and to you."

"Listen, I'm glad you found him. Seriously, I think that's great. But my closure came the day I went down to the courthouse and filed the paperwork to have him declared dead. If I could have done that the day he filed for divorce, that would have been even better."

Whew. She definitely hated the man, but there was something in the way she spoke that made him actually question whether or not she was the one who'd murdered him.

It was like she wouldn't have been as angry if she had been the one behind it. Pierce would imagine that perhaps he would have been more sedate and less toxic.

It was a strange logic, but he just had a feeling.

"Do you know anyone who would have wanted your husband dead?" he asked.

She rubbed her finger at the corner of her eye, smearing some of her black eyeliner. "You could start with any of the number of women he was sleeping with. Maybe one of them found out about the other, that's what I told the police when he first went missing. You can look up their names in one of the police reports. I don't know if the numbers are still accurate for their phones but have at it." She waved him off.

"I'm assuming since the police did not make any headway on that," he said, looking over at Emily who almost imperceptibly shook her head. "That your theory about his mistresses or girlfriends didn't pan out. Do you have any other ideas about people who would want him dead? Business partners? Colleagues?"

She glared at him like he had stepped out of line by going against her in any way about Donovan's mistresses. "I hardly ever knew what he was doing at work. He was always at dinner with someone. Usually it was with women, and I don't know if those were actually work dinners or 'working dinners.'" She made quotation marks with her fingers. "I finally had enough of him. I told him no more women. I said if I caught him with any more that we were done."

"So, you caught him with a woman?" Emily asked.

"One of my friends saw him walking into a hotel with a woman who worked for the US Marshals' office. She sent me pictures of them walking inside and standing at the lobby desk. She waited, and then she sent me pictures of them leaving a few hours later." There was a flatness in her voice that told him she had retold this story many times, to the point that she had become desensitized.

"That's a good friend." Emily nodded.

The woman shrugged.

"Why didn't you just leave him at that point?" Pierce asked.

"I loved him. I thought I could forgive him." Carey stared out the front windows as though she wished she could use them as some form of escape. "I have thought a lot after he first went missing about what could have happened to him. That initial period of time, I really thought he had just holed up with some woman and he was being a jerk and playing some stupid legal game with me that I didn't understand. I'd never been through a divorce before. He had, so I didn't know."

Emily leaned forward and she touched the woman's knee. She must have been feeling something for this woman's plight as well. When they had gotten here, he had never in a million years thought he would have left questioning his assumptions about this woman.

"The only thing I can come up with that I didn't discuss with the police when he initially disappeared was a business deal he was working on with the park. I don't know much about it. I just remember hearing him talking about a merchandising option with the city and the park, and money exchanging hands." She shrugged.

Pierce leaned back on the couch. A branding deal with the park would have included their marketing team, and he didn't know a ton of people in that department. He'd have to ask around, but it was worth looking into. Just like everything else with this case, it seemed far-fetched and a probable dead end.

"That's super helpful, thank you," Pierce said. "You said that you were willing to forgive your husband for his problematic behavior, but then he went ahead and filed for divorce. Is that correct?"

She nodded.

"That strikes me as unusual. Normally, in these situations, at least by what I know about national averages, women are the ones who initiate these types of divorces. Why was he the one to file? And how long after the fact, and you finding out, did this filing take place?"

"It was probably six months, maybe more. I don't have a head for dates. We'd had a pretty nasty fight—he told me he never wanted to see me again. He just picked up and left."

"What was this fight about?" Emily asked.

The woman moved away from Emily's hand and her body closed off. "I don't recall."

She was lying. Her body language and her words didn't align. What she had just said had been well-coached by a lawyer.

Carey stood. "I need to get back to work. I appreciate you letting me know about Clyde. As for his death, I've given you everything I know. If you have any other questions,

I'm working with the DB Law Group. You can contact me through them." She motioned toward the door.

As Pierce stood to leave, the empathy he had been feeling for this woman slipped away. He wasn't sure if she was innocent or just a really good liar who excelled at playing the victim.

Chapter Seventeen

Jamie watched as Emily and Pierce walked together toward the pickup. Their heads were low and they were deep in conversation. She couldn't tell from the looks on their faces how the meeting had gone, but it had taken much longer than she had anticipated.

When they had arrived at the cul-de-sac, she wasn't even sure that they would go into the house. In the end, they had spent more time with this woman than they had with the judge. It made her wonder how much the woman had told them. Now, she wished she had gone inside, but it really hadn't been her place, and it would have been awkward.

She rolled down the window as they neared. "How'd it go?"

Pierce looked at her and she could see the confusion in his face. He looked more lost than when he had walked in. *Interesting.*

"She had a lot to talk about," Emily said. "In the end, she ended up lawyering up."

"Isn't that a sure sign that somebody's guilty?" she asked, looking at Pierce for some unspoken tell.

"In this case, I really don't know if she is or isn't, and we are going to have a hard time proving it if she is. I don't know if she's really smart or just a really good liar," Pierce said.

Emily nodded. "I have the same feeling. I don't know if she's guilty or not. But she's definitely made a life of getting what she wants regardless of who she hurts."

She seemed to be guilty of something, even if it wasn't the crime they were there to investigate. She might deserve to go to jail, but time would tell how things would play out. If she had played a role in Clyde's murder, and if she knew that she was being investigated, it wouldn't surprise her if this woman ran. They needed to find answers, and now Jamie hoped they would get them before this woman disappeared.

Pierce looked down at his watch. "Hey, we need to get running. My patrol captain was chomping at the bit to get an update on the case. I'm sure your captain is as well."

Emily nodded. "Given the family name, you know my captain's on my ass. I wouldn't be surprised if Judge Donovan has already talked to him. I'm sure I'll be sitting at his desk in the morning, being dressed down about how I need to work faster and find out exactly who was the one pulling the trigger."

"I have a feeling both of our necks are on the chopping block. There's a lot at stake." Pierce sighed.

"Let's plan on meeting up again in the morning and hitting it hard. We'll come up with a game plan and go from there. I'll send you over all the investigation reports into Clyde's initial disappearance. You can study up tonight," she said, her gaze slipping to Jamie. "That is, if you're not too busy." She sent her a little devious smirk.

Jamie felt the heat rise in her cheeks. She quickly looked away.

"I will be studying," he said, checking Emily's little attempt at humor.

"Oh, you guys are no fun," Emily said. "You two make a cute couple and there's nothing wrong with you spending the night together." She winked at Jamie. "We won't expect you back at the ranch tonight—have fun." She turned and waved as she hurried off. She didn't give her the option for a ride home.

Jamie was glad.

She wasn't sure she was ready to jump into bed with Pierce, but she was ready to spend more time with him, even if that meant sitting around with him while he read police reports. "If I'll be in the way, you can run me back. Or I can get a ride," she offered.

Emily got into her Suburban and waved as she passed by. Jamie stuck out her tongue. Pierce laughed. "Don't worry about being in the way. I want you around. Besides, my boss and his wife are expecting us for dinner. I would hate to have to tell them you stood them up. It would be horrible for my reputation."

"Oh, your reputation? Is that what you care about?" she teased, playfully ignoring the bit where he had admitted he had wanted her around.

He tilted his back with a laugh as he made his way around and got into the truck.

As they hit the road, he slipped his hand into hers, and it felt so natural as he told her about their interview with Carey that she almost didn't hear what he was talking about. Yet, it was so interesting—the duality of the woman, the victim and the antagonist.

In some ways, it felt like the duality of this moment, her hand in his. Hers callused by leather reins and bailing twine. His softened by time behind steering wheels and telephones. Yet, he was arguably the stronger and tougher between them.

It was striking how quickly life, feelings and the world could change.

As they arrived at the cabin on the outskirts of West Glacier, tucked back into the mountains, she was taken by the quaint charm of the place. It looked like something out of a Thomas Kinkade painting her parents used to have. Complete with the cabin's wraparound porch and a chimney with white smoke pouring out into the dusky summer sky.

As they stepped out of the truck, the air smelled of barbecued meats and baked potatoes, and her mouth watered. It had been hours since they'd had breakfast at the greasy spoon and though it had been that morning, it didn't even feel as if it had been the same day. So much had happened, it felt as though had been weeks ago.

There was a small ramp up to the porch and her boots thumped on the plywood as they made their way to the door. It opened before they even had a chance to knock. "Hey, guys," a brunette woman said, giving them a thin-lipped smile.

The woman was beautiful, curvy, and had sparkling brown eyes. "Come in, come in. We have been waiting for you," she said, excitedly, waving them inside.

The house was sparsely decorated and the leather furniture that was there was kept wide apart so Eliot's wheelchair could maneuver more easily through the space. There was a table off to one side that held a collection of medical devices, items to help the man breathe, including what she recognized as a nebulizer.

Though Jamie had realized the man had significant health problems, she hadn't known how much of his body had been impacted by his paralysis. It did make sense his lungs would have issues. It made her wonder how he continued to work, but she was impressed.

"Thank you so much for having us in your beautiful home," Jamie said, motioning toward the fireplace where they had a small fire going. "I love how you've done everything. I've always wanted a rock fireplace."

"I know it's summer and it seems silly to have fire, but it still gets a little chilly up here at night. Plus, I just think it's fun to have a fire for guests. You know?" The woman smiled brightly at the compliment as she glanced at the warm flames. "Thank you. And, oh, by the way, you can call me Nicole. I'm Eliot's wife. He's outside watching the barbecue for me while I was getting the door. I heard you guys coming up the road. You know how it is out here in the timber—you can hear people coming from a mile away." She laughed.

From the chipper way the woman spoke and from her drawl, Jamie guessed she was from somewhere down south, maybe Mississippi. She seemed like a nice woman, if a little too chatty—but perhaps it was just nerves at having strangers coming into her home.

"It's nice to meet you, Nicole. I've heard really great things about you."

She waved her off as she looked demurely away. "Oh, come now. It's all lies."

Pierce didn't argue with her, and it made Jamie wonder. Most people she knew would have politely bantered with the woman—especially given the fact it was his boss's wife.

"I'm going to head out to the grill," Pierce said, motioning outside. "Mind if I grab a beer?"

Nicole shook her head. "Wait, let me grab you a cold one. You don't need to serve yourself here. You're our guest."

She hurried into the kitchen, which was attached to the living room in an open-concept design, and grabbed two beers from the fridge. She opened the drawer with the clatter of silverware and rummaged around until she pulled out a bottle opener and clumsily flipped off the lids, letting one fall to the floor.

Her hands were shaking slightly as she handed the first brown bottle over to Pierce. "There you are. Tell Eliot I'll get him some water when he comes in."

Pierce lifted the bottle in thanks. "You got it." He turned on his heel and made his way outside.

Jamie hadn't really seen Pierce be this curt before and she was slightly taken aback. She would have thought this was Pierce in a professional setting, but this wasn't even the same Pierce she had seen in Eliot's office—just here, with Nicole. It was almost as if she made Pierce uncomfortable.

As he stepped outside and closed the door behind him, some of the tension seemed to leave with him. Nicole sighed as she reached over and handed her the other bottle of beer before grabbing one out of the fridge and opening another for herself. "He *really* doesn't like me," Nicole said, just confronting the elephant in the room and surprising Jamie.

"I don't think it's that. Pierce hasn't said anything to that effect about you to me." She tried to take some of the sting out of the woman's assumption, even if Jamie wondered the same.

"I don't know why, but he has never really warmed up to me. Tonight, though, he seems really *off*. Maybe you're right, it's probably just to do with this case with the former mayor. I heard it was a homicide investigation now."

The woman knew more than Jamie had expected, but then she was a patrol captain's wife. It made sense that he would take his work home and talk to her about his day.

"It is. Gunshot wound. I don't think they've found the gun."

"David and Vince are up there with the dogs. If it's there, they will find it. Those guys are great. Vince is a good ranger. Very *thorough*."

"I met him this morning. He seems like a good guy."

"Who did you meet?"

"Vince."

"Oh, yeah." Nicole smiled as she picked at the edge of the paper label on her beer bottle before taking a sip. "He is. He was supposed to be in Pierce's wedding party. Did you know that?" Nicole jerked her head up. "Oh, did Pierce even tell you about that?" She motioned toward her, awkwardly, and squished her face.

"He did tell me about it, yes."

"That was a sad deal. She was horrible to him. Damaged the whole family. I think he may still love her, though." She glanced at Jamie like she was goading her for a response.

She still didn't really want to discuss Pierce or his wedding with this woman—especially if there was some reason for tension between her and Pierce. If Nicole was one for gossip and drama, that could have been exactly what the problem was and why Pierce had high-tailed it outside.

In fact, she was going to give him a piece of her mind for leaving her as the fall guy with this woman when they were alone again. And, if he still loved his ex, which she was darned near sure he didn't, she would be giving him a whole lot more than a piece of her mind.

"What do you do for work?" Jamie asked, trying to gently change the subject.

Nicole leaned against the counter. "I used to be a certified nurse's assistant at Logan's, but when Eliot got hurt, I decided to stay home and become his full-time health-care provider. Social security pays me a salary, and it's actually more than I was making before at the hospital, so it works out great."

If she wasn't mistaken, it sounded like Nicole was almost grateful her husband had gotten hurt. There was no wonder Pierce didn't like her.

"That's nice that you can and are willing to provide him with the care he needs, but he seems pretty independent and capable in his daily life."

Nicole scowled, like Jamie had somehow offended *her* by questioning the validity of her taking on a full-time role when Eliot clearly didn't need it. "He needs a lot more help than most people realize."

Jamie put her hands up in submission. "I'm sorry, you are absolutely right. I'd had a grandfather who spent the last few years of his life with limited mobility, and he relied on a wheelchair to get around. I know it can be a challenge."

"That's not the same as a man being paralyzed."

"Again," Jamie said, dropping her head in apology, "you're correct. I'm sorry. I'm just trying to relate with your life and what you must be going through, but I know I have no real idea of what it must be like for you. I'd be happy to listen if you want to tell me about it, though." She felt like such a jerk, but she had been well intended.

"Eliot cannot take care of his personal hygiene adequately. So, several times a day, I have to move him from his wheelchair, with the help of a lift and make sure he is clean and dry. Often, he has sores because of his position in the chair. Because he can't feel the sores, they can quickly get out of control if we don't pay attention." Nicole let it all pour out, as if she had been waiting for someone to let her just vent. "And that is to say nothing about when he runs his legs into things—he has broken his foot twice and he had no idea until I took his shoe off and his foot was black and blue."

"It has to be so hard to be a personal caregiver."

"It is. And it is taxing. I love him, but he isn't the same since his accident. It's like I'm married to a man I don't even know." She picked at the label until a piece tore off. "I feel more like a nurse than I do a wife, but he wants me as both. It can be *hard*."

She had not liked the woman, but as Nicole opened up to her and poured her heart out to her, Jamie found herself warming to the woman. Clearly, she didn't have anyone to talk to and she just needed to have a safe space to let out her thoughts and feelings. Tonight, that could be her.

Jamie was grateful that when she'd been going through her darkest days, she'd had Matt by her side. He'd been there to talk to about all her memories and then how they were going to move through the future. Sometimes it had been hard to even move from day to day with his help. She couldn't imagine what it was like for Nicole—and it wasn't like she could talk to her husband.

"You should come out to the ranch. I was thinking about starting a riding clinic or equine therapy or something. It could be something to get you out of the house while Eliot's at work and it could be something you do just for yourself. I mean if you are interested in something like that?"

Nicole smiled, and for the first time Jamie noticed her

right canine tooth had a large chip in it that made it appear almost straight. "That would be great. I had been seeing a therapist for a while, but that didn't work out. I went to a few, but none of them really helped and I just decided to stop. Maybe therapy with animals would be better."

"Do whatever helps. In order to help others, you must take care of yourself. You know, that whole *put your own oxygen mask on first* thing." Jamie took a sip from her beer.

"Did I tell you I ran into one of your ranch hands the other day in town?" Nicole asked, tilting her head like a confused dog.

"Oh really? Do you know who it was?"

There was the creak of the back door as it swung open and there was the whirr of the electric wheelchair as Eliot rolled inside. "Hey, Jamie, how's it going?" he asked, moving the chair forward with the black knob in his hand.

"It's going, Eliot. Thanks for inviting me over for dinner. It's appreciated." She sent Nicole a grateful smile. "Ranch food is great, but when you raise beef, it's steak every night for dinner."

Nicole laughed. "Well, you're in luck, tonight we made brats." As she spoke, Pierce walked in through the back door carrying a tray of blackened brats and toasted buns.

They looked delicious and her mouth started to water.

"Do you need me to do anything?" Jamie asked, motioning toward the cupboards. "I can set the table or whatever you need."

Nicole nodded. "Step over here and I'll hand you the plates. We will just load up here in the kitchen and make our way over to the table." She pointed in the direction of the adjoining dining room where there was a large log table, sans one chair where Eliot must put his wheelchair. "Pierce, you can put that tray down on the stove there."

They all moved through the kitchen like a well-orchestrated dance thanks to the maven's commands. Eliot moved toward the dining room. "I'll have one brat," he called back to Nicole. "And a baked potato. No salad."

Nicole rolled her eyes at the order. "You can say 'please,' Eliot." There was a noticeable chill in her tone.

Eliot huffed. "Please. Thank you. Whatever."

Nicole opened the microwave and pulled out a plate of steaming potatoes crusted in salt. She placed them on the stove next to the tray and then she grabbed the plates out of the cupboard and handed them to Jamie. "Can you put these over there," she said, pointing to a space on the counter. "I'll grab the salad that Eliot will most definitely be having." She looked back at her husband with annoyance.

Pierce sent Jamie a look, like he wanted to know if she could feel the thick animosity between the couple as much as he could. She lifted one shoulder. After what Nicole had revealed to her, she could understand some of the woman's frustrations with her marriage. She was in a hard place. Now, Jamie wished she'd had a chance to ask her if she still loved him. If Nicole didn't, it would make it even harder to watch.

Maybe this was why they didn't have a lot of dinner guests.

She would just have to eat fast.

Nicole placed the bowl of salad beside the potatoes and moved to grab the condiments for everything from the fridge. Jamie turned to the silverware drawer and pulled out what they would need, to speed things up.

Grabbing a plate, she dished up food and handed it over to Pierce. "Here you go."

Nicole turned with a bottle of ketchup in her hand and looked at his plate with the bratwurst with a tilt of the head. "Um, do you need this?" she asked, offering him the bottle.

He shook his head. "Nah, I'm good." He glanced at Jamie and smiled.

He must have read her mind about wanting to get out of this place.

"Can I get Eliot's plate together for you?" Jamie asked, grabbing the next white plate in the stack.

"No, that's fine," Nicole said, taking the plate and starting to put things together. She sliced up the bratwurst and put the ketchup and mustard on the side of the plate for him to dip. She dropped some Caesar salad on the side and a mashed up baked potato, topped with butter and salt and pepper.

As she worked, Jamie prepared a light plate. She was hungry, but she made herself a simple brat and salad so she could plow through. She moved to the table and sat down next to Pierce. He touched his elbow to hers; a simple gesture but one that was greatly appreciated.

Nicole placed the plate on the table in front of Eliot along with a larger gripped fork. His arm trembled as he picked up the fork and stabbed it into the first piece of meat and dipped it into the ketchup. "So, David called tonight and said that they have a hit on the location the guy died. The anthropologists came in and started the dig. We are going to have the results back from that tonight, hopefully." Eliot looked at their plates. "Go ahead and start eating, you don't need to wait for her."

Pierce cleared his throat and gave a nervous laugh. "No,

that's okay. She cooked, we don't want to offend our host." He sent Nicole a smile as she came walking over to the table with a plate.

Nicole slipped into the chair one away from her husband after setting down a glass of water for him by his plate. "Thanks, Pierce. Really, you guys can dig in. We want you fed. You've been working hard."

Pierce picked up his fork. "It sounds like the park team is the one who has been working the hardest."

Eliot's phone pinged but he glanced down at it and ignored it. Instead, he chewed his bite for a long time before swallowing. He took a scoop of potatoes, but carefully avoided the salad. "How did the notifications go? How did Judge Donovan take the news?"

"You didn't get a phone call?" Pierce asked, sounding surprised.

"You know I did. I think every high-ranking official involved with this case got a phone call. He did tell me he was impressed with you. I don't know what you said, or did in there, but good job." Eliot lowered his arm, letting it relax on the table. "That being said, he also made it clear you have by the end of the week to wrap this up, or I'm to make sure you are no longer working at Glacier National Park."

"He doesn't have the right to do that," Pierce countered, anger in his voice.

"I said the same thing, though slightly more tactfully." Eliot let out a long exhale. "He and I had a long talk. There were many threats—to both of us. You just need to get this handled. Quickly."

Eliot's phone pinged again.

Pierce's phone buzzed in his back pocket.

"You guys probably need to answer that," Nicole said,

motioning toward Eliot's phone. "We all know when you guys get calls at the same time, it spells trouble."

Pierce pulled out his phone and answered. "Hello?"

Jamie looked at his face. At first, it was pinched with anger from the conversation with Eliot, but as the person on the other end of the line spoke, his gaze moved to her and his eyes widened, and she could see the color drain from his cheeks.

"What happened? What's wrong?" she asked, suddenly very afraid.

She tried to think of anything that would make him look at *her* like that. She wasn't involved with anything that was happening, she had just been helping with the case. What had she done?

Pierce nodded. "I got it, I'll be right there. Thanks for calling me." He clicked off the phone and stood up from the table. "Eliot, Nicole, we have to go. I'm sorry. Thank you for dinner." He held out his hand and Jamie put her shaking hand in his as he helped her to stand.

"What's going on?"

He shook his head as he looked at her. "I'll tell you outside in the truck. We have to go. Now."

She nodded as she let him lead her from the table. As they neared the front door, she remembered what she had been doing. "Yes," she said, looking back over her shoulder at their hosts, "thank you for dinner."

"Any time," Nicole called after her as they walked out the door and clicked it shut behind them.

Pierce didn't let go of her hand as he pulled her toward the truck and helped her inside. He gave her hand one last clutch before letting go and closing her door.

He got in, put the truck in gear and hit the gas, hard. He

kicked out dirt and gravel as they sped off down the dirt road and back toward the highway.

"Are you going to tell me what is going on or keep me guessing, Mario Andretti?"

He exhaled and the action made her stomach clench with nerves. "Something's happened to Matt."

She felt like she had gotten punched right in the gut. "What? What *happened*?"

"A man found him down outside The Mint Bar in town. Someone got their hands on him and beat him pretty bad. He is in the hospital. They have him intubated. He's in a medically-induced coma, and not doing well."

She had been so wrapped up in Pierce and what they were doing that she had barely been thinking about Matt. He was her best friend, and she had just left him to do his thing for the last couple of days. What kind of friend was she when he had come up here for her to help at her family's ranch and make sure she was settled?

Her thoughts moved to Eliot and Nicole. She would have to call Sally in Juneau and have her come down to see her husband. Sally was not going to take the news well. She had been freaking out over the cat attack, and now this. She was going to be a mess.

Once again, it struck her how quickly things could change and how, in this moment, Sally was going to do as she had once done—she was going to rush to a man who was on the brink of death. Hopefully, she would make it in time.

Chapter Eighteen

When they arrived at the hospital, the staff turned them away as it was after visiting hours. Pierce had tried to argue their way in, telling them about the situation and flashing his badge, but they'd made no special concessions as they weren't immediate family. He felt as though he had failed Jamie.

He looked out the window toward the parking lot, where she was standing beside the truck, talking on the phone. Tears were running down her cheeks and she was rubbing them away with the back of her free hand as she spoke.

She had told him she was calling Matt's wife, Sally. He'd offered to make the call for her, and watching her in this pain, he wished she had taken him up on his offer. It killed him to see her crying; his entire body yearned to go to her and do anything to staunch her agony.

There was so little he could do to help, but he could at least see what the local police were doing to find the person who had done this to Jamie's best friend. He pulled out his phone and called Emily. She answered on the first ring. "Hello?"

"Did you hear about Matt Goldstock? You know, the attack at The Mint?" he asked, not bothering with niceties.

Emily shuffled the phone, and it sounded like she must have been in bed. "Yeah, I saw the call-out, but I don't know anything about it." She sounded tired.

"Matt is the guy who was on the trail with Jamie. I don't have proof, but I think this attack might have something to do with our case."

There was a pause and the ruffle of linens. "Why would you say that?" she asked, sounding more alert.

"Matt didn't have any enemies here. Jamie said he isn't the kind to run his mouth and cause problems." He ran his hand over his face. "I know this guy's attack isn't your call, but I'd appreciate you getting involved and looking into it. You need to look through the lens of our investigation. Who has ties to our guy?"

He could hear Emily getting out of bed and her footfalls. "I'll get on it."

"Hey, I'm sorry if I woke you up."

"It's part and parcel of the whole genie gig." She exhaled a thin, tired laugh. "Where are you guys right now? Are you safe?"

"We are," he said, worriedly glancing out the window at Jamie. He hadn't wanted to think about what Matt's attack could have meant about their own safety, but the potential for their being attacked next had been moving through the back of his mind. "We're at the hospital right now. I was hoping she could get in to see Matt. He's in the ICU, but they're not letting us in. Honestly, it's probably not a bad thing. He's in pretty bad shape, according to what I heard from my friends at Dispatch."

"Is he going to make it through the night?"

He rubbed his face as he leaned back against the white hospital wall. That was something else he had tried to avoid thinking about. "I'm hoping so. The hospital staff won't release any information to us because we aren't family. Jamie is on the phone with the guy's wife now. Maybe she can get more out of them."

"You know, if they're not letting you in… It's probably a good thing they are sticking to visiting hours in the ICU. A lot of time, they will bypass those kinds of rules for people who are actively dying."

It wasn't great, but it was at least something he could give Jamie to make the night go by a little easier until they could see Matt in the morning.

"Let me know if you get any more information on the beating."

"I'm sure we can pull footage from around the bar, they have cameras up all over around that place, for obvious reasons." Emily exhaled, like she was pulling on a shoe. "I'll call you when I get something." She hung up the phone.

He appreciated that she wasn't messing around, but it probably expedited the process thanks to the fact that Matt was an employee at her and her husband's ranch.

He walked through the automatic door that led outside just as Jamie was hanging up. Her eyes were puffy, and she rubbed the bottom of her palms against them to try to control herself. "He's going to be okay."

"Did you talk to one of his doctors? Did they tell you something?" she asked, sounding hopeful.

"No," he said, taking her by the hand and trying to comfort her, "but I spoke to Emily, and she reminded me that if staff is under the impression a person is on the verge of death, they often let friends into the room to say goodbye. They don't want anyone to have to be alone or without those they love. So, they must be confident he is stable enough that he will make it through the night."

She sniffled and tilted her head back, shaking out her hands. "Good, that's good. I'll tell Sally that. She'll like it. It will make her feel less stressed while she makes her way here."

"So, she is on her way?"

Jamie nodded.

At least he knew Matt would be in good hands if his wife was going to come in from Alaska. He hated hospital policies sometimes, especially in cases like these where no one from the family was near. It wasn't the same to simply talk to a doctor or nurse on the phone instead of standing with your loved ones while they received hands-on care.

THEY WERE JUST about to the ranch when Jamie turned to him. "Can we go back to your house? I don't want to be here tonight." She motioned to the rusted metal sign with their brand, which listed gently in the moonlight from where it hung on the log over the driveway.

"As you wish, you know you are always welcome. I'm glad you want to," he said, laying his hand on the console between them and putting his palm up.

She slipped her hand into his.

"I just don't want to sleep alone tonight if there is someone out there who is upset we're looking into Donovan's murder. I'm tough, but I'm not close to 'Matt tough.' I'd be an easy target."

"Until we know if this was related to our investigation, you are right, we need to just assume it is and prepare for the worst. It is better to be as safe as possible." He also didn't hate the idea of her in his bed—even if he was to kiss her again. "But I hope you don't think you need to be afraid. I won't let anything happen to you. Ever."

She caught his gaze and smiled so sweetly that it made his heart ache from swelling.

"I won't tell anyone how sweet you really are, okay?" she teased.

"What?" he asked with a laugh.

"You kinda acted all tough around Nicole and Eliot at dinner tonight."

"Oh." The joy fell from him.

"You don't like her, do you?"

He looked out the windshield like he suddenly needed to really concentrate on the darkened roads. He didn't want to tell her about Vince's admission to him about his sleeping with Nicole around the time of Eliot's accident.

"Why don't you?" She clearly didn't have to get a verbal answer for the first.

It was impressive how well she already knew him.

"I can't tell you, but what I know isn't the only reason I avoid her. She has a way of just..." He made a knife-dabbing motion with their entwined hands.

"Oh, I know exactly what you mean. She told me you are still in love with your ex."

He jerked the wheel so hard, they nearly drove off the road. "Are you effing kidding me?" He corrected and slowed down. "Pardon my language. But seriously, no way. I wouldn't have anything to do with her if my life actually depended on it."

"That's what I told her."

"I am over the entire situation. All of it. I'm angry at Nicole for trying to get under your skin and start a problem between you and me, but as for the rest of it with Haven, I'm apathetic. She made her choices. I'm just glad it saved me from having to go through a lengthy and painful divorce."

"Well, that's one way of looking at it."

He shrugged. "Obviously, she never really loved me."

"She made a huge mistake, but if she hadn't, I wouldn't be holding your hand. I guess there's always a silver lining."

"I'm glad for every second I've gotten to spend with you. I was so glad when you came back this morning. Why did you?"

She looked at their entwined hands. "You couldn't help the timing. Fate is funny. I think it was a way for me to take a second and realize that it was okay for me to move on."

He lifted their hands and kissed her fingers. "Tonight can be whatever you want it to be. It's been a long day. If you want to take a shower and just hit the rack, I'd completely understand. I have a great watch list and popcorn."

She leaned her temple against their hands and didn't say anything as they pulled into his driveway and he parked. He kissed the top of her head and touched his forehead to where he had just kissed. The action was so simple, but so filled with love, that he wanted to pull her into his arms and over the console and just hold her to him, but he reminded himself they were almost inside.

She sat up and moved to open the door.

"You wait right there," he said with a smile.

He got out, hurried around to her side and opened her door. "You've worked enough today. Tonight, let's give you the princess treatment." He scooped her up into his arms and kicked the door shut.

Her giggle carried out into the night, threatening to lure the sun up with its warmth.

"I could listen to you giggle forever. Did anyone ever

tell you how beautiful your laugh is?" he asked, smiling as he walked her to his front door.

She pulled her arms tight around his neck. "You don't have to be so sweet. You already have me swooning."

"Oh, do I? Was it obvious that I was trying?" He laughed. "I always thought a woman wanted to be swept off her feet."

"I don't know that they meant literally, but I definitely like it. You can do this any time."

"Any time?" he asked with a quirk of the brow. "You promise?"

She giggled and kissed him. It was so unexpected and sweet that he dropped her to her feet so he could hold her in his arms. He loved the feeling of her in his arms, the weight of her and all she represented—love, strength, partnership, and thoughts of more.

Her tongue traced the edge of his lip and he slipped his hand down her back, cupping her ass. He pulled her tight against him with his other, pressing into the center of her back. She gasped at the pressure, and he smiled as he moved his kiss down her neck and then back to her lips.

He was hungry for her; he needed to taste every part of her.

JAMIE HAD BEEN fantasizing about this moment in flashes since she had first met Pierce, not that she would have admitted it to anyone but herself. She loved the way his body was hot as fire against her skin. He wanted to possess every part of her, and she yearned for him to take just as much.

She broke his kiss and took him by the hand. "Let's take this inside," she said, motioning in the direction of the house.

He glanced at the front of his house and then out toward

the lake. "You know what… I have a better idea. What do you think about a campfire?"

She put her hands over her mouth and nodded excitedly. "Oh, yeah, that would be so much fun. I haven't had a campfire in a long time. They are so much fun. We can sit out by it, listen to the waves crash on the beach and watch the stars."

He smiled. "You read my mind." He slipped his hand in hers and they made their way into the house.

She liked his place and its quaint charm—even the antique green couch that was far more comfortable than she would have first expected. It was so unpretentious, and it just *fit* him.

"Why don't you grab a blanket from the living room, and I will run outside and start putting together the fire. Give me fifteen minutes, or so, and it should be going." He walked over to her and gave her another kiss, soft and languid, before slipping out the back door.

She walked into the kitchen and stood at the sink, washing her hands and watching him grab a large log. He picked up an ax that was sitting against a boat shed at the side of the property. The way he walked was so strong and self-assured.

He pulled off his uniform shirt, exposing a skintight white T-shirt he was wearing beneath. Her mouth actually began to water. She wasn't sure how, with all the rangers who worked in the park, she had been lucky enough to have him be the one who'd shown up to help.

Then her thoughts moved to Matt. That night when they'd found Anthony.

She shook the thoughts away. Matt was going to be okay tonight…and if he knew she was here and doing what she was doing, he would kick her butt for ruining the night by being all wrapped up being worried about him. She smiled at the thought of her best friend.

There were so many things he would need. But she would be there for him—tomorrow. Tonight was for her and Pierce.

They had nowhere to be. No one to answer to. They were safely tucked away together in his home. Or, as safe as they could be, as they were together.

Together. The word reverberated through her soul.

She embraced the feeling.

There were never any guarantees when it came to the future—her past had taught her that—so she was going to make the most of this night with him and this time. If this was the only stolen time they were granted, she would treasure it and honor it by making it the best night she could.

Jamie watched him splitting the wood, his shoulders pressing against the fabric of his shirt and his core tightening as he swung. He was an incredibly handsome man. She didn't want to, but she finally turned away when he moved to pick up the pieces of wood he'd split and started to place them in a tent shape in the rock-edged fire ring near the edge of the lake.

Walking into the living room, she grabbed a patchwork quilt that looked as though it had been made about the same time the couch had been manufactured, thanks to the orange and green fabrics and gaudy giant flowers complete with brown centers. She remembered her grandmother having these kinds of patterns on her furniture when Jamie had been a kid.

She picked up the blanket but then put it back down on the couch. The last thing she wanted to think about while she was with Pierce and lying out under the stars, was her grandmother, or his. She chuckled at the thought.

Instead, she walked over to the chair in the corner and picked up a plain green fleece blanket that would probably pick up everything on the ground and require several shakings to flip the pine needles loose. It was worth it, and it *was* soft. She lifted it to her nose; it smelled of fabric softener and Pierce.

She loved that smell.

On her way out, she grabbed a couple of beers. She'd be lying if she said she wasn't a little nervous. It had been a while and though she was pretty sure she was ready to take things to the next level, it was still a big step and one there was no coming back from.

There was thick smoke rising up from the fire pit as she walked outside. She'd probably not waited as long as he'd said, but she didn't care. It wasn't that cold of a night, and she had a blanket if she needed it. What she didn't want was to miss another minute with him. If this was their only night together, she wanted to take advantage of every second.

Pierce was squatting next to the fire, making sure the burgeoning flames were getting enough oxygen. They were still the bright orange, not yet hot enough to put off a great deal of heat, but they would give plenty of ambience until then.

She cleared her throat in an attempt to get his attention in the darkness and so as not to surprise him.

He turned and smiled at her. "You can put the blanket there," he said, pointing behind him. "Normally, the wind comes in from the direction of the cabin and rolls over the lake at night. That way, the smoke shouldn't blow in our faces, at least, not too much."

Following his directions, Jamie set down the beers and laid out the soft blanket behind him on what turned out to be a small patch of green grass. She sat and wrapped her arms around her knees in front of her, watching him work.

As he finished up, he came back to her and sat behind her, putting his legs on each side of her body. "Here, lean back," he said, touching her side gently.

She leaned into him, and he wrapped his arms around her body. He motioned toward the constellation in the sky. "See that right there? Those three stars?"

"Yes." She nodded.

"That's the summer triangle. It's made of Vega, Deneb and Altair."

She smiled as he pointed at each of the bright stars.

"Right there—" he pointed at one "—is Deneb. It is in the constellation of Cygnus the Swan." He took her hand and led her finger to the next. "That is Vega, in the constellation Lyra the Harp." He moved their entwined hands to the last of the three bright stars. "And that is Altair in the constellation Aquila the Eagle."

"How did you learn all that?" she asked, turning back slightly to look at his face glowing in the firelight.

He smiled at her and gave her a gentle kiss on her forehead and let go of her hand. "I used to sit out here with my dad at night when I was a kid. We would fish off the dock and he'd tell stories about the constellations to help me learn them. I guess some of them stuck."

"It sounds like you had a really special dad."

He nodded. "I did. I miss him a lot." He pressed his face into her hair like he was kissing the back of her head, but she wasn't sure. "Someday, I would like to do the same thing with my own kid, or kids."

Her stomach clenched a little, but she wasn't sure if it was with nerves or excitement at the prospect of talking about the future. "How many kids would you like to have?"

"I don't know. At least one. I just want a healthy house, full of love and laughter."

She nearly melted. "Me, too. And I want to teach my kids how to ride. It's an expensive lifestyle, but it's a non-negotiable for me. It's something so important to me, I couldn't imagine having a life where my kids weren't involved in it as well."

"I completely understand that." He pushed the hair away from her neck. As he did, the hair tickled her and brought goose bumps to her skin.

"I…" She started, but found it hard to form words as his warm breath caressed her neck. His kiss fell on her soft skin, forcing all thoughts from her mind. "I… I don't remember what I was going to say," she said, her voice airy.

"Good." He reached down for her legs and pulled her around until she was facing him.

She put her legs around him as their lips found each other. He tasted so good, and he smelled of campfire and sweat. He was intoxicating in every way.

What she felt for him wasn't just lust or longing, though she was feeling both right now…she wanted him, badly. Yet she found herself wondering as he kissed her neck if the ache in her chest was love.

She ran her fingers through his hair as he moved his hands down her and cupped her breast as he kissed. She tilted her head back as he squeezed her nipple through the thin fabric of her T-shirt and bra until it was so hard it throbbed.

He reached and pulled her shirt over her head and threw

it onto the ground. He stopped for a moment, looking at her silhouetted by the firelight that radiated warmth off her.

She reached back and unclasped her bra as he sat and watched her. Sending him a seductive smile, she held up the cups as she slipped the straps from her shoulders. When they were free, he reached for her arm holding the bra up and gently pushed it down, and she let her bra fall free of her breasts.

The summer air felt cool on her skin and her already firm nipples grew impossibly harder. He leaned in, drew the left one into his mouth and gently sucked. Her body clenched with want. Reaching for him, she pulled his shirt loose and over his shoulders, exposing his tanned muscles she'd seen rippling against the offending fabric earlier.

His kissed her violently and their lovemaking turned hurried and fevered as they fell to the ground. Pants stripped off. Thrown. She yanked at her panties, fighting them as he pulled off his T-shirt. He lowered his boxers as they sought to reunite their lips.

She crawled on top of him, leading his body to her. Her wetness covered him without his penetrating her and she smiled as she looked him in the eyes and rubbed her body against his hardness. He felt so good pressing against her. He was so close to being inside. One simple movement, one thrust, and his tip would slip between her folds.

She slid forward on his length, reached down and pressed his tip inside her as she looked into his eyes. There was a beautiful ache as he spread her open and she stretched around him. She groaned as she gently moved on top of him, letting her body ease into the pressure of all he had to offer.

He was so much bigger than she had expected.

Pierce took hold of her hips and rocked her body on him, helping her to roll her hips with the action of his body. Their bodies were in tandem with each other, giving and taking, and she felt the tingling of excitement of the initial smaller climax that was her norm.

The sensations took hold of her as she drove harder against him, letting her folds rub against his body and intensify the enjoyment. She slowed her hips as she felt the ecstasy flow through her. Small aftershocks riddled through her body, making her shudder.

"Did you?" he asked, looking at her with a devilish smile.

"Oh, that is only the start, cowboy. I'm not a one-and-done kind of woman." She answered his devilish grin with one of her own as she leaned down and devoured his kiss.

She picked up her speed, bouncing atop him in the night.

He leaned his head back and his eyes closed as he let out a guttural moan. "Oh my God, you feel so good."

She laughed; the sound dark and heavy with lust. "Watch me ride you."

His eyes opened wide, and he looked down at where their bodies connected. He groaned as she kissed his neck and worked her hips, bouncing on him like a jockey.

She could feel him harden inside her. He was close, so close.

"Jamie…" He said her name like it was a wish.

"Give it to me, I want it." She smiled as she sped up.

He called out, the sound carrying like a wild animal in the night. Primal. Freeing. Unforgettable.

She leaned into his ear. "There are some things cowgirls just do better."

Chapter Nineteen

The morning came far too quickly for Pierce's liking, and that was after they had slept well past his alarm and hers and several phone calls of people looking for them. They just hadn't cared. She had checked on Matt, who had remained stable through the night, and beyond that, everything else had waited.

Jamie was lying in bed as he slipped out. Her arm was over her eyes, blocking out the thin light of the sun as she soaked in the last tendrils of stolen sleep. She looked perfect in her naked form. They had made love until the fire had gone out and only the hot, glowing, orange coal was left in the fire pit.

There had been a thin edge of light on the horizon and promises of the coming morning as they had slipped into the house for rest.

He could easily say it had been one of the best nights of his life. She had told him last night that it had been the same for her, but he wouldn't hold her to it. He smiled at the thought and at her as he took one more look at her before slipping out of the room and silently closing the door.

He was an incredibly lucky man.

His phone pinged with a message as he looked out and

checked that the fire was dead. Pouring water in the coffee maker, he started a pot and then picked up the device and checked his message. It was Emily. They had pulled video footage from The Mint. She'd sent him an encrypted email with film.

Opening up his email, he had to wait a moment, but it didn't take long for the email to pop up. He pulled up the video.

The video was clear. It showed Matt walking out of the bar, a man Pierce didn't recognize along with him. The man held up some keys, saying something, and then he walked off toward what Pierce assumed was the parking lot.

Matt stood there for a moment and pulled a can of Copenhagen out of his pocket. Opening up the lid, he took out a pinch and placed it in his bottom lip. As he was putting the can back in his pocket, a person wearing a black coat and a black mask approached from the opposite direction, carrying a metal bat.

Matt, with his back turned, didn't see the first blow to the back of the head coming.

He landed on his knees and fell forward, his face hitting the ground and his arms falling limp at his sides. There were splatters of blood on the sidewalk around his face.

The attacker came up and swung the bat, hitting him in the back. Then again in the back of the head, hard. The blood began to seep from Matt's head and pool on the ground around him as the person kicked his body.

The attacker hit him one more time between his shoulder blades. The person looked up in the direction where the man with the keys had disappeared to, and then turned and ran.

Pierce wondered how long the beating would have gone if they hadn't been interrupted by something off camera.

A black Dodge with the ranch's brand pulled around in front of the bar and parked. The man who had left Matt jumped out and pulled out his phone. There, the video ended.

He watched the video three more times, zooming in on the person in black. Based on their body size, which was about the same as Matt's, that made the attacker about six-foot and over 200 pounds.

He assumed the attacker was male, but beyond that, there was not much information. He texted Emily.

Got the video. Thx. What do you make of it?

It didn't take long for Emily to get back to him.

I'm hdd 2 the hospital. They r extubating Matt. Going 2 question him. Meet me there.

He fired back a text.

Okay. See ya soon.

He didn't want to wake Jamie, she had been sleeping so peacefully, and after everything they had been through in the last few days, she needed the reprieve. In all honesty, so did he.

His thoughts drifted to her sitting in front of the fire, her beautiful body silhouetted by the light of the flames. It had been the night of his dreams. Actually, it had been better than anything he had ever imagined.

If he could have things his way, he would only go back in that room to make love to her again.

The coffee steamed and gurgled as it finished brewing. He grabbed a mug, poured himself a cup, and leaned against the counter and stared outside at the place they had first made love. From that moment forward, that would forever be her spot and anytime he looked out at the lake, he would think of her—no matter what the future brought in their lives.

Thinking about the future, he sighed. He was in deep. His heart was hers and he knew there was no way he could tell her. He liked her so much and now it had shifted into the territory of love and longing, but it was too soon and dangerously fast. Given the trauma and volatility of both of their lives, allowing his emotions to get involved was figuratively playing with fire. In many senses, he could be feeling what he was because she was a safe place in the chaos of his life—was what he was feeling trauma bonding?

He couldn't allow himself to overthink it.

Pierce shook his head as if he could shake out the intrusive and unwelcome thoughts.

Sometimes he wondered if there was such a thing as being too emotionally intelligent and aware. Maybe ignorance really was bliss.

He forced himself to watch the video again instead of picking apart his moments of happiness and contentment.

The attacker was wearing black-and-white Hoka running shoes. He didn't know much about the shoes; he'd only seen the brand at the local sporting goods store a few times when he'd walked through. However, seeing them gave him an idea. It was a stretch, but it was a small town, and if the person wearing them had purchased them, maybe there was a record of the purchase.

It was a needle in a haystack, but it was a place to start.

He puttered around, making a little extra noise as he moved through the kitchen, cleaning up from the night before and starting the dishwasher.

He sent Emily a quick text message about his idea of looking into the shoes. She quickly reminded him that to get any information that they could use in court, he would need to apply for a search warrant.

As it so happened, he knew just the judge who could talk to the federal judge he'd have to send the search warrant through, stating he believed the beating was in connection to the federal case they were currently investigating in the park.

He jogged out to his truck, grabbed his computer and set to work writing out the application. After thirty minutes and some great writing, if he had to say so himself, he sent the application to the federal judge and fired off a text to Judge Donovan to let him know he'd sent the application to the federal judge with the video and a request he make a phone call to get the process expedited.

He had the search warrant signed and in his hands within ten minutes.

That was, hands down, the fastest search warrant he had ever gotten in his life. For the federal government, that was definitely some kind of record.

He sent Judge Donovan and Judge Casper, the federal judge who signed the order, a quick thanks.

Closing his computer, he sauntered back to the kitchen. He had a feeling it was going to be a productive day.

He grabbed a second travel mug and poured Jamie a cup of coffee to go.

Just as he was about to give in and walk down the hallway to wake her, Jamie came out down the hall, dressed and ready to roll. "Good morning," she said, a wide smile on her face. She looked just as beautiful as she had in the firelight.

"You look stunning," he said, walking to her and giving her a kiss before handing her the cup of coffee. "Are you hungry?"

She shook her head. "My abs are sore this morning. I don't know if it's from laughing or from…*other things*." She sent him a guilty grin.

He laughed. "I like knowing it's a toss-up."

"Thank you for last night. I had no idea how badly I needed…well, all of it." She motioned toward the lake and around the house. "And I didn't mean to sleep like that, but, oh man, it was so nice. I hope Detective Monahan isn't upset."

He shook his head. "Not at all. I've been talking to her. You and I actually need to run to Sportsman's Outlet. I got a search warrant for sales records. Matt's attacker was wearing a certain brand of shoe, and I want to look into anyone who may have purchased them. It's a long shot, but the shoes looked relatively new and I'm hoping maybe we can catch a break."

"You do know people buy shoes online all the time, right?"

He nodded. "Yeah. I know, but these are higher-end shoes. Running shoes that, if I was buying, I would want to make sure fit my foot before committing. I'd want to try them on in person."

She tipped her hand, like she was conceding the point.

IT DIDN'T TAKE long for them to get to the store. Thankfully, the store manager was working, a man named Brent Grant. He was an older gentleman with graying hair and a friendly smile. When Pierce had presented him with the search warrant, he had been more than happy to help.

Now, he and Jamie were standing with Brent and his tech lady in the main office upstairs in the warehouse-style building. The industrial-like complex smelled like solvent, gun powder and leather, and he had to admit it was a great mix—second only to Jamie.

As the tech lady, Traci, set to work tapping on the keys of the computer as she pulled up the sales records for the last year, Pierce sent Jamie a smile. He couldn't help but let his thoughts drift back to memories of last night's fun.

Brent turned to him. "So, can you tell me a little bit about your case? Why are you looking for just this kind of shoe?"

Given how much the small community seemed to know about the Donovan case, he wasn't sure how much fodder he wanted to feed to the gossip fire. But Brent and Traci seemed like great people, and he could give them some tidbits in an effort to advance their search.

"We are looking for a suspect who was wearing these while they committed a crime. They were wearing all black in the camera footage, and this was their only identifiable feature. We aren't even sure if this person was male or female."

Brent waved him off. "Oh, I might be able to help you a little bit there. Those are men's running shoes. Women's have a different color pattern. I would say you are looking for a male. Here, at least, I don't believe we've ever sold a pair to a woman for her use. Traci?"

She was grabbing a few pages off the printer. "You can

take a look." She placed the freshly printed pages on the desk so they could all see each of the four pages of sales.

It appeared that since the shoe had gone on sale, the store had sold twenty-two pairs.

"I worked in our shoe department for more than a decade," Traci said. "If you let me see the brand, I could probably give you an estimate on the person's size. That would narrow our sales list down."

He pulled up the video and zoomed in on the attacker's shoes before handing the phone to Traci.

"Do you mind if I zoom this out a little? I need to see the shoe in contrast to the person."

"Do whatever you need." He motioned toward the screen.

Traci tapped and, as she did, she started to get a self-satisfied grin. "This is definitely a male, based on his gait. And he's wearing a size 9 shoe. Which, interesting enough, is actually smaller than the national average for his height." She handed him back his phone with an air of pride.

He was impressed. Brent reached over and gave her a soft pat on her back. "Now, what about sales in that size?" Brent asked.

Jamie pointed to the page on the far right. "There was a pair sold just recently. Here." She put her finger on a transaction record.

Traci stepped next to her and picked up the paper. "Yep. It was paid for with a Visa card. Let me get back on the computer and see if I can get the details." She sat down and tapped away. "First, there have been only three pairs sold that match our description." She pressed more keys as she spoke. "Here we go. Okay." The printer kicked on.

"Did you find out the names of the people who bought the shoes?" Pierce asked.

Traci nodded as she grabbed the paper off the printer and handed it to him. "Here you go. Do you need me to do anything else?"

He took the page and stared, disbelieving at the name at the top of the list—David Slayton.

It didn't make sense. David had only met Matt on the mountain. What reason did he have to want to beat Matt nearly to death?

Chapter Twenty

Jamie was so confused as she listened to Emily and Pierce talking animatedly on the phone as they raced toward Glacier Park, "running code," as Pierce had called it with his red and blue lights flashing.

She couldn't reconcile why David, the man who had helped to discover Clyde Donovan's body, would have wanted to beat her best friend. Now, it left her wondering if she and Pierce had been wrong about the attacker wanting to send them a message or threaten them about Clyde's murder.

Unless David had had something to do with the murder?

If he did have something to do with the murder? Then why would he have wanted to work so diligently in uncovering the evidence? He and his team had been the ones to find the speed loader. And, if she recalled correctly, he was also the one who'd suggested that they call in the dog handlers to see if they could locate the exact location where Clyde had been killed, or at least decomposed.

It just didn't line up. Nothing about this made sense.

Had Matt had a run-in with David that she hadn't been aware of? Matt hadn't said anything to her about him fighting with anyone to do with the case, or the rescue of Anthony. He would have, if he had thought anything was amiss. He wasn't the kind to hide anything from her. Sure, they hadn't talked a lot in the last few days since the cat attack, not with everything that had happened, but he would have called her with big news.

She checked her phone for messages, even going to all her social media platforms in case she had missed something from him, but Matt had sent her nothing. So strange.

She texted Sally to check on her progress. Sally was quick to text back. She was in Seattle. It wouldn't be long before she was on the ground. From Seattle to Kalispell wouldn't take long. With the layover and flight time, she would be on the ground in two hours.

With the click of a few buttons, Jamie texted her brother to let him know that he would need to pick up Sally at the airport and take her to the hospital to see Matt. He sent a thumbs-up a few seconds later in true brother form.

Pierce hung up his phone and threw it on the dashboard. "Detective Monahan and her team are working another angle," he said, sounding angry.

She wasn't sure she had heard him call Emily "detective" before, and she wasn't sure what had happened during their phone call to make him suddenly be so angered with her, but she didn't like the shift, and it made her feel even more on edge. "Is everything okay?"

He sighed. "We will see. She doesn't think there is validity to Traci's work. I think there is, she is an expert in her field. The other people on that list have no ties to this investigation or the crime."

"Do you think he killed Clyde?" Jamie asked, rubbing her pointer finger and thumbnail together nervously and making a clicking sound.

He looked at her fingers. "I don't know. It doesn't make sense if he did. He started as a ranger just a short time before the mayor went missing. I don't think he had any ties with Clyde before that as he came out of Dillon—straight out of University of Montana Western with a degree in environmental science."

"How did he get a job in the law enforcement side if he was studying environmental science?" she asked.

"That program works directly with the United States Forest Service, so it's not a big leap. They are just looking for people who are dedicated and willing to work for the government." He gave a dry chuckle.

"So, you don't think there was anything nefarious about his getting a job? Anything which could have led to him having a run-in with Donovan?"

"Short of him screwing his wife—which I don't think, given his short stint here before his disappearance—"

"Do you think David was sleeping with Carey? That he killed Clyde and got rid of his body up here?"

He looked over at her. "I'd be lying if I said the thought hadn't crossed my mind."

She wasn't completely surprised given what she knew about the woman, but before he'd hurt Matt, she would have thought a man like David was well outside Carey's league—that was, unless he had some kind of mother fetish.

In some ways, it seemed too easy.

"Did you ever see David and Carey together? Did he ever talk about dating someone to you?" she asked.

Pierce tapped on the steering wheel for a moment, like the tick helped him to think. "When he was first on the job, he trained with me. I don't remember him saying he had a girlfriend or was in a serious relationship of any sort. We talked about girlfriends and stuff. I remember we talked about my being with Haven, we weren't engaged at that point."

She bristled at the thought.

"He told me that he didn't believe in marriage."

She was confused. "He didn't believe in it?"

He nodded.

Maybe he did have something to do with Clyde's murder.

They pulled to a screeching halt in front of the headquarters. There were several other trucks, just like Pierce's, parked in front.

There was only one other open parking space on the entire street, and it was a stark contrast from the last time she had been at the building with only the patrol captain and the secretary.

Jamie followed Pierce as they rushed inside.

The building, which was filled with empty desks the previous day, was now filled with the comings and goings of officers. The desk in the middle of the room with the nameplate that read David Slayton sat ominously empty.

There was no way David could have known they were coming for him. No one besides the two of them and the employees at the sporting goods store knew what they had discovered. As far as anyone else was concerned, they were still just watching the video and picking at thin threads, hoping to find a decent lead.

Not even Reynolds knew what they had found yet.

She looked toward the office at the far end of the building. It was shut up and dark inside.

Pierce walked toward the office and peeked in through a crack between the edge of the window and the shade. "It doesn't look like Reynolds has been in today." He pulled up his phone. "He is on the schedule and he's not really one for being late. I'm surprised he isn't in."

"Does he drive himself here?"

Pierce shook his head. "We work on government salaries—those kinds of rigs cost a ton of money. I know we have a GoFundMe going for him to get one, but he's not met his goal just yet. For now, Nicole has to bring him in their wheelchair-accessible van."

"Maybe you should give him a call."

"Let me ask if anyone else has heard from him first, I don't want to freak out over nothing." He walked over to the woman they had seen the last time she'd been in the building and started chatting. She couldn't really hear them over the chatter in the building and the clatter of keyboards and phone calls. The woman looked over at her and frowned. She shook her head, and from her body language, Jamie could tell the woman hadn't seen Reynolds.

Pierce came back and motioned for her to follow him outside.

She said nothing as she followed him, but she was dying to know what the woman had said.

As soon as they stepped outside, he looked around and, like he was making sure no one else he worked with was within earshot, he said, "Reynolds called in last night and let his secretary know that he wouldn't be in for the next week. She said she asked why, but he wouldn't tell her if he was sick or what. She said he sounded upset, *off.*"

"I didn't think things went that badly at their house last night. I mean I didn't exactly hit it off with Nicole, but that shouldn't have caused a problem between them. At least, I wouldn't have thought so," Jamie said. "I mean, we got along okay *enough*."

Pierce shook his head as they got into the truck. "Who knows what's going on with him. It's not like him. Even after his accident, he came back to work as soon as they had him fitted for a wheelchair. He didn't miss a beat. His work is his life. But he may be sick." He shrugged, but there was a worried expression on his face.

Jamie had a sickening feeling in her stomach. Something was wrong.

He tapped on his phone as he drove. "Maybe Emily was right. Maybe it wasn't David in the video."

"If it wasn't him, then why wouldn't he be at work?"

He ran his hand over his face with exasperation. "Right. I know." He exhaled. "We need to find him. That way, at least, we can either eliminate him as a suspect in Matt's attack or find justice."

EMILY HAD SUNK her teeth into Carey as a potential suspect in Matt's attack. She just couldn't believe that the attacker was a man based on the gait and that they were men's shoes. According to her, those types of things could be faked or used to throw off investigators.

Pierce didn't completely disagree with her. Carey had some motive to go after Matt. However, he hadn't heard of any connection between the two. In fact, he wasn't even sure that Carey was aware of Jamie taking part in the investigation. Even if she had seen Jamie sitting in his truck while he and Emily were questioning her, Carey wouldn't have had reason to suspect Jamie of any major role, so targeting her best friend from the ranch seemed like a stretch.

That was, unless she was just going after Jamie to get to him. But Jamie hadn't been with Matt, at least not that

Pierce had known of, since they had found Clyde's body on the mountain.

Pierce scratched at the stubble on the edge of his chin as he worked through all the possibilities.

Emily was still at the hospital with Matt, and Pierce didn't want to interfere with her questioning by bringing Jamie there. Emily needed to get as many answers from him as he could provide. However, Pierce would be surprised if Matt remembered much from the attack. From the camera footage, the attacker had come from behind—it was likely he'd never even seen the face of his assailant thanks to the mask, even if he did remember anything about the event.

Pierce tried to call David, but his phone call went straight to voicemail. Pierce told him to call as soon as he got the message. He did the same with Eliot. Then Nicole. It was as if they had all fallen off the planet.

He had no reason to believe the three of them were connected. David worked with Eliot in the same capacity he did, but beyond that, he knew of no deeper connections.

Nothing was lining up.

"What are you thinking?" Jamie asked, almost as if she could read his mind.

Pierce shook his head. "I'm at a loss, but I'm thinking maybe we do need to listen to Emily and look deeper into Carey and her life until we can connect back up with David. It can't hurt. Right?"

Jamie chewed on her top lip. "If we go over there, Carey isn't going to be happy to see you. Did you say she wouldn't speak to you again without her lawyer present?"

He nodded. "She did, but she also wasn't detained at the

time she stated that. So, we are free to go to her residence and question her as necessary. She hasn't been Mirandized."

"If she isn't, can anything she tells you be admissible in court?"

He shifted his head back and forth. "Ninety-nine percent of the time the admission will be thrown out. However, if she confesses to something, it makes it a lot easier to hang her up on the stand. Plus, we know where to start to get the evidence we need to prove that she was guilty with or without her confessing if she gets behind a lawyer who keeps her buttoned up."

Jamie gave him a devious look as she nodded. "Then I think we need to go talk to her again. It can't hurt, and then maybe—if Emily is on to something—we can get ahead of it."

He picked up his speed and it only took five minutes to get to the cul-de-sac with the obnoxiously ordinary house. There was a brand-new black Cummins Dodge diesel parked in front of the house that hadn't been there the last time they had been there. The truck was so new, it only had the temporary registration hanging in the back window instead of a license plate.

The truck was lifted and everything on it was top of the line down to the custom deep-dish wheels. It was at least an eighty-thousand-dollar pickup. It seemed out of place in front of the cookie-cutter house with the horrible witch inside.

He really couldn't understand how she had ended up married to a mayor. If this truck belonged to another man, well… He shuddered at the thought.

Apparently, there really was a lid for every pot.

He took a moment to collect his thoughts and plaster on

the fakest smile he could muster before he moved to get out of the truck. He started to tell Jamie to stay in the vehicle, but before he had the chance to, she was already out and closing the door. He didn't blame her for not wanting to be left behind, but he didn't like the idea of her coming along.

In reality, though, given how the last meeting had gone with Carey, it was unlikely that they would get anywhere with their questions, so it really wouldn't matter. It was only a fifty-fifty chance that she would even answer the door. She didn't have to—he didn't have a search warrant, and there was no probable cause to come after her in relation to Matt's attack or Clyde's murder.

He was unexpectedly nervous as he made his way up to the door. Jamie walked in step behind him. As he neared the front door, he could hear the sounds of a male and female arguing, and he put his hand down on his sidearm in the holster on his utility belt.

He put his other hand up, motioning for Jamie to stop where she was behind him. "Call 9-1-1, tell them there is a domestic disturbance and I've instructed you to call. I'm Special Agent Hauser with the National Park Service, badge number 406."

She nodded.

"Stay outside. Do you hear me?" He didn't mean to be commandeering, but the last thing he wanted was for her to walk into a hornet's nest and end up getting hurt.

Jamie looked at him with fear in her eyes. "Pierce... Be careful."

He reached back and gripped her hand, giving her a reassuring squeeze. "I will, trust me. You, too. Go back to the truck."

She nodded.

He turned and knocked on the door. "Special Agent Hauser, I'm entering your home!" he yelled. "Put down your weapons and come forward with your hands up!"

His heart thrashed violently in his throat. He dealt with bears, mountain lions and rogue angry tourists, but he had never had to enter a house to stop a partner/family member assault—which was what this sounded like from outside the door.

The screaming from within the house continued. He unholstered his weapon as the door eased open and he stepped inside. He cleared the foyer before walking into the main entertaining area of the house. The man was yelling as though he hadn't heard him announce his presence when he'd entered the building. "You are such a goddamn slut! Why don't you just admit what you did?"

Pierce was careful as he moved smoothly in the well-practiced roll-step used by law enforcement officers throughout the United States.

The last thing he wanted was to walk into a volatile situation and surprise the people in the room—that was how an officer was shot and killed. At least, in a situation like this. Sometimes, an element of surprise was necessary, but not when emotions were running high and weapons may or may not have been in play.

"Carey!" he yelled. "Carey! If you are in here, you need to answer me!"

The screaming continued; a woman was yelling expletives and telling the unknown male where he could go and all the things he could take with him.

Pierce swept the hall leading to the kitchen, clearing the area before making it down to the screaming persons. It sounded like there were only two people, but he'd learned the hard way never to assume. He announced himself again, but the din of yelling didn't change and there wasn't even a pause. It was as if they didn't hear him in the slightest, or maybe they just didn't care.

He pressed his body low against the wall that led into the kitchen, and he could hear Carey and the man shouting about Clyde inside. They were talking about the murder and shooting, and Carey was denying her involvement over and over again. She sounded frightened and desperate. The part of him that despised her didn't feel sorry for the woman, but the honorable civil servant in him felt for her desperation.

"Please," she begged. "I didn't hurt him. I loved Clyde. You have to know I loved him."

"Then why did you file for his death certificate? That isn't something someone does who doesn't have a role in their husband's death." The man sounded so angry that there was almost a whip in his words that even Pierce could feel lash over his skin.

"I needed to get through probate. I had to get things in my name so I could move forward with my life. *You* of all people should understand." The way she spoke made him desperate to look around the edge of the door frame to see the face of the man she was talking to, but if he did, he would be in the direct line of fire if the man held a gun and held a penchant for killing.

"Don't lie to me. I saw the video. And I listen to damn liars every day of my life. You are a fool if you think you can get away with that crap with me." The man gave an angry, dark laugh. "You are just lucky I ever let you live this long."

"Why did you?" Carey asked.

The man's laughter stopped. "Because I held out one last desperate hope that I would find my son alive."

Chapter Twenty-One

Pierce slowly peered around the corner of the door frame and spotted Judge Donovan standing tall over Carey. She was sitting down at the kitchen counter, her hands on the cheap marble surface as she stared up at the man.

He had been right all along. Carey had played a role in Matt's beating—at least from what he'd just heard Judge Donovan allege. She did fit the physical description of the person in the footage, in the loose-fitting black clothes. There must have been some moment when she had put together the pieces and somehow connected Matt to their investigation, but she would have to explain for him to really understand.

Like any breaking investigation, there were always pieces of information that at first didn't seem to make sense or have relevance, but then…*boom,* it all became clear.

There was the metallic sound as the judge slid back the slide and jacked a round into a pistol that Pierce couldn't see, but he knew the sound only too well. He carried a weapon each and every day. He glanced down, instinctively, at the Glock in his hands.

"Judge Donovan, put down your weapon!" he yelled,

refusing to step out from behind his cover until he heard the gun hit the ground.

"Who's there?" the man answered.

"This is Ranger Hauser. You need to put your weapon down! You don't need to make this situation any worse by involving guns. Let's talk this out." He noticed a framed painting on the wall across from him of a woman and a dog. In the reflection in the glass, he could see Donovan and Carey in the kitchen.

Donovan looked from her to the gun in his hands. He appeared confused, as if he wanted to put it down and follow orders but was at an impasse with her.

Though he'd trained to always assume the man would remain a threat until neutralized, this was his moment, and he had to act.

Pierce moved around the corner.

The judge dropped the gun onto the countertop. "You know I wasn't going to shoot her. The gun was for my own protection."

"That's good. Just don't touch it. Do you understand?"

The judge nodded. Clearly, he was a man who knew his legal rights and where and what he could do while remaining safely within them and protected.

He could hear sirens wailing in the distance. His racing heart started to slow. The judge didn't seem hell-bent on killing.

"Carey, are you okay?" he asked.

The woman nodded. "I want to press charges."

Of course she does.

"You are delusional if you think they will stick. I have video evidence of you beating Matt Goldstock. You are the one who is going to go to prison," the judge seethed.

"I will make sure of it. Don't you know who you are messing with? And that's saying nothing about your role in my son's death."

"I told you," she said, looking between the judge and Pierce, "I didn't kill your son, and I didn't hurt this guy Matt. I don't even know what you are talking about."

"You don't know Matt Goldstock?" Peirce asked.

"No." She shook her head vehemently.

"Where were you last night between the hours of 6:00 p.m. and 8:30 p.m.?" Pierce asked.

"I was with my boyfriend. Mark. He will tell you the same thing. We were here. I promise." She spoke fast. Desperate.

Innocent.

He looked over at Judge Donovan. His face was contorted with rage. "You don't have to lie."

Pierce put up his hand, silencing the angry father. "If I call your boyfriend, right now, would he tell me the same thing?"

She nodded but chewed on her lip as if she was thinking about her answer. "Actually, you don't even have to call him. There are pictures I took of us together last night on Snapchat. I was talking to my friend Jessica. She and I were talking about him."

"What were you saying about Mark?" he asked.

"I have been thinking about breaking up with him." She stopped. "Don't tell him. Please. I don't know what I want in the relationship. Which was why I needed Jessica. I sent her a snap of him talking to me about a fight we were having."

"Can you show me this on your phone?" he asked.

The judge shoved his arms over his chest and looked

away. "I can't believe you are listening to this woman. She should be handcuffed, in your vehicle, and on the way to being booked. You know I'm right about her."

He looked at the judge. "Do you remember what you told me the other day?"

Donovan glared at him. "What?"

"Rumors are often true, but they never hold up in court."

"You will never prove anything, I'm telling you." Carey took out her phone and put it on the counter, opening up the videos in her gallery and pushing Play.

They watched as she and a blond man, inside the kitchen where they were now standing, were talking about some kind of fight they were having over moving in with each other. From what Pierce could piece together, Carey wanted Mark to take things to the next level in their relationship, but the man was not having any of it. The time stamp was three minutes after Matt had been attacked at The Mint.

Carey had been telling the truth. She couldn't have been the one swinging the bat and hurting Matt—there wasn't even enough travel time between the two locations.

She was innocent. At least, when it came to beating Goldstock.

"Just because you didn't beat Matt, that doesn't mean you didn't kill my son," the judge countered, but some of the fight had left his voice.

Carey slapped her hands down on the counter, her right hand was millimeters away from the grip of the Glock. "I have effing told you!" she screamed. "I wanted him out of my life. I did. But I'm not a damned murderer." She looked at the gun.

Pierce could see what she was going to do, and time slowed down.

"Don't touch that gun, Carey," he ordered, but as the words came out in slow monosyllabic sounds, her hand curled around the grip of the weapon.

He raised his gun and aimed it at her.

There was the sound of the front door slamming open and footsteps coming down the hall toward them.

A wave of relief filled him. It sounded as if two people were rushing to help be backup.

The timing couldn't have been better.

Goddamn this woman.

Carey's hand tightened around the Glock, and she lifted the weapon as she pointed it directly at the judge's center mass. "You are just as narcissistic and self-righteous as your son. No one can ever be right but you. I hope you know your son *hated* you."

"He didn't think you were a damned *peach*, either, darling."

He appreciated the judge's tenacity for a good fight, but now wasn't the time to piss the woman off.

The footsteps stopped behind Pierce and he wanted to see who had come to cover him, but he didn't dare turn his back on the gun-toting woman with an anger issue in front of him.

"Carey, I'm only going to ask you one more time. Put the gun down. If you don't put the gun down, you are putting your life on the line. I don't want to have to shoot you."

There was the sound of a woman's laugh behind him and it caught him so off guard that he turned and moved toward the wall.

Standing behind him were Nicole and David.

David stared at him, a deadly look in his eyes. "Just let her shoot him. He came here to kill her. She is within her rights—as long as she shoots him in the front, it's all castle doctrine and self-defense."

"What are you doing here, David?" Pierce asked, turning his body so he could easily see everyone around him.

His skin crawled as he realized he was standing in the death zone if this thing turned into a shootout. There was no worse position for a person to be in. He slowly tried to edge back, but his back was pressed against the refrigerator and there was nowhere for him to escape.

"I'm here to help," David said, a strange, crooked smile on his lips.

"With Nicole? Shouldn't she be outside?" Suddenly, his blood ran ice-cold. Jamie was outside. Had they come here to hurt Carey? Him? Jamie?

What if they had already killed her?

Panic filled him, but if they hadn't seen her, he didn't want to point out her presence to them. He scanned David's clothing; he was wearing the exact same black-and-white Hokas from the camera footage from outside the bar. David *had* been the one responsible for Matt's beating. But why?

He looked at Nicole and she reached over and touched David's arm, the action almost intimate. She was wearing a blue-and-white sundress that seemed wickedly out of place for the moment. Thankfully, neither seemed to have blood on them.

He had to hope Jamie was safe and unharmed.

"Nicole is just fine with me." As David looked at Nicole, it hit Pierce—the two had been sleeping together.

Had Matt seen them together? Was David afraid Matt would out them to Jamie or him? It had to have been why he'd tried to kill. He must have meant to finish the job. But when he hadn't… That was why they were here.

His stomach sank.

They were here not only to kill Carey, but they were also here to kill *him and Jamie*.

They had to make sure no one had seen them together.

There was the sound of a machine and the squeak of tires. He recognized the noise, and he peered around the corner to see Eliot coming down the hall in his wheelchair.

What? Wait.

"You guys didn't have to leave me in the van. I was coming." Eliot sounded annoyed.

David laughed.

Pierce had absolutely no idea what was going on, but he felt deeply threatened. He looked at the judge and at the gun in Carey's hands. She'd lowered the weapon and had it on the counter, still pointed at the judge, but even she seemed at a loss as to what was happening and why these people were in her house.

"Dammit, David. Just get it done," Nicole said. "You're taking too long. If you don't hurry up, the other units may arrive. We can't screw this up."

David turned to Carey and in one swift motion, lifted his SIG Sauer and pulled the trigger. *Tap. Tap. Tap.*

Carey looked at David with shock in her eyes as she peered down at her chest like she couldn't believe what had just happened. Blood started to ooze out of the three holes in her chest, just over her heart, staining her gray T-shirt. She reached up and touched the blood. As she did, her body slumped and she fell forward, falling from the chair with a *thump* as she hit the floor.

Oddly, Pierce didn't feel anything except panic that David would turn and shoot at him next.

Pierce couldn't take the risk and acted before David had

a chance. He pointed his gun at the man who had been his friend. He fired once, hitting the man squarely in the wrist. The gun flew from his hand as blood sprayed violently from the dangerous wound.

Pierce rushed to the gun, grabbing it as David called out in pain and moved to cradle his arm.

Nicole lunged for the gun, but she wasn't as fast. She landed on Pierce. He thrust his elbow back, hitting her in the nose, hard. It made a crunching sound. He could feel the warm wetness of blood on his arm and she pulled back and yowled in pain.

From the corner of his eye, he saw Eliot wheeling toward him with a gun in his left hand and the joystick in his right. Jamie was running down the hall behind him. Taking David's gun, Pierce slid it on the ground down the hallway toward Jamie, hard and fast. "Stop him!"

She picked up the gun as it slid by Eliot, who stopped.

The sirens outside grew louder.

Nicole was crying on the floor beside him as she held her nose. "This is all Eliot's fault. He did it. He killed him." She sobbed. "He killed Clyde Donovan."

In every single scenario in his mind's eye, he'd never ever thought Eliot could have possibly been Clyde's killer. It didn't make sense.

He looked at the gun in Eliot's hand as Jamie walked up beside him and stripped it away without even hesitating. He put his hand up to stop her, but it was too late. She'd already gotten the gun away from him. Eliot moved his wheelchair backward, like he was going to try to escape, but as he did, Jamie reached behind the machine and removed the power cable from the battery.

"She is crazy!" Eliot yelled. "I didn't do anything to Clyde."

"What did you do to my son!" The judge jumped to his feet, but Pierce stood up and pushed his hand into the man's chest, forcing him to fall back and into his seat.

He made sure to keep his gun pointed at David, even though he was sobbing in a heap as blood poured from his arm.

"Pierce!" Emily yelled as she ran inside. "Are you okay? Neighbors reported gunfire!"

"We are in here, Detective!" he called. "We're going to need an ambulance and a coroner." He looked over at Eliot. "Why did you kill him, Eliot?"

Eliot looked from Pierce to Nicole, who was in a heap and crying on the floor. "Before I was injured, I used to care that my wife was unfaithful." He gave a dark laugh. "I caught her in bed with Clyde. I lost it. I shot him in my bed, without a second thought."

Pierce could only imagine the horror of the moment.

"So, you dumped his body?"

Eliot nodded. "I thought the bears would get him long before he'd ever be found. I made a mistake with the speed loader—it must have fallen out of my belt or something when I was dumping him."

Pierce glanced at Nicole. "Why didn't you just get a divorce?"

Eliot scoffed. "I should have, but hindsight... Right?" He looked at his wife.

"He told me he'd kill me if I ever left him...or, if I told anyone what happened that night," Nicole said between sobs. "I never wanted to stay."

"She is lying," Eliot countered. "She has a free ride. I

pay for everything. Then...after my accident, you get even more—don't you, woman?"

Nicole gave a single dry laugh. "I wish you had just died."

"Sometimes I wish the same thing," Eliot said with a sneer, and he looked at Pierce. "Now you can tell, the joke's on me. With me, she has stability, a house and all the money she could want. And now, I have to watch her take lovers and because of my body and my inability to perform as a husband should, I feel like I can't say a damned thing about it. Karma has come full circle. I'm at her mercy. She has to care for me."

Nothing the man had said was justification for what he'd done or the choices he'd made. There were so many other choices he could have made instead of pulling the pin on the grenade that was homicide. If he was stuck in his life of evil, he had done it to himself. He wasn't going to find a moment of pity from him.

Pierce couldn't help the judgmental chuckle that fell from his lips. "Well now, Eliot, you won't need her anymore. From here on out, you will get all the care you need in prison."

Chapter Twenty-Two

The ranch was abuzz with the comings and goings of ranch hands and community members who had been invited for the inaugural Fourth of July picnic Emily and Cameron had decided to put on to help raise funds for Matt and Sally for his recovery.

There was a local band, Shane Clouse and the Dawgs, playing country music from the stage setup in front of the barn. They'd even gotten a dance floor set up and several couples were already out there dancing.

At the edge of the dance floor, Stephanie and Vince were holding hands and chatting with several other rangers from the park. They made an adorable couple.

Anthony Lewis, the man she and Matt had saved, was there. His arm was still in a cast, and he was wearing a patch over his eye, and from what he'd told her, he would need several surgeries. While he had a long road to recovery, he had been grateful for all they had done for him. His girlfriend, Cynthia, had cried when extending her thanks when they'd arrived.

Brent and Traci were there from the sporting goods store and Jamie had recently found out they were married. She'd had no idea when they had been going over the footage, but now it was obvious thanks to the way Brent looked at his wife. She could see the love in his eyes. He was devoted to the woman in a way that made Jamie glance to Pierce and smile.

Almost as if he could feel her gaze, Pierce looked over at her and sent her a wink and a warm grin. She loved him so much.

"You guys are sickening," Matt said, laughing loudly at her as he caught their little wordless exchange.

Ever since he had gotten out of the hospital, Matt had been doing pretty well, but he needed a cane to get around due to the injuries sustained to his lower back. David had done a number on him in his attack.

At sentencing, the federal court had given David twenty-five years for one count of attempted homicide. For his killing of Carey, he'd received life in prison. All his sentences were to be served concurrently in a prison in Arizona.

She felt a little sense of justice in the fact the man would never see mountains again.

Eliot and Nicole had also been given life sentences for their roles in the murder and subsequent cover-up of Clyde Donovan. Nicole was going to do her time in a women's prison in Nevada and Eliot was going to be in California.

The thought of the three murderers and the justice that had been wrought upon them brought a smile to Jamie's face as she looked around at the crowd. Judge Donovan was there, celebrating.

She wasn't sure how she felt about Donovan getting away with his coming into Carey's home and threatening to kill her, but given how everything had played out—no charges had been filed against him and he had walked free.

If Jamie ever had a son, she could understand the man's

desire for revenge. He was just lucky he had been saved by Pierce getting there in time to find out the truth. If Pierce hadn't, it would have been the judge who would have been sent to prison. She couldn't imagine a judge would survive a single day in a prison filled with the men he'd put inside.

Pierce came sauntering over carrying two iced teas. "You doing okay?" asked. "You look like you have the weight of the world on your mind."

She nodded and smiled. "I'm good. Just thinking about how far we've come in just a short time."

He nodded. "I hear you. It feels like we've known each other for years, doesn't it?" He handed her the iced tea. "Two sugars, no lemon, just like you like it." He gave her a kiss on the cheek.

Matt and Sally were sitting at one of the picnic tables and as Pierce kissed her, Matt smiled and waved her over.

She turned to Pierce. "Do you want to go sit with them?" she asked, pointing toward her best friend and his wife.

"Sure." Pierce smiled. "Are you hungry? The hot dogs and burgers are just about ready. Of course, I think your brother is even grilling some steaks. What would you like?"

She waved him off. "I'm okay. Let the guests eat first." She looked over at the grill where her brother was standing with a beer in his hand and chatting animatedly with some people she didn't recognize.

There was a long line of folks at the food table and even more where they had the raffle baskets and silent auction set up. It amazed her how many people had come out in support of the ranch, her family, and her friends. This place had come a long way in repairing their reputation since her father's passing and she couldn't wait to see how far she and her family would continue to take the cattle ranch.

As they sat down, Matt looked over at Pierce. "You didn't tell her, did you?" he asked, sounding more excited than she had heard him in...well, years.

Pierce shook his head. "This moment is all yours, man. Have at it, but you probably want to grab Emily and Cameron."

Matt turned and waved at her brother and his wife. Emily smiled widely as she spotted them, and she smacked Cameron at the grill. He looked over and he gave them a big thumbs-up. Putting down his tongs, he said something to his friend before he and Emily came sauntering over toward the table.

"What is going on, you guys?" she asked. She looked at Sally. "Are you pregnant?"

Sally tilted her head back and barked a laugh. "Oh gawd no. We need to get things settled first before we jump into that kind of shark-infested water." She looked pretty with her dark black hair that glistened in the summer sun.

It was so good to see her and Matt happy that it almost made Jamie's heart burst.

Cameron flopped down at the end of the table and Emily gently slipped next to him on the bench. "Okay," Emily said, "tell her. We are dying for you to give her the news."

Matt smiled widely. "So, Jamie," he said, looking over at her, "we have all been talking."

"Are you kicking me off the island?" she joked, trying to figure out why they seemed to all be so excited. It was making her uncomfortable.

"Just shut up and listen, sister." Cameron laughed.

"Your brother and Emily have agreed to have it at the ranch, and John's parents reached out and they received some money from his life insurance, and we have all pooled

our money together," Matt said. "We started an equine therapy business in your name. Everything you need, as far as
the legal and business side is concerned, is good to go. We
called it the JMac Foundation, in honor of you and your
boy. There's enough money to buy a few horses, do some
high-end marketing, and hire some reliable live-in staff at
the ranch." Matt pointed between himself and Sally and
loudly cleared his throat.

Jamie threw her hands over her mouth in surprise. "Oh
my... No... You guys didn't!"

She didn't know what to say. Until now, she'd wanted this
but hadn't a clue how she would have been able to make it
all happen. To get it up and running like this had to have
cost them at least a half-million dollars.

Tears streamed down her face.

Pierce put his arm over her shoulder.

Matt smiled. "It was all Pierce's idea. He was the one
who talked to the attorney and got the ball rolling while I
was in the hospital. He was even going to get loans until
John's parents heard what he was doing and reached out
to me. They want you to know they are incredibly proud
of you and how you are moving forward with your life."

Her tears intensified. She wanted to be embarrassed for
her display of emotions, but she didn't care. She loved these
people; everyone at the table loved her. They were her life.

She turned to Pierce. "Thank you, babe. Thank you so
much," she said amidst grateful sobs.

He reached up and softly cupped her face between his
hands. He leaned in and kissed her forehead. "You deserve
everything you want in this life. I love you."

She let the tears run. "I love you, too." She turned to her
friends and family. "And I love all of you, too."

"Do it now, brother. Do it now," Cameron said in his low baritone voice.

Pierce shook his head as he looked over at her brother and he dropped his hands from her face. He took her hand with his. "I don't want to take away from this. This is about Matt."

Matt shook his head. "We are best friends, we don't compete. We support each other and we share our greatest moments. Do it, brother."

Pierce got up from the table and moved down to one knee beside her.

She wasn't sure her heart could take any more. That, or she would run out of tears.

"Jamie Trapper, would you do the honor of—"

She threw her arms around his neck and buried her face in him. "Yes!" she exclaimed, not waiting for him to finish and not waiting for him to take out a ring.

None of that mattered. She didn't care about material goods. After all she had lost and all she had gained, what she truly cared about and treasured was in her arms and surrounding them at the table.

No matter what life brought them, they would be grateful for the moments that they were lucky enough to spend together in the bonds of love.

* * * * *

COLTON IN THE WILD

JUSTINE DAVIS

This one is for all the people of the glorious, beautiful and amazing state of Alaska, which is at the very top of my wish list of places to visit. I hope my admiration comes through and that any mistakes are minor enough for you to forgive.

Chapter One

Spence Colton was just too pretty for his own good.

This wasn't the first time Hetty Amos had had that thought, and this likely wasn't going to be the last time, but it was just as annoying every time.

And, just as usual, the client flirting with him now only cared about his good looks—she didn't actually care about *him*. Hetty understood, to an extent. With his thick, dark brown hair and bright blue eyes, and that six-foot muscular form radiating a subtle power built by years of an essentially athletic sort of work—hiking, skiing, paddling—he was nothing short of eye-catching.

So, yeah, she understood. She just didn't like it.

She'd watched the dance between him and attractive female clients so many times she should be numb to it by now. She didn't know—not for sure anyway—if he ever took any of them up on their blatant offers. Didn't want to know. Because, of course, she had absolutely, utterly, definitely no interest in the guy's love life. None whatsoever. He was simply someone she had to work with. Had to put up with, even with his annoyingly juvenile habit of flirting right back at female clients…and maybe more.

Had to, because Spence wasn't just the premier guide

of her employer, Rough Terrain Adventures. RTA was the number-one tour company in Shelby, and one of the top-ranked in the entire state of Alaska. And Spence was also a part owner of the business. He was the son of Ryan Colton, one of the two founding brothers of the company. He was someone she had to get along with, since they often had to work together. As a pilot who specialized in getting to the more remote places—RTA's bread and butter—she needed to stay on good terms with the star. And that required pretty much ignoring Spence outside of work.

Which was easy, because she had no interest in him outside of work at all. None whatsoever.

The denial rang hollow even in her mind.

"—be sure and look me up when you come to LA!"

"I'll do that, next time I set foot there."

Hetty wondered if the woman even noticed the undertone in his voice. Or maybe she was only imagining it, being the one here who knew Spence would hike to the Bering Strait before he'd set that foot in Los Angeles.

The unquestionably lovely blonde finished sending her phone number to Spence's cell phone from her own, smiled brilliantly at him, lifted the phone to snap a final photo of him and actually giggled as she turned away and headed for the car waiting to pick her up and her thankfully much more reserved girlfriend.

Spence was grimacing now, but Hetty was certain he'd look great in the photo. Because he always did. Other people looked silly when caught off guard, or had some unflattering expression on their face—she tended to a brow-furrowed, mouth-twisting, wry expression herself—but not Spence. Never Spence. No matter the angle, the lighting, or the situation, he always managed to look like he'd stepped off the cover of some men's magazine. Something about the bone structure of his face, especially when lit up by his signature flirtatious grin, got almost any female thinking appreciative—and often racy—thoughts.

But not her. Never her. All he did for her was spark her temper, which was already on a short leash.

Still, she watched as he ran a finger down a page then signed off on the paperwork for the enamored client and put it in a folder for Lakin to get to when she could. Which would be soon, Hetty was sure; Lakin Colton was her friend and Spence's cousin—not to mention her brother's girl-friend—and Hetty knew she was both quick and efficient.

Then he went back to his phone, fingers swiping it open then tapping on the screen. And out of nowhere the snark arose and the words were out before she could think bet-ter of them.

"Going to call her already?"

She saw his fingers pause. Then he went back to tapping and, without looking at her, said flatly, "Deleting."

She felt her cheeks heat and she hated herself for giving in to the urge to make that wisecrack. But then it struck her to wonder if that was what he always did when one of those female clients—and for all she knew maybe a few males, too—insisted on giving him their number.

Deep down, she wanted to believe it. To believe that all this silliness and flirting was just on the surface. To believe that underneath all that, he still had the depth of the Spence she'd known in school. The Spence she'd once worked with so closely but could now hardly stand to be in the same room with.

The Spence who had needed her then but now saw her as merely another RTA employee.

The fact that she missed the days of him needing her was like salt poured over an open wound. She had everything she'd ever dreamed of. She'd worked hard, studied, gone to flight school as she ached to do ever since, as a child, she'd looked upward to see float or seaplanes traversing the wide-open Alaska skies. Since the state had more registered pilots than any other, it happened often. The family story was that, from the first, as a toddler, Hetty would reach toward the aircraft, as if she wanted to snag one for herself.

And now she had. True, she didn't own the Cessna 206. RTA did. But she was the only one who flew it, except for Will Colton occasionally. Spence's uncle had been RTA's fixed-wing pilot back in the early days, flying his old single-engine Beaver, and still kept his hand in by taking flights now and then. But for the most part, the Cessna was hers and she saw to it with the intensity of the experienced pilot that she was, who loved the plane that let her fly.

And if that meant she had to put up with the irritation to her soul that Spence Colton was, then so be it.

She hated him.

She hated him, and the sooner he admitted that, at least to himself, the better. Spence didn't blame her. And in fact, he should count it a success. After all, didn't he go overboard with attractive clients for precisely that reason? Sure, he'd always been a bit of a flirt, he admitted that. It was a skill he'd developed early in his life when he'd seen it work. It diverted people. Kept them from pushing into areas he preferred to keep well-hidden.

Now, he also did it because he knew it annoyed Hetty. And he needed to keep that safe distance between them.

But the safe distance he'd wanted had turned into a gulf

he doubted could ever be bridged. And he hadn't anticipated how much that would bother him.

*Brilliant, Colton. Work hard to keep your distance then
whine about her being unreachable.*

Maybe the brain quirk that made it hard for him to read
like other people had screwed up more than just that. But
thinking of it only reminded him of why he was able to
function at all with such a quirk. There was one reason:
the tutor who had discovered a way for him to utilize his
memory and his ability to visualize and convert that tal-
ent into his atypical version of reading. It worked, and it
had saved him.

True, he had kept to his decision not to go on to college.
He'd been relieved just to make it through high school with
decent grades—although much better than decent in math
classes—thanks to that tutoring. He'd never been hot on the
college idea anyway. He knew, had known from childhood,
what he'd wanted to do with his life. And now he was doing
it, spending his days exploring this place he so loved. And
if the people he was leading on these explorations weren't
always as appreciative as he was, he just considered it the
price he had to pay to do what he wanted to do.

As for the women, if they flirted, he flirted back. If
they were single. He might be a bit loose with one-on-one
teasing, but that was a line he would not cross. Of course,
he could only take their word for that single status. When
one suggested—or outright demanded—that it go further,
he wiggled his way out. Because for him the banter was
the end of it. His family might worry about it, to the point
of them strongly suggesting he never do any trips without
someone else along, but to him it meant nothing. In fact,
the game was a bit taxing these days, but that was because

Hetty was usually his pilot when a trip required a plane. And keeping up the front when she was there was much harder.

He'd catch her watching him with those amazing green eyes, not even bothering to hide her disgust. It stabbed at him, painfully, but he kept going. Because, in the end, that was the goal. The more Hetty disliked him, the easier it was for him to keep his distance. So yeah, he might go a little far with the flirting, but it was for a good cause.

Because Hetty Amos was not for the likes of him.

"How'd it go?"

The call from the hallway leading to the office wing of the RTA headquarters broke through his miserable thoughts and turned him around.

Uh-oh. Both of them?

He might be the premier, most-requested guide at RTA, but Ryan and William Colton *were* RTA. His father and uncle had founded the business nearly three decades ago. They had both pulled back a little now, especially since his cousin Parker had stepped into the main management role, but they essentially were still RTA. It wouldn't exist without them. And he would likely be stuck doing some other job he'd hate because it would be hard for him. He could do it, thanks to the tricks that tutor had taught him more than a decade ago, but he wouldn't like it.

And he certainly wouldn't like it the way he treasured every minute of being out in the wilds of this state that was a part of his soul.

So, in a way, he owed this life that gave him so much enjoyment to that long-ago tutor. That teenaged girl who had taken the job so seriously, worked so hard at it. That tutor who had realized the contradiction in the fact that he was great at math but sucked at word-based math problems, and had made the intuitive leap that had helped him go from floundering to being able to get through. That tutor who had taught him how to apply his knack for visualizing things to words and letters and sounds, enabling him to read so much easier, even if it was in a way that was different than most people. That tutor who had showed him how to function in a world where he wasn't the norm.

That tutor who had, in essence, saved him.

That tutor named Hetty Amos.

Chapter Two

"Great," Spence belatedly answered his father's question about how this last trip had gone.

"Come on back to the office," Uncle Will said.

Spence wondered if a lecture was in the offing. Maybe Hetty had complained about Ms. Merchant. He discarded that thought immediately. She wouldn't do that. She might call him out to his face, as she just had, but she wouldn't complain behind his back. It just wasn't her way.

He stepped through the door into the RTA manager's office, which these two men had once shared but was now staked out and claimed by Will's son, Parker, who was currently out on a short morning trip himself. Parker kept his hand in on the guide side, not just the business side. Spence didn't envy his cousin. As good as he himself was with numbers, the manager's job seemed daunting. Probably because there was a lot of reading involved, which he could do—thanks to Hetty—but didn't like much. Not that he didn't like books and stories, he did, but audio was his method of choice for consuming them. Which reminded him he wanted to finish the book he'd started a couple of days ago. And then—

"—would you suggest?"

Damn, he'd tuned out. He glanced at Uncle Will but then focused on his father, who had spoken. He'd put on a little weight since he'd semiretired, although it seemed to Spence he wasn't relaxing, not when he was regularly trekking out for his day-long fishing trips. There was only a touch of gray hair at his temples and his blue eyes—the ones Spence had inherited—were as bright and lively as ever. If it wasn't for the frequent hints that he would like to be a grandfather sometime soon, he'd be the perfect father figure.

He is the perfect father figure. You're the one who's out of step.

"Sorry, Dad. I was thinking how much I'd hate doing any other job, so if you're going to fire me, I don't want to hear it."

His father snorted audibly, but Will laughed outright. Spence smiled at his uncle, just slightly more salt-and-peppered than his father but with the same blue eyes. Also semiretired yet seemingly unable to slow down, he worked as hard at promoting Aunt Sasha's pottery business as he had when he'd helped run RTA full-time.

"Like we'd fire the most in-demand guide in the state of Alaska," Uncle Will said, still chuckling.

Spence shifted his feet, gave his uncle a crooked grin. "Not quite. Maybe in Shelby."

"Ha. I've read the reviews, son," Dad said. "You're going to top that statewide list before you're through."

"So," Uncle Will said, "now that we've cleared that up, back to the question."

"Uh…which was?" Spence asked.

"Your father and I are in need of a good spot for a nice,

long day of fishing, now that we've survived the Fourth of July rush."

Spence blinked. The holiday rush wasn't over for him, by a long shot, but he was more puzzled by the question.

"You're asking me?"

They both had lived here longer than he'd been alive. Not by much, true, but still…they knew the local environs as well as anyone, and better than most.

"We know all the usual spots," his uncle said. "But we want someplace we've never been."

"For a nice, long, uninterrupted day," Dad said pointedly.

"And productive, fishwise," put in Uncle Will.

"And scenic." Dad again.

"And private."

"And a ways out there—"

"I get it, I get it," Spence said, laughing now. "You want a day where nobody will find you or bother you or ask you to talk or expect anything trickier than reeling in a ton of fish."

Both men grinned at him. "Exactly."

"I knew you'd get it," Dad added. "It'll be our last chance before things start getting really hectic for the rest of the summer. So you know a spot that meets all that criteria?"

Spence grinned back. "Most of Alaska?" he suggested.

"Yeah, yeah," Uncle Will said. "But specifically? We know the closer-in spots, but they've gotten a bit more populated than we'd like for this. Hence we ask Mr. No Place Too Far."

Spence couldn't deny he felt a bit flattered that these two men, of all people, were asking him where to go.

"You want to hike in or fly?"

"Weather looks good for the next week, so I can fly us

in, in the company helicopter," Dad said. "It's clear on the RTA schedule for that long, nobody signed up for the more inaccessible locations. And the first ones who do, Hetty can fly in aboard the plane, now that the ice is pretty well broken up on the lakes."

Spence grimaced, but only inwardly. He had a couple of backcountry trips booked, and he'd hoped to use the chopper for at least one of them. But his father and uncle so rarely asked for anything for themselves, he wasn't about to put a damper on this.

"So, can I safely presume you don't want to just jump over to Robe Lake?" he asked teasingly, referring to the closest to town and therefore most popular lake.

"Along with every summer tourist arriving in the next month? No, thanks," Dad said.

"Figured," Spence said with a crooked smile to tell his father he'd only been joking.

He walked over to the big map on the back wall of the office. He studied it for a moment, eliminating the most popular places and the places he knew they had already been, although he doubted he knew them all. Alaska was simply too big to know everything. Shelby alone was close to eight national parks and wildlife preserves, plus had about twenty tidewater glaciers that ended at Prince William Sound, the highest concentration in the world.

Someone had once said Alaska was forged by fire but ruled by ice, and Spence thought that was a good description. It was huge, vast, magnificent, forbidding, and often deadly. Visit But Don't Stay was Spence's motto when it came to their clients, who had no idea of just how dangerous this place he loved could be. This place with fifty active volcanoes, two of which usually blew up every year.

This place bigger than the next three largest states combined, yet with only five thousand miles of paved road, a thousand less then New York City alone. No, it took a certain kind of spirit and heart to call this wild place home.

Finally, he reached up and tapped a spot on the map.

"How about Tazlina Lake? If you can dodge all the rafters who want to tackle the river, there are a couple of good fishing spots. Especially at the north end. Weather can still be iffy up there this early in the season, so you'd have to pay attention to that, but I'd bet there'd be nobody else to bother you."

"Sounds good to me," Uncle Will said.

Spence opened his mouth to warn them that they'd be heading into higher country, and that while there might not be many two-legged visitors, some of the four-legged inhabitants could get interesting. He shut it again, knowing they both knew that perfectly well and would appropriately prepare.

"Good call," Dad said, his smile telling Spence he'd known exactly what he'd been about to say. "We may have sort of retired, but we haven't forgotten a thing about living in Alaska."

"I pity the bear or moose that tries to take you two on," Spence said and all three of them laughed. "So, when's this expedition taking place?"

"Assuming no shift in the weather pattern, we'll be off in the morning."

"Enjoy," Spence said. Then, a little warily, he asked, "Do I need to check in on Mom and Aunt Sasha while you're gone?"

"I believe they're planning to enjoy this as much as Dad

and Uncle Ryan." The words came from behind them as his cousin Parker entered the room.

Spence laughed at that. Parker was probably right. The two women were very close. They had no shortage of things to talk about in that way women did, which seemed never-ending to him.

Parker shoved back his longish, shaggy, dark brown hair. He'd skipped the morning shave again, and Spence knew his always clean-shaven uncle had finally resigned himself to the fact that the stubble was likely going to be a permanent feature.

"You're back early," Spence said.

"It was an easy trip, and my people were quick to settle in at the fishing camp. I'll go back and get them in three days."

Although they specialized in the more remote trips, RTA didn't turn their nose up at more local jaunts if requested. The customer was the one spending the money, after all.

"Nice milk run," Spence said with a grin.

"Yeah, yeah," Parker growled it out in mock irritation. "But I'll take that over your next one."

Spence rolled his eyes. His next scheduled trip was to a remote lakeside fishing spot most easily accessible by floatplane. Which meant more time with Hetty, although that wasn't why he rolled his eyes. He did that because it was a honeymoon trip. He'd made a few of those before and they'd always been a little too…gooey for his taste. All that lovey-dovey stuff seemed a bit over the top to him.

Dealing with it in the closed-in space of the plane cockpit with Hetty was something he didn't want to think about.

"Hetty's pretty excited about getting back into the air again," Parker said.

"Yeah," Spence said noncommittally. Going for a quick subject change, he asked his cousin, "You have all the supplies lined up?"

They were going to restock the permanent campsite they had set up at the lake, which had gotten a lot of use last year. He'd already checked the big, sturdy, wood-framed tent they used for that location, one that fit neatly onto the permanent foundation they'd built so it was a bit more solid than one that just sat on the ground. The still chilly ground.

"It's all ready and waiting in the storage building," Parker said, nodding toward the outbuilding that sat about fifty yards from the main office building they were in now.

"Good. I want to get it loaded on my truck, so I can get it aboard the plane early."

Parker grinned at him. "You just don't want to hang around the newlyweds any longer than you have to."

"Yeah, yeah," Spence muttered, not looking at his cousin.

Later, as he headed out to the storage building to gauge how many trips it would take him to get everything to the dock where the floatplane would tie up, he thought about how true Parker's jab was. He really wasn't looking forward to that aspect of this trip.

And you are not going to waste time analyzing why.

Order to himself given, he pulled open the big sliding door and made himself focus on the task at hand. Parker hadn't lied, it was all here, neatly stacked. The restock supplies, plus the state-required equipment for any flight, food for each person for a week, signaling devices, fishing tackle, an ax/saw combo, fire starter, mosquito nets—the old jokes about bush planes being taken down by a squadron of mosquitos seemed a lot more believable when you spent some time fighting off the huge Alaskan variety—and personal locator beacons.

True, he'd have to figure out what order to put it in the plane's cargo space, and track the weight for load capacity purposes, but he was used to that. Numbers were no problem for him.

He picked up the clipboard that sat atop the stack of boxes and crates and saw the individual weights already listed next to each item, in his cousin Lakin's careful hand. He silently thanked her. That would make up for any extra time he had to spend making sure he was reading the item description right.

And not for the first time, he was thankful for this place, this work, and most of all, this family of his.

Chapter Three

"Want some help?"

Spence looked up to see his sister Kansas standing in the doorway. She wasn't in uniform today, although her long, dark hair was pulled back as usual. She said it was because it got in her way when she was working. Kansas was a state trooper assigned to the search and rescue unit, and if there truly were jobs some people were born to do, his sister had been born for that one.

"Shouldn't you be out rescuing someone?" he teased.

"I am. You," she shot back. Spence laughed. Kansas smiled and shrugged. "Seems everyone's being careful out there today."

"First time for everything," he said wryly.

She pitched right in and they began shifting boxes and crates. He was not at all surprised at how much Kansas could lift. He knew well enough how strong his little sister was. He thought the "little" part but didn't say it, because it irritated her—*Two years isn't that much difference,* she would say—and she was helping him out, after all.

He was mentally gauging the space left in his truck, comparing it to what was left on the inventory list, and deciding which crate to move next when he heard a notification tone unfamiliar to him. He knew from the way Kansas stopped dead and yanked her phone out of her pocket that it was probably something official. He wondered if it was a call-out, if somebody out there had stopped being careful, or if Alaska had decided to teach some puny human a needed lesson about life in the wild.

Kansas swiped the screen, read what was there, smiled, tapped out a couple of quick sentences, sent the message, and put the phone back in her pocket.

"No emergency?" he asked.

"No. Just a text from Scott Montgomery, a guy who works with Eli. A forensics guy. He looked up something on an old case for me."

"An old case?"

"Yeah. That kid we found last year, out in the Kenai Wildlife Refuge."

"I remember that. The kid you found with that herd of… what were they? The ones that look like mountain goats only with killer horns?"

"Dall sheep. I'd never seen one up close before. It was funny, how they almost seemed to be protecting him. Like they knew he was young and harmless to them. Anyway, I wanted contact info, to see how the kid's doing, and Scott just happened to answer the phone. He was nice about it, like he always is, and looked it up for me."

That was very Kansas, following up on something she was hardly required to. She was nothing if not passionate about her work, as he knew from the times a search ended badly. She took it hard, was occasionally even distraught at what she saw as failure. And he'd heard she had no qualms about unleashing her anger on people she didn't feel were as dedicated to the work as she was. The Coltons were not a retiring bunch.

She was coming back from the truck for another box when she unexpectedly said, "You ever wonder what we'd be doing if Mom and Dad had never left San Diego?"

"Nah," he said. "All that heat, concrete, asphalt, traffic?" He gave an exaggerated shudder. "Too scary."

She laughed. But then her tone changed to very serious. "You really love it here, don't you."

It wasn't really a question, more of an observation. Of the obvious, he thought, but he answered her anyway. "I do. I would not want to live anywhere else."

"Neither would I," she said quietly. "And not because of what happened down there."

Spence stopped, shutting down the jokes, sensing his sister was in a serious mood at the moment. He put down the crate he'd started to lift and turned to face her.

"You okay? What brought this on?"

"I talked to Eli this morning. He had a question about one of our rescue cases from a few months ago. Which was what made me think of the Kenai kid. Anyway, he sounded kind of…something. I asked what was wrong, and he just said it was the date." She grimaced. "It took me a while and a calendar check to understand. It's…or it would have been, Aunt Caroline's birthday tomorrow."

Spence grimaced. "Damn."

He knew the family story, of course, but it wasn't in-grained in him, or Kansas, to the point where the date would have even occurred to them. When he'd gotten old enough to understand tragedy and trauma a little better, he'd tried to imagine how Eli must've felt. Spence had never known Caroline, but Eli had. What would it have felt like to be there when the body was found?

She'd been beautiful; he'd seen the pictures. A rising star in the modeling world at a young age, still in high school, she had attracted many fans. One of them in particular was mentally unstable and vicious. That twisted, sick fan had come to the house to kidnap Caroline. Instead, he had brutally murdered the grandparents Spence had never known, Edward and Mia Colton. He hadn't stopped there, continuing with the apparently unplanned murder of Caroline herself. The killer had then arranged himself with Caroline on the living room sofa and taken his own life. When Uncle Will and Eli had arrived, it had taken them a moment to realize they were both dead. And then they'd found her parents, slaughtered upstairs.

Spence couldn't imagine ever being able to put that out of your mind.

To him and Kansas, it was history, but Eli had lived it. At five years old, he had been old enough to have the ugly scenes and the trauma etched into his memory. Spence had always figured it was why Eli had chosen the career path he had.

It had also been big news, in all the headlines, and he knew the day Uncle Will had found the media camped out in front of Eli's school had been the day the decision had been made. And three months later, the Coltons were in Alaska, far from the chaos of Southern California.

"I'm glad we didn't have to live through all that," Kansas said. "Although I think we might understand it all better if we had."

"Maybe. What I try to focus on is afterward. That, together, Uncle Will and Dad built this, and because of that I'm able to do what I love."

"And I found the one thing in life that I was meant to do," Kansas agreed. "Maybe…maybe because it's that day, we should say something."

Spence's brow furrowed. "Say something?"

"To Dad and Uncle Will. About how glad we are they did what they did, and how sorry we are that they had to go through…that. That we know the life we have now is because they got through it."

That was so like Kansas. When she cared about something, she went full bore. Not that that made him any more comfortable with the idea of getting all sappy and emotional with everybody. But maybe she did have a point. Maybe it did deserve acknowledgment, at least.

"I don't want to make a huge deal out of it," he said, "but I see your point."

"I don't think they'd want a huge deal, either. I know Eli didn't, because I tried and he changed the subject so fast it was dizzying. But I still think they need to know that we know. That just because we were born after it all happened doesn't mean we don't know and care about the hell it must have been."

For a long silent moment, Spence just stared at her. And then, because it was the only thing he could think of to do, he crossed the three feet between them and hugged her.

"You're really something, little sister."

"You're not so bad yourself. For an annoying big brother, that is."

He laughed. "Well, if you're going to say something to them, do it now because both Dad and Uncle Will are heading out tomorrow…"

His words trailed off as something that should have been obvious hit him. No wonder the two men wanted out of town tomorrow. And that decided him. Kansas was right. He should at least acknowledge what had happened even if he'd never known their sister, the woman who would have been his aunt. He wanted them to know he understood.

"Thanks, sis," he murmured and hugged her again.

She was right. His family had always been there for him, so he could—and would—do no less in return.

Chapter Four

Hetty stifled an early morning yawn as she read the email Parker had forwarded to her last night before she headed downstairs from her apartment to her car. It was from a client whose family she'd flown down to Kodiak Island, raving about what a great time they'd had. And while it was mostly about their guide, which of course had been Spence, there were some very kind words about their pilot as well. Her.

The note made her smile and she sent a quick thanks back to Parker. He was pretty good about that. She doubted he realized how she and Spence grated on each other sometimes—or at least how Spence grated on her, since Spence didn't seem to show much of anything behind that jovial exterior—but he took care to send them all the responses like this one. And despite everything, when it came to their jobs, she and Spence always did their best. If she did say so, their best was pretty darn good.

Even if too many of the rave reviews from female clients were mostly gushing praise of her partner.

It doesn't matter, she told herself.

And it didn't, really. It didn't matter if every client gushed over him, or flirted with him. Or if he flirted back.

It mattered nothing at all, to her anyway. She just did her job, and darn well. To be honest, so did he. He just had more one-on-one time with the clients, and so it was only natural there would be more of a…relationship. Of sorts.

Besides, it was quite obvious Spence only flirted with those he found attractive—who else?—and they were all coquettish and a bit shallow-seeming to her. So, obviously, that's what appealed to him. While she herself was businesslike, levelheaded, and maybe a bit brusque. So it was clear that, if the kind of women he flirted with were what he wanted, he'd certainly want nothing at all to do with her. Not in that way, anyway. Which was just as well. That was a company pool she did not want to swim in. Especially with him.

At least she knew, because he was a Colton and they couldn't care less, it had nothing to do with her being biracial. Her mother, the contributor of her darker skin, had sat her down when she'd become a teenager and explained that there were those it would matter to. It had been her beloved late father—he of the green eyes—who had told her bluntly to tell them to get lost. His anger at the very idea of someone insulting his daughter had warmed her heart, as he so often had. And he had also greatly respected the Coltons, and she knew he would have been pleased when she'd gone to work for RTA.

But that didn't mean he would have wanted her dating one of them. That she didn't swim in the dating pool at all, with anyone, was another matter. She simply didn't have the time.

She repeated the oft-used—most often with her mother— excuse to herself. It wasn't just an excuse, it was the truth. What little spare time she had she preferred to spend in the quiet solitude of her own living room, reading, catching a movie or keeping up on developments in the flying world. Maybe it was an overreaction to growing up in a big family, or maybe she simply liked the peace.

Already weary of these unusual thoughts that had caught hold of her this morning, she made herself focus on today. She grabbed up her small backpack, the one she took on every trip just in case, filled with extra clothes and toiletries. They had a lot of gear already in the plane, but she just felt better if she had this with her. Hers was nothing compared to Spence's though, which was three times the size; a fact she never failed to rag on him about. She didn't know what all he lugged around in the thing, beyond a first-aid kit and the RTA radio for the times when they were out of cell phone range, which was often.

He was the one who also went armed, which thankfully saved her from having to do it. The state law requiring pilots to be armed had been changed after 9/11, but no one who knew anything ventured into the Alaskan wilds without protection of some kind. And for them, that fell to Spence, who happened to be an excellent shot with that rifle of his. True, he didn't carry it every minute, but it was always fairly close by. She appreciated that, and that he did it without comment, except for joking he didn't care if he could hit a pine cone at a thousand yards with it. He cared if he could carry it on a twenty-mile hike, climb and still stop a berserk moose if he had to.

Hetty knew how to shoot, she understood the necessity, but hitting a living target was something else altogether. She wasn't sure she could shoot an animal regardless of the situation. She didn't begrudge those who did, it was a huge part of Alaskan culture, but it wasn't for her.

At least she didn't have to have her usual battle on the usual topic with herself before a trip with Spence. Half the time she wanted to call in sick when she knew she was going to be partnered with him for an excursion. For all her rationalization, watching him flirt rubbed her the wrong way and she had to work to hide her reaction to it. It was a distraction, and she did not want distractions when up in the air. For all the joy she got from flying, she took her work very seriously.

But today's flight was a honeymoon couple and the bride would—she assumed—be so wrapped up in her new husband she'd barely notice their handsome, sexy guide.

I wonder if Spence will feel slighted?

As soon as she thought it, she quashed the idea. For all his nearly provocative come-ons, it only happened when the interest was obviously mutual. He never made the first move—well, in words anyway, it never went beyond that, that she knew of—and if the other party didn't start, he remained as businesslike as she herself did.

And she had to give him credit…he was always so good with the shy ones. Adults or kids, Spence worked to draw them out as much as he could, to make sure they enjoyed their venture into this land he so loved.

Yes, there was much to like about Spence Colton, and if the irritations sometimes outweighed that to her, that was her problem, not his. He was who he was, he'd overcome problems that sidelined many in life—and who knew that better than her?—and if he chose to use his other assets a bit up front, then who was she to judge?

That settled, she headed for the door. She went down the stairs quietly, care she always took so as not to disturb whoever might be in the usually hushed art studio downstairs from her small apartment. The owner of the building had given her a break on the rent because of the need to be quiet, but since it was her nature anyway, she would have stayed without the perk. It was enough of a novelty to be away from her big, sometimes chaotic, family.

Of course, she was now working for a big, sometimes chaotic, family. And even if she wasn't, she'd be spending time with them anyway because her family had always been close with all the Coltons. In the case of her younger brother Troy, very close; he'd been dating Lakin Colton since he was fifteen.

She smothered an inward sigh. Her little brother had his personal life pretty much in order, while she still drifted. Not that she hadn't ever dated, she had, and once it had been serious. Or so she'd thought. But when she'd realized the man in question had city life in mind, preferably someplace big and highly populated, she'd known it would never work. She didn't mind a visit now and then, but after that, coming home always felt like escaping.

Spence never left this wild place at all, if he could help it.

And there she was, thinking about her annoying partner again. And no matter how often she told herself it was natural to think about the guy you worked with so closely so often, it didn't seem to help much. It was still maddening that she couldn't keep her thoughts from veering in his direction, most times with no warning whatsoever. Her normally quick, decisive mind always slipped the leash where he was concerned.

By the time Hetty got to the RTA headquarters, she thought she had herself well under control. She would focus on this trip and nothing else. And if watching a newlywed, happy couple together ate at her, she would keep it hidden. Well hidden. She didn't need that as part of her life.

But did she want that...a husband? A family of her own?

She sighed inwardly as she got out of her car and walked toward the familiar building with the A-frame roof over the entry. She was one of seven kids, so family was part and parcel of who and what she was, as was the devastating loss of her father. That was still an ache, even several years later. But she also savored the peace and quiet of her apartment alone, away from all of her family's well-meaning machinations. She wasn't quite sure she wanted to follow the path her parents had, producing kid after kid. Besides, if she was pregnant, she'd have to stop flying, at least for a while, and she didn't like that idea. At all.

The absurdity of worrying about the impact having children might have on her life while at the same time avoiding any serious dating struck her, and she was practically laughing at herself by the time she went through the door.

"Did I miss the joke?"

She managed not to stop dead when she heard Spence's voice the moment the door closed behind her.

She didn't turn to look at him. "You often do," she said, making sure her voice was so cheerful that no one else in the room—Parker and Lakin were both there—would take it as a jab.

"Oh, he's not that bad," Lakin said teasingly, defending her cousin.

"Ha," said Parker, leaving Spence nothing to do but take it as a joke.

"Yeah, yeah," he muttered. He looked at his cousin. "The big bosses get off okay this morning?"

Parker nodded. "Left right on schedule."

"Of course," Lakin added, grinning. The senior Coltons were nothing if not efficient.

"So," Spence said to Parker, "what's the big news?"

Hetty, having just set her backpack down on one of the chairs in the lobby area, turned to look at Parker, curious. Big news?

"Well, let's just say your day suddenly got freed up."

Spence frowned. "What?"

Lakin sighed audibly. "The Greshams canceled."

Hetty drew back in surprise. "Just now?"

Parker nodded. "Seems Mr. Gresham took ill last night. Must be serious, if they're willing to take the cancellation hit."

Hetty knew there was a percentage fee for cancellations within twenty-four hours before an excursion was scheduled to begin. Perhaps oddly, she was disappointed. She liked this particular flight to her favorite lake. And besides, she'd been waiting excitedly to get back in the air now that the ice on the sound and most of the nearby lakes had finally broken.

"Well, that leaves a gaping hole in my weekend," Spence grumbled, sounding as if he was as disappointed as she was. And he probably was. For all her frustration with him, she'd never denied that Spence loved this work as much as she did. His passion for the land and its inhabitants rang through in his voice whenever he spoke to their guests.

She thought quickly and then looked at Parker. "I want to take the plane up anyway, make sure everything checks out. I can do a circuit, check the usual sites and fishing camps, see how everything looks before we get really deep into the season."

"Not a bad idea," Parker agreed. He looked at Spence.

"You need to do the restock of this destination site anyway, right?"

Rats. She'd forgotten that one of the tasks at hand had been to resupply the campsite they'd been headed to.

"Yes," Spence said.

"You don't have to go this time," Hetty said quickly. "The next excursion up there isn't until a couple of weeks from now, right?"

Spence shifted his gaze to her, and those blue eyes felt even more intense than usual. "I've already got the plane loaded up. It would be silly not to just get it done now."

She had no argument. She should have checked the plane first, before she'd come here to the office, then she would have known and wouldn't have embarrassed herself trying to talk him out of going with her on this first flight of the season.

"Oh," she said rather lamely.

"You two go get that done, then we'll be ready to go for the Radfords in a couple of weeks," Parker said. He added, with a grin, "Then we'll be back to all aircraft assigned and out, and Lakin and I can take the day off."

She knew that was about as likely as...nothing.

"And we've got another reservation for next week, for the Soundview site," Lakin put in. "After that, we're booked pretty solid for the rest of the summer. You two are going to be working hard this year."

And the brother and sister who essentially ran this place most of the time turned and walked back to their offices, unaware of the kick in the head they'd just delivered to their chief pilot.

Chapter Five

"Hey, where's your passengers?"

Spence looked at Jake, the teenager who worked part-time maintaining the docking facilities. "They canceled, last minute."

Jake frowned. "Oh. There was someone down looking at the plane, I thought it was your guy. Must have just been a tourist."

"'Tis the season,'" Spence said. He glanced at Hetty, who wasn't looking at either of them. "We're going to make the trip anyway, to drop off the new season supplies, since I've already got them loaded up. Thanks again for the help with that, by the way."

The boy grinned. "Thanks for the freebie at The Cove. It'll smooth things over with my girl."

Spence grinned. "Bring her some flowers, too. My mom said they just got a delivery in at the market in town."

"Good idea," Jake said.

The kid walked away, whistling happily. Spence smiled to himself. He wasn't going to use that gift certificate a client had tipped him with anyway, so it might as well go to a good cause, smoothing over a tiff between young lovers.

"You gave him that certificate for a free dinner and dessert Mrs. Barnes gave you?"

He turned to find Hetty looking at him quizzically. He shrugged. "I wasn't going to use it. Somebody might as well."

"Why not?"

"Exactly."

She blinked, figured it out and grimaced at him. "I meant why weren't you going to use it?"

He shrugged. "I just wasn't."

He didn't really want to discuss his love life—or decided lack thereof lately—with Hetty of all people. It had become almost a chore to keep up the lighthearted, flirty exterior in front of her. But he felt like he had to. It was a barrier of sorts between them and he needed it to be there. Why, he didn't want to delve into, now or ever.

"Nice of you, then," she said.

"It happens, despite what you think," he said and immediately regretted the jab.

"I've never disputed that you can be a nice guy, when you want to be. When you're not being—"

She cut herself off so sharply he was sure he knew what she'd been about to say. She had said it, more than once. *When you're not being a shameless flirt.*

She'd been saying it since high school, when that flirting and his looks had been all it had taken to charm almost anyone on campus. Anyone female, that is. Well, except Hetty, who had apparently been immune then and clearly still was.

It had taken his prowess on a baseball diamond or his skill on skates and with a hockey stick to impress the guys. And his willingness to take a hit, if it would help the team.

That was something he'd learned early on. Because his family—which to him meant all the Coltons, not just his own parents and sister, but Uncle Will and Aunt Sasha and his four cousins, too—was a team. A team with an unbreakable bond, who all pulled together under any circumstances. Because they'd paid the highest price once, for not doing just that.

And the aunt he'd never known, Caroline, had paid with her life for the lack of that bond back then.

Believe.

It was the Colton family motto now. If you had a problem or were in trouble, the one thing you could be sure of was that the family would believe you. Because, long ago, they hadn't.

Spence gave a sharp shake of his head, wondering why his mind was wandering off like that. Maybe to avoid having to deal with Hetty. If so, it had worked, because she'd walked away to do her safety check before they took off.

He checked his backpack of what he considered standard gear—never mind that Hetty teased him mercilessly about the size of it—one final time. His Kimber Mountain Ascent was strapped to one side. He knew some folks didn't agree with his decision to carry the very lightweight rifle, which was under five pounds without any added gear like his scope. And if he was out here to hunt big game, he'd agree and carry something heavier. But he didn't carry it for that. It was for protection, and all he cared about in that mode was that the bullet went where he aimed it. He wasn't out to be a sniper, he just wanted that bear or ticked-off moose to decide he had better things to do than go after a piddly little human.

He also checked his Blackfoot knife in its sheath attached

to his belt before he slung the backpack over his shoulder. Since Hetty's pack was also right there on the dock, he picked it up, too, and lugged them both into the plane and stowed them carefully in the racks just behind the cockpit. He stood there for a moment, staring at the copilot seat.

On flights like this, he was usually back in the passenger area, talking to the clients, explaining a few specific things about their destination if they were old hands, explaining a lot more if they were newbies. But today there would be no one and no reason for him to be back there. No reason for him not to sit up front. Except one.

Spence felt suddenly as if a battle was raging inside him. His brain was saying, *Of course, sit in front. It would be silly not to.* Besides, he liked it up front, where he could look out over this place that stirred him like no other, where he could spot the locations he'd been to fish or hike or just breathe in that Alaskan air.

Not to mention his other favorite view, which was her.

But his gut was saying, *Stay back there, as far away as you can get.* Because it would be torture. And Hetty wouldn't want him up front anyway. Or would she? Whenever they had clients who wanted to sit up front, or who wanted their kid to, she'd never seemed to mind, and even found things for them to do. But that was a paying client. Not her RTA partner she could barely stand to be around.

He could ask, he supposed.

Now there's a concept. Just ask.

He could almost hear his cousin Mitchell, the ever-practical lawyer, the one who cleaned up messes for all the Coltons, saying the words with a roll of his eyes.

He went back down the steps to the dock. Hetty was just finishing up her exterior check. She glanced at him then went back to making a note in the small notebook she carried. Old school, perhaps, but necessary here. It always came as a shock to some of their guests that there were actually places where WiFi didn't exist and you were actually offline the entire time you were there. They had it at the headquarters building, courtesy of a satellite link, but out at the camp, there was nary a cell tower nor an internet connection in sight. And he kind of liked it that way.

"We need to top off the avgas?" he asked, thinking about the necessary fuel for the flight.

She shook her head. "We're good. We'll be flying light, even with the cargo load, without the two intended passengers and their gear."

He nodded in acknowledgment, hesitated, then said it. "You mind if I sit up front, or would you prefer me out of your way?"

She went still, her hand stopping midnotation. It was a moment before she looked at him and he wondered, rather urgently, what she was thinking.

But all she said was, "Your choice."

He didn't know whether to be pleased or disappointed that she hadn't made the decision for him. At least she hadn't said, "Stay out of my way."

Up front it was then. He'd just sit, keep his mouth shut and enjoy the view. He'd go through it in his mind, thinking about how each place was on foot. As they passed over the east end of Chugach State Park, he'd ponder his last hike at Columbia Peak. Then the lakes. He'd always loved the symmetry of them, all of similar shape, crescents that were laid out in order of size from the smallest Tonsina to the largest, Tazlina.

He had the thought he should tell Hetty not to buzz too

low at Tazlina, or his dad and uncle might think they were searching for them. He turned to look at her, but the words died in his throat.

Hetty Amos made that plain, RTA shirt look…well, sexy. He couldn't tell if she was wearing makeup, but if she was she was doing it right, because, well, he couldn't tell. All he knew was she looked amazing.

He turned back to looking out the window. He'd best just sit here and enjoy that view.

And avoid the other view he loved.

WOULD YOU PREFER me out of your way?

Yes! She'd wanted to say it. She'd wanted to shout it. But she already knew, in her gut, that having him out of sight did not equal having him out of mind. So if he was going to be in her thoughts anyway, he might as well sit up where he could see better. She knew how much he loved watching the landscape unroll before them, and she wasn't cold enough to deprive anyone of that.

Besides, of all the fishing camps they flew to, this one was the closest, so it wasn't going to be a long flight anyway. Which was probably just as well. She was already twitchy.

She walked to the end of the dock and looked out toward the sound. While it wasn't rough, it wasn't anywhere near glassy smooth, either. Which was good, since she hated dealing with the excess surface tension of glassy water. She would have liked a little more wind to head into for the takeoff, but this would do. At least once they taxied out of the marina there would be all the room the Cessna needed to take off. Unknowing passengers were sometimes surprised at how much room a seaplane needed to take off because of the hydrodynamic drag of the floats.

No, it should be a normal takeoff; one she'd done hundreds of times. But there was no plane less forgiving of sloppy piloting than a seaplane, so she knew better than to take anything for granted.

She did a final check of the cargo, although she knew Spence was always careful. He might not be a pilot, but he understood the center-of-gravity concept, and how important it was in flying floatplanes.

He also knew enough to help Jake push them off from the dock and then quickly make the jump aboard before she turned on the engine. A floatplane under power was moving, whether you wanted it to or not.

Spence chose the front seat, as she'd expected. At least he turned off auto-flirt when it was just them. And she knew he knew the basics of the instruments and controls, just in case.

She lowered the water rudders and upped the power to the engine until they were taxiing away from the RTA dock at a pace she was comfortable with. For some reason, a memory came back to her from a picnic-style gathering of RTA people the owners had hosted. She been the newest hire at the time, and as always, was grateful they'd taken a chance on her, a relatively inexperienced pilot. She'd been afraid she'd have to leave Alaska to get that first job. When she'd said as much, Ryan Colton, Spence's dad, had smiled at her and said, "We like when we can hire people we already know and trust."

"Too bad you can't handle a boat, too," one of their crew had joked. "I could use a break now and then."

"The heck she can't." Spence had jumped in. "That plane's a boat until it's airborne."

She'd wanted to hug him, and might have if there hadn't been so many people there, including all of his family. That was the Spence she remembered, the boy with more discernment than anyone gave him credit for. Looking back now, she thought it was probably the moment when her high school crush on Spence Colton had reactivated. And refused to die, even when she watched him flirt with clients, because she knew, she just knew, there was more to him.

She even had proof, like the time they'd been prepping to take the Alexander family out to the main fishing camp. The parents had been worried the kids would get bored with no internet, so he'd talked to them a bit and found out they liked this one board game even if it was hopelessly old school. So, Spence had gone out and tracked down an edition of the game in a secondhand store and packed it up with the rest of the gear. When she'd realized what he'd done, she'd practically melted inside. That was the Spence she knew lived beneath the casual, carefree exterior. The Spence she remembered from the hours they'd spent together fighting through his quirky way of learning.

The Spence she'd never forgotten, for so many reasons. Even if the man sitting beside her now seemed like a surface imitation.

The takeoff was uneventful, as she'd hoped. Their destination, when they got there, would be a different matter. Partially because the lake was so much smaller and she'd have to taxi them out from the campsite to where she could utilize more of its length for takeoff. But it was also usually a bit windier there, which would help with faster liftoff.

She chuckled inwardly at herself. *Get there first, before you worry about leaving.*

"Something funny?" Spence asked, sounding wary.

"Just me getting ahead of myself," she said.

"You always think ahead. It's a requirement, isn't it, to be as good as you are?"

Yes, that was one thing about Spence she could always count on. He never failed to compliment her on her flying. He might joke about everything else, might be a goofball sometimes about some things, but not about this.

"I do try to think ahead," she agreed. "And thanks."

He shrugged. "Truth is truth."

Yes, it was. And the truth was the same as it had always been since the first time she'd laid eyes on Spence Colton and had felt a totally unexpected jolt of attraction. And that she knew she could never, ever have him, didn't ease that feeling one bit.

Chapter Six

Spence wondered if the jolt of adrenaline he always felt when they took off was even a tenth of what she felt. One sideways glance at Hetty, at the sheer glow of exuberance, made him doubt it. Then again, when he looked out over the landscape below them as they banked and turned from the sound toward the mountains, he felt that burst of energy that always followed the knowledge that he was once more headed into the wild. So maybe it was just as powerful as what she felt, only different.

He looked down over the foothills—which would be considered mountains themselves in many places in the world—and saw that even the patches of snow that usually lingered in the shady, sheltered spots were gone. He wondered if he was strange, for being almost sad to see the last of the snow melt away. Maybe it was because they had fewer clients in the dead of winter, and he was more free to go trekking on his own. He knew his family worried when he, or Mitchell, took off alone as they were wont to do, but he was extra careful, always prepared, and then more careful.

This area was fairly close to Shelby and wasn't as wild as some of the places he visited. Especially including those he kept to himself, never taking clients there even though to him they were the most beautiful places he'd ever been. There was nothing like standing looking at a gorgeous, crystalline lake, and only having to turn your head to see an unstoppable glacier creeping down from the peaks. Or having the eagles soaring overhead and sparing barely a glance for the insignificant human below.

He never felt more alive than when he was out in the vastness of it. The wildness was the reason he went to those places, and he didn't want that to change. Didn't want them on the list of places RTA took people. Selfish, perhaps, but there were some things he just wanted to keep to himself.

As he scanned the horizon ahead and on both sides, he felt the urge to go higher, so he could see more. Almost in the same instant, he felt the shift, the climb, and knew that she was already doing it. He turned his head to grin at them being in sync, just as she said, loudly enough to be heard over the noise since he hadn't put on the plane's headphones yet, "I just want to check the status of the main spots."

He nodded and belatedly reached for the headphones, activated them and slipped them on.

"Just what I was going to suggest," he said. "Last year the north camp didn't become accessible until the beginning of August. Need to know that before we start booking anything there."

She bobbed her head. They banked smoothly into a turn, and since she was intent on the maneuver, he felt free to watch her. It was so clear in her face, in her eyes, that she loved what she was doing, it might as well have been written in neon above her head. She loved flying as much as he loved exploring this place where he'd been lucky enough to be born.

He tried to remember, back in the days when it had just been the two of them in a classroom as she'd tried to help him figure out what seemed to come so easily to other kids, if she'd talked about learning to fly. He couldn't remember that she had, but he'd been so focused on his own frustrations that he might not have noticed. He'd had a few appointments with people who could supposedly help him with his reading issues. None had. He knew his parents had been worried, so his mask of it not mattering to him got thicker, even with them. He'd hidden his problem from his friends for so long, feeling ashamed, they thought the times when he made some mistake were intentional, all part of that joking façade.

But because Hetty was practically family, and had volunteered to tutor him through a school mentoring program—and because he knew her well enough to know she would never use it against him—he had finally let it out.

And to his amazement, once he had explained, she'd made it her mission to find a way to help him. And she had never lost her temper with him, had never chastised him or gotten irritated or thrown in the towel. Never thought he was stupid, just different. And she ever and always ended a session with, "We'll try again."

And it had been Hetty who had come up with the idea that had finally worked, so that he was able to function almost normally in a written-word-driven world. And he would never forget that. He trusted her more than any person who wasn't blood family, and all her teasing and jabbing couldn't change that.

Too bad telling himself that's all he felt for her wasn't working so well.

Soon they were circling over the small high-country

clearing that got less interest than the fishing camps, but got a lot from people looking for isolation, a respite from the madness of the everyday world. He understood that. It was sort of what he was sad to see go when summer and the high-traffic tourist season rolled around. Although he tended to like better those who had never been here before who came wanting to see the more remote places. He'd always figured they had something in common under the surface, more so than he had with those who just came looking for the best fishing spot.

But that season was what allowed him to live the way he wanted, so he wasn't about to complain. RTA was supporting his preferred lifestyle and keeping his cousins Parker and Lakin busy as well. Not to mention all the other people they employed.

Including the woman beside him, handling the controls of the Cessna with such calm competence. And who much preferred this season for flying. She'd told him once that with the stark, unbroken ice white of winter, it was too easy for pilots to lose the sense of how high—or low—they really were. And she didn't like the retractable skis for snow landings, or the extra bounce. Give her a smooth water landing any time.

Her long, dark hair was pulled back as usual, he guessed in part so it didn't get in the way of the headphones. He'd asked her once if the noise canceling didn't impair her ability to hear a potential problem with the engine, and she'd explained that it helped instead, by toning down the constant steady drone, so that anything unusual in fact actually stood out more.

He yanked his focus away from her and shifted position so he could look down below.

"That quaking aspen went down," he murmured to himself, making a mental note. He'd noticed the last time he was up there that the thirty-foot tree was leaning rather precariously. He'd taken a close look and seen no sign of damage or infestation, but there had been a large root making its way from a neighboring spruce and he'd suspected that was what was tilting the much smaller aspen. He'd need to come up here with some equipment and cut into logs, then split, since it didn't dry well in the round. The wood wasn't something he'd want for lots of heat or length of burn, but it was great to get things started, especially for people who might not be expert fire builders.

"Good excuse to get up here, huh?"

Hetty's voice in his ears told him he'd muttered that louder than he'd thought he had. But he didn't deny it. Just looked at her and grinned as he said, "Yep."

"Learn to skydive and I'll drop you off," she quipped.

His grin widened. He liked this Hetty, relaxed and willing to joke. Usually quite brisk and businesslike around clients, she would never kid around.

"My luck, I'd land on the chainsaw I need to bring."

She laughed before saying, "You have what you need?"

Not really.

His gut knotted at his own thought. Because what he needed was this Hetty, lighthearted and at ease. And he needed her a lot more than he wanted to admit.

"Yeah," he said, his voice a little rough as he fought down his unwanted response to her cheerful mood. "Everything else looks good."

She nodded and banked the plane to turn toward their next flyover, the fishing camp RTA had built a few years ago, which had become one of their most popular. As he

usually did coming out of that turn, he remembered the
flight when a thick cloud layer had dropped in, masking
the mountains around them. Then the wind below it had
kicked up and they'd been a bit tossed. Staying under the
clouds but not being trapped in a valley between mountains
without room to turn around, or any place to land, had been
the real trick. Hetty hadn't turned a hair and handled it as
if it were any routine flight. Because that's what she did.

But today was clear and he had a great view. He could
see nothing from the air that indicated any problems, so
he checked the camp off his mental list.

And finally they were done with the airborne survey
and headed for their destination. He glanced at his watch.
After noon, but they'd still have time for him to get all the
gear, food and other supplies off-loaded, and the tent he
jokingly called a "canvas house" put in place for the next
excursion. The Radford family were regulars and he knew
they'd never missed a trip once it was set.

It wasn't long—or didn't seem that way because of his
mood, which was in turn because of Hetty's mood—before he spotted the gleam of the sun on the lake up ahead.
They circled above first, so he could take a look at the area
surrounding the cleared campsite. He didn't see anything
amiss and was about to give the okay to take them on in
when he heard an odd, high-pitched sound he didn't recognize. He looked at Hetty and realized she'd changed. Gone
was the relaxed, easygoing woman of a few moments ago.
In her place was a taut, focused pilot.

"That squeal?" he asked.

She didn't answer, only nodded again, clearly focused
on all her instruments and the controls.

He remembered her once saying the plane talked to you,

if you knew how to listen. A change in pitch, the variance between engine noise and airframe noise, it all meant different things. She'd explained, in almost professorial tones, how hearing was second only to vision in maintaining awareness while flying. And that sounds had three variables that all provided data. "Frequency, intensity and duration," she'd quoted at him.

He also remembered asking her if frequency meant the pitch of the sound or how often it happened. She'd given him that now-all-too-rare smile that he'd first seen when he'd begun to make rapid progress back in those tutoring days, when the pieces had started to fall together visually in his mind.

"Both," she'd said approvingly.

He snapped out of the memory, special though it was, to focus on the present. Which, judging by her demeanor, might not be pleasant at all.

He looked up front to see, thankfully, the propeller still spinning normally. Then he shifted his gaze back to her, awaiting any sign or request—no, judging by the set of her jaw, it would be an order—that he do something.

"Fuel's dropping too fast. We're going straight in to landing—" She broke off in the same moment the prop stopped turning.

They were definitely going down.

Chapter Seven

Everything she'd ever learned raced through Hetty's mind. She'd been through the drill countless times, her flight instructors shutting the engine off and leaving it to her to get them down safely. She'd done it multiple times, on both land and water. It wasn't as catastrophic as civilians thought it would be—an engine failing. Of course, it was a bit easier when you'd known the instructor beside you would take over if need be.

But still, it wasn't like they were in a helicopter, after all. An airplane without a functioning engine became, in essence, a glider. A not particularly efficient one, true—and the pontoons of a floatplane made it even worse because of all the drag—but a glider nonetheless. A machine designed to fly. Which meant they had time. Not much, but some.

Her mind raced, assessing. They were, or had been, at about five thousand feet. As she had already said to herself, floatplanes didn't have the best glide ratio, but there was currently no headwind to slow them down further. But distance wasn't really the concern, since they were essentially over their destination landing spot.

Minimum descent rate.

She chanted the words as she tried to restart the engine.

No good. She banked slightly as they lost elevation. Tried again. No go. She couldn't figure out what had happened, but time enough for that once they were safely down. Since they were directly over what had been their intended touchdown location anyway, she decided to use the momentum they had left to land safely, with enough left, hopefully, to get them ashore. They had the inflatable kayak on board to use if they had to, but she would prefer not to have to use it.

I'd prefer to have my engine still running!

She gave it a third and last try, with the same result. That decided the issue. She would have to land this ungainly glider without power.

Hetty adjusted her approach heading so that they'd be aimed straight for the small beach that helped make this such a popular spot. There would be no turns after the last visual reference. She'd touch down as close to it as she could and still have room for the drag of the water to slow them enough.

When she was set, when they were committed, she said to Spence, "Call it in. I have a feeling we won't be going back the same way we got here."

She saw him reach for the radio. It was the last thing she saw other than the controls and the water below as they dropped. They were going to hit faster than usual because they'd need the speed to be sure they had enough flare, so she adjusted to make sure the pontoons didn't dig in and flip them. She talked to herself, running through her mental checklist continuously, so focused, she only vaguely heard Spence on the radio talking to RTA.

The touchdown was a jolt, but not that much stronger than usual. The slowdown was immediate, the water dragging them quickly. She adjusted the flaps to maintain as much momentum as possible. When they'd reached a safe enough speed, she dropped the rudders, although she was happy to see she'd judged that about right and they were headed straight for the beach.

She concentrated on keeping the Cessna straight, since she couldn't maneuver with anything but the rudders and what forward motion they still had left.

Hetty thought back to the last time she'd been here. They had been tied up to the small dock then. But she didn't have the option for that kind of finesse this time. She'd walked the beach here regularly, just in case, to see if there were any changes she needed to know about. That precaution paid off now because, unless there had been a new rock-slide in the interim that had sent something big rolling all the way down, the beach was wide enough and smooth enough that this should work.

She spared a split second to be thankful RTA had gone for pontoons tough enough to withstand some grinding, because they were going to hit that beach. She thought it with an inward smile, a combination of pride in the organization she worked for and, to be honest, a little pride in herself for pulling this off rather neatly. They would run out of speed a little short of grounding, but not by much.

She turned her head to tell Spence he was going to have to get a little wet, but he was already moving. A moment later, he was thigh-deep in the ice-cold water, without even a wince. He'd grabbed the tie-off rope and used it to pull the plane the last few feet. And he made it look easy, although she knew that essentially towing even a floatplane was no simple task. Sometimes she forgot just how strong he was, even though she knew. She'd certainly watched him enough times; the way he hefted the big supply crates, the way he climbed when out on a hike, the way he—

Stop it!

She wrote off her sudden veering into forbidden territory to the at-last-ebbing adrenaline. What she needed to be thinking about right now was what had gone wrong, not the very apparent physical prowess of Spence Colton.

Hetty felt the shift when the plane was a land creature once more. She picked up the radio to notify RTA they were safely down, and after the relieved congratulations, got the news she'd expected—with all aircraft out on excursions, they were there until morning.

She shut down everything, clambered out and down to the port pontoon, walking to the front end and hopping off, getting only her boots wet. As opposed to Spence, whose jeans were wet past his knees as he tied the Cessna off to a large, heavy-looking log half buried on the beach. He leaned into it as if to make sure it would hold, then straightened and turned.

As soon as she was on the beach, he ran at her, startling her. He caught her in those strong arms she'd just been admiring and, with an almost wild-sounding laugh, he lifted her up and spun her around.

"You are the best, Cap'n Amos!"

She started to laugh herself but it died in her throat. Died because he'd planted an enthusiastic kiss on her cheek. Because he'd planted a kiss on her cheek and that's not where she wanted him to kiss her.

"We're alive," she managed to get out with difficulty because he was still holding her tightly. "It could have been worse."

"Sure," he said, laughing with what she recognized as

an aftereffect of an adrenaline spike. "We could have been in a helicopter."

Despite her nervous state—from his embrace, not the landing—she mastered her usual response. "That's why I fly the machine that wants to fly, by design, and not the one that wants to tear itself apart with opposing forces."

He laughed again, joyously. Then he let go of her. And, contrarily, she now regretted the loss of his touch, when mere moments ago she'd been silently wishing he'd let her go.

She bit the inside of her lip as she confronted once more the clash of her feelings about the man.

"You radio home we were down and okay?"

She nodded. "They copied and reminded me we're… stuck. Until morning, at least."

"Yeah, I figured," Spence said as if it didn't bother him at all. "Everybody's out, even Dad and Uncle Will, on their own trip."

She hesitated then said, "I know they'd come get us if they knew, but I told Lakin not to interrupt them." For a moment, Spence just looked at her, and she started to feel uncomfortable. "I should have talked to you first, but Lakin told me what day it was and—"

"No. No, you did exactly the right thing." That Spence smile flashed again. "But then, you always do," he added, gesturing back toward the plane, "or we wouldn't be here talking about it."

Not for the first time, she thought she could hear the difference in his voice between when they were talking like this and when he was chatting up some client who'd turned on the charm at her first sight of him. She'd like to think what she was hearing now was the real Spence, was sincerity, and all the rest was…well, not fake exactly—he wasn't a liar—but part of an act.

Hetty suddenly recalled the last time—and maybe *the* last time, given the gushing—she'd read a review of RTA on one of the travel websites: "Ladies, if you want some lovely scenery—and I don't mean just the landscape— check out RTA out of Shelby, and ask for Spence as your guide!"

She remembered how he'd deleted that last guest's phone number as soon as she was out the door, and how she had wondered if that's what he did with all of them.

What she should have been wondering about was why it mattered to her.

She knew he almost never left Alaska, only a couple of times to see friends down in Seattle. But even that was a while ago, and he'd said after the last time he doubted he would be going back because things weren't like they used to be.

She'd dwelt on that one for a while, too, wondering if it was a sign that Spence couldn't move on, if maybe he really was still that high school flirt. She'd later felt badly about those thoughts when she'd heard his dad talking about how the Seattle friends were all leaving the city for various reasons. She told herself sternly she needed to quit judging present-day Spence by the teenager she'd known. He'd proved her wrong then, when, on the edge of giving up, they had figured out how to use the quirk he did have to compensate for the one he didn't, but she hadn't learned, apparently.

You need to stop judging, period. Nobody appointed you judge or jury.

She came out of her reverie, almost embarrassed at hav-

ing mentally wandered off. But at least this time it had
served a purpose; the last of the adrenaline had ebbed and
she was back to calm and steady.

As long as she stopped trying to figure out Spence Colton.

Chapter Eight

Spence put the last crate in the bearproof—well, as much as anything was up here—storage outbuilding. He straightened up and spared a moment to be thankful that that was the last of it. It was quite a stretch from the beach to this hilltop campsite and, of course, the heavy-load part was on the uphill side. He needed to talk to Parker about some kind of motorized transport for the site, since it was one of their most established and often used destinations.

Too much for you, old man?

He could just hear Parker's laugh as he ragged on him for being a whole year older. He doubted his cousin dared do the same with his older brothers. Eli was too intimidating and Mitchell the same but in a different way. You took care with Mitchell because it was him you'd need if you were ever in trouble.

A faint sound from outside made him pause. Something in the distance, down toward the lake. It didn't repeat and he heard nothing else out of the ordinary. They hadn't seen any fishing boats on the water, but that didn't mean they weren't there now. Or hikers in the vicinity, though that would be beyond rare out here this early. Or simply a big elk getting fired up for a summer of fun.

Still, he stepped out of the building and looked down toward the water. He couldn't see the beach where the plane was tied off, but the part of the lake he could see was empty. He watched for a minute then went back to work. He stacked the crates in a logical—to him, anyway—order, settled them to be sure they were stacked solidly, then straightened, finally done. His back was probably going to remind him of this tomorrow.

Hey, at least you'll be around to be reminded. Thanks to Hetty, Ms. Cool Under Fire.

And now I get to look forward to—he glanced at his watch, the chronometer his dad had given him on his twenty-first birthday—*twelve more hours here, at least.* Twelve hours of unexpected leisure. Twelve hours he could spend fishing. Or hiking. Or paddling out on the lake. Since it never got really totally dark this time of year, the options were pretty open. Or he could take this gift of twelve hours and just relax.

Twelve hours with Hetty.

Sure. Relax.

He started walking around, inspecting the camp. Looking for something, anything, that needed attention. But everything seemed in working order. The tent—or the "tabin," as the little boy of one of their clients had called it once, a combination of tent and cabin—had no holes or rips, even the roof was clean. Which he of course knew, because he'd been the one to clean it when they'd taken it down last fall. The indoor woodstove was in good shape and vented properly. The camp stove outside was the same. Everything had wintered well.

So there, he'd killed a couple of those twelve hours. Now what?

Maybe he should radio headquarters. Ask Parker if there was anything he wanted done up here, as long as he was stuck anyway. He only had the basic tools that he always carried, back aboard the plane, and the tools that were always here, but he could make do, if his cousin had a project in mind. He'd be happy to tackle anything.

Anything that would keep him too occupied to think about being up here with Hetty for hours on end. All night. Alone.

All night. Damn.

He darted toward the tent. He'd lugged the folding camp beds down from storage along with the tent, without even thinking. But the original plan had been the big double one, for the honeymooning couple who would obviously be sleeping together. But there were a couple of singles, too, so he needed to be sure those were set up. And as far apart as possible. Hell, he should think about grabbing his sleeping bag out of the back of the plane and sleeping outside tonight. It wouldn't be that cold. And at least he might actually sleep, instead of lying awake all night, knowing she was just a few feet away.

Hetty was already inside. And she already had the singles unfolded and set up. On opposite sides of the tent. She glanced up as he came in, looked puzzled at his rush. He tried to think of something to say, something logical, reasonable. Words failed. There was something about standing in an area meant for sleeping, with Hetty Amos, that made him almost forget how to talk at all.

"Wood," he muttered finally. "We need firewood."

Her head turned as she looked at the woodstove and the neat rack of compressed-energy logs beside it. "There are ten of these, and they each last about two hours once it's going, don't they? And it's July, after all. Not like it's going to drop below zero."

"Kindling, then," he said almost desperately. And before she could question that, he turned on his heel and strode back outside. He knew perfectly well there was kindling and even some fire starters also there in the rack beside the woodstove, but he had to get away.

He tried to remember the last time they'd been alone together for any length of time. Usually there was family around, his or hers, or clients. And what time they did spend alone was usually filled with prep work, planning, or her doing her flight check while he got things loaded up. But now...

He stood outside on the hill, for one of the few times in his life too distracted to fully soak in the beauty all around him. Too distracted to savor the crisp, clean air, to gaze out at the expanse of the lake below, where the plane she had brilliantly brought down safely was just out of sight behind the edge of the stand of trees to the north.

He tried to tell himself he was so focused on her because she'd just saved them both with her skill. But he knew better. He was distracted because, when she was around, he seemed to lose control of his thoughts and they rocketed off in directions he should never be thinking. He was distracted because he knew it was futile, that she would probably forever see him as that kid she'd had to tutor in high school. He was distracted because she seemed only to dislike him now. Ironic, in a way, that she constantly ragged on him about flirting with clients when the only reason he did it was that the pull to do it with her was so strong.

And then the main source of that distraction came out of the tent cabin behind him.

"Adrenaline crash?" she asked as she halted beside him. Startled, he looked at her. "What?"

"After an incident like this, I know the drained feeling that happens once the initial shock fades. You get kind of numb. And tired."

"Oh. Yeah," he said, gladly agreeing with her to avoid the real reason he was so...flustered.

Maybe that really was part of what was wrong with him. Maybe it was the letdown after a supremely stressful moment. Nothing like thinking you're going to die in a plane crash to get that adrenal gland going strong. Maybe it wasn't solely the idea of spending the night with her that had him so revved up and scattered at the same time.

Sure, Colton, keep telling yourself that.

"So...who's fixing dinner?" the ever-practical Hetty asked.

And now she'd disconcerted him again. "I... I sort of figured we'd just eat one of the prepacks," he said, referring to the bagged-and-sealed main courses with the long shelf life always kept in stock up here. "I saw there's some of that chili you like."

She was the one who looked surprised now. What, that he'd remembered she liked that particular version of the meals? Why would something that basic surprise her?

How would you feel if you knew I remember that you hate Brussels sprouts, that your favorite song is Hendrix's classic "All Along the Watchtower," and that your favorite color is that almost lime green of your jacket that makes your eyes practically glow? Or that you want to see the Eiffel Tower someday, after the Statue of Liberty, because you like the French connection between them?

His list of things he knew about her could go on and on.

Not because she'd ever told him all these things, but because whenever he was around her he was glued to every word, no matter who she was actually saying them to. Which was almost always someone else, since she rarely spoke to him directly other than on work-related things.

"—fine with me," she was saying, making him tune back in. "I like it warm, though, so I'll get the fire going."

She turned to head back but paused for a moment, looking intently up the hill.

"What?" he asked.

Hetty shook her head. "Nothing. I saw something move up there, or thought I did. But I don't see anything now."

"Maybe it was our moose, coming for a visit," he joked, still trying to shake off the odd feelings he always seemed to get when he was alone with her. "I'll go grab a couple of those meals," he said, glad of the reason to take a hike, in all senses of the saying. He also needed to grab the Kimber out of the storage shed where he'd set it down to wrestle with the bulky stuff. Nobody in their right mind would be holed up this far into the Alaskan backcountry without a weapon at hand to convince some of the local wildlife that they would taste horrible.

They each turned to follow their stated intentions. But before he'd taken two steps, Spence saw a chunk of bark fly off the tree they were next to, for no apparent reason. A moment later, he heard a loud but distant crack of sound. Hetty looked puzzled, but Spence knew. He knew, and he dived for her, taking her down to the ground in a fierce tackle. She tried to pull away, but he held her fast. He played it back in his head in an instant; the lesser sound of the impact with the tree and the loud report. He knew he was right.

"What—"

"That was a shot."

"There are always hunters around—"

"It was aimed at us."

Chapter Nine

He was crazy. She'd heard the sound but assumed it had been a tree branch breaking, as often happened out here.

He was imagining things. That had to be it.

Except, Spence was far from crazy. He didn't go around imagining things. And when it came to almost anything here in the backcountry, at least on the ground, he had more experience than she'd ever have. And he'd certainly had more experience with firearms.

He was also lying on top of her. She was finding it a little hard to breathe and had a suspicion it wasn't solely because of his solid weight pressing down upon her. And he didn't seem to be breathing at all. Then she realized he'd lifted his head just slightly and tilted it as if listening. For another shot?

Another shot.

Someone had actually shot at them. She was beginning to get past the shock and process it now.

"Did they think we were a deer or something?" she asked, whispering by instinct as if the likely faraway shooter could hear her.

"Possible," Spence muttered. "But given where we were standing and that it came from further up the hill, not likely." His mouth curved into a wry half smile. "Not to mention the color of your jacket."

It was proof of how rattled she was that she hadn't even thought of that. Her lime-green puffy jacket would be hard to mistake for a deer or any other wild creature.

Some dirt a couple of feet away seemed to jump of its own accord and a moment later she heard the same kind of crack she'd heard before. And now that Spence had told her, it seemed obvious.

"He's not giving up," she said. "We need to move."

"My rifle's in the shed." He shifted as if he were about to get up.

"But that would be going toward him," she protested, a nightmare scenario flashing through her mind of Spence lying on the ground, bleeding out.

"The tent isn't going to stop a rifle round. Only other option is the plane, which is immobilized."

"But there's the radio," she said quickly, liking this idea much better. "Call for help."

"Which would take too long to get here to be much help."

"The plan is still more solid than the tent," she said. "It might not stop a bullet, but the walls of the plane would at least slow it down, wouldn't it?"

"Point taken," Spence said.

She felt a flash of relief at his agreement. She would feel better, safer, whether it was true or not, in her beloved plane.

A third shot hit the dirt, barely missing her left hip. She couldn't stop her instinctive flinch.

"We need to move," Spence said urgently. "Zigzag down to the big rock then cut right to the tree line."

Hetty nodded. "On three?"

She saw that familiar Spence grin that so captivated her flash for a split second. That he could do it under these circumstances impressed her more than she wanted to admit.

"On 'now,'" he said. "Like...*now!*"

She wasn't sure how he did it, but almost instantly he was on his feet and had pulled her up with him in one smooth, graceful move, reminding her yet again how strong he really was. How powerful.

And then they were running, and with the zigzag course he set, it was all she could do to both stay on her feet and keep up with him. It felt like a wild, wacky made-up game of some kind. Except for the very real threat as more shots rang out.

She felt a little safer as they passed the big rock and then dodged into the tree line. Something about the heavy cover of thick branches and solid trunks made this nightmare seem survivable.

"Is he just a bad shot?" she asked when they'd slowed slightly in the shelter of the big trees.

"Or maybe too far away," Spence said. "Given the time between the shots hitting and the sound, I'm hoping for the latter."

That made sense to her, since even she could hit a target if she was close enough.

"You piss anybody off lately?" he asked sourly.

"Only you," she countered, an edge in her voice; this was no time to be joking around. Even if you were Spence Colton.

He half turned to look at her. "You never piss me off. Irritate, yes, but full-on pissed? Nope."

She had the strangest feeling there was more depth to that seemingly teasing answer than he was letting show.

Maybe it was the way he was looking her straight in the eye. But this was no time to get lost again in her meandering wonderings about Spence Colton.

They worked their way down to where the plane was beached. She stopped dead the moment it was in sight.

"It's further out," she said.

"Yeah," Spence agreed, and he didn't sound happy. "And I know I tied it off securely."

When they got close enough, she could see the mooring line must have come undone, allowing the plane to drift offshore a few yards, the line trailing through the water.

Her brow furrowed. She knew Spence was right. He'd never not make certain things were absolutely secure, so it had to have been untied, maybe even pushed free of the beach.

He didn't hesitate, even though he had to get wet again. Although, only knee-deep this time, just far enough to retrieve the rope and pull the plane back in. She ran to help, knowing a little extra weight on the line couldn't hurt. When the plane was beached again, and he was tying it off, she scrambled onto the float and then up into the cockpit, while Spence grabbed his emergency pack out of the bin in the back. Once she was in the pilot's seat, it took a moment for her to process what she was seeing.

Every reachable wire in the cockpit had either been yanked free or cut. Panels had been pulled free to expose more wiring, also cut. Most of the screens and dials had been smashed and every knob appeared broken off. She had little doubt, but tried the radio anyway. And got what she'd expected and feared. Nothing.

"What the hell?" Spence's words as he leaned into the cockpit were short, sharp and vehement. He almost immediately pulled back and looked around, scanning the water and landscape around them.

Hetty snapped out of her stunned state and realized he was looking for any trace of who had done this. The idea that the vandal might still be lurking around—and that there may be someone *additional* targeting them other than the shooter—terrified her. She wasn't normally so slow, but the impossible question of who would do this had rendered her normally sharp mind sluggish.

Was it the same person? Was the hand that had done this damage now holding the weapon that was firing at them? But why?

"Damn," Spence muttered. "That's what I heard."

"What?"

He didn't look at her when he answered, but kept scanning the area around them. "Back when I was stacking the crates in the shed, I heard…something. From down here. But I couldn't tell what it was, and it didn't repeat, so I figured it was probably a fishing boat in the area, or an elk or some other animal." His jaw tightened. "That'll teach me to assume."

"Do you think it's the same person who's shooting?"

"Out here this far, let's say the chance of it being two different people, one shooting at us, another destroying our means of communication, is pretty low."

"Unless they're working together."

His head snapped around to look at her. He grimaced and let out a compressed breath. "There is that," he muttered.

"But…why?"

"That's the big question, isn't it? There's nobody that—"

The lower right corner of the windshield shattered into a starburst. Spence dived sideways and down. He took her with him and they slid toward the floor. She gasped audibly. Had he been hit? For an instant, she froze at the idea. Then she erupted into motion. She squirmed around in the cramped space. Her heart slammed in her chest when she saw blood trickling down the side of his face.

"Stay down," he hissed.

She breathed again. He was alive. "How bad are you hurt?"

"I'm fine. We've got to move."

"But you're bleeding!"

As she said it, the blood reached his right eye and he swiped at it. He winced, but it seemed more in annoyance than pain.

"We've got to move," he repeated. "He knows we're here, and it sounds like he's using high-velocity rounds, so this isn't going to be a shelter after all."

He was clearly coherent and aware, so she shelved her immediate panic. "Move to where?"

He was silent for a moment, clearly thinking.

Hetty tried not to move, which was difficult. What was more difficult was ignoring the feel of Spence's body pressing down on her.

"Remember the cave?"

She knew immediately what he meant. Before they'd set up this semipermanent campsite, they'd explored the surrounding area thoroughly. "The one northwest of the camp?"

"Yes. If we can make it to the tree line, we can head west then up."

"All right."

"I'll take lead and you—"

"I will. You're hurt."

"I'm fine," he repeated.

"You're the one who's bleeding."

He swiped again at the trickle of blood on his face. "I just got nicked by some glass or something. It's just a—"

"If you say it's just a scratch, Spence Colton, I will knee you hard enough to make you scream."

She saw him realize she was in the perfect position beneath him to do just that. And to her surprise, he laughed. "That's my girl," he said.

Before she could ask what exactly he meant by that, he was moving.

Chapter Ten

By the time they were halfway to the cave, Spence knew a couple of things. One, the shooter was either inexperienced with his weapon, or not at home out here. Was it because he was used to cities with lots of buildings, not trees with branches that moved with the wind? Used to more noise to cover his movements? Crowds to blend into? That, he didn't know. And it didn't matter. He only knew he was glad of it. Otherwise, one of those shots might have hit.

They scrambled up a steeper slope, still sheltered by the thick trees. He had only slung his pack over one shoulder initially, but now slid his other arm through the second strap. And aimed a rather fervent curse at himself again at the lack of his rifle usually secured on that side. If he had it, he could resolve whatever this was in a hurry.

The going was a bit rough, especially in spots where only a thin layer of earth covered larger—and more slippery—rocks. He'd gone down on a knee once already and it had been an effort to bite back the yelp of pain. But now that they were out in the open air, moving, any sound could easily carry to the hunter and betray their location.

He spared a split second to hope the guy had gone down a couple of times himself, but Spence never stopped moving. And Hetty, tough, stubborn woman that she was, kept up with him.

That last slip made him think of something else about the shooter. That maybe he was used to level ground—like asphalt or concrete—under his feet all the time. At this point, Spence would take any edge he could get, and that would definitely be one.

He paused to look around, to make sure he was headed in the right direction. It had been a while since he'd been up here. But if they made it to the cave, the situation would shift completely. With its entrance mostly masked by a large boulder and a huge Sitka spruce, most newcomers to the area would never realize it was there. The entrance was narrow, although the cave itself opened up quite a bit once you were inside. That meant anyone coming in after them would have to present themselves in the restricted space. Spence might not have his rifle, but he had his knife. He'd never used it on a human before, but if it came down to the assailant or him, he would.

If it came down to the assailant or Hetty, he'd not only use it but tear him up like a grizzly.

A faint rustling behind them made him spin around. Hetty froze in place. Spence visually searched down low, where the sound had come from.

"Stoat," he whispered to her, having spotted the small brown-and-white weasel in the underbrush. Summer was definitely here, since the wiry creature had shed its winter-white coat completely. It gave them a tilted-head assessing look and, apparently deciding they weren't worth any more attention, scampered off into the trees.

They moved on, carefully, stopping to listen every few yards. They heard no more movement and, more importantly, no more shots. Had they lost the shooter? Spence didn't know for sure, and he wasn't about to gamble that they had. Not when the stakes could easily be Hetty's life.

Cursing himself once more for setting the rifle down in the storage shed—and hoping he lived through this, so he could never repeat that carelessness—Spence started moving again. The incline of the slope had lessened a bit, making the going easier, but the trees were also thicker, with branches barring almost every path, making moving silently and invisibly nearly impossible. Practically crawling—actually crawling would probably be a good idea—was the only answer.

He didn't stop to explain their pace to Hetty. She might not be a hunter, used to skulking around in the woods, but she knew they were under serious threat and she would understand why they were being so cautious. And why he was being so quiet. Besides, she knew this terrain almost as well as he did. That had been a requirement of working for RTA; to know the crucial things about where you were taking people who didn't know anything about it.

He thought of those days when he'd first been assigned— by his father, so he couldn't say no—to showing her to and around all their various destinations. One of the things he'd done was to teach her various hand signals. At that time, they had been intended to be used to avoid spooking game, or in the case of some of the critters of the wild, to avoid drawing their attention. Now he had to hope that she'd been paying attention to those lessons and remembered how to communicate silently.

The moment he had the thought, he almost laughed at himself. This was Hetty, and if there was one thing she consistently did, it was learn and remember. If that wasn't true, he wouldn't be here now. They'd both be in the drink, along with a crashed plane, probably both dead. But she'd pulled off a safe landing, saving them both.

And now here we are with some crazy person with a rifle trying to take us out, and I don't have a single damned idea who or why.

He stopped again, scanning ahead, searching for any sign of movement, listening for any sound. Then he felt a touch on his arm and quickly looked back at Hetty. She nodded to their left and slightly lower, making a motion with her hands at her head that it took him a moment to figure out. He couldn't stop his smile when he realized it was from back on that day when she'd asked if there were signals for particular animals and he'd jokingly put his hands up on both sides of his head to signify a moose's antlers.

He looked where she'd nodded, saw nothing at first. But Hetty also didn't make mistakes, so he waited. And after another minute or so, he saw movement: a large, brown, antlered head reaching down for some no-doubt tangy green summer growth.

They waited, watching. Most people who had never encountered one didn't realize the threat an angry moose could be. If he decided you were a problem he wanted to be rid of, you'd better get gone. And fast.

The big animal looked their way, as if he'd known they were there all along. And he probably had, Spence admitted. This was his neighborhood, not theirs, and any and all intruders were likely noticed, assessed and either ignored or driven out. And unlike their other pursuer, chances were good he wouldn't miss.

He went back to his meal and Spence looked at Hetty and nodded up the hill. Once more, they started inching their way forward. The moose looked again, but this time seemed satisfied that they were vacating the premises and stayed where he was.

Spence glanced back at Hetty and saw that she was smiling. She'd always loved it when they encountered the various wild creatures that inhabited—heck, owned—this countryside. She would never hunt them, but she loved to see and watch them. And apparently that hadn't changed.

Then again, Hetty didn't change much. Even in high school, she'd been like this—smart, quick and endlessly patient when necessary. She always had been that way with him, and he was sure he'd put quite a strain on those qualities, especially the patience, in those days. Heck, he was sure he put a strain on them now, although it was for completely different reasons.

At the time, it had been because he'd been sure, with all the certainty of a teenager, that nobody could help him. Hetty had proved him wrong, then. Now, it was because he had to keep some distance between them, otherwise he was going to say or do something utterly stupid and make it hard for them to work together. And they had to work together, because they were one of the main supports RTA was built on.

And so he kept his distance, upheld the front of flirting with every receptive female who came along, telling himself he had to maintain that space between them. He supposed it was the inner urge to do just the opposite that made him push the envelope, go further than he wanted to, which resulted in a weird feeling of both success and irritation when he succeeded in bringing on that disgusted eye roll of hers.

He shook off the tired old thoughts and speculation.

He needed to be paying attention here. Just because there hadn't been any shots fired since they'd made it into the trees didn't mean the guy had given up. And wasting energy trying to figure out why wasn't helping, either. Right now that didn't matter, the why would come later. Assuming the shooter didn't find them and finish the job. He winced inwardly at the thought of his dad and uncle trying to figure out what had happened to them.

Once they were out of sight of the moose, he picked up the pace as much as he thought he could without advertising their presence. This plan obviously wasn't without risk, especially since they were essentially moving in the shooter's uphill direction, but if they made it to that cave, they'd at least have time to think and figure out what to do.

He paused at a break in the trees, to assess the two possible ways past the small clearing in front of them. He was trying to decide if they'd be better off heading to the left to get past that downed spruce or to the right on what looked to be a longer path that would keep them concealed among upright trees, when he heard…something.

His head snapped around and he held up a hand to stop Hetty. She froze where she was, about five feet behind him. He searched the direction of the sound—a faint snap, as if a branch had broken—had come from, but saw nothing; no movement, no moose, no human. He heard a faint sort of chattering—an animal—and wondered if it was the stoat and his clan. It sounded kind of weasel-like.

The area had fallen back into silence and still he waited. Only when several minutes had gone by did he start to walk again. Hetty never protested, only moving when he finally lowered his hand.

At last, they reached the huge outcropping of rock he recognized. The cave was about midway along and he could see from their position that the huge Sitka spruce still stood. But the stretch from here to there was like the clearing down the hill. Too open for comfort.

He turned to Hetty and whispered, "I want to check and make sure the cave isn't…occupied."

It was unlikely, this late in the year and at this time of day, but still possible that some creature or creatures were sheltering there. The opening was too narrow for a bear of any size, but smaller wildlife had used the cave before, leaving evidence of nests, droppings and food debris behind.

"Okay," she answered just as quietly. "I'll go check on that little waterfall that was over there." She glanced to her right.

He remembered the small rivulet that ran down the south side of the rocks. He'd prefer she stay put, but he also knew they needed water. He was already thirsty after the long hike and she had to be, too. So, reluctantly, he nodded. Thought about saying, "Be careful," or some such other warning, but stopped himself. Hetty knew as well as he did to take care up here and not just because that shooter might still be in the area. She was aware that with one wrong step, she could take a tumble she wouldn't easily recover from. Especially as completely out of touch as they were now.

And then she was gone, moving as silently as he had been. Jaw set, he headed toward the cave. It was awkward, doing it in a crouch, but safer in case the shooter had perhaps spotted or heard them.

He made it to the cover of the big tree and took his first full breath. He edged around the slight outcropping of rock, hoping nothing had happened to block off their planned shelter's entrance. The narrow opening was just as he'd remembered. He stopped, listened, but heard nothing from inside. Still, he had his knife at the ready when he moved again. He had to find the perfect middle ground between stooping and staying constricted enough himself to get through it.

It was, thankfully, empty. There were signs that perhaps a coyote or three had wintered here, including bones leftover from whatever the clever carnivores had caught for several meals.

As long as we don't add any human bones to that pile...

His thoughts went immediately to Hetty and he turned to exit the cave. He needed to tell her they were good and to get her into the shelter. He didn't want her out there any longer than necessary. He could use a drink of that clear, mountain water himself, if the little creek was still running.

The moment he got back outside, he heard something. A sound that was half gasp, half scream. His entire body tensed.

An instant later, he heard a sharp unmistakable crack of sound.

Another shot.

And another scream.

Hetty.

Chapter Eleven

The fiery pain in her left thigh made her want to scream a third time, but Hetty knew that first loud gasp of shock and surprise was what had given her away. She hadn't been able to stop it, not after what she had found in the trees just past the tiny waterfall. She had the feeling the horrible image would be with her for the rest of her life.

Assuming she didn't bleed to death right here and now.

She couldn't get to her feet, was afraid she'd scream again if she even tried, so instead she rolled over, biting her lip fiercely to keep from crying out as her wounded leg took her weight for a moment.

Shot. She'd actually been shot.

She kept rolling, knowing the sooner she got out of sight in the trees, the better. The bullet had gone from the front of her thigh through the back, and she knew enough to know the exit wound would be the worst. But as far as she could tell, it hadn't hit the bone, so the big thing she had to worry about was the femoral artery. She kept as much pressure as she could on the wound while still getting herself under some kind of cover. She tried to blank the pain by concentrating on working out exactly what had happened.

She'd taken a grateful drink of the clear, cool water,

straightened and… Had she started back down yet? Or had she been in his line of fire simply by being at the waterfall? Had he known where it was and that, needing water, they would end up there? Had he spotted her and followed? Or had it just been chance that they'd both wound up within sight of each other?

Within sight.

That's what she should be thinking about. The fact that she'd seen him, although only a glimpse. Enough to tell he was indeed male, tall and with longish, wavy blond hair trailing down below the edge of what had looked like a knit cap. She thought she'd seen a mark on his face, a scar maybe, on his left cheek, but it could have just been a smear of something.

And he was wearing some sort of camouflage. The gray-and-black stuff. Which didn't work so well. She felt a spark of disdain for the man who clearly had thought it was always snow and rock here, when in fact so much burst into greenery this time of year.

She wondered if the guy—

"Hetty!"

It was a low but powerful sound, a whisper, yet projected all the way to where she was now lying in the shelter of the trees.

"Here," she answered, trying to get the same power into her voice as he had. She did, but only by letting some of the pain drive it. She thought she heard him swear, low and harsh, and knew he'd read the undertone.

It was probably less than a couple of minutes before he found her, although it seemed longer as she grasped at the bloody hole in her leg, still trying to stem the bleeding. He was on his knees beside her in an instant, edging her hands away from the wound.

"Spence, I found—"

"Shh. Let me check."

She hushed. Her apology for bringing this down on them could wait. So could the reason for it, for the moment. She concentrated on not screaming as he examined her leg. It took her a moment to realize what he was doing when at first he simply held her leg and watched it bleed, front and back.

"The artery?" she asked, trying not to let her fear into her voice.

"I don't think so. It's not pulsing, just bleeding. But it's bleeding a lot, and we've got to stop it."

He yanked off his belt free and wrapped it around her leg as a makeshift tourniquet.

"But he's out there—"

"I know." He tightened the belt hard enough she nearly moaned. "So we're moving right now."

"But I don't think I can—"

Before she could finish the sentence, Spence was picking her up. More easily than she would have thought possible given she was not a small woman at five-eight and she had a lot of muscle. She opened her mouth to protest but it died in her throat. If him carrying her hurt this much, it was obvious she couldn't walk. He got to his feet as if she weighed no more than that stoat they'd seen. Cradling her carefully, he started toward the cave.

It was a strange feeling for her, this helplessness. She'd fought it all her life, vowing at an early age to never be that helpless sort of female. Or, for that matter, male, like the scared-of-his-own-shadow kid from her first computer class back in high school. She'd felt an odd sort of pride that she hadn't been as nervous as he'd been, and never had been. Thanks to her mom and dad, she had more faith in herself than that boy'd had.

But now she didn't seem to have the strength to fight that helpless feeling. Or maybe it was just because it was Spence and she knew that, in this, she could trust him with her life. Because when the chips were down, Spence Colton would come through. He always had, and he always would.

Hetty surrendered to the weakness she'd always fought. She didn't ever want to be seen as weak, by anyone. She wanted to be like her mother, tough, strong, bending but never breaking no matter what life threw at her. But that was one more thing; Spence would never hold this against her, or throw it back at her the next time they fought over… well, the only thing they ever fought over.

She let her head rest against his shoulder, taking what comfort she could from his strength, his heat. The pain from her leg did not lessen, but it seemed to matter less at the moment. That was a marvelous knack he had. She'd seen him calm others when something happened on a trek. He always managed to take the edge off a situation, no matter what it was. He was especially good with kids, which she'd always found appealing.

Come on. You find everything about him appealing, except the fact that every other woman seems to feel the same way.

She'd never minded competition. In fact, she thrived on it in many arenas. Except this one. The one she couldn't handle: competing for attention from the man who had once been the tangled-up teenager she'd tutored in high school. The kid who had had to fight so hard to do what other kids their age did easily. The kid who had lit up when she'd made that crucial suggestion one day years ago and it had worked.

And three days later, after he'd practiced the visualization idea with words and sounds over the weekend, he'd showed up at their session and given her a huge, fierce hug that had made her breath stop and her heart race. She had—

She snapped out of the hazy reverie when she realized they were at the cave entrance.

"I'll set you down here. You hang on to my arm and try using your good leg to slip through. Stop there until I get in, and then we'll pick a spot for you to get off that leg."

It took her a moment to process what he was saying. It made perfect sense. It should have been easy to understand. Was she in shock? God, was she bleeding out? Was that why her head was fuzzy?

It took all she had to accomplish the simple thing he'd asked of her. And when she was inside, she had to lean on the cave wall to stay upright. Just seconds later, Spence was there and sweeping her up into his arms again.

To her surprise, he walked straight back then cut right slightly. He must have had time to explore a little or else he remembered the layout of the cave from the last time they'd been there. Knowing him, it was probably the latter.

A large piece of rock jutted out from the wall and he went past it. Then he stopped and lowered her gently.

"Why…?" she began, but didn't have the energy to finish asking why all the way back here, away from what light was coming through the entrance.

"If somebody just looks in from the entrance, they won't see anything," he explained. With her current sluggishness, she didn't realize right away that she hadn't even gotten the question out, but he'd answered it anyway. As if he'd read her mind or something. And, for some reason, that gave her the strength to get out a complete thought this time.

"You think he could find it?" she asked, tamping down the apprehension that flared. "I mean we only found it that first time by accident."

"Depends on if they know the territory at all."

He didn't even look at her when he spoke, he was busy checking her wound. He loosened his belt around her leg. Even that made her clench her jaw. But there was something she needed to tell him.

"I don't think he does," she said. "I saw him, Spence."

He froze. Looked at her. She told him what little she knew, including about the color of his attire.

"Huh. You'd think somebody from here would know better," he said.

"Exactly what I was thinking."

"So maybe an import," he muttered as he shrugged his pack off. He dug into it, bringing out the red box that was his basic first-aid kit. He dug out what else he wanted, went back for one more thing, then, oddly, wrapped what looked like a wooden tongue depressor in gauze. He handed it to her.

"Bite down. This is going to hurt, and we don't want him to hear you."

"Think I'm going to scream?"

He gave her a solemn look. "I would."

She sighed. She'd had no room to talk, it had been her shocked cry, after all, that had drawn the shooter's attention. She had nobody to blame but herself for ending up lying here with that burning agony swirling out from her leg. But who wouldn't have done the same?

"I had reason, Spence," she said, rushing the words out. "There's a body out there, right by the waterfall."

He went still once more, this time in the act of using his knife—carefully sterilized with a wipe from the kit—to cut a bigger hole in her jeans so he could work on the wound. "He's already killed someone?"

"I don't think so. It looks like it's…been there a while. She. It's a woman. Half buried."

That information, that the body wasn't fresh, was apparently what he'd needed to shove the revelation into a compartment for later while he worked on the here and now. He'd always been good at that, too—putting things aside in order to tackle the present.

It turned out she did need the gauze-encased wood to clamp down on as he worked. The exit was the worst, and he used the one haemostatic sponge he had there to stop the worst of the bleeding. He used the kit's tourniquet up above the wound, a much better option than his belt. Then he dug out the roll of gauze and hoped there was enough.

When he was done, and the best bandage he could manage was in place, she let out an exhausted breath. The pain ebbed to a pulsing throb and she had to force herself to think.

"I don't think I can walk, not over the terrain here. And I know I couldn't keep up with you like this, even if I could walk."

"You're not even going to try," he said in a determined, decisive tone she'd only heard in tense situations. Situations where Spence did what was necessary. It was one of the things that had proved to her that the depth she'd first seen in him all those years ago was still there.

"I agree. So—"

"I slowed down the bleeding, but if you try walking, it'll be back to square one. You need medical attention."

It was as if he hadn't even heard her agree with him. Was he so used to her disagreeing with him he hadn't even noticed she wasn't? She spoke with more emphasis this time.

"I know that. So you'll have to go down past the lake until you can get a cell signal and let RTA know they need to get here ASAP."

He stopped with the debris from his work on her in his hand, which, at her words, had curled into a fist. "That's at least ten miles."

She gave him a puzzled look. A ten-mile hike in this wild country might be daunting to many, even most, but not to Spence. He did it for fun whenever he had a day off.

"I'm not leaving you alone here, unarmed, with a shooter out there. No way, Hetty, I'm just not."

Oh.

She felt heat rise to her cheeks, knew if they were out in the sun, it would show despite the darker tone of her skin. And if they were, she knew he'd notice. Mr. Sharp Eye never missed a thing. She turned her head instinctively, shielding her reaction to his words.

The movement shifted her balance, just slightly, but that was all it took to send a stabbing reminder through her leg. She winced, but managed not to cry out.

Spence's jaw tightened and he turned back to the first-aid kit.

He came up with a small paper packet of pills and a collapsed silicone circle. He tugged at the outer edge until it expanded into a small cup, then handed her the packet. "These should take the edge off. I'll go get some water for you to get them down."

Leave it to Spence to remember, even now, that she sometimes had trouble getting pills down. Then something else drove that out of her mind. "But he could still be there, watching that spot."

"I'll be careful." He hesitated then said, "And I need to go look at…what you found, anyway."

She should have known. Of course, he would. With a smothered sigh, she nodded. She looked at the pills then back at him.

"These won't make me groggy, will they?" That was the last thing she needed right now. She was having enough trouble keeping her act together, she didn't want to be drugged into more sluggishness.

"No, it's nonnarcotic. And like I said, it'll only take the edge off."

"That's all I need."

He gave her a smile that made her think of that moment in the plane when she'd threatened him with a knee applied to sensitive body parts and he'd laughed and said, "That's my girl."

And suddenly there was an ache inside her that almost surpassed the physical pain.

An ache that reminded her of just how long she'd been wishing that were true.

Chapter Twelve

It was hardly a waterfall, little more than you'd get from a
healthy faucet, but it was consistent, clean and cold. She'd
be able to get the pills down. Spence climbed the last few
feet slowly, carefully. He scrounged a broken branch off the
ground and tossed it ahead to see if it drew any fire from
their invisible hunter. Nothing.

The Midnight Sun wouldn't allow for the cover of full
darkness, but the tall trees made it seem darker than the
perpetual summer twilight normally would, so while he
could see, he was still on uneven ground and paid attention. Every couple of yards, he paused, listening carefully
as he approached the small, clear spot around the rockslide
that formed the path of the rivulet. Listening for any out-
of-the-ordinary sound.

Like somebody reloading a rifle.

He suppressed a shudder as the image of the bullet
wound in Hetty's leg slammed into his mind once more,
shoving aside all else. He'd never seen her hurt or injured
before, other than a sprained ankle she'd incurred playing
basketball in school. After a beautiful, leaping dunk shot,
she'd been jostled by an opposing player and come down
wrong. Being Hetty, she'd made them tape up the ankle

and gone back in to finish the game. Which they'd won, thanks to that shot of hers.

And during it all, she'd never let out a sound. She'd barely even winced. So that, if nothing else, told him the level of pain she was enduring now.

These won't make me groggy, will they?

Shot in the leg and she worried about that, when just about everybody else he knew would be asking for a large dose of groggy.

He scanned the ground around the small water flow and was starting to wonder if what she'd thought she'd seen had somehow been a trick of the light. If perhaps the trees had cast enough shadows in the everlasting twilight to make it seem as if—

And then he saw it himself. What she'd seen. *Who* she'd seen.

He swore under his breath.

The body was only partially buried, the head and arms— no, just one arm—were above ground. It was barely recognizable as a woman, and he was only guessing at that because what hair was left was long and wavy. Oddly, it also looked as if the tresses had once been spread out neatly, although now there were leaves and probably less benign things tangled in it. She'd been fed upon, which was hardly surprising out here.

He had to look away. He didn't think he was easily disturbed, but this did it. This desiccated corpse that looked as if it had been...arranged, got to him on more than one level. Then, as something belatedly registered, he glanced back, thinking he couldn't have seen what he thought he'd seen. But he had. The one arm that was above ground was the left. And encircling the bones of the left ring finger was a gaudy, huge diamond ring. Or at least something that was supposed to look like one.

The part of his brain that was still functioning was telling him the ring had to be fake. Because why else would whoever had put this woman here leave the diamond behind if it were real? If it was, the piece would be worth tens of thousands, and he just couldn't see a killer walking away from that. So whoever had left her here, with that ring, either hadn't known or hadn't cared.

Or…had put it there on purpose?

He gave a sharp shake of his head and yanked his gaze over to the calming trickle of the waterfall. It seemed pristine…untouched, but what wouldn't after that sight? No wonder Hetty had screamed. He almost had, and he'd known what to expect. Well, almost; he'd never seen a body like this, in this decomposed condition, but at least he'd known it was there. Thanks to poor Hetty.

He grabbed his cell phone. It might not get a signal here, but the camera still worked. Not for nothing did he have a sister and cousin in law enforcement, who often spoke of crime scene photos and how the sooner they were taken, the better. Obviously this poor woman had been here a while, but still… Besides, putting the phone between him and the ugly scene made looking at it a tiny bit easier.

After taking several images from several angles, he shoved the phone back in his pocket, went and took a long drink from the stream himself, then filled the cup and headed back to the cave. And wondered all the way if whoever was after them now had something to do with that corpse. Was he protecting this site, afraid if the body was found, so would he be? Had he chosen this place because of its remoteness?

Or were the two totally unconnected? Was it just a freak accident that had left a body half buried there? Was this anonymous gunman hunting them for some other nefarious reason? That didn't seem likely, as Spence could think of no reason for someone to shoot at him or Hetty, but he freely admitted he might not be thinking with total clarity.

He tried to go carefully, quietly, keeping hidden, but he was suddenly in a rush to get to Hetty. When he got back to the cave, he gave her the water and watched as she downed the pills. As soon as she had, she looked at him carefully.

"You found her."

"Yes."

"You agree it's…a woman?"

"I think so."

"How long do you suppose she's been there?"

He grimaced. "No idea. I think freezing temperatures affect…decomposition. And up until a couple of months ago, we were still getting three or four feet of snow up here."

Hetty lowered her eyes and he thought he saw her shudder. "It was…awful."

"Yes," he agreed softly. "Sometimes I don't know how my sister does what she does, or my cousin."

The thought he'd shoved aside while focused on the unsightly discovery came back to him now. The reality of what he'd been looking at, the dead body half buried on an Alaskan hillside, had made the memory of the Colton family tragedy fade, but now it came back. Hard.

His expression must have changed because she asked, "What?"

"I was just remembering…a family story." He hesitated, but decided it may be a good distraction. For her, from the pain and the shock, and for him, from the long night ahead alone with Hetty. "Did you know I had an aunt?"

Her brow wrinkled. "I remember your dad mentioning his sister who died, before they ever came here, before you were born. And Lakin told me that was the reason for the fishing trip with your dad and uncle."

"Aunt Caroline was the reason they left San Diego."

"That's quite a switch, from sunny San Diego to Alaska."

"They needed a big change." He paused, took a deep breath and went on. "Because in San Diego, my aunt and my grandparents were murdered."

Hetty let out a shocked gasp. "Spence," she said with a shake of her head. "I didn't know that."

"They don't talk about it much anymore."

"Who did it? Did they…ever catch him?"

"They did. His name was Jason Stevens. He was an obsessed fan of my aunt's."

"Fan? She was famous?"

"When she was still in high school, Caroline was…discovered, I guess they call it. She became a model and was very successful very fast. Did a lot of ads, until it seemed like her picture was everywhere. And with that came a lot of attention, not all of it good. Stevens stalked her for months, and she was a wreck over it, my dad says. But… their parents didn't take it seriously."

He had to stop for a moment. He'd never known his aunt, but he'd been very aware of the pain of his father and his uncle during the first few years of his own life, when they were trying to rebuild here in Alaska. Hetty, bless her, didn't push or prod, she simply waited, silently. Bracing himself, he went on.

"The police found his journal, and he'd been planning

this for over a year. His delusion was that Caroline was his girlfriend and her parents were keeping her away from him. The original plan was to break in, kill them and take her away with him. He got the first part done. He stabbed them to death in their own bed. Then he drugged Caroline, dressed her and started to carry her out of the house. But…she woke up."

"And she fought," Hetty said softly. "She was a Colton, so she fought."

It was odd, to feel a spark of warmth amid this shocking, sorry tale, but her words had done it. He was also a little puzzled that she hadn't yet asked why he was telling her all this. But now that he'd started, he kept on. Because if there was anyone he knew who would listen and understand, it was Hetty.

"Yes, she did. And he ended up strangling her to death. Then he put her on the living room couch, sat down beside her and arranged them in…a loving pose. Then he committed suicide with an overdose of what he'd drugged her with. Uncle Will and Eli found them."

Her eyes widened even further, reflecting what light there was. "No wonder Eli does what he does."

Spence nodded. "Took me a while to put the two together, but yeah."

"You weren't even born when all this happened."

"No. And they didn't talk about it, like I said."

"Too painful," she guessed. "I'm so sorry, Spence."

He shrugged. It wasn't burrowed as deep into his psyche as it was with his father, Uncle Will and Eli, who had been eight years old at the time. Mitchell had been barely five and Parker only a baby, so their experience was much like Spence's. But Eli had been older, and had been at the scene.

He used to think he could never imagine what it must have been like for his cousin to see those bodies.

Now he had a much clearer idea. He was going to carry the image of that woman out there for the rest of his life.

"Anyway," Spence went on, trying to shake it all off, "that's it. The press never quit on it, harassing the family, even showing up at Eli's school, so they finally packed it in and moved here."

"I'm glad about that part."

Hetty hadn't sounded like herself when she'd said it. In fact, she'd sounded almost shy. He wanted to interpret her words as she was glad he was there. But big as his ego was, he couldn't quite do it. And she went on so quickly, changing the subject, he was sure he was right.

"I wonder...do you think that woman out there might be someone authorities were looking for and never found?"

"Could be. That's what I was thinking, so I took some pictures." Her eyes widened and he hastened to explain. "Something I picked up from Kansas. They need a record of the scene."

She nodded in understanding and gave him a small smile. "Kansas taught you well."

"She's just always talked about not disturbing the scene if they find...someone dead."

That Hetty could have also died, had the assailant been a better shot, was something he didn't want to dwell on. He went over to where he'd dropped his backpack and dug for a couple of the emergency ration bars he always carried. There was a pack of twelve inside, which was enough to get them both through until somebody from RTA got to the site.

At least you didn't leave the pack in the shed, idiot. Spence sighed in frustration.

"What's wrong?" Hetty asked.

His anger at himself must have showed on his face.

"Nothing," he said sourly. "Other than the fact that I could have taken that guy out by now if I hadn't left the damned rifle in the shed." He doubted he'd ever forgive himself for that.

"There was no reason to expect...this."

He grimaced. "And what's that saying that's practically the state motto? Expect the unexpected?"

"'North to the Future' isn't doing it for you, huh?"

The grimace became a tight, wry half smile. "Not at the moment, no."

"We'll be fine," she said quietly. "RTA will be here in the morning, and we'll be back home by noon, I bet."

"Maybe."

"We'll probably hear them when they arrive. You know how sound carries up the hill out here."

"Yeah."

"Spence, stop blaming yourself. Frankly, I'm much happier waiting it out here than having you out there hunting something that can shoot back."

There was no doubting the genuine concern in her voice. He knew what he wanted to think, but quickly quashed it, telling himself it wasn't that she'd be worried about him, she just didn't like the idea of being left here alone, injured and pretty much immobilized. And who would?

He dug back into the pack and pulled out the emergency blanket. If it was just him, he wouldn't worry about it this time of year, in the shelter of the cave. But Hetty was hurt, and she'd lost enough blood she could get colder than normal, and faster. He also dug out the small pack of candles.

It might not get dark outside this time of year, but it was pretty dim in this protected corner of the cave.

"That's my boy," she said. He turned back sharply. "Always prepared."

As she echoed his earlier sentiment, his rattled brain rocketed to other circumstances where that might be an appropriate statement. Circumstances he'd never be in with Hetty, no matter how much he might want to be.

He managed a rather tight smile. Then he studied her for a moment. She looked a little better, the furrow on her forehead had smoothed out a bit. "Feeling better?"

She nodded. "Those pills did take the edge off." She looked at the things he'd brought over to where she was propped against one wall of the cave niche. "You're going to have to restock when we get back."

"Yeah." He always made sure the backpack was ready to go, and he personally tested everything in it himself, so he'd know exactly what he had to draw upon.

"When was the last time you did one of your survival jaunts?"

He didn't like her using the word survival at the moment, but answered simply. "Spring. But early, when it was still cold enough to really test things."

"You mean when it only gets down into the twenties instead of the teens?"

"Or negative numbers. I'm careful, not crazy."

She laughed then winced as if it had hurt, and all his amusement vanished. He was down on his knees beside her in an instant. "Hetty?"

"I'm all right," she said, although she sounded a tiny bit breathless. "I just…jostled it, I think." She glanced at the blanket. "I do think we may need that later, though."

We? He'd planned on putting it just over her tonight, but now that she'd said that—and once he got the delicious idea of snuggling with her under one blanket out of his head— he knew she had a point. The reflective blanket did reflect body heat, after all. That was the whole point of it, and so he should add his own heat, for her sake.

So he would find himself in the position he'd always longed for but never expected to have. Snuggled up to Hetty Amos, under a single blanket, in what dark there was, with practically zero chance of interruption. And imagining what might be happening if she wasn't hurt.

It was going to be a hell of a night.

Chapter Thirteen

"Talk to me," Hetty said, not liking this strange feeling that was overtaking her. Every little sound made her pulse kick up, which in turn made her oddly lightheaded, which then scared her even more.

She wasn't used to being scared. And telling herself she wasn't used to being shot, either, wasn't helping much.

"About what?" Spence asked, sounding wary.

"Anything. Everything. I just don't want to fixate on what happened when I can't seem to think straight."

"You were shot, Hetty. Of course you can't."

She was pretty sure Spence would be handling it better. She'd bet his brain wouldn't have disintegrated into turmoil, bouncing from here to there to over there, unable to settle on any one thought or idea.

"Talk about something else. Tell me about... I don't know, tell me about Gwen."

He blinked. At least, she thought he did; it was pretty dark back here, and he'd said he didn't want to light one of the candles unless they had to. But she hated that she couldn't see well enough to really read him, as she usually could.

Or thought she could.

"Uh...who?"

Despite everything, she almost laughed. "Gwendolyn Merchant? The woman so entranced with you she demanded you take her phone number?"

"Oh. Her."

Hetty couldn't deny the fact that his apparent inability to remember the woman's name had made her feel oddly better.

"She'd be crushed," she said, trying to make her tone light and teasing. "She thought you were entranced with her."

She was able to see him shrug then. "It's an act. It's always an act."

He'd never actually admitted that before and she felt further mollified by his admission. And before she thought—she seemed to be having trouble with that at the moment—she asked, "Why?"

"Protection."

She heard him suck in a sharp breath, and thought she heard a muttered oath, low and harsh. As if he hadn't meant to let that out and regretted that he had.

"From what?" she asked.

"Never mind."

"Sorry, you don't get to call that back."

The idea that Spence Colton thought he needed protection from anything was rather unsettling, and went entirely against the mask he usually presented. The flirting, the lightheartedness, the certainty verging on the edge of cockiness but with none of the obnoxious aspects. Which left her with one big question.

What could the brilliant, handsome Spence Colton need protection from?

His response to the question turned out to be total silence. He went back to the cave entrance periodically, she supposed to look and listen. Each time he returned and she asked, he shook his head to indicate there had been nothing to see or hear. But he still didn't speak.

She was starting to feel a little fuzzy-headed. She supposed a combination of it being well after midnight now and the chill starting to take effect. Plus that little fact that she'd been shot.

"You cold?"

Later, Hetty thought, she'd appreciate that it was concern for her that had made him break his self-imposed silence. But right now she was too busy realizing he was right.

"Yes," she said, barely suppressing a shiver.

He reached for the emergency blanket. The next thing she knew, he was lying next to her, arranging the blanket over them both. Loaning her his body heat. Her slightly dizzy mind wanted to romp off in ridiculous directions at that idea, so she bit her lip to remind herself to keep her thoughts to herself and her mouth shut.

She savored his warmth, only then realizing how cold she'd actually become.

"Thanks," she murmured.

"Mmm."

Nice, noncommittal response. They lapsed back into silence.

She didn't know how much time had passed when Spence finally spoke. Quietly, softly, soft enough that she could probably have slept through it, had she been asleep. But the sleep she'd assumed would be easy to come by seemed to have vanished the moment he had laid down and wrapped the blanket—and himself—around her.

"Do you remember," he whispered, "what I was like when you first started to tutor me?"

As if she could forget, even if it had been over a decade ago. "You haven't changed all that much," she said.

"I know. Always a smart-ass."

"I didn't mean that. I mean you still work hard, and when you find something that works for you, you run with it. You're brilliant. You just had to find a way to express that in terms the rest of the world could understand, and find a way to understand how they express things."

He'd gone very still. She didn't even think he was breathing for a moment. Finally, he said, in an almost awed tone, "You thought that? Back then?"

"I knew it," she said with a shrug she knew he'd feel even though he couldn't see it.

"You never made me feel stupid, like others did."

"Because I knew you weren't. I knew you weren't just a pretty face."

"I...played on that. The looks and the flirting, I mean. It was part of it." Another pause before he said, "That's what I meant about protection. It was the...façade, I guess. Shelter. The looks were just part of the act, part of the cocky wise-ass routine that kept people from seeing the real me. The stupid me I always thought I was until you showed me another way."

Hetty felt a fierce, aching tightness in her chest. She'd known he was grateful to her for pointing him in the direction that had enabled him to break free, but she hadn't known how much of his attitude was based in this. Beyond curious, she had to ask.

"And the flirting now?"

"Habit, I guess. And still a bit of that protection. Because it's obvious I'm not serious."

"You might want to rethink that," Hetty said dryly. "Because I'm pretty sure some of our clients thought you were serious."

"You saying I'm too good at it?" There was a touch of teasing in his tone.

"Too good for my comfort," she admitted.

He went utterly still again. "Why?"

She couldn't tell him the truth. She just couldn't. So she dodged. "It's uncomfortable to be around."

"It's not easy to do," he said. "Especially when one of the things it's covering up is…my real feelings. About somebody else. But I don't know how to act around a woman when the feelings are…real. I never have. So she has no idea."

It was her turn to go still. There was somebody else? Someone he had real, genuine feelings for? She couldn't stop herself from asking, "Who?"

"Somebody I've had a crush on for a long time." She heard his deep intake of breath. Felt his body tense, as if he were steeling himself for a blow. "Like since the eleventh grade."

Eleventh grade. When she had begun to tutor him. Surely, he wasn't saying…what she wished he was saying. It had to have been someone else.

"Where is she now?" she asked, trying for a merely curious tone.

Again there was a pause and a renewed tensing. And then he said it. "Right here."

Her breath slammed to a halt in her throat. She couldn't speak.

He went on. "In my arms. At last." And then the old,

smart-aleck Spence reappeared. "Of course, she didn't have much choice."

She swallowed. Gathered her nerve. Spared a second to think how it figured that they would reach this point here, in this remote place in this backcountry they both loved, trapped in a freaking cave, waiting for rescue. And then, knowing she had to at least match his courage, she said it.

"If she'd had a choice, she would have chosen this."

It was another silent moment, one in which she could still feel his tension. He raised up on one elbow before he said, tentatively, "Hetty? You...mean that?"

"I think...it's why I get snarky with you so often."

He reached out with his free hand, brushed the back of his fingers over her cheek. "I never knew. Never dared to even hope. And I was afraid I'd...ruin our friendship, so I really locked it down."

She looked up at him, able only to see a profile in the dim light. She thought she would have recognized him anyway, even if she hadn't known it was him next to her. Hadn't she memorized his face all those years ago? And he truly hadn't changed that much on the outside, either. His jaw stronger, more masculine, the line of him lean, having lost any lingering softness of youth.

"And I'm just me, and you were a Colton, the big name in town."

He let out a wry chuckle. "I love my family, and I'm proud of what they've built, who they've all become, but sometimes it's a pain in the backside."

She couldn't help smiling, widely. "It's only me. You can say ass."

The chuckle became a laugh this time. Then he dropped back down off his elbow and wrapped his arms around her again. "And that's another reason," he said, sounding both amused and delighted.

And genuine. More important to her than anything, there was no doubting the utter sincerity in his voice.

Spence Colton may have been a flirt in front of her countless times, but never had he ever given any of those women the authenticity and certainty he'd just given her.

Where they went from here, she didn't know. And right now she was too weary to think about it. It was simply enough to lie there, wrapped in his arms and the blanket that so nicely reflected their body heat back to them.

And imagine a night when they might generate an entirely different kind of body heat.

Chapter Fourteen

Spence was in the middle of a strange daze…half awake, half asleep. The asleep part of his brain was manufacturing a crazy dream in which the thunder of a running herd of moose somehow morphed into the steady thwap-thwap sound of a rotor blade.

A big rotor blade.

A helicopter.

The moment the sound registered in the half-awake part of his brain, he jolted upright. Hetty didn't wake, so he tried to move carefully, until he was clear and could make his way to the cave entrance.

He had to step out into the small clearing to get away from the echo from inside the cave walls. He scanned what sky he could see, much brighter now that it was nearly five in the morning and the sun that never set was higher in the sky.

Bless RTA, someone had to have rolled out the moment it was safe to fly by sight.

Spence could still hear the helicopter, but it sounded like it was down by the water. That made sense, if it was the RTA chopper, which was the only thing that made sense. And then he caught a glimpse as the bird rose and became visible above the trees downhill from him. He recognized the Bell Jet Ranger instantly, the RTA logo clear on the side, matching the one on the plane.

He ran back into the cave, smiling as he dug into his backpack.

"They're here," he said quickly when he realized Hetty was stirring, raising up on one elbow and looking toward him. "Don't know who's flying, but it's the RTA bird."

He grabbed the two things he needed and raced back outside. He turned on the small walkie-talkie. Used mainly for contact when they were working with a large group and more than one guide, for the guides to keep in touch if they were out of sightline, it didn't have the greatest range, but it might just reach the radio on the helicopter.

He held the walkie up to his mouth, keyed it and spoke, using his initials as his moniker, as usual.

"RTA bird, this is SC. Do you copy?"

Nothing but dead air. He waited until the helicopter made another circle, obviously scoping things out before making a landing. When it was at its closest point to him, he tried again. This time, the walkie-talkie crackled back.

"SC, this is RTA One." Spence had never been so relieved to hear his father's voice. "Your location?" Ryan Colton asked.

"Northwest of you. I'll fire a flare, but I don't think there's room for you to land up here."

"Fire."

He aimed the small flare gun he'd retrieved from the backpack upward, straight, for a more accurate pointer. He fired it, the little rocket soaring and trailing a stream of red smoke.

"Got it," his father said. A moment later, the helicopter was directly overhead, hovering. Spence waved widely. And this time the audio on the walkie-talkie was much clearer. "You're correct on the landing. You'll have to meet me back by the plane."

"Hetty's hurt, Dad." He started to explain then realized his father didn't know yet about the shooter. "And be on the lookout," he said sharply. "There was somebody out here either playing some kind of twisted game taking potshots, or trying to kill us."

"What?" His father's voice was harsh.

"No sign of him since last night, but be aware. You're armed?"

"Of course. Can you get her to where you beached?"

"I'll manage. We'll start now, but it'll be slow."

"And be careful," Dad said warningly.

"Absolutely."

On his way back he detoured momentarily to the site of the body, thought a moment longer about the idea that had struck him, then reached into his pocket for the little packet he'd grabbed. He crouched down beside the hand with the ring. If this was a mistake, he'd have to live with it, he thought.

When he was done he straightened, and headed quickly back uphill. When he got into the cave he found Hetty had struggled to her feet, although she was extremely wobbly. She tried to stand straight as he ran over to her, taking her arm to steady her.

"Take it easy," he said. "It's Dad, and he knows the situation. He can't land here, so we have to head back to the beach, by the plane."

She only nodded. She was trying to fold up the blanket, but he grabbed it and what was left of the four emergency ration bars he'd taken out, and stuffed it all into the pack. He'd straighten things out and restock the bag when they got to base. Or maybe the next day, after he'd had about twelve hours of sleep and time to recuperate from the terrifying fear of losing Hetty.

Once he had the backpack settled on his shoulders, he turned to look at Hetty. She was propping herself up against a cave wall, but, even so, looked far too unsteady for his comfort.

"Don't get mad at me…" he began.

"I've sworn off." She managed a smile, but it was a bit wobbly. "Temporarily anyway."

"Good. Because we need to get back to the beach ASAP, and you trying to walk is going to really slow us up." He didn't mention it could well start her bleeding again, and she'd already lost too much.

"I can—"

He cut her off. "I have no doubt you could, if you had to. But you don't have to, Hetty. You're not alone."

That was when he moved and, in one swift but very careful motion, picked her up in his arms, settling her against him as he had before.

"Spence, no," she protested. "From where I was shot to here is one thing, but all the way back—"

"Hush." He pushed away the errant thought that he would like to hush her by kissing her so hard and deep she couldn't talk. But this was hardly the time, and she was in no condition. And he was starting to wish he'd never let loose his feelings to her last night, because they seemed to think they now had free rein. "It'll be fine."

He knew it would be. She was no lightweight. She was only about four inches shorter than his own six feet, and she was fit, with lots of muscle, but now that getting her out of here and to medical help was within reach, he felt like he could run a marathon carrying her. He just had to hope the adrenaline pouring through him would last long enough to get her to the helicopter.

It was tough going, and having to make sure there was enough clearance between the trees to get her long-legged frame through without jostling her wound, made it even trickier. Plus he had to be alert to everything around them, just in case the shooter really was still around.

He didn't know how long it really took, but it seemed far too long before they broke clear of the tree line and he saw the RTA helicopter sitting in the clearing above the beach where the plane was tied off, just as they'd left it. And climbing out of the plane's cockpit was his father. As nimble as ever, Ryan Colton jumped from the portside float to the beach and headed toward them at a run.

When he reached them, Spence could see his father's expression was grim and angry. He'd obviously seen the mess in the cockpit, the bullet hole, the ripped-up control panel, broken dials and destroyed radio. But he took one look at Hetty and instantly his loving father was back.

"Don't you worry, Hetty. I radioed ahead to the trauma center and they're on standby for us. You'll be fine."

She managed to smile at the man who was acting more like doting parent than boss at present. "I'm okay. I just feel a little woozy, that's all."

Spence wanted to hold her the entire way, but it wasn't practical inside the 'copter. So they stretched her out on the second row of seats, secured her as best they could, and his father went back to the controls.

Dad glanced at him, gaze fastening on the cut on his forehead.

"I'm fine," he said before he could ask. "It's just a cut from the glass, I think."

"You'll need to strap in for takeoff," his father said with a nod toward the copilot's seat as he put the headset back on. Then he gave Spence a sideways look. "After we're airborne, you can get up to check on her every five minutes if you need to, but you buckle up the rest of the time."

"Yes, sir," Spence said, because when Ryan Colton gave an order in that tone, that's what you did. And he had to admit, he felt a little comforted when he watched his father's competent hands work so swiftly. He put on the copilot headset, but kept one ear clear so he could hear any sound from the back.

"Hey, it could have been worse," Dad joked, clearly trying to lighten things up. "You could have really crashed."

"With Hetty flying?" Spence said. "Not a chance."

"Good point. Okay then, you could be driving."

Spence gave a half-hearted laugh at his dad's obvious try at Alaskan humor—applicable because driving to a medical facility would be impossible due to the simple fact of no roads that didn't take them a hundred or more miles out of their way.

And hours of time Hetty might not have.

He'd noticed that there had been some fresh blood at the wound site when they'd put her down across the three seats that formed a bench in the back. Not a lot, but any was too much as far as he was concerned.

"Dad?" he said quietly. His father looked at him as the

rotor picked up speed and volume. Spence couldn't help the tightly wound tension in his voice when he added one word. "Hurry."

"All possible speed," Dad promised, and Spence knew he meant it. And it wasn't just because Hetty was a crucial part of RTA. She was, but she was also a part of the extended Colton family. And if there was one thing he was utterly positive about in life, it was that Coltons came through for family.

It was a lesson they'd learned the hard way.

Chapter Fifteen

As promised, staff at the trauma center was ready and waiting. There was no helipad per se, just a marked-off area in the parking lot. With his typical skill, Dad set the bird down so gently, Spence wasn't even positive they were down until the crew with the gurney started heading toward them.

They handled her as gently as he ordered them to. He caught Hetty watching him as he gave that order. She had an odd look on her face, and somehow he knew she was thinking of those hours last night when feelings they'd kept buried for over a decade had broken free. Once she was up and around, they would have to go there again, but for once he didn't dread what would surely be a talk with a capital T.

Hetty didn't hate him.

The moment when they wheeled her past those swinging doors and they closed after her, shutting him off from what would happen next, put him in mind of a million movie and TV scenes. In reality, he felt more than a bit nauseous, his gut churning as she disappeared. One of the staff asked if the cut on his forehead needed attention, but he said no. Nothing mattered right now but Hetty.

He stood there staring at those closed doors for what seemed like a long time. Then he started pacing. Dad appeared with a cup of hot coffee. He drank it for the jolt, if nothing else.

It seemed like forever before someone came out to talk to them. A weary-looking woman with the hospital cap holding back graying dark hair. "It missed the artery and there doesn't appear to be any damage to the femur. She got lucky there," she said, "but she's still lost a lot of blood. We're transfusing now."

"If you need more..." Spence began, but the doctor, whose name tag said "W. Masters" followed by some letters he had no idea the meaning of, shook her head.

"Not for her, but donations are always welcome at the blood center." It sounded like something she was saying by rote, but he supposed that was a reflexive, and normal, request for an ER doctor. "We found no pieces of the bullet, and cleaned out all the other debris that we found, which should hopefully prevent infection. We've placed a drain for now. We'll be moving her into the ICU. You won't be able to see her for a while, so see to yourself for the moment, Mr. Colton."

When she'd gone, his father put an arm around his shoulders.

"Come on, let's go outside. I think you need a bit of non-hospital-smelling air."

He couldn't deny that, but couldn't seem to remember how to move. Dad had to practically push him toward the doors. Once they were outside, he automatically sucked in a long, deep breath. He closed his eyes for a moment, as if that could make it all go away, but it only brought the image of Hetty, down and bleeding, vividly back into his mind.

"She's a tough girl, Spence. She'll be all right." Spence looked at his dad in time to see him grimace. "And in the meantime, I'm sure there will be some folks with badges who will need to talk with you eventually."

The rest of what had happened out there slammed back into him. "Dad… Hetty found a body out there."

Ryan Colton went rigidly still. "This guy killed somebody else?"

"Not unless he's been at it and gotten away with it for a while. That body was…not fresh."

Spence could almost see his dad processing, and thought he should get it all out before he had to spend what would probably be a couple of hours with the state troopers. So he quickly poured out the whole story. He watched his father frown at the news of the plane's engine losing power then smile briefly at Hetty, getting them down safely. Ryan frowned again hearing about the shots fired near the campsite, the plane's radio being taken out, the shots fired there, their escape, and finally what Hetty had seen in the moments before she'd been shot.

"She saw the guy?"

"At a distance, but yeah."

"Does he know she saw him?"

"I…don't know. I was…"

"Preoccupied with keeping her alive overnight. I get it, son." He looked past Spence suddenly, and when he turned to see what had caught his eye, Spence saw two men headed their way, one in uniform, one not.

Dad nodded slowly. "I see they've already notified the authorities."

"Gunshot wound, I think they have to."

"Probably," his father agreed, watching the two men approach.

"I was half expecting Eli," Spence said with a grimace.

"If they knew about the body, it probably would be him," Dad said.

Spence guessed he was right. Crimes didn't get much more major than murder, and as a lieutenant in the Major Crimes Unit of the Alaska Bureau of Investigation, his cousin Eli Colton, a big believer in being involved, had a lot of say in when and where he got assigned to cases. In fact, he wouldn't be surprised if the Colton name was what had netted them a two-person response instead of just the local in uniform.

"So once they find out…" he began then stopped as the men got nearer.

"We'll likely be seeing him," dad agreed.

The two men reached them and stopped. Both Spence and his father nodded to the one in the Shelby PD uniform. Bobby Reynolds was familiar to them both; they'd dealt with him on a few occasions back in Shelby. For him to be here now, he must have come in by air, maybe on a state agency bird. The man shoved a hand through his light brown hair and there was what appeared to be genuine concern in his face and voice when he spoke.

"How's your flygirl?"

"She's going to be fine," Spence said firmly.

Reynolds nodded then introduced the man in plain clothes as Detective Sam Barton, from the Alaska State Troopers. Since Alaska had no counties, there was no county sheriff to turn to, and the AST handled…well, almost everything.

"Mr. Colton, Mr. Colton…you're Eli's uncle and cousin?" Barton asked.

"Yes," Dad said.

"He's a good man," the investigator said.

"He is," Ryan confirmed.

Then Barton shifted his attention to Spence, but without, Spence noted, asking Dad to leave them alone. The Colton name again, he guessed.

"Obviously, we'll need some details about what happened up there," Barton said. He nodded toward the small park across the street, fairly empty at this early hour, although Spence knew it would fill up later as people rolled out to enjoy the predicted summer weather for the week. Of course, any of the locals could tell you weather predictions for the area were notoriously inaccurate and to be taken with a pound of salt. He remembered the day when it had been sunny in town, windy out on the sound and snowing up in the pass. None of which had been predicted.

They found an empty picnic table in the park and sat down.

"This guy had a rifle?" Barton asked.

"Yeah. High-power, I'd guess." He grimaced. "Didn't have time to dig out a spent round for you, but there's one in the cabin of the plane, somewhere in the back. And I can get you to a tree I think has another one buried deep."

Barton looked appreciative. "Learned from Eli, have you?"

"And my sister. She's on the SAR team."

"Kansas Colton. Stationed locally, right?"

"Yes."

"All right. Now, about the shooter—"

Spence nodded. "I never saw the guy, but Hetty got a glimpse of him right before he shot her. Probably why he shot her."

"We'll need to talk to Ms. Amos, of course—"

"When the doctors say you can," Spence said firmly.

The two men blinked. Exchanged glances. "Of course," Reynolds said.

Spence had the feeling they wouldn't stop short of applying a little pressure to those doctors if they felt they had to. So he'd just be darned sure he was around in case they tried.

"Any idea why he'd come after you? For that matter, which one was he after?"

"None. And he shot at both of us, as it happened. Maybe he just likes taking potshots at people. Or he decided that camp is his. Or that the whole hunting area is, and we trespassed. Or he hid something he didn't want found..."

His voice trailed off. He knew he had to tell them, and the sooner, the better, but that didn't make it any more pleasant. The two men waited, as if they sensed this would go more smoothly if they didn't push. He wasn't a suspect, after all.

"There's something else..." he began. "We found a body up there. One that's been there a while."

The two men went very still. "A body?"

Spence tried to remember the way both Eli and his sister talked about cases, when they did. Tried to give the kind of concise version they always managed.

"Appears to be a woman, long dark hair, mostly buried, but with her head and left arm above ground." He got out his phone and brought up the string of photos he'd taken. He picked the one that best showed the position and condition of the body and showed it to them. They went very still.

"Arranged," the one in plain clothes murmured.

"What I thought," Spence agreed.

Dad had gone stiffly still beside him. Rigid, in fact. Belatedly, it hit him. He looked at his father apologetically. "Sorry, Dad. I didn't think about—"

Ryan Colton let out an audible breath. "It's all right, son. I just wasn't prepared for that."

The two cops were looking at Dad with interest. "It's ancient family history," Spence said quickly. "Almost thirty years ago ancient."

Both men nodded then and he wondered how much of the Colton history was common knowledge around here. He'd never wondered that before, and he felt rather guilty that he'd so successfully put it out of his mind. True, he hadn't even been born yet, but it had shaped his father and older cousin, and he should be more aware.

"Is this connected to the shooter you encountered?" asked Barton.

"No idea. Like I said, it looked like she'd been there a while."

"What's that on her hand?" Reynolds asked, peering closely at the image on the phone.

"A fake, I'd guess," said Barton. "Nobody'd leave a real diamond that size behind."

Spence hesitated then reached into his pocket and brought out the small bag with the ring they were staring at in the photo. "I know removing evidence isn't good, but there were signs of recent animal predation in the vicinity, and I thought it would be better to have it than get there and find it's vanished into some rodent den or something."

The two law enforcement men stared at the bag. Barton reached out to take it, almost gingerly.

"I didn't touch it directly," Spence explained. "I used some sterile gauze that was in that bag, and it went right back in."

Because I used all the rest of that gauze on Hetty's leg.

"Look," he said abruptly, "I need to get back and see

how Hetty's doing. If you want to talk to me more, come on inside."

"We'll need a formal statement from both of you," Barton said, then, rubbing at his jaw, changed it to, "Two formal statements from both you and Ms. Amos."

"Right now," Spence insisted, "I need a formal statement from the doctor, saying she's going to be all right."

He didn't get that when they first went inside. There was no news yet, he was told, and to please take a seat. After a brief conversation with the woman who appeared to be in charge of the emergency intake, Barton led Spence over to a private meeting room. He went, after his father nodded at him encouragingly, saying he'd stay right there and interrupt with any word on Hetty.

The room was very small, a table with two chairs on each side, and not much else. Except a painting on one wall that looked to Spence to be of a spot along Thompson Pass. A spot he'd been to a time or two, he thought as he studied the piece. He wondered idly who had painted it as he sat down.

It didn't hit him until the two other men sat across from him that this was likely the private room where bad news got passed along. He suppressed a shiver, thinking about people who had probably had their lives upended in this room with word that their loved one or family member had not made it.

He shook it off and looked at Reynolds and Barton.

"You want this in chronological order or order of importance?" Not to him, of course. To him, Hetty was the most important, but he'd been around Eli and Kansas enough to know what these guys would consider important.

"Let's start with the as-it-happened version," Barton said. Spence walked them through it, from the engine shutting down, Hetty's skillful landing, them radioing for help, checking the area for any wildlife to be cautious around, setting up the campsite, even, embarrassedly, admitted he'd stupidly left his rifle in the storage shed, thinking he'd already checked for natural threats and he'd be right back anyway.

He'd never expected a human threat.

He went through the rest, ending with Dad's arrival, thinking that *We spent the night in the cave* was far too simple an explanation for what had really happened in those intervening hours.

"And you never saw the shooter?" Reynolds asked again.

"No. All I can tell you is what she told me." He went through Hetty's description of the man, including the possible scar that might not be a scar.

He didn't know how long they'd been sitting there, going over it again and yet again, before the door opened. Rapidly, without even a knock. His father was there, a look of pained worry on his face.

"Dad?" he asked, a little shakily as he got to his feet.

"She crashed, son. It's bad. They…don't know if she's going to make it."

Chapter Sixteen

Spence didn't think he'd ever heard the term "traumatic shock" before, and he certainly had never heard of "hypovolemic shock." He had heard Dr. Masters say something about an overwhelming inflammatory response, in turn causing acute respiratory distress, and heard about the possibility of something called MODS—multiple organ dysfunction…syndrome, he thought—but he wasn't really processing all the words.

All he was certain of was the doctor's grim expression and the words, *It doesn't look good right now.*

Even the woman's assurance that if Spence hadn't done what he'd done so quickly, this could have happened out in the cave and he would have had only a body to bring home, didn't help much.

"But she was…fine. Hurting, but fine," he finally said, feeling more than a little lost. And a lot guilty. How could he have left Hetty and gone off with the cops while she'd been fighting for her life? It didn't matter that she'd seemed fine when she'd gone in, she'd been shot and he should have stayed with her.

How had he not realized how seriously injured she was?

How could he have just watched them wheel her away and then take off for essentially a chat in the park?

"It happens," Dr. Masters said. "Adrenaline and other reactions to being under stress, as you two obviously were, can keep someone going beyond what we'd expect. But then when the crash comes…" She hesitated. "We'll have to watch her very carefully. She's in serious condition, Mr. Colton. The next several hours are critical."

"Can I see her? I…need to see her."

"Not just yet. When we get her settled in ICU with all the monitors we need, we'll let you know."

It wasn't until the doctor walked away that Spence realized his father was staring at him. He must have sounded as desperate as he felt.

"I know going through something like this is…intense," Dad said very quietly. "But…is there something else going on here, Spence?"

Like what? That we both confessed during the night that we've always had feelings for each other? Since eleventh grade? And now she's in there fighting for her life. Should I have kept my stupid mouth shut? I should have—

His father's arm around his shoulders cut off the runaway train of thought. An image from long ago, when he'd been a kid, flashed through his mind, of his father explaining why the Colton family motto was Believe.

Your aunt Caroline deserved to be believed, Spence, and because she wasn't, she ended up murdered, along with our parents. A high price to pay for a lesson we'll never forget. If you have a problem, if something's wrong, tell us. If you can't tell me or your mom, tell your uncle or aunt. And do it knowing we will first and foremost believe you.

He could talk to Mom about it. Maybe not Dad, who

seemed to be on a "When am I going to get grandchildren?" binge of late. And that was something Spence wasn't ready to deal with. He wasn't sure he ever would be. But then, he had been certain he could never be honest with Hetty, either, yet last night he had been.

He gave a shake of his head. It seemed much longer than mere hours since he'd finally admitted his feelings for Hetty.

He opened his mouth to speak but closed it again. They had been so wrapped up in the revelation that they'd both been hiding how they'd felt about each other for so long, they'd said nothing about where things would go from here. Nothing about future plans.

And now Hetty might not have a future.

"Later, Dad," he said finally. "When I'm sure she's going to be all right."

Because if she wasn't, there was no point. To anything.

"All right, son. Just know that we love you and whatever you decide, we're with you."

Spence wasn't sure he understood what his father meant, because there was no way he could know what had happened up in that cave. He shoved it aside for now, because only one thing mattered.

The ICU nurse was kind and gentle, but Spence suspected she could be tough as nails. He'd encountered the kind side first when she'd let him stay in the room with Hetty while she went about her business.

He found he could only watch Hetty for so long before he got twitchy because she wasn't moving. Hetty being still was a rare occurrence; she was always on the verge of motion. Seeing her lying motionless only pounded home to him how bad this really must be.

His mind was whirling as if it could make up for her stillness by racing in all directions at once. Was life really this unfair that it would take her away the moment they'd admitted the surface tension between them had always been just that, on the surface? That it had masked something else they'd both thought had to be kept hidden? So—what?—they realized it, admitted it, and then it was yanked away?

Or was it that they had to go through this? Was it that nothing less than some kind of near-death experience was what it took to blast through the decade-thick barrier they'd built between them, Spence mostly with flippancy, Hetty with biting sarcasm? Maybe it took this to shatter those two solid facades?

But why her? Why not him? Spencer wished it had been. Not because he thought he was tougher than she was—he wasn't at all sure of that—but because he hated to think of her in such pain. Hated to think of her hanging on the edge like this. He'd rather it was him than to be sitting there watching her like this.

He should have realized. He should have known how badly she was hurt, never mind that she'd kept saying she was all right. He should have known by the way she had opened up and talked, if nothing else. Hetty never did that. Not with him, anyway.

Had she known? Had she somehow realized this was going to turn bad on her? Was that why she'd opened up last night, why she'd admitted that he hadn't been the only one feeling attraction since all the way back in high school?

That idea jabbed at him worst of all. Why wouldn't she have told him if she was feeling that bad? He would have figured out a way to get her out of there sooner if he'd known she was going to crash like this. Somehow. Even if he'd had to carry her every step of the way.

Spence would have sworn the clock over the door had somehow been piped through a loudspeaker because he could hear every ticked second as if it echoed off the walls. Every second that went by that she didn't move, didn't wake up. The nurse glanced at him now and then, smiling in understanding, and he wondered how she could stand this kind of work. People weren't nearly appreciative enough of individuals in this profession, until it came to hellish times like this.

He'd muted his phone an hour ago, when he'd first come in to sit at her bedside. Out of the need for distraction he pulled it out and saw a screen full of missed calls and texts. He knew Hetty's brother Troy was out on an oil rig so he wasn't surprised that there wasn't anything from him. Every other sibling she had, which meant five, had all texted. Then there was Dad, checking back in, and Mom, saying she'd be there in an hour. Hetty's mom, who was out of town, had left a voice message saying she was on her way back. His cousin Lakin, who was very close to Hetty, had also texted she was on her way.

And at the end of the list, a brief text from his cousin Eli, only saying he'd see him soon. So he probably had been assigned the case of the body they'd found. Something Spence was having a little trouble caring about at the moment.

A quiet whisper of his name came from the doorway and he looked up to see Parker standing there. He got up and walked over to him, and they stepped outside the room, although Spence made sure he was standing where he could still see her.

"How is she?"

"Not great." He couldn't help the grim tone in his voice.

"She's as tough as she needs to be, Spence. She'll pull through."

She has to. She just has to.

He didn't say it aloud, afraid it would come out as nothing less than a whine.

"Let me know if anything changes, will you?" Parker asked. "I'm going to head out with Chuck to see what can be done about the plane."

"Okay." Then, as his brain woke up to what his cousin had actually said—that he and the RTA mechanic were going to the campsite where it had all happened—he added sharply, "Hey, wait, we don't know if that guy is still out there."

Parker's mouth quirked. "Aw, cuz, you care."

Something hot and sharp welled up inside him. "Don't joke around when Hetty's lying in there possibly dying."

Parker looked startled then thoughtful. "Well, well," he murmured.

"What's that supposed to mean?"

"Nothing," his cousin said almost cheerfully. He turned to go then looked back. "Except it's about time."

Spence stared after his cousin. What was *that* supposed to mean? And when had that become the question of the day?

For a moment he just stood there, feeling a little stunned. Was he wearing a freaking sign or something? First Dad, hinting that he'd known something was brewing. Now Parker, acting like he'd known all along that all the sniping and poking at each other was a cover.

He let out a compressed breath, shoved all that aside, too, and went back into the room where the only thing that really mattered right now lay so very, very still.

Chapter Seventeen

Spence had lost track of who all had come and gone. He'd vacated his spot for Hetty's family, but not for just friends. All of the siblings except Troy had already been, he thought, but with seven total, he could be wrong. He hadn't had much, if any, sleep since things had gotten bad.

He was back in the almost-comfortable reclining chair next to her bed, dozing in and out, when he heard the nurse talking to someone fairly close by.

"—and he hasn't left her side since. It's actually very sweet," the nurse was saying to whoever it was.

He opened groggy eyes to look, and felt a jolt when he realized it was her mother. He swung his legs over and got to his feet, although it took him a moment to steady himself.

He was startled when the petite woman came straight to him and clasped both his hands in hers.

"Thank you, Spence."

He blinked. "For what?" *Taking her out where she got shot? For assuming she was going to be okay and deciding to stick the night out up there instead of carrying her down to somewhere Dad could have picked her up even at night?*

"For saving her and getting her here alive."

"Should have gotten her here sooner," he said gruffly, unable to meet her eyes.

"But the doctor said this didn't happen until after she was here. It's not your fault."

"It is. I'm the one who thought she'd be okay once the bleeding stopped. But she lost more than I realized and I—"

"Spence, stop. You're the one who stopped that bleeding, or she would have died out there. She wouldn't have even had the chance to fight."

He should have protested, should have explained exactly how he'd been stupid about it, not realizing how severely injured she'd actually been. But when Hetty's mother leaned up and planted a kiss on his cheek, he couldn't say a single word.

She then rushed over to Hetty's bedside, taking her daughter's hand in hers gently. He knew she was close to all her kids—all seven of them—but guessed there was a special, different kind of bond with the only girl. He remembered when Hetty's father, Charles Amos, had died of a fast-moving cancer. He had been an executive with an oil company where he had started out working the same job his son Troy now had on the oil rigs. His death had left Hetty's mother with seven kids to finish raising, but she'd never faltered.

He watched the two for a moment then realized he should probably leave them some privacy. He stepped out into the hallway and leaned wearily back against the wall. So wearily that the ICU nurse even paused to ask if he was all right.

"I'm all right as long as she is," he said with a nod toward the room behind him.

When Mrs. Amos came out some time later, he'd finally

sat down on one of the benches outside Hetty's room. She took a seat beside him, reached out and laid a hand over his. He looked down at them, so tired, he caught himself comparing skin tone, how Hetty's was somewhere in between his and her mother's. But the green eyes? They were the forever gift from Charles Amos, and he wondered what it was like to see that both loving and painful reminder every time you looked in a mirror.

When Mrs. Amos spoke, it was with quiet certainty. "That old saying about hindsight being twenty-twenty is true, you know. You had no way of knowing this could happen. The blame lies squarely on the predator who did this, not you."

"I still should have—"

He stopped when her mother shook her head. Because you just didn't argue with this matriarch. "No. You did everything you could and should have. And you've stayed with her, by her side, through it all. My only girl, our treasure, has a chance, thanks to you, and your father." She paused then gave Spence an odd sort of smile. "You've been a big part of her life for so long, I'm not surprised you'd be the one to help her through this."

When she'd gone back to her daughter, Spence sat running those last words through his weary mind over and over again, wondering if there was some deeper meaning there.

He should leave, he belatedly realized. Her mother was there now, she didn't need him. And when she had needed him, he'd completely missed how bad things really were and she'd nearly died because of it. Because, when they'd been huddled under that survival blanket last night, all he could think of was her, how good she felt and how much better he felt after finally letting out the secret he'd carried all these years.

And how amazing it had felt to hear her admit to pretty much the same thing. All those times when she'd jabbed at him, when she'd sniped at him, it had been for the same reason he'd always flirted with clients or other women in front of her; to hide the truth. They'd been playing this silly game, each of them hiding their feelings behind differing masks, until fate had stepped in and slapped them both upside the head.

"Wake up, Hetty," he whispered to the momentarily empty hallway. "You've got to wake up."

WHEN HETTY FIRST heard the low hum of…something, she thought… She wasn't sure what she thought. It didn't sound like her plane, and she wouldn't have been sleeping if it was. But then she remembered that jolt of adrenaline when the engine had died…then the shots. The searing agony of the bullet tearing through her flesh. Her next thought was that she had died and this was what it smelled like. That startled her into opening her eyes.

She had to blink several times against the unexpected brightness. She had the fleeting notion that this was some kind of waiting room where you went after you died. Or maybe when you were in the process of dying.

But then there was movement and a moment later she was looking up into Spence's face. Still groggy, she was struck with the horrible fear that he was dead, too. Had the shooter gotten him? Had he been hurt and she hadn't known? Her pulse kicked up and suddenly she was a bit more awake.

"Hey," he whispered. "Welcome back."

"I...what? Where?"

"Easy," Spence said soothingly. "We're in Wasilla. Do you remember my dad coming for us?"

"I..." She scrunched her eyes closed then opened them again, determinedly shoving back at that groggy feeling. "Yes," she said.

And she did remember lying across the back seats of the RTA helo, held in place by seat belts. Looking up at the sky as they'd wheeled her into the emergency room. Most of all, she remembered the look on Spence's face when they'd gone through those swinging doors, leaving him on the other side. And that was about the last thing she remembered.

The rest, the before part, came back to her in a rush now: last night huddled in the cave, the things they'd said, the things they'd finally admitted. She would have probably felt her cheeks heat if another question hadn't arisen almost immediately.

"How long?"

"You've been pretty out of it for almost twenty-four hours. It's Tuesday morning."

She frowned. "Why? Did they drug me? I wasn't feeling that bad, did they have to—"

She stopped abruptly when Spence reached out and cupped her cheek. Yesterday—no, two days ago apparently—that would have been unthinkable. Now, it was... She wasn't sure what it was. Other than it felt good.

As she lay there looking up at him, she saw an odd sheen in his deep blue eyes. Tears? Why on earth would Spence Colton be tearing up?

He reached down and pressed a button on a cord that ran along the bed rail before he looked at her and said, "You crashed, Hetty. Pretty hard. Traumatic shock, they called it. From what they said, I guess once the adrenaline ebbed away, once you didn't have to fight anymore, your body finally realized you weren't doing so great."

"Oh."

She didn't know what else to say. So she simply looked at Spence's handsome face and, for the first time since they'd been kids, allowed herself to truly appreciate his good looks. Looks she had always had to pretend to assess scornfully as the major tool he used to entrance clients.

Words came back to her then, in his voice, as he'd said them that night in the cave.

The looks were just part of the act, part of the cocky wise-ass routine that kept people from seeing the real me. The stupid me I always thought I was until you showed me another way.

She had never realized he'd thought himself stupid. Perhaps because she knew better, because she'd dealt with that agile mind so closely during those tutoring sessions. She'd seen the quickness of his thinking, the way he solved puzzles, the way complex mathematical problems never fazed him, the way he designed things that would actually work simply because he liked doing it.

Anything that didn't involve traditional reading, he whizzed through. This was far from the first time that she was grateful for the study she'd read that had suggested a way to use that visual acuity of his, that design ability, and relate it to the kind of language and writing the majority of the world used.

The memory that shot into her mind then was the day he'd come back for a session after they'd started using that technique and thrown his arms around her in a thank-you that was nothing less than joyous. Maybe because that was the way he was looking at her now. And that alone told her how serious these last hours she wasn't even aware of must have been.

"Thank you for getting me out of there," she said, aware her throat was a little sore and wondering if she'd had some kind of tube rammed down her throat at some point. She'd ask, later. The doctor, she decided, since she didn't really want Spence to have to tell her about the worst of it.

"Thank Dad, he did the flying."

"But you did the heavy lifting," she said, wishing now she hadn't been hurting quite so much so she could remember better how it had felt to have this man carrying her. But all she remembered was how steady his pace had been, how careful he'd been not to jostle her, how he'd held her as if she were some precious thing he hadn't dared drop.

"You're not heavy." A flash of the old Spence grin warmed her. "It's just all that muscle, girl."

A woman in scrubs came in, quickly rushing to her bedside, saying how glad she was to see her awake. Spence started to move aside, and instinctively Hetty grabbed his hand. She didn't want him to go.

"She needs to check some things," he said soothingly. "And I need to call your mom. She went to get some rest. And text Troy. And the rest of your family, who've all been here, several times. My family, too. Everybody was worried."

She nodded, feeling a little tired as it started to register just how bad it must have been, to pull everyone here. It might only be a hundred and ten miles as the helicopter flew from Shelby to Wasilla, but it was about two and a half times that if you tried to drive. And her mother had been in Seattle with friends, taking a well-earned and long-delayed vacation.

She watched him go, phone in hand, as he left the room.

"That boy," the woman beside her said with a smile as she made notes from the monitor readings at the head of the bed, "has not left your side since you were moved in here. He gave your mom some space, but nobody else. He was a better guard dog than my German shepherd. He must love you a lot."

Hetty felt her pulse leap at those last words, and the nurse laughed as it registered on the monitor.

"He'd kick-start my pulse, too, honey, but he's only got eyes for you."

No matter how the woman poked and prodded, Hetty didn't feel much of anything after that.

Chapter Eighteen

Hetty didn't realize she'd dozed off again—which was irritating in itself, since she had been lying there for a day and a half and thought she should be feeling better—until she opened her eyes to see Lakin Colton standing there. The woman who was the office manager at RTA and also her brother Troy's girlfriend since elementary school, was looking down at her with obvious worry in her warm brown eyes.

"Hi," she said with the best reassuring smile she could manage. She realized she was feeling a bit better, so she had to reluctantly admit that the sleep Spence had kept urging her to get was doing some good.

"I've been so horribly worried," Lakin admitted. "I was afraid we were going to lose you."

"I'm too stubborn," Hetty said, keeping that smile going.

"I'm glad," the younger woman said. "I'd be lost without you. We girls are outnumbered at RTA. All those Colton boys."

Yes, those Colton boys. Hetty had to hide her reaction to the observation. Until she and Spence had a chance to talk about the changes that had—she hoped—happened that night in the cave, she didn't want to sharpen the already-too-perceptive gazes of said Colton males by saying anything that would start them prodding Spence for answers.

"Four of them, three of us counting Kansas," Hetty said. "That makes us pretty much even."

Lakin was smiling now. "You would know. You're the one girl among six Amos boys, and you still rule."

Hetty laughed at that. She held her own as the middle child of seven and the only girl, but rule? She didn't think so. "They might dispute that."

"Troy wouldn't. He was really worried about you, too. I've never heard him so upset about being stuck out on the rig."

"Well, he should be more upset about leaving you alone for months at a time," Hetty said firmly.

Lakin might be reluctant to criticize him, but Troy was Hetty's little brother—well, the first of the three younger ones anyway, which balanced out the three older ones—and she had the right and felt no hesitation. She knew Lakin loved Troy, and thought that he really did love her back, but if he didn't start getting his head in the game and paying more attention to her rather than assuming she would always be there waiting, he was going to blow it.

Funny how easy it was to fix her brother's situation, but how long it had taken to address hers with Spence. Assuming, of course, that they had. He'd been reluctant to talk about it while she was in here, and she understood because there was always somebody around, hovering, and she didn't like the idea of strangers listening in on that particular discussion, either. Or family, for that matter. At least not until they'd worked it all out between themselves.

Although she had to admit she was starting to wonder if maybe she'd jumped the gun a little. Maybe that night had been a moment of weakness Spence regretted now. Maybe he wanted to go back to their old, sparring ways, keeping some distance between them at all times.

Lakin looked a little embarrassed at her words and Hetty wondered if it was because she'd had a similar thought. "I don't want you two breaking up," she said firmly. "I've got my heart set on having you as a sister, Lakin Colton."

"I'd like that," Lakin said almost shyly. "I love my family, but I love yours, too. And I'd like to see us all…connected, you know?"

"Now that," Hetty said, thinking of the seven Amos siblings related to the four Coltons, "would be an amazing family."

After Lakin left a little while later, Hetty thought she would love to see this woman who was a dear friend have that kind of combined family behind her. She was aware of the fact that Lakin, abandoned by her biological parents, had been left at a local grocery store.

She'd been given to a foster family, but when Sasha Colton, Will's wife, had encountered her, she had instantly fallen for the bright-eyed, intelligent child. They'd taken her in, and all three of the Colton boys had promptly followed suit, doting on the endearing, smart newcomer who'd quickly returned the favor by adoring her new big brothers. Hetty suspected that Lakin barely even remembered she wasn't a Colton by birth, and that the rest of the Coltons rarely thought of it, either.

The rest of us just got born. You got chosen.

Hetty remembered Lakin telling her about those words, spoken to her at a young age by her ten-years-older brother Eli. Words that had made her feel so special that she had let down the last of her barriers and fully become a Colton.

Become a Colton.

Sometimes Hetty felt like one simply because she was an integral part of RTA, but also because the entire Colton family, from Will and Sasha and Ryan and Abby to all the cousins, had made her feel that way. They were a tightly knit bunch, in some ways tighter than her own spread-out clan.

And now I know why.

The story Spence had told her of the slaughter of his aunt and grandparents had chilled her beyond even the worst Alaskan weather. She couldn't imagine having to deal with something like that. Even though Spence hadn't yet been born, it had to have affected him indirectly given the devastation it had wrought on his family.

And that story had made her appreciate the senior Coltons even more than she already had, simply because of the courage it had taken to relocate and build the entirely new and different and rock-solid life they had. Which included her, since she had the life she had—the life doing what she loved most—because of them, because they'd been willing to take a chance on a young inexperienced pilot.

She had, in part, Lakin to thank for that, for she knew her friend had pushed Will to take that chance. Which had made her, in turn, utterly determined to make sure they didn't regret it.

You could have really crashed.

With Hetty flying? Not a chance.

She doubted Spence and his dad realized she'd heard them. But she had, and it had done more to ease her nerves than anything short of knowing rescue had arrived.

And that Spence had said it was the most soothing balm of all.

THERE WEREN'T MANY men who could make Spence feel undersized, but his cousin Eli was one of them. He didn't know if it was that the guy was a couple of inches taller than his own six feet, that he was so strong and broad-shouldered, or simply that air of authority he carried around. With good reason, given his position in the Alaska Bureau of Investigation's Major Crimes Unit.

"Landed the case, huh?" he asked when he first saw Eli in the hospital hallway.

"Never mind that yet," Eli said, his eyes warm with obvious genuine concern. "How's Hetty?"

Points for that, cuz. Eli wasn't part of RTA, and although they'd never discussed it, Spence suspected the fact that he'd been with his father when they'd found the body of Caroline Colton and her killer had shaped his future. But that didn't mean his cousin didn't care about the family business, and he knew Hetty.

"She's going to be okay," he said firmly, as if the more confidently he said it would make it true. Although now, three days after those doors had swung shut on him and they'd taken her away, he really did believe it. She'd stabilized, they told him, and would be moving out of the ICU this afternoon. "They're going to move her into a regular room later today."

Eli let out a long breath then nodded. "Good." Then, visibly, he settled into business. "Thanks for thinking to take those pictures. And even though our lab guys are finicky and don't like anybody touching their evidence, I think you made the right call on the ring. I've been up there now, and the scene has already changed a little, likely from those animals you recognized were around."

Spence grimaced. The image of the dead woman was

going to be one he'd probably carry forever. "Any idea who she...was?"

"Not yet. We're checking missing persons' reports, but no hits so far, and we can't assume she was a local."

"But it was a murder." He didn't really have any doubts, but he needed to hear it from the man who would know.

"Not much doubt about that. They've moved the body to the forensics lab. Montgomery jumped at the case, and he's good. Even if he does have a thing for your sister."

Spence blinked. "Scott's got a thing for Kansas?"

"Definitely." Eli grinned. "And it pays off for me, because if I need something in a hurry or after hours, he's always willing. Anyway, they're running DNA, but no definitive results yet."

Eli shifted subjects, a signal Spence recognized as meaning he'd shared all he could on the body they'd found.

"Locals have any idea on the shooter?"

Spence shook his head. "Theories range from some hunter who misfired but knew Hetty saw him so decided to take us out to just some random nutcase."

"Nothing connected to the clients who canceled?"

Spence blinked. That, he had to admit, had not occurred to him. Leave it to Eli. "I...don't know. I don't know if they've even considered that yet."

Eli gave a one-shouldered shrug. "Just a thought."

"I'll ask."

Could it be? Could the shooter have maybe been after the newlyweds, and shot at them by mistake, not knowing the Greshams had canceled at the last minute? Had this not been some random hunter run amok, but a...a hitman or something? Surely, he'd have known what his targets looked like. Or had he just assumed, at that distance, and based on location? But then, how had he even known where they were going?

So many questions tumbled through Spence's mind, it was a little dizzying. And he found himself staring at his cousin.

"What?" Eli asked.

"How do you...do it? What you do, I mean?" He realized when he said it that Eli might think he meant the kind of work he did, especially after being there when their aunt had been found. So he quickly added, "Start at the end and work back, I mean, when there are so many directions it could go in?"

Eli smiled widely. "Leave it to you to put it in a nutshell. That's exactly what it is, a lot of the time. Start with the results of the crime and work backward. And yeah, it means a lot of dead ends sometimes." Another shrug, as if it were nothing instead of a crucial part of civilized life. "Process of elimination."

"I'm glad we have people like you out there," Spence said, meaning it.

But that was not what lingered in Spence's mind after his cousin had left. It was the idea that both terrified and thrilled him at the same time.

The idea that he and Hetty might have been mistaken for newlyweds.

Chapter Nineteen

"When do I get out of here?"

Hetty didn't mean to sound sharp, but she was about out of patience. She hated being cooped up here, hated the constant interruptions as someone checked on her, or made noise as they checked on someone else, or any of the other multitude of interruptions. She'd been spoiled, used to being in control, used to her quiet environment at home. The move out of the ICU was an improvement on a couple of fronts, noise among them, but she still wanted out as soon as possible.

The only good thing about this whole mess was Spence. He seemed to spend more time here than not, even though she knew there were clients booked for the rest of the summer. *Clients*, she thought with a sour twist of her mouth, *she should be flying*.

And that was the thought at the top of her mind when Spence came back into the room.

"Do they know what happened with the plane?" she demanded before anything else. He had told her his dad and Chuck were practically taking the thing apart to find out what had happened.

He didn't look startled at the abrupt question, or the lack

of greeting. She wondered if that was because she got like that when she was intent on something and he was used to it. She had a temper, she knew, and after three days in this place, it was a bit close to the surface.

No, he didn't look startled, but he did look a bit uncomfortable. "Spence?"

He let out an audible breath and said, in a tone so neutral it had to be intentional, "They have an idea, but it's not confirmed yet."

"I'm already tired of that phrase, whether it's about the plane, the shooter or when I'm getting out of here."

"You've always been a yes-or-no kind of person," Spence said dryly.

"If that means I don't take well to stalling, then yes."

"In this case, it's simple truth. They're looking at everything, and that takes time. And that," he added with that upward quirk of his mouth that used to irritate her but now seemed...charming, "applies to all three of your questions."

She made a face at him, one that had always made him laugh back in school, because she didn't want him to think she was upset with him rather than just the circumstances. All of them. She thought she saw him smother a laugh.

"I did talk to Eli, though," he said.

That caught her attention. "You did?"

He nodded. "He stopped by to see how you were. Your brothers were still here, so he said to just tell you hello and to get out of here soon."

"Well, I'm with him on that," she said the words heartfelt. "But does that mean he did get assigned to investigate...the body?"

Spence nodded. "They haven't identified her, or the manner of death yet. They moved the body to their lab and will have one of their best people working on it."

"But she was murdered, right? The way she was...arranged..." She suppressed a shudder.

"He thinks so."

She had the feeling there was something more, something he wasn't saying, but if it was something Eli had told him to keep in confidence, that was what he would do. Spence Colton was a man of his word. He would never break a promise. Or a vow—

Her thought was abruptly cut off when two people came through the door. Not hospital staff, as she would have expected, but two people she didn't recognize, at least until Spence greeted the first one in, a man in a pair of khaki pants and a casual jacket over a dress shirt. When she heard his voice, she realized he was the detective who had questioned her right after she'd awakened, the one who was working the case of their shooter. She'd still been a bit foggy then, so it took her a moment to place him.

A rather shy-looking woman in a pair of baggy jeans and a loose, flowing blouse in an almost Hawaiian print followed him in. She carried a small case of some kind, but the sketchpad in her other hand told Hetty why she was there. Spence had mentioned they wanted to try to do a sketch of the man she'd glimpsed, and had promised they understood it had only been a glimpse and at some distance.

"We usually do this at the station," Detective Barton said. "We've got a computer that does it, but frankly, I think Amy here is better."

The woman smiled. "Sometimes humans are better at humans." Then, to Hetty, she said, "I'm glad you're feeling well enough to do this now."

"So am I," she said fervently.

Hetty found herself oddly distracted after Spence had bowed out and left the room, and had to make herself focus on the task. She had been sure this would be pointless, but the artist asked some either/or questions that had her realizing she might have noticed more than she'd thought.

After the artist had finalized the sketch, and Hetty had said that was the best she could do—it didn't look like anybody she'd recognize if she saw him again, but the hair was right—Detective Barton asked her some other questions, mostly about the weapon the man had used.

"We know the caliber fit a 6.5mm Creedmoor from the rounds we recovered at the site…" he began.

That surprised her. She hadn't realized they'd gone back there already. But then, she'd barely realized how much time had passed, she'd been so completely out of it. He went on.

"That's a common sniper round. Causes less recoil, and the trajectory—" He cut himself off. "Sorry, that's not what you need to think about. Think about the weapon itself."

She closed her eyes for a moment, trying to replay that moment in her mind. "All I know is it looked all black. Not a wood stock. And it had some kind of optical sight. But that's all I could see."

Barton nodded. "All right."

"You're sure he's gone?"

The man nodded. "We did a full sweep of the area before we went in to gather evidence."

"One round hit the plane," she said. "He almost hit Spence." Just saying it gave her a little chill. And not just because if he'd also been hurt, they both could well have died out there.

The man nodded. "Your partner told us about that one, so we got that." *Your partner...* She wasn't sure how she felt about that term. "Guy did a number on the electronics there, didn't he."

It wasn't really a question, so she only nodded. She wondered how they were going to get the plane back from the lake. Wondered why there had been a problem in the first place.

"But that was after. It doesn't explain what happened to make the engine quit in the first place."

The detective grimaced. "It appears the fuel pump was tampered with."

Her brow creased. "The fuel pump? But that wouldn't kill the engine, not in that plane."

"So I was told, by your partner." *That word again.* "He said the pump is only for extra juice on takeoff, landing, and pushing for altitude, because of the location of the fuel tanks, in the wings."

Hetty nodded. "It's a high-wing plane, the fuel is gravity fed."

"Apparently our suspect didn't realize that, any more than I did," Barton said rather ruefully. "But the theory is whatever he did to mess with the pump eventually shifted and blocked the fuel line."

A sudden memory shot into her mind and her pulse kicked up. "You need to go talk to Jake, the teenager who works down at the RTA dock. He mentioned right before we left that there had been some guy down looking at the plane."

The detective went still. "Did he now," he said quietly, obviously seizing on the idea.

"He thought it was just some curious tourist," Hetty explained. "And all my preflight checks were fine, so I didn't think anything more about it."

"We'll get right on that," Barton assured her. "Anything else?"

"I don't think so," Hetty said, feeling as if she had scraped the very bottom of her memory bank.

"All right. Thank you."

He turned to the artist, who nodded to indicate she was done. And as he moved, his jacket slid back enough for Hetty to see the sidearm he wore on his belt. And suddenly something else floated up from that bottom. A brief but vivid flash of memory. And she felt she needed to say it, even if it might be pointless.

"I don't know if this means anything, I'm not that experienced with weapons, but..."

"Go ahead, please," Barton said.

"When I saw him, he was holding the rifle in his left hand."

Again the man went still. And then he smiled at her. "Well, now, that may just turn out to be very helpful. Get well, Ms. Amos."

"Working on it," she said, feeling quietly pleased that she might have actually helped to find the man who had put her here in this hospital bed.

Chapter Twenty

Spence was yawning as he stepped outside, but it cut off with an awkward cough when he realized he'd almost walked into his father's fist, raised to knock on his door.

He'd come home for a shower, a change of clothes, had almost dived into his bed for a nap, but told himself the shut-eye he'd caught in the reclining chair at Hetty's bedside would have to be enough. He needed to get back there. He didn't like being gone even this long. He'd only left because she'd had a physical therapy session. She was working hard at getting back on her feet, but she was going to be needing those crutches they'd given her for a while, no matter how much she obviously hated them.

Belatedly, he realized his father was holding out a bright blue mug with the familiar Roaster's logo. The café down on Main Street had the best coffee around, probably because it roasted its own beans. It was a standing joke among the locals of Shelby that you could always tell a tourist because they were drinking from one of the Roaster's paper cups instead of the refillable mugs all the regulars had.

But right now, all Spence cared about was the smell of that coffee and the caffeine jolt it promised. He grabbed it gratefully and his father let him take a long sip before he said, "We need to talk."

There was a grim undertone to the voice and Spence wondered if he had enough energy left to brace himself for whatever was coming. He stood aside for his dad to enter and they walked over to sit at the small dining table he rarely used. He waited. When his father didn't speak, he finally gave him a wry one-sided smile and said, "Just hit me with it, Dad."

Ryan Colton nodded. "All right. Two things. Chuck says there was a partial cut of the line to the fuel pump, which is why it only gave out when it tried to turn on for the controlled landing. And a piece that was cut off the line, he thinks maybe accidentally since it was just floating loose, blocked the fuel intake from the wing tanks."

That made sense, to him anyway. Hetty would be the one to really ask, but he didn't want her getting all wound up about that yet. Time enough when she was well enough to be released from the hospital.

"And second," Dad went on, "there may be a connection between RTA and your shooter."

Spence blinked. He remembered Eli's question and wondered at the instincts his cousin had developed that got him places long before anyone else. "What connection?"

"It's not certain, just a possibility," Dad cautioned. "In fact, it's a pretty slim possibility."

"Nothing in the last four—no, five—days has been certain," he said, his tone a little sour. "Just tell me."

"Well, you can thank your sister for this one…" his father began.

Spence drew back slightly. "Kansas?" Search and rescue was her bailiwick, and she was one of the best at it, but why would she have gotten involved with this, after the fact? "What did she find?"

A brief smile flashed across his father's face. "This time it's not what she found, it's what she thought of. Something no one else did. She called a friend of hers who's a cop in Portland."

Portland. Where the newlyweds who had canceled were from. So, both his sister and Eli had made the mental jump. He supposed that's what happened when you were in their line of work, your mind naturally went there.

"She'd be here to tell you herself but she got a call on a job over in Chugach," Dad went on, referring to the state park just down and across the sound from them. "Anyway, it turns out the new hubby's ex-wife is quite the piece of work. She's well known to the officers assigned to the district your couple lives in. Several domestic incidents with her on file."

That threw a whole different light on things. He frowned. "Hetty's positive the shooter was a guy, and I don't think she'd misjudge that. Which would mean…what?"

Dad gave a single-shouldered shrug and a shake of his head. "No idea. Friend? Relative?"

"Or…she hired someone," Spence said, feeling a little silly even saying it. Who on earth would hire a…a hitman to try and take out your ex? *A lot of people. You know that.*

"That did occur to me," Dad said grimly.

The pieces were tumbling around in his head. "But why would he come after us if the ex is the target? Not like he could mistake us for them. And is the guy who tampered with the plane also the shooter? Did he follow us out there? How else could he even have known where we were going?"

"Slow down there, son. One step at a time. How long were you there before it all started?"

"A couple of hours, maybe."

"Enough time for somebody to get there," Dad said. "But that'd pretty much mean it has to be a local, because some guy from Portland isn't going to be able to just find his way out there."

"Unless he hired somebody to take him there," Spence said.

"Good point," Dad admitted. "I think I'll head down to the marina and ask around a bit before I get you back to Wasilla. Maybe I can find something."

"Aren't the cops supposed to be doing that?" Spence asked, grateful that he didn't have to explain to his father than he had to get back to Hetty. That he was already restless and nervous being away from her.

"There's only so many of them," Dad said. "Shelby PD is small, and you know how strapped Bobby Reynolds always says they are. Besides, this is kind of a wild hair that might well be a dead end."

"Yeah," Spence agreed, even though his brain was latching onto the idea as the most logical. It made more sense to him than some random guy out there just taking it in his head to shoot at a couple of total strangers.

But if it was true, what did it mean? That he didn't know what his targets looked like and thought they were the couple? He and Hetty?

If only.

Spence mentally stomped on the urge to pour out what had happened up in the cave that night to his dad. He wasn't ready for that, wouldn't be until he and Hetty had a chance to talk without family, friends and an entire medical staff lurking about. But setting that aside—which took more of an effort than he was used to—and after Dad had left to head down to the marina, he thought it through.

The ex hired a guy. If she'd somehow found a local, that answered the next few questions. Otherwise, she'd hired someone from Portland who'd came up here. Either the woman had to have known her ex had booked with RTA, or maybe the hitman had found out somehow. It wasn't like they'd kept everything secret. In fact, Lakin, in all her cleverness, had arranged some newlywed-type trappings from local suppliers for the trip, so it could easily have gotten out that they'd had a booking of that kind.

So, he tried tampering with the plane, but didn't know enough about them to realize that a broken fuel pump wouldn't bring down a gravity-fed system. And what? Got lucky that he had managed to do some damage that later did bring it down, as things had shifted during the flight?

He pushed that aside and went back to visualizing the plan. So, the plane was not supposed to land safely—*Didn't count on Hetty being as good as she is, did you, jackass?*—and the guy went to their destination just to be sure it didn't? To make sure he'd completed the job? How, by searching the wreckage for bodies? Or if his sabotage effort had worked, would he have just assumed when they hadn't arrived that it was mission accomplished, that they were down in deep water and beyond help or rescue?

And then what? He sees the plane land safely—thanks to its stellar pilot—but then realizes his quarry was never aboard and…what? Panics? Decides he has to kill them anyway? Or maybe he had just been trying to drive them away so he could escape unseen. That made more sense. Except, Hetty had seen him, which had changed everything. He wouldn't want to leave a witness behind, so he'd started to hunt her, and Spence because he was with her. Was that it?

He gave a sharp shake of his head. It was crazy. The whole freaking thing was crazy. The only thing he was really sure of was that the shooter knew Hetty had seen him, which was why he'd tried to take her out so many times. And had come too damned close to succeeding.

Frankly, for him, that was all the certainty he needed. And as soon as Hetty was well enough, he was going to see to it that the guy never had a chance to try again, if he had to go out there and hunt him down himself.

Spence suddenly understood how his parents and his aunt and uncle had found the courage to leave everything they'd known behind and move here to Alaska, changing their lives in so many ways. Because this had already changed him, somewhere deep inside. Between finding that half-buried body and nearly losing the woman he'd finally admitted he cared so much for, he was feeling a bit beyond fierce.

He'd never hunted a man before. But all it took was the image of Hetty hooked up to every medical machine he could imagine, barely clinging to life, to convince him that he not only could but would.

Chapter Twenty-One

Hetty was certain that if she didn't get out of here soon she was going to explode. This was day five of her stay and she'd had enough. She was surprised her blood pressure wasn't through the roof every time they came in and wrapped the cuff around her arm. It was in no small part because she knew Spence had put everything on hold to be with her. To be with her practically every moment she was awake. And, judging by the times she'd awakened in the dark—they used blackout curtains to simulate actual darkness at night in the hospital—most of the time when she was sleeping, too.

Which meant RTA had to be scrambling, minus their premier guide who had been booked solid all month, and down a pilot. This had to have thrown them into complete chaos. If only she'd noticed that guy sooner. If only she'd realized something was wrong with the plane. If only, if only, if only…

But on second thought, she wasn't sure she'd trade that night in the cave with Spence, when the truth between them had finally come out into the open, for anything.

Even for not being shot.

She wrapped her arms around herself. She was anxious

to talk to him, really talk, without anybody else around to interrupt. But she had no idea when that might happen. She had sent her mother back to finish her vacation, insisting it was the first real break she'd taken in years, and that she would be fine. She'd told her brothers to back off; that she needed to concentrate on recuperation and didn't need them dropping in five times a day. She'd even—with ulterior motive—told Troy that if he wanted to call multiple times a day to see how she was to call Lakin instead, so she could focus on healing.

She did not, however, tell Spence to back off. She couldn't bring herself to do it, not when she got so much quiet pleasure out of waking up and seeing him there, so close at hand, or when she thought he'd finally left but then he strolled in the door a few minutes later.

Hetty pushed herself extra hard at therapy that morning, both to vent her frustration and because the harder she worked at it, the sooner she'd get out of here. She was exhausted after the hour and a half session, which alone told her how much farther she had to go. At one time, she could have done everything the therapist asked her to without even breathing faster. Now, it was an effort unlike anything she'd had to make before, except for that night at the lake when she'd been in such pain from the gunshot wound. And even then, once Spence had found her, she hadn't had to do much, since he had carried her. Carried her with such ease, such care, such...tenderness.

But she would make the effort. Every day if she had to. She had learned to handle the crutches, although she didn't like it. If they would get her out of this place, she'd deal. Although now she was almost tired enough for a nap. But no sooner was she back sitting on the edge of the bed in her room, pondering if she dared try lifting her injured leg up under its own power or if she should use her hands to maneuver it, than the door opened.

She sucked in a breath and tried to paste on her cheerful face, something else she'd adopted in her effort to escape. But when she turned to look, she was sure the expression had frozen.

It was Spence. And he was pushing an empty wheelchair. Well, empty except for a small duffel bag on the seat. And with him were his parents. Ryan and Abby Colton were smiling widely. And, in their case, it was for real, unlike the effort she'd made. Abby's smile in particular was warm, and her short, bouncy bob suited her so well. Her eyes were green, although a different shade than her own, and they were actually sparkling, as if she was delighted to be there.

"You ready to get out of here?" Ryan—she always had trouble even thinking of him by his first name, no matter his insistence, because he was, in essence, her boss—asked, his smile becoming a grin.

"Out?" She almost yelped. "Seriously?"

"Well, it'd be a pretty lousy prank if we weren't," drawled Spence.

"And we need to hurry before I get accused of bribing a source on the biggest story this town has had in years," said an also grinning Abby, obviously referring to her job as a reporter for the local newspaper, the *Shelby Weekly*.

Hetty winced inwardly at the reminder of not only the man who had shot her, but the body they'd found, but she selfishly let the personal news outweigh it. She was getting out.

"I don't need the chair, really," she said, experiencing a burst of energy that made her feel as if she'd already healed.

"You don't," Spence agreed easily, "but the hospital requires it." He flashed his own grin at her, which somehow had a lot more impact. "How about we let you climb into the bird on your own?"

She blinked. "You flew here?"

"So I'm impatient," Spence quipped.

"Besides," his father said, "I think that drive in a car would be a little much for you right now." His mouth quirked. "And for me, for that matter. I'm spoiled, I much prefer flying."

They all seemed so happy, as if they were rescuing one of their own. They had always said she was family, and had always treated her that way, but if she had any doubts left that they really meant it, they were vanquished by the happiness that now filled the room. And she found herself grinning right back at them, the unexpected gift of freedom too much to hold in.

"Now, you're still under doctor's orders," Abby said in the same kind of tone her mother used when she was giving instructions to one of her brood. "So you have to take it easy."

"And we'll enforce that, if necessary," Ryan said. "We have your room ready and waiting—"

"My room?" Hetty said, staring at Spence's dad.

Abby laughed. "Leave it to him to put the end of the story first. You're staying with us, dear."

"But—"

Abby hushed her with a wave. "Not up for negotiation. The only reason they agreed to release you was our promise that you'd be in a place with no stairs. So, your upstairs apartment does not cut it. Now, I talked with your friend Dove, and she told me what clothes she thought would work, and told us where the extra key was hidden, so we went and gathered those for you," she said, indicating the bag on the wheelchair seat.

Redheaded Dove St. James ran Namaste, the small yoga studio on Main Street in town, a place Hetty frequented when she needed some calm. So, often. Often enough that she and Dove had become good friends. And since her studio was right down the street from Hetty's apartment, it was a handy spot to stash a backup key to her place.

"She'll also look into some special techniques that might be helpful, when the doctor says you're ready," Abby went on, leaving Hetty feeling like her head was spinning a little. All the things she'd been trying to figure out—including how she was going to manage the stairs to her apartment— seemed to have magically been solved.

"Wow," she said. "Got a problem, turn the Coltons loose on it."

They all laughed, and she knew she'd found the right words to thank them. Spence had stayed mostly quiet since his first wisecrack, but Hetty had the feeling that if she dug down deep enough, she'd find that he had started this.

"Absolutely," agreed Ryan. Then, his tone suddenly solemn, he added, "After all, RTA got you into this fix. You wouldn't have been up there if you weren't working for us."

"And you'll be needing somebody around in case you need help with something," Abby continued. "You'll need to keep your leg elevated, the dressings changed and probably ice packs for any swelling at first. I've arranged to work from home for the next couple of weeks, so we're all set. And your mother can enjoy her vacation without worrying that you're alone while you're healing."

Hetty sat silently for a moment, staring at this couple

she'd always admired. She didn't know what to say. She truly had been worried that her mother might cancel this first vacation she'd taken in years, to rush home and take care of her. She'd almost done it when she'd first arrived at the hospital, but Hetty had convinced her to go back to her plans and that she would call her if she needed help.

And now she had all the help she could possibly need, and she hadn't even had to ask.

Because Spence had asked for her. She was sure of that now. And his family had come through, like they always did.

She remembered what he'd told her that night in the cave; the horrible story of the murders of the aunt and grandparents he'd never known. Whether that was the genesis of the Colton trait of helping whoever needed it or not, she didn't know, but if she had to guess, she would say it probably was. And this time she was the lucky recipient.

On some level beneath the joy, she registered the discomfort as Abby helped her get dressed in the comfortable and thankfully easy-to-put-on clothes they'd brought, and was almost glad to sit in the wheelchair when it was done. Abby also kept talking and, by the way Spence's mother kept glancing at her, Hetty knew it was to distract her from the pain.

"You'll have to sign some papers at the desk on the way out, but Spence gave them all the info so you won't have to spend an hour filling out the rest of the forms," she was saying.

For the first time since he'd cracked the joke about flying here to get her because he was impatient, she looked up at Spence.

"Thank you," she said vehemently, hoping he understood she meant not just for the paperwork but for…everything.

He smiled at her, and she hoped she wasn't kidding herself when she thought she saw understanding in his beautiful blue eyes.

Using her good leg to do most of the work, she actually did manage to step up into the RTA helicopter mostly on her own. Somehow knowing Spence was right there to brace her and keep her from falling made it easier. She looked around the interior for a moment, thinking about the last time she'd been in here, lying across these seats, hurt and bleeding.

Spence climbed in and sat next to her, fussing with the seat belts he'd used then to hold her in place. His mother took the copilot's seat while Ryan settled in and prepared for takeoff. And as the bird came to life, and things started to whir, Abby looked back at them.

"All set?"

"We're good. Let's get out of here."

Abby smiled widely. "Yes, let's. And thank you, Hetty."

Startled, she said, "For what? You're doing everything for me."

"But as long as you're with us, at least we know we'll see a lot more of Spence."

His mother was grinning as she turned back to face front as the sound of the engine increased. Hetty risked a glance at Spence. He was staring out the window as if he hadn't heard a thing.

But he was smiling.

Chapter Twenty-Two

Ryan and Abby's house was a lovely, almost sprawling place on a rise, with the vaulted roofs and ceilings familiar to Alaska. But the house almost seemed insignificant compared to the view from all sides. Out the back, the mountains towered. From the front, there was a sweeping view all the way down to the sound. Hetty thought she could easily sit in either place for hours and, as it turned out, she sometimes did. In fact she was delighted when, after she'd gotten the okay from the doctor, Abby suggested she do the exercises the therapist had ordered out on the back deck, where she could see the country she would be able to visit again once she was back to a hundred percent.

She'd expected, because she knew what kind of people the Coltons were, that they would see to it she had everything she needed. And she did. The room they'd provided had a queen-sized bed—which she ended up in embarrassingly early, running out of steam shortly after the lovely dinner they'd had—and its own bathroom, and was a very short walk to the huge kitchen. A walk she'd been able to manage alone—with those crutches she both hated and loved—this morning, the day after her arrival.

In part inspired by the luscious smell of something baking in the oven.

What she hadn't expected was to find just about everything she liked to eat and drink on hand, neatly arranged on the counter and on one shelf in the fridge. They didn't know her that well, did they?

"If you want anything else, just let us know," Abby said from where she was setting up a coffee maker. "Spence did the shopping the day before you were released, but he might have missed something."

Spence had done that? How had he known? Sure, they'd eaten together sometimes, when the length of a job required it, or when it was an RTA gathering, but...had he really been paying that close attention to what she ate? What she ordered at The Cove when the gathering was at the quiet waterfront restaurant? Or what she brought on flights that were going to be long enough she wanted something to snack on?

It seemed impossible, but how else would that specific brand and flavor of crackers be there on the counter? Or, to go with them, that container of her favorite hummus— sold only by that small specialty market—sitting there in the fridge? Even her family didn't know about that particular craving of hers.

So did that mean that, all this time, even amid all the jabbing and poking at each other, he'd still been noticing small things like this? A memory floated up out of her mind and she knew the answer. She thought back to those days in high school, when she'd been assigned to tutor him. The very idea of tutoring a Colton had had her almost wishing she'd never volunteered for the program, for all that she'd been flattered when they'd approached her about it. But the idea that a Colton had needed tutoring had been enough of a surprise that she'd gone ahead.

And one of the first things she'd noticed about the then sixteen-year-old Spence Colton was that he noticed *everything*. He'd been so visually oriented that he seemed to observe and remember everything. And that had eventually been the key, the answer, to his problem with traditional reading.

So why was she surprised now that he had noticed something as simple as what she liked to eat?

"You are all being so kind," she said, feeling awkward enough that it sounded in her voice.

"You," Abby said firmly, "are a crucial part of not just RTA, but the RTA family. And thus our family." She looked over at Hetty as she closed the refrigerator door. "And this was the only way your mother would stay and finish her vacation. Which she needed. You seven have kept her busy for a very long time."

"We have," Hetty said. "But she's been a rock for all seven of us, especially after Dad died. She still is. And if this is what it took for her to get that break she deserves, I thank you all over again."

"I know."

The oven timer dinged and Abby grabbed a potholder and went over to pull out a tin full of wonderful-smelling muffins. She set them to cool then glanced at Hetty, who had taken in a deep breath of the scent, which in turn had made her stomach growl audibly. Abby grinned and tugged one of the muffins out by the paper liner, plopped it on a small plate and slid it over to her, along with the butter dish.

"Butter it now, but I'd give it a minute or two to cool before you stuff it in your mouth."

Abby Colton, Hetty decided then and there, was a delight. She didn't know her as well as she knew her husband, having worked with him for quite a while now, but she should have guessed that a nice guy like Ryan would be married to a nice woman. And luckily for her, she was also someone who baked a wicked-good banana nut muffin. Hetty savored the taste, marveling again at how good food tasted away from the hospital. Alaska might have to import ninety-five percent of its food because of the permafrost, so that even in summer when the surface was green, a few feet down was still frozen, but the Coltons sure brought in the good stuff.

Hetty was used to being on the move most of the day, so it was a bit mentally difficult for her to stay still when her leg started seriously aching. But a perusal of the well-stocked bookshelves she found in Abby's home office made her quickly decide maybe this wouldn't be so bad, after all. She also wasn't used to tiring out in the middle of the day—especially after doing nothing more difficult than getting up now and then from the chair she'd staked out for reading—but they'd warned her it would happen. And so, reluctantly, she'd accepted that an afternoon nap was going to be on the agenda for a few days.

When she woke up after that first nap to a vase full of her favorite flowers, the Alpine Aster, the delicate lavender blossom with the bright yellow center, she felt as if she'd landed in some expensive, full-service hotel.

Having learned the hard way with a near tumble, she moved very slowly to get up, using the crutches she'd this time left next to the bed. The house seemed quiet at the moment, but the door to Abby's office was open, so she peeked in. Spence's mother had been reading something on the screen of a laptop, but immediately looked up.

"Well hello," she said. "How are you feeling?"

"Rested. And better, I think."

"The two go hand in hand, I suppose."

Hetty smiled. "The flowers are lovely. Thank you."

Abby smiled back at her as she got to her feet. "Don't thank me, I only provided the vase. Thank Spence. He stopped by to see how you were doing, and brought those with him. He stopped to gather them on his way here, said they were your favorites."

It was a moment before she could react to that. Spence had been here? In her room, while she'd been asleep? Although, it made no sense that that made her pulse kick up, not after the night they'd spent in the cave. Or maybe it was that those circumstances had been so unique, it didn't count; it was all part of the craziness of that day and night.

"They are my favorites," she said, her throat a little tight.

Was there nothing the man hadn't noticed? She'd bet there were friends she'd had for years who couldn't have come up with everything he had. And to handpick that bouquet...

"This scared us all, Hetty," Abby said quietly. "But especially Spence. I think he had this image of you as indestructible."

Hetty's mouth quirked. "Feeling pretty fragile right now, and I don't like it."

"I'm just glad you're going to be all right, no matter how long the path to get there is."

And that, Hetty decided, was the outlook she needed to adopt. She was going to be all right, eventually. And it very easily could have been worse.

"I might have bled to death, if Spence hadn't been there. If he wasn't always so prepared for anything."

"His father taught him well," Abby said.

"I will never again tease him about lugging that backpack everywhere."

Abby laughed then said, "He's got a run to make today, to one of the fishing camps, but he'll be here for dinner. And he'd better show up because he's supposed to bring dessert from the bakery."

Hetty wondered if he'd hit a home run on that, too, somehow remembering her favorite pecan pie. She decided she wouldn't expect it, but at the same time wouldn't be in the least surprised if he did.

"Now, how about a snack to tide you over until then?"

Abby walked beside her down the hall, matching her slow pace but not making a big deal of it, which Hetty appreciated. She took a seat on one of the high stools at the kitchen counter, grateful, if for no other reason, that they were easier for her to get on and off of since it required less exertion of the very muscles trying to heal. The doctor had told her it would take several weeks for her to be back to her old strength and control, and that, for the first few of those weeks, she'd be seeing a physical therapist here in Shelby.

Belatedly she realized something her joy at getting out of the hospital had pushed to the back of her mind. She wasn't going to be able to drive for a while—at least not her rugged little Jeep, which was a manual transmission that required a functional left leg—but she needed to get to the south end of town three days a week.

"That didn't look like a happy thought," Abby said as she set one of the muffins she'd baked and what looked like a mug of luscious hot chocolate in front of her on the counter.

"I…just realized I can't drive my car for a while," Hetty said. "It's a stick, and I'd never manage the clutch. But I have appointments with the therapist the hospital referred me to in town and—"

"Don't worry, we've got it worked out," Abby said cheerfully. "I'll take you tomorrow, Ryan on Wednesday, and Spence will drive you on Friday and all the next week."

Spence, all week? "Can he afford the time? I know we were booked pretty solid."

"Parker's doing more of the fieldwork for a bit. And he's liking getting out of the office more. And Ryan and Will haven't forgotten much, you know, despite their…semiretirement."

Abby rolled her eyes as she said that last bit, and Hetty couldn't help laughing. "If that's retirement, I'll just keep working, thanks."

"My sentiment exactly," Spence's mother agreed then went back to the subject at hand. "And then, as soon as you're cleared to drive, you can use my car until you're healed enough to get back to the Troll."

Hetty burst out laughing; she'd had no idea anybody outside her family knew her nickname for her army-green, slightly battered Jeep.

But then, she was now realizing just how much a part of the Colton family she already was. Which in turn made her think of Spence and wonder what, if anything, would come of those revelations divulged in the shadows of a cave here in the land of the Midnight Sun.

Chapter Twenty-Three

"No proof yet," Bobby Reynolds said. "But the new wife says the ex would be more than capable of something like that."

Spence's jaw tightened as he listened to the officer's blunt statement. Reynolds was one of the most senior members of the Shelby Police Department, and while he was a bit stiffly by-the-book, he took any crime that happened in or near his town very seriously. And when it was as serious as this was, he dug in. He might not be the most sympathetic guy around—probably ran out of that years ago, Spence thought—but you could depend on him to find what needed to be found, no matter how long it took.

"They're trying to track her down now," Reynolds said, running a hand over his short, light brown hair, "but she's apparently out of town and no one seems to know where."

"Convenient," Spence muttered with a grimace.

"My thought exactly. They'll keep on it. And if they don't, I will."

"What about the shooter himself?"

"I sent copies of the sketch to all the departments in the area both of your clients and where the ex is—as far as we know—living, to see if anyone recognizes him. In the meantime, everybody here is on the lookout. We'll be talking to anybody who even has the same shoe size, I swear."

Spence knew they'd found some tracks up at the scene because they'd come to look at his hiking boots, to check the sole pattern to eliminate them from the search. They'd also verified his guess on the caliber of the rifle, having found the spent bullet in the tree he'd directed them to. He decided then to go ahead and share his theory, even though it was nothing more than just that, a theory.

"My gut says he's a city guy, but I have no proof of that," Spence said. "Just the way he moved. He made more noise than somebody familiar with the woods and hills would make, so I was thinking he was used to having more noise to cover him, like in a city. Or maybe he wasn't used to a lot of tree branches moving around him."

Reynolds's gaze turned inward, considerately, then he nodded. "It makes sense."

Encouraged, Spence went on. "And he was either trying to miss, is a lousy shot or not used to that rifle. Thankfully."

"More used to handguns in that city of his?" Reynolds asked.

It didn't seem to be a jab, but still Spence said only a cautious, "Maybe. Like I said, no proof, just speculation."

"But the speculation of someone who does know how to move in the backcountry." A slight smile curved Reynolds's mouth, and a glint of amusement showed in his brown eyes. "And someone who's used to carting around people who don't."

"That, too," Spence agreed a bit ruefully.

"I'll keep you posted if anything turns up."

And he would, Spence acknowledged when the man left to take a call. As he'd thought earlier, Reynolds was nothing if not dependable. And he tended to take anything that disrupted the peace of his little town kind of personally. They were lucky to have the guy.

As he walked back to his car, glad he'd run into Reynolds because it had saved him trying to track him down, he pondered the revelation of that last realization. He'd never thought much about such things like Shelby being lucky to have a cop like him. Or Melissa in the bakery, who, day after day, turned out luscious things like the pecan pies Hetty loved, one of which sat on the passenger seat beside him right now.

Hetty.

That was why he was thinking that way. They'd nearly lost her, so naturally he was thinking that way.

He'd nearly lost her.

He had to suppress the shudder that rippled through him at the thought. He didn't know what would happen next, or where they would go from here, but at least he had hope. That small hope could have been destroyed before it had ever seen the light of day. If their attacker had been a better shot, she could have died out there. That night in the cave would never have happened and he would have spent the rest of his life regretting never having told her the truth, and never knowing that her sniping had been as much a cover as his flirting.

As he headed for his folks' place, a movement above caught his eye. An eagle, not low and searching the water for dinner, but soaring high, in that way Spence had always thought of as flying for the love of it. Kind of like Hetty. He'd never doubted she loved what she did, as much as he loved what he did. Which made them both lucky, he guessed. Loving your work wasn't something everyone had in life.

And now, maybe they would work on something else not everyone had. Another kind of love. The kind he saw every day between his mom and dad, his aunt and uncle. He knew Hetty had seen it, too, in her parents before her father had died. Had she also doubted she would ever find that kind of bond with someone? Could they take whatever they'd started in that cave and build on it?

Damn, you're starting to sound like Lakin, mooning about Troy. When did you become mush?

He knew the answer to his own silent question. He'd turned to mush when he'd found Hetty down and bleeding and thought she was going to die.

He picked up the pace the moment he hit his folks' long driveway up to the house and parked as close as he could get to the front porch. When he got inside, he found his mom and Hetty sitting in the great room, laughing at something. The scene tightened his chest. And when Hetty looked at him with those amazing green eyes, when she saw the pie box he was carrying, with the word *pecan* scrawled on it, she smiled. And no matter how much he tried to tell himself it was because he'd gotten the pie she liked, he couldn't help thinking there was more to it. More to the way she was looking at him, smiling at him.

Maybe even a foundation.

Let the building begin.

IF IT WEREN'T for the occasional little spike of nerves and the more frequent throb of pain from her leg, Hetty would have enjoyed this evening as much—well, even more, if her little brothers were arguing—as dinner at home with her family. Being able to ask Ryan Colton about the founding of RTA, and how he and his brother had decided to do it in the first place, the stories of how he and Abby had met in San Diego, was fun. They'd skipped the gruesome events that had precipitated the move and gone straight to how much they loved their adopted state.

"Alaska's no place for wusses," Ryan said, and there was pride in his voice, no doubt at how well and how completely his family had adapted.

"She knows that, Dad," Spence said, his gaze fastened on her. "All she has to do is look in a mirror."

"Truer words never spoken," Abby agreed, but Hetty barely heard her. Spence had taken her breath away, not just with those words but with the way he'd looked at her when he'd said them.

In my arms. At last.

The words he'd said that night when they'd been wrapped around each other under the emergency blanket. Courtesy of that huge, ever-present backpack she would never joke about again.

But tonight all she'd been able to manage was to thank him for the lovely flowers. And suddenly she was face to face with the downside of staying here in this lovely house, with people who were taking such good care of her. She couldn't seem to get a moment alone with Spence. He didn't seem particularly concerned about it, and just went on with what probably was, to him, a normal dinner at home with the folks. It was only when she began to doze off on the couch, in spite of the interesting conversation, that he acted.

"Come on," he said, taking her hand and jolting her back to alertness. "You need to get some rest."

Her first instinct, born of years of having to prove herself, was to protest and say she was fine. But she wasn't fine, on a couple of fronts, so she tamped down that reaction and let him help her to her feet. And then startled herself with a sudden wish that he would sweep her up into his arms and carry her, as he had out there in the wild. She even thought about stumbling, intentionally, to see if he would, but that didn't seem fair. Or smart, since his parents were watching and would then think she was weaker than she actually was and hover even more than they already were.

Instead, he handed her the crutches. She grimaced inwardly. But then he said encouragingly, "When your leg's a little stronger, we'll try it with you just leaning on me."

Did he mean that in more than a practical way? Did he mean for her to lean on him in the way a…a girlfriend might?

The moment they were out of sight in the short hallway, she gave into the urge and said, "We need to talk. Don't we?" She hated that she'd ended with that question and in an edgy-sounding tone.

"That can wait until you're stronger, too," he said as he ushered her into the room she was using. Just as she was about to interpret that as avoidance because he'd changed his mind, he leaned in and whispered, "So hurry up, will you?"

And then, to her shock and delight, he backed her up against the wall and kissed her.

Chapter Twenty-Four

He shouldn't have done it.

Spence stopped just outside the bedroom door he'd closed as he'd left, not ready to face anyone at the moment.

He shouldn't have done it because all his good, responsible resolutions had just been blown to hell. He'd intended to wait until she was well, at least well enough to function on her own. He'd intended to simply be there when she needed him, if only because he knew how stubborn she was about accepting help. He'd intended to be the support she needed right now, nothing else.

He'd never intended to kiss her, especially under his parents' roof, although that modifier made him feel like a rowdy teenager again. But she'd been right there, looking up at him with those eyes. And her lips had parted slightly, as if she'd suddenly needed more air, just as he had. The temptation was overwhelming and he hadn't been able to resist. He simply had to touch, to taste. It wasn't just an urge, it was a necessity.

And then reality had wiped everything out of his mind except for the taste of her lips under his. The feel of her long, taut body against his.

Nice job, Colton. She's just out of the hospital and you're pushing her up against a wall.

It had made the rest of the process of getting her to the bed—and blocking any and all thought about joining her there—awkward and uncomfortable. Not because she'd pushed him away. Oh no. She'd reached up and pulled him closer, as if she'd wanted more. And more. Which had made backing off hard.

Among other things...

Only remembering the doctor's words about getting enough rest and not pushing too much too fast—as if he knew Hetty's nature already—had enabled him to back off. But it hadn't enabled him to do it easily. Or willingly.

Spence gave a sharp shake of his head, gritted his teeth and steeled himself to go face his parents. And stopped dead just inside the great room entry when he realized they were snuggled up on the couch together...kissing.

His first thought was the silly idea that there was something in the air. Something that had not only made his control snap, but theirs.

Vivid memories flashed through his mind of the times when as a kid he'd walked in on them just like this. "Ew, gross!" had been his usual reaction. But now, he felt an odd sort of knot in his gut. After all that had happened, after everything they'd been through, and everything they'd accomplished in spite of it, his parents were still rock-solid, still able to feel like this about each other. And he realized, at the far-too-late age of twenty-eight, how damned lucky he was to have them as an example.

"Hetty all right?" his father interrupted the kissing to ask.

He nodded, hoping they couldn't guess from his unsettled state what had happened right down the hall. He tried to focus on what came next, without relating it to what he'd just done. He had to make a charter drop-off tomorrow, early, as much as he would rather stay close by just in case. But they'd already had to shuffle things around so much, he couldn't mess it up even more by canceling now that Hetty was home safe.

"You're taking her to therapy tomorrow?" he asked his mother, who nodded in turn.

"And I've got her on Wednesday," Dad put in. "After that, she's all yours. We've got your calendar cleared on those days through the end of the second week."

All yours... Did he have to put it like that?

"And if I know Hetty," Mom said, "after that, she'll be stubbornly back to trying to handle everything herself, so you'd better hover."

All he could do was nod. Because, if he spoke, he was afraid he'd give everything away, and he had no right to do that until he and Hetty had had that *talk*. The one he didn't want to have here, where there was every likelihood of an interruption.

"I'll check in when I get back from the drop-off tomorrow," he said as he headed for the front door, thinking that at least he didn't have to worry about Hetty being in good hands. And then, with the door already pulled open, he stopped and looked back at them. "I love you," he said.

Their eyes widened and he took it as proof he didn't say that nearly often enough. The smiles they both gave him made him realize that needed to change. Now.

Nothing like a brush with death to wake a guy up.

The next day, he got back to the RTA office after making what happily turned out to be a routine run to one of their fishing camps further down the sound, and was still filling out the report for Lakin—in that unique but efficient way he had, thanks to a certain high school tutor—when the door opened. He looked up to see his cousin Mitchell stepping in.

"Hey," he said in surprise. As a very successful attorney practicing corporate law, Mitchell—who winced if you shortened it to Mitch—didn't spend much time at RTA, although, like any Colton. he'd be there in an instant if need be. "I thought you were in Anchorage."

"I was. Got back last night, but it was late, so I got some sleep and waited until today."

"How'd it go?" Spence asked, knowing Mitchell had been there giving testimony on a case filed against some bureaucratic agency that had overstepped. It hadn't been his case, but he'd been called as an expert witness.

Mitchell smiled. "The opposition wasn't very happy with me, so I'm taking that as a win."

"Sounds good to me," Spence agreed with a grin.

His cousin lifted a brow at him. "I hear things have been a little crazy around here. How's Hetty?"

"She's going to be fine," he answered firmly. "She's at my folks' place, and Mom's working from home this week to be there with her."

Mitchell smiled. "No wonder I didn't see her at the *Weekly* when I got in this morning." Spence nodded, knowing that his office was right next to the *Shelby Weekly* office. "That sounds like Aunt Abby."

"Yes. It's just like her," Spence agreed, his throat tightening a little all over again at how both his parents had leapt into action when needed.

Mitchell glanced around the RTA headquarters, empty

right now, except for Spence. "Kind of kinks things up a bit around here, though, doesn't it, being down a pilot?"

"For a while. But Dad's filling in, and we're using the chopper until the plane's repaired."

Mitchell frowned. "I ran into Officer Reynolds outside my office this morning. He said it had been tampered with?"

Spence nodded, the warmth fading as the barely sublimated anger welled up again. "If anybody less than Hetty had been at the controls, I probably wouldn't be standing here talking to you now."

"But who would ever—"

Spence held up a hand and shook his head. "We don't know for sure yet. Might be somebody connected to a client, or totally unrelated, just some nutjob taking potshots. They're working on it. You know how slow that can go when you're working with little scraps of evidence."

"Too well. Speaking of which, what's this about Hetty finding a dead body up there?"

Quickly, Spence told his cousin what he knew, once again ending with the same exasperation at the lack of progress.

"But your brother is on that one, so I'm betting it'll go faster," Spence said, meaning it.

"It will if Eli has anything to say about it," Mitchell agreed.

"So, what's up for you now?"

The other man grimaced slightly. "I don't know. Things have been pretty quiet. I've got nothing on the docket at the moment. I mean that thing in Anchorage wasn't even my case."

"So you can go fishing or climb mountains for a while,"

Spence said. "By yourself, as usual," he added with a wry grin because, just like himself, it was his cousin's habit to trek out solo whenever he had some spare time.

He knew, and he was sure Mitchell did, too, that the family worried about that. Just a little, but some, because... well, Alaska. But to Spence it was worth the risk, to fully experience the vast expanses, to enjoy literally endless summer days and cope with winter nights and single digit temperatures. To savor the pristine white of snow and the crackling ice of the glaciers. And above all else the towering peaks that put what they called mountains in the continental U.S. in a distant second place. He supposed it was the same with his cousin.

"Actually, I'm thinking maybe I should be worried," Mitchell said. "Every time I have a lull like this, something big seems to come along."

"I've had enough of big things for a while," Spence said, his tone dry. "So the next one's yours."

Mitchell gave him an exaggerated side-eye. "Thanks a lot, cuz."

Spence was still laughing as his cousin left. And knew the only reason he had the heart to laugh at all was his family and the fact that Hetty, indeed, was going to be fine.

And it flitted through his mind that he wanted the day to come when he didn't have to separate the two.

Chapter Twenty-Five

Hetty had been many things in her life, but pampered was not one of them. Her father had been loving but brusque, and had left them far too soon. Which had left her mother too harried with seven children to spend a lot of time coddling each of them. Yet Mom had always been there for her, for all her siblings, caring and caretaking, and Hetty counted herself lucky for that.

But right now she was thinking she could get used to this. Oh, not the rigorous rehab she was going through, although she'd had to take a break just now, after an hour of pushing as hard as she could short of doing new damage. But now, while taking a break out on the back deck, looking up at the mountains whose towering peaks were never clear of snow, making for a beautiful contrast with the summer green of the lower altitudes, she seized on other things to think about so she wasn't so focused on her body's soreness. And life here in the Colton house was quite a change.

It had been three days of both pain and bliss. The rehabilitation part was tough, but if there was anything she needed, anything she wanted, Spence saw that she had it. Sometimes even before she realized she wanted it. To the point where it was making her think about things like mind reading and psychics. One day, it was the cinnamon roll she'd been thinking about. The next, it was that book she'd been wanting to read. And the next, it was the cane she wanted to try as soon as the therapist said she could. That one he'd leaned against the wall right by the door to the bedroom.

"Keep the goal in sight," he'd said simply, and with a casual shrug, as if going out of his way to do this was nothing special. But Spence Colton was definitely something special. Even when she'd been the most irritated at him, she'd never doubted that.

She remembered how in high school she used to watch him with the girls, watch how they all flirted with him, looking at him with what her mother laughingly called "sheep eyes." With his looks, his name and the fact that he'd been the star of both the school's baseball—weather-short season and all—and hockey teams for bait, they'd circled him like hungry fish. She supposed that was how he'd learned to deal with the come-ons so well, because he'd been the target of them from such a young age.

She, on the other hand, had not. Not that there hadn't been interest because as one of the few biracial students on campus she'd been a bit of a novelty, but because she'd had no patience for it and it had showed. That had been why, when she'd been given the tutoring assignment for him, she'd dreaded it.

Suddenly, vividly, a memory shot through her mind, something she hadn't thought of in years. That first day, when Spence had walked into the small study room that was dedicated to the tutoring program. She'd seen him earlier, out near the gym and the baseball diamond, smiling amid a cluster of girls laughing delightedly at something he'd said. But the smile he'd worn then was nowhere to be seen now. And her irritation had broken through the mask of indifference she'd tried to put on.

"Sorry to take you away from your fan club," she had said sharply as he'd entered and dropped a couple of books on the small table.

His head had snapped up and he'd stared at her. And then, in a voice she'd never forget, he had said, "If they knew I was stupid enough to end up here, they wouldn't be interested."

She'd been taken aback, not only by the chill in his tone but the self-disgust, and had truly regretted what she'd said and how she'd said it. Because she knew he wasn't stupid, the director of the program had told her about his math and science and engineering scores, that he was borderline genius in all of those areas. She'd vowed then and there that she would find a way through whatever his problem was, find the method that would work for him.

And she had, she thought now, with no small amount of satisfaction. And it had, as he'd told her with solemn sincerity the day he'd found out he'd passed all his final exams, changed his life. Forever.

She supposed maybe that was the moment. The look in his eyes, the genuineness in his voice when he'd thanked her for saving him, the nothing-less-than-fierce hug he'd given her... She thought maybe that was when she'd fallen. Fallen for the real Spence, the one he kept so well-hidden but that she had seen in every session they'd had.

Of course she'd shoved the feeling aside, because Hetty Amos had had no time for something as silly as high school romance. Or any romance, for that matter. She'd had plans for her future, and even though she'd admired and loved her mother dearly, they hadn't included getting married and having a bunch of kids.

And she had done it. That reaching for planes in the sky she'd done as a child had become her true passion on a school-sponsored small-plane flight to Anchorage for a ceremony for award-winning students. She'd been beyond fascinated not only with the flight but the plane itself, how it worked, and the intricacy of the controls. She'd been so entranced, even the pilots had noticed and had let her sit in the copilot seat part of the way. That was when she'd been certain of her destiny.

Over her mother's fears, as soon as she'd finished high school, she put herself through flight school. Her determination never wavered. It was what she'd been born to do, and she would let nothing stop her. One of her flight instructors, Andrew West, a former military pilot who specialized now in teaching the younger students, seemed to recognize a kindred spirit, and had taken a personal interest. He'd not only taught her, he'd pushed, prodded and demanded her absolute best.

Flying in Alaska is unlike anywhere else in the world. It's not just the mountains, and the fact that dead-end canyons are everywhere, or that you'll be flying at lower altitudes and so have less time in an emergency, or that magnetic variation can be as much as twenty-five degrees, it's also that you're flying over water that's always frigid. Never forget the 1-10-1 rule.

She'd committed that to memory early on. First minute in the water was pure cold shock. After ten minutes, you had muscle failure. And after one hour, you'd be unconscious from hypothermia, and therefore dead. And even if she hadn't memorized it, the test training she'd had to go through would have pounded it home. Nothing like being dumped in that icy water and having to get yourself out of the mockup aircraft and to a pier a hundred yards away to sear it into your brain.

You've got it, Amos. You've got that passion, and you've got the knack, you just need to hone the skills. You need to work harder at it than you've worked at anything, even that fancy top-of-the-class diploma you got.

Hetty smiled at the memory, sighed aloud and went back to work stretching her leg. That, if she set the pain aside, was perhaps the most unsettling aspect of all of this. She was a goer and a doer, and didn't normally spend much time lost in thoughts of the past. But she had twenty-four hours a day now where her brain was free to roam, and even when she was working on the injury, they happened. In the beginning, she had let them, as a distraction from the pain, but now the recollections seemed to be happening all the time.

Except when she was fantasizing about the future. A future she had no guarantee would really happen. Not until she and Spence had that talk they had both hinted at.

So get to work in the now. Start planning instead of remembering. You can fly a freaking airplane, you can figure this out.

Self-directed order given, she began to do exactly that. There had to be a way. Maybe the next time he was here, she could claim cabin fever and ask him to take her outside, somewhere, anywhere. Anywhere away from potential interruptions. Anywhere they could have that discussion. Because she couldn't stand to just loll around here and wonder any longer.

She didn't want to just reclaim the life she'd had, she

wanted to start building that new one, the one she'd never really hoped to have until that night in the cave had let her know it might be possible.

You need to work harder at it than you've worked at anything...

Captain West's words came back to her again and, for the first time, she thought they could apply to more than just learning to fly.

Or perhaps it would be a different kind of flying.

Her resolution settled now, she went back to her stretching. She'd done the hardest part of the routine, now it was a matter of keeping the injured tissue and muscles from tightening up too much, keeping the scar tissue to a minimum. She didn't know just how much of a scar she was going to have, but she'd resolved early on that she'd consider it a souvenir, a reminder of that night.

She wondered if there would come a time when she would be telling the story of how it—they—began in a dark, hidden cave, one of those nights that never really became night and—

"You're not pushing too hard, are you, Hetty?"

Abby Colton's voice as she stepped out onto the deck was light, cheerful, and obviously sincere. It had taken Hetty a bit of effort to see the woman as an individual rather than just as Spence's mother and the wife of the founder of RTA, but Hetty felt as if she knew her much better now. And liked her. She'd always read her articles in the local paper, mostly—or so she had told herself—because of her connection to her employer.

But now she was at the point where she could admit it was also because she was Spence's mother.

"I'm through the hard part," she said.

"Good," Abby said as she sat down on the chair closest to where Hetty had stretched out on the mat she did her sessions on. She held out a glass, which Hetty recognized as full of that luscious strawberry lemonade she frequently made.

"Oh, I love this stuff."

Hetty accepted the glass thankfully. She took a long swallow, let out a sigh of satisfaction and appreciation, then licked her lips to be sure she hadn't missed any.

Abby smiled widely. "Now that's the best kind of thank-you."

Hetty took another long drink, then decided what the heck and finished it. Toying with the now-empty glass, she said, "Speaking of thank-yous, I don't know how I'll ever thank you for this," she said, gesturing with her free hand at the house, the deck, the view.

"You're one of the most important components of RTA. It's the least we can do." She grinned. "Besides, I'm under strict orders to see to you today, since Spence is off collecting your baby."

Hetty blinked. All the possible meanings of that phrase shot through her mind and her voice was a little wobbly when she said, "He's what?"

"I know, your precious plane's been sitting up there all this time, but this is really the first chance they've had, with the schedule so messed up."

Oh. The plane. She felt a flush rising to her cheeks and looked away. Abby went on.

"And as Chuck said, it was a bear to get all the parts out here, and it wasn't like anybody could really steal it. But he says he's finally got it flyable, so Ryan flew Spence and his uncle Will out to get her this morning. Then he'll shadow them coming back, just in case."

Hetty knew Will Colton was a fixed-wing pilot, although he hadn't done as much for RTA since they had hired her. But that fact didn't matter to her. What mattered was that it had finally registered exactly where they were going.

"Spence is going back there?" she almost yelped. "To where the shooter was?"

Abby looked puzzled. "To where the plane is. He's the one who knows."

"But what if that guy is still around? What if he's still out there?"

A sudden image of Spence lying on the ground in a pool of blood, dying, shot through her mind and, for a moment, she couldn't breathe. She felt a shudder go through her, tried to stop it, and failed.

"No," she finally blurted. And then all the fears tumbled out in a single rush. "No, he can't go back out there, that guy saw him there that night, too, and he might think Spence saw him, if he's still there he could see him now, and maybe he won't miss this time and—"

She stopped when Abby left her chair and came down beside her on the mat, enveloping her in a rather fierce hug.

"Shh," she soothed. "They're ready for that, Hetty. Armed and ready, I might add. I promise you they are. Ryan and Will would never, ever, let anything happen to Spence. We've been there before, and if there's a vow we Coltons will never break, it's that one. Nothing happens to our kids."

Hetty gulped in a breath and tried to suppress the shakiness that had gripped her the moment she'd thought of Spence being back where the shooter had tried to kill both of them. It took her a moment or two of clenching her jaw, but she finally got her breathing back to normal.

"Now," Abby said, still in that soothing tone, "would you like to tell me what that was about? Is there something going on between you and Spence I should know about?"

Hetty's gaze shot to her face. She looked away quickly, but was very much afraid she had betrayed herself. "I can't...talk about it."

I can't talk about it until we talk about it. Talk. Talk, talk, talk. When had that become the watchword?

"All right," Abby said. "But may I say one thing?"

Hetty looked back at the kind, caring woman who was Spence's mom. She didn't trust herself to speak, so only nodded.

"I hope it's true. That there's something going on between you. Because you would be the best thing that could happen to him."

With that, she got to her feet, took Hetty's empty glass from her, and went back into the house. Leaving Hetty staring after her, her eyes stinging a little at the pure honesty and hope that had been in those words.

Chapter Twenty-Six

His father hadn't had time to look around up here before, when the focus had been on getting Hetty to the trauma center. And then, after that, it had been a crime scene. Actually, two crime scenes that overlapped. And with his son involved in one, and his nephew investigating the other, Spence should have guessed Dad would want to look around now. Neither his father nor his uncle would ever take a threat to one of their offspring lightly. Not with the family history being what it was.

Once Spence had pointed out where the areas involved were, he'd left them to it. He was happy just doing what he could to clean up the cockpit of the plane. Chuck had gotten the fuel pump fixed so that it wouldn't be an issue during takeoff, which was the main time the high-wing aircraft needed it, but there was still a bit of debris from the window that had been shot through, and he didn't really want to chance sitting on broken glass.

And then there were the markings the forensics people had made, showing where they'd found evidence for the photographs they'd taken. He didn't want those there when Hetty was able to get back to the pilot's seat.

He'd thought about trekking up the hill with them, to

where the body had been buried, but decided there was no reason. If he knew his cousin Eli, they'd combed that area so thoroughly they'd probably scared away any scavengers for weeks. And there was no way seeing the spot now would erase the image in his mind of the half-buried body. Besides, he'd had no real desire to revisit the grim site anyway.

The cave, now…

The moment the idea hit, he was seized with a sudden need that seemed undeniable. He climbed out of the plane and jumped down to the beach. He headed up the hill, not quite sure where this urgency had come from. He made it there a lot faster than he had that night, although the memories were so vivid they made him feel just as wound up as if it were that night again, and Hetty was in his arms and bleeding.

He barely slowed for the steeper parts of the climb, and managed not to even look over toward the little waterfall where it had happened.

You think you're rattled? She found the body and then got shot, she's the one who should have been a basket case. But no, not Hetty. She held it together, because that's what she does.

He stepped behind the big Sitka spruce and sidled through the narrow cave entrance. He had to stop for a moment to let his eyes adjust to the dim light. It didn't look like anyone—or anything—had been in there. He supposed whatever scent they'd left behind had kept the wary wild creatures clear. Stupid, vicious humans, however, were another matter, so he trod carefully.

Once he was certain the cave was empty, he walked over to the little alcove where they had spent that long, emotion-filled night. He hadn't really intended to do this, so he only had the flashlight from his phone to use to scan the area. He found some paper wrappings from the gauze, which he automatically picked up and stuffed in his pocket. His instinct about keeping the wilds free of unnatural litter was strong.

His stomach clenched when he found some bloodied cloth lying where Hetty had been. He'd forgotten he'd pulled one of his spare shirts out of the pack and used it to try to staunch the bleeding. The dread he'd felt then washed through him again now.

The next thing he knew, he was crouched down near the cave floor, feeling as if his legs had suddenly given out. The light from the phone lit up a dark spot on the floor of the cave. He knew it was blood, Hetty's blood, and nausea churned his gut. He should have known then how badly hurt she'd been. He should have tried to get her out of there and on the way to help right then, shouldn't have tried to wait until morning even though she had insisted she'd be fine. He should have—

"Spence!"

Even coming through the speaker of the RTA walkie-talkie clipped to his belt, his father's voice sounded…sharp. Harsh. Angry?

At his next thought, dread suddenly swamped him all over again. Had that not been anger he'd heard in Dad's voice, but fear? He hadn't heard any unusual noise, certainly not a shot, but…

He spun on his heel and ran to the mouth of the cave. Froze there, listening. Automatically, his hand slipped down to his belt, checking his knife.

"Spence Colton, get your sorry butt back here right now!"

He heard them both now: anger and fear. But if Dad was calling him back, the threat wasn't there, or wasn't active. Or anywhere near…or he wouldn't be shouting. So he scrambled out of the cave and down the hill, trying to focus on getting there rather than what he might find when he did.

The moment he cleared the tree line, he saw Dad and Uncle Will standing near the helicopter. Had it been tampered with? Was the crazy guy still around? He started to run, and both men turned then, obviously spotting him. For an instant, he thought they both almost sagged a little, as if they'd each let out a huge breath. Of relief?

His brow still furrowed, he slowed when he got closer. He stopped a few feet away, warily. Because both his father and his uncle were not only holding their rifles, they looked…furious.

"What the hell were you thinking?" His father rarely yelled, and even more rarely swore, but he was doing both now. "Taking off like that and not letting us know?"

"I just went back to the cave because—"

"I don't care where, or why, damn it. You were out of sight without a word, when we're within a few yards of where some nutjob tried to kill you!"

Belatedly—far too belatedly—realization hit. His father had been scared, all right. But not for himself. For him.

It all tumbled into place; another time when a Colton had been found too late. The aunt he'd never known, who had been his father's little sister. And for the first time Spence thought of that family history in today's terms, of how he would feel if something had happened to Kansas. He would carry the scar forever and it would influence his reactions for the same length of time. He realized that now because he already knew he would carry the memory of his panic over Hetty the same way, for that same forever.

"I'm sorry, Dad," he said humbly. "I didn't think." He glanced at his uncle. "You, too, Uncle Will. It was stupid. I should have at least used the radio to check in first."

The two men looked a little surprised. And a bit deflated, which he hoped meant he'd taken a bit of the anger out of them. Not that they didn't have the right to be, but he hated the feeling and wanted it gone.

Uncle Will, ever a wise man, nodded in acceptance then excused himself from the scene to go down to the plane, leaving them alone. And when his father spoke again, it was calmer, although a bit of an edge remained.

"Why did you go back to the cave?"

"I…wanted to clean up," he said, gesturing with the shirt he was still holding. His father's gaze locked on the blood-stained garment and he winced. "We left kind of a mess, in all the rush to…to…"

"Save Hetty's life?" Ryan Colton suggested softly.

Spence met his father's steady gaze, swallowed tightly and blinked a couple of times before giving up on speech and simply nodding.

"I get the idea something else happened up there that night that made you want to go back there."

Not ready for this, not until he knew for sure where he and Hetty stood, he muttered, "Just wanted to be sure we hadn't lost anything up there."

"I think," Dad said slowly, "that you didn't lose anything. But just maybe you found something."

Dad had always been too smart to fool for long.

Chapter Twenty-Seven

Hetty was glad when Spence left her alone at the therapy clinic. Not that she wanted him gone, she would much rather have been someplace quiet and private with him now that they were finally away from his parents' house. But she was still new at this therapy thing, and she didn't want him seeing her whimper when the therapist pushed her.

The fact that she had asked the woman to push her as hard as she could without doing damage—she wanted to be back on her feet, sans crutches or even the cane, as soon as possible—didn't mean it didn't hurt like crazy or that she didn't yelp now and then.

And so she'd asked Spence not to hang around and watch, and Mrs. Cowell, who dealt with him like the former marine she was, convinced him of the wisdom of finding something else to do for a couple of hours.

This was not, Hetty thought as she gritted her teeth to do another leg raise, like it was portrayed in the movies. And the next time she saw a film where the protagonist got shot in the leg and the next day was up walking around with barely a limp, she was going to boo and hiss audibly. Maybe throw something at the screen if she was at home.

She pushed harder, until she could feel the tears gathering in her eyes from the pain. Her gut wanted her to push on through, but the therapist had cautioned her the first day that that could be one of the worst things to do.

"You need to listen to your body," she had said warningly. "A little pain is fine, and expected. Agony, not so much. It will set you back, give your body more healing to do, and this will take even longer."

With that echoing in her mind, Hetty eased up until it only hurt, not felt like her leg was tearing apart.

"I have to say," Mrs. Cowell said when she finally called a halt and led her to one of the tables where she would do some massage and heat therapy to promote further healing, "you're the most determined patient I've had in a long time. You're doing well, Hetty."

"Enough for you to give me an estimate on when I'll be back to normal, Mrs. Cowell?"

"I think you'd better call me Liz. We're going to be seeing a lot of each other. But in answer, I'd say a year or so," the older woman said as she worked with nimble hands on Hetty's leg. "That's assuming there's no permanent nerve damage too great to ignore."

Hetty felt a chill ripple over her. She focused on the time span rather than the maybe in the statement, because right now that's what scared her most.

"A year?"

With a tiny quirk of her mouth that told Hetty she was about to get one of those comparisons she loved to make, the therapist said, "I assumed you meant back to where you were before this happened. I'd say you'll be back to functional much sooner, if you keep working this hard. Another week like this, and maybe you can try that cane your man came in and got for you."

Hetty let out a breath of relief. But then the last of the woman's words truly registered. "Wait, who got the cane?"

Liz's brow wrinkled. "The guy we just chased out of here? Spence Colton?"

Hetty felt a flood of warmth inside her. She knew that Spence had brought the cane into her room for inspiration—which she'd needed after the worst parts of these sessions—but she hadn't realized he'd been the one to actually come here and get it.

They were wrapping up before Liz spoke about Spence again. "He's a good man," she said, her tone devoid of any of her usual prodding or teasing. "I'd hang on to that one if I were you."

"We're…still working that out."

The therapist smiled widely. "Judging by the way he looks at you, it's already worked out in his mind."

Hetty's gaze shot to her face. She'd already realized the therapist noticed everything and sensed even more, so she risked the question. "You really think so?"

The tough, relentless woman's expression softened in a way Hetty had not seen before. "He looks at you the way my Matt used to look at me."

Used to? Hetty glanced at the woman's left hand, where a simple gold band adorned her ring finger, then back at her face. The truth was there in her eyes, in the aching sadness, before she confirmed it with words.

"I lost him a few years ago. He was KIA overseas," the woman said quietly.

Hetty couldn't stop herself, she reached out and clasped that hand, her palm over that ring. She didn't want to say the usual, trite platitudes, which had always seemed useless to her. So instead she said, just as quietly, "He chose well."

The woman's eyes brightened and she knew somehow she'd found the right words. "We were good together."

There was a sound from the doorway and they both looked. It was Spence, who apparently had just made the other therapist—a young man about a foot shorter than he was—laugh. Liz looked back at Hetty.

"Don't waste time you can never get back," she said softly, and there was an amazing combination of remembered pain and goodwill in her voice and her expression.

"You're right," Hetty said decisively. "That ends today."

Back on the crutches—which she was now determined to be rid of after that two weeks Liz had mentioned—she made her way toward the door. Spence was still just outside the door, now looking at something on his phone. She didn't think she'd made any noise, but his head came up sharply and he turned to look as if he'd somehow sensed her coming.

And she thought she'd go through any amount of this hell to see the smile that spread across his face when he saw her.

He looks at you the way my Matt used to look at me...

She was done wasting time.

"Do you have a run this afternoon?" she asked him without preamble.

"No," he said, sounding startled. "I cleared the day. I've got nothing until tomorrow."

"Good. We're going to have that talk."

He drew back slightly, either startled again or...wary. Well, if it was wary, she wanted to know now. Before she let herself fall any further than she already had. Maybe he'd decided that night in the cave had been a mistake, or a hallucination, or maybe he'd only been trying to placate her because she'd been hurt. She didn't know, but it was past time she found out. It wasn't like her to be this indecisive, to have let this drift along for nearly two weeks. But she wanted this so much, maybe she was just afraid of the answers she'd get.

So when did you become a coward?

She wasn't, she told herself firmly. The dodging ended now.

"Where are we going?" Spence asked after they were back in his SUV, still sounding somewhat nervous.

"Somewhere where we can look at this place we love," she said.

Yet again, he looked surprised, but she saw one corner of his mouth twitch, as if he liked what she'd said. She'd meant it, she did love this place, although maybe not quite in the "get out there and learn every inch of it from the ground up" way he did. No, she preferred flying over it, where she could see the incredible vastness, the amazing range, from the water of the sound to the towering mountains, with every variation in between.

She especially savored this time of year, despite the lack of an actual nighttime. She loved the way the snow forever on the peaks contrasted with the fresh green of new growth below and, in turn, with the deep blue of the water. It made her heart swell; made her feel lucky that this was where she'd been born and raised.

"I got a text from Officer Reynolds," he said as they stopped at one of Shelby's few traffic signals. "He said Portland may have a line on the ex-wife, and he'll let us know."

"If it turns out to be her, remind me never to set foot in Portland again," she said as the light changed.

A few minutes later, when Spence pulled the SUV to a stop atop a slight rise just outside of town, where they could

sit and look at everything she'd just thought about, she wondered not for the first time if the man could read her mind.

Her stomach gurgled a little but she ignored it. Food
could wait. This could not. And then Spence reached into
the back seat and came up with a small cooler. He opened
it, dipped in, and showed her a bundle wrapped in paper.
She knew at her fist whiff that it was one of the delicious
roast beef sandwiches from the shop just above the marina.

"They said it was your favorite," Spence said.

"It is," she agreed, impressed yet again, both that he'd
thought of this at all, and especially that he'd bothered to
find out what she particularly liked. And in view of that,
she decided eating could come first. But she'd do it fast.

"Then let's go sit down out there and eat. You're burning
up a lot of energy in that therapy," he said. "Mrs. Cowell
is quite a taskmaster."

"She said I should call her Liz. I feel like I've been hon-
ored."

"I can see why."

"We're pushing for me to be off the crutches after two
weeks." She gave him a sideways look. "And on to using
the cane you got for me."

He didn't even react. As if it were the most obviously
normal thing in the world for him to go out of his way to
both pick up the device and think to place it where it would
inspire her to work toward it.

*Judging by the way he looks at you, it's already worked
out in his mind.*

She hoped the taskmaster was right.

Chapter Twenty-Eight

Spence was really glad he'd stopped and picked up lunch. He knew it was just a delaying tactic. But so what? Was any guy ever not nervous about "the talk"?

He got out of the SUV and grabbed the tarp he always carried in the back, because you never knew up here when you might need to protect something from an unexpected burst of rain or snow. He walked over to the spot he frequented himself, with the best, most glorious view down to the marina, over the sound and to the mountains on the other side.

He busied himself a little more than necessary before going back to get Hetty. And lectured himself while he did it. Either she had meant what she'd said in the cave, or she hadn't. Hetty was inherently honest, but maybe she'd been too rattled or hurting too much to dig deep. Or maybe she had been thinking she needed him to get out of there, so she'd better not make him mad.

No. That wasn't Hetty. She would never admit to what she had that night if it wasn't true, even if she was in pain.

Would she?

When he'd helped her over to the chosen spot and they'd settled in, she took the sandwich while he reached into the small cooler, brought out and popped open two cans of soda.

He chewed his own first bite of roast beef sandwich a bit more thoroughly than was really necessary. What did he know about it? He'd never in his life been serious about a woman before. At least, not as serious as he was now.

Maybe because you were waiting for her.

He stopped chewing. Sat there staring out over the vista that felt like a part of him down to his soul, with a mouthful of meat, cheese and the tangy sauce that gave it the kick he liked.

Could it be true? Could that be another reason, maybe the real reason, he reacted the way he did when clients would come on to him? He'd never really considered it before, but after that night in the cave, he'd thought about it a lot. He had realized that it was like flipping a switch; that he'd be going along just fine until some woman started the game and, almost with an audible click, he'd turn on that Spence, the one who could banter like the biggest playboy in town. And all the time, underneath, he'd known he was anything but. That it was the mask he put on. The protection.

But he'd never really wondered if there was another reason he did it, why he made certain to keep those interactions on the surface, essentially meaningless. Never wondered if there was a reason he'd never been even slightly tempted to hang on to one of those freely given phone numbers after the client—and some of them had been pretty darned attractive—was on the way back to wherever she'd come from.

But now he wondered if it was that, somewhere down deep, he'd known it would never turn into anything because that part of him was already taken.

By Hetty Amos.

He finally swallowed that very well-chewed bite. Stared down at the sound below, at the sunlight dancing on the water, at the cargo ship heading out after unloading whatever portion of its load had been sent to Shelby. He knew in some places they were considered unsightly, but in Shelby they were welcomed, bringing in things from far away. Of course, pretty much everything was far away from Shelby, so if something you wanted or needed was out of stock, you waited. And waited. His gaze shifted to the ever-snow-capped mountaintops, and once again deemed it well worth it.

"It's wonderful to love where you live, isn't it."

Hetty said it as if it were a given, not a question. And suddenly he realized this was the key, this was the way to say what he wanted to say, because he knew she would understand.

"Yes. And I especially love the hidden places I've never told anyone about, places where I never take anyone."

She drew back slightly, her head tilting as she studied him. Hetty-like, instead of asking what places, she asked simply, "Why?"

He sucked in a deep breath and took the plunge. "Because they're special to me, and I wouldn't want to show them to anyone who wouldn't love them as I do. There's a spot up on the ridge—" he gestured up and to the east "—where you can see three of the lakes, the sound, and on a clear day all the way to Mount St. Elias. There's a place in Wrangell where I've been watching a family of Canadian lynx grow up and coexist with a herd of Dall sheep. And a spot lower down where I actually collided with a flying squirrel. Or vice versa."

She was staring at him now, and he knew she hadn't missed the significance of this outpouring, right after he'd said he never told anyone about these special places. But he said what he needed to say anyway.

"I want to show you all of those, Hetty. And so many more. Places so beautiful you have to remind yourself to breathe. So amazing, you're thinking it has to be special effects. Places I've hoarded, kept to myself, because there wasn't anyone who'd look at them or from them and feel what I feel."

"I would," she said softly.

"I know. That's why you need to get well fast, so I can show them to you. All of them."

"Spence."

It was all she said, and he didn't quite know how to interpret it. A spark of fear careened through his brain, that he'd misinterpreted everything. It wouldn't be the first time. But he had to know, and he had to know now. And so it came out a little bluntly.

"I meant what I said that night in the cave. Did you?"

He thought he saw her take in a breath. Then she looked up, holding his gaze steadily. And said, softly, almost reverently, "Every word."

His heart seemed to miss a beat then race to catch up. "All this time…" he said and stopped because he had no idea how to finish. But Hetty finished it for him.

"We've been hiding, me behind sarcasm, you behind flirting. We've wasted a lot of time."

"We have. That stops now."

"Agreed."

A vista as vast as the one they were looking at in reality seemed to roll out in his mind. A future, built on a foundation started more than a decade ago, starring the woman who had changed his life then and would change it again now.

He reached out and with his thumb gently wiped away the trace of that tangy sandwich sauce from the corner of her mouth. That mouth... He wished he had leaned in and kissed it away. Her lips parted, and her tongue crept out as if to taste that spot he'd touched. It was too much and his resistance—resistance that was merely habit, now that they'd admitted out here in the brilliant light of day as opposed to under that Midnight Sun—vanished.

He slipped a hand around the back of her neck in the same moment she reached up to cup his cheek, sending a ripple of luscious sensation through him. And then his mouth was on hers and the ripple became a wave. He let her lead, because it seemed the thing to do. And she did, tasting, probing, until his control snapped. The next thing he knew they were sprawled on the canvas he'd laid out, arms around each other, deep into a kiss he never wanted to end.

It was everything he'd ever thought it would be in those rare times when the idea crept around his defenses and into his imagination. No, it was more. It was incredible. Staggering. Maybe even astonishing.

What it wasn't was impossible. Not anymore.

After all these years, after all the sniping and mocking, and his own fakery and pretending, this was what was real. This was what they'd been hiding.

This was what he'd always wanted but been afraid to go after.

And when they finally broke the kiss, they simply stared at each other, blue eyes boring into green, and Spence knew he had never in his life felt anything more right than that kiss and Hetty in his arms.

He wondered if the smile that he couldn't stop looked half as goofy, as giddy, as he felt. And if Hetty's smile in return was at how silly he must look or because…she felt the same way. He didn't have to wonder long.

"That," she said softly, "was almost worth the wasted time."

An emotion he'd only ever felt when looking at one of those special, secret places he was going to take her to welled up inside him. The only word he could think of for it was beyond corny, but it was the only word that fit.

Joy.

"I guess we really needed our cage rattled to get out of our old rut."

"Well, that's one of the better mixed metaphors I've heard lately," Hetty said, and he knew she was using that old, familiar, tutoring tone of voice on purpose.

Spence laughed and the elation he was feeling practically echoed in the sound of it. He wanted to seize this moment and hang on to it forever.

Just as he wanted to do with Hetty.

Images of the life they could build, here in this place they both loved, unrolled in his head like some video stream. She could move out of her tiny apartment, maybe into his place. Or if she didn't want that, they'd find a new place for both of them. Some place private, where they could pursue this electric connection they had.

He wasn't foolish enough to think there wouldn't have to be some give and take, some adjustments on each side, but they'd do it. They'd do it because it was meant to be, they'd just been fighting it for years. They would—

A loud cough from rather close by made them both jump. They jerked around to see Officer Reynolds standing there.

"Sorry to bother you," he said, "but I saw your SUV up here, Spence, and had some news you need to hear."

Spence went very still. He heard Hetty suck in a breath. They both started to get up, but Reynolds crouched down until he was at eye level with them. His normally neutral, sometimes-thoughtful expression had been taken over by a furrowed forehead and concerned eyes. Bobby Reynolds took his job very seriously, and Spence again had the thought that he hadn't appreciated the small-town cop nearly enough.

"We heard from the PD in Portland, finally. They're really strapped right now, so it took them a while, but…they found your client's ex."

The man hesitated and Spence braced himself, already guessing what was coming next from his somber demeanor.

"Get it said," he told him, reaching out to grip Hetty's hand in his, squeezing it gently.

Reynolds nodded. "All right. They kept on her, and she finally admitted it. She hired somebody to follow her ex and his new wife up here and kill them both."

Chapter Twenty-Nine

Spence heard Hetty's smothered gasp at Reynolds's words, but he wasn't surprised at all. He'd been expecting this ever since he'd heard about the ex-wife. Still, his voice was tight when he spoke again.

"Hired...who?"

He knew the answer to that, too, before Reynolds spoke. "We don't know. All we have is the name Strauss, and it's probably an alias." The cop grimaced. "Barton told me that was the cover name of one of the most prolific hitman ever known, who committed from a hundred to five hundred hits for Murder, Inc., back in the thirties."

"History student or delusions of grandeur?" Spence asked, his tone sour.

"Who knows," Reynolds answered. "I'd lean toward delusions, given his inefficiency."

"For which I'll be eternally thankful," Hetty said fervently, the first thing she had said since this had started.

As will I. Again the image of her down and bleeding tried to take over Spence's mind, but he made himself focus on the subject at hand. "The Creedmoor round isn't going to help much if you don't find the weapon, right?"

Barton nodded. "It's efficient and cheap, so it's all over."

"Low recoil," Spence said, remembering his thoughts about the shooter being maybe a city guy. "Maybe the he's not used to rifles. Or more used to up-close-and-personal weapons."

"Could well be," Reynolds agreed. "They're working on it down in Portland, and we're doing what we can from here. The ex said she found him online, through a connection she wouldn't give up. We don't know how she found out RTA was who they'd booked the trip with, but apparently she did."

"So he knew right where to look," Hetty said.

Reynolds nodded. "Yes. And he told her he'd been to Alaska once before."

Spence couldn't help snorting. "Like that makes him an expert."

He hated people like that. People who thought they knew it all when they knew nothing. It made him recall how neighboring Valdez had begun as a landing port for miners during the gold rush in 1897, and how they'd been conned into thinking something called the Valdez Glacier Trail existed and would lead them directly to the rich, untouched gold fields. That it had turned out to be a hoax promoted by steamship companies to sell tickets, a hoax that had cost many lives and was a sore spot with any local who knew the history.

"I get the feeling that if he was as good as he told her he was, we wouldn't be here talking now," Reynolds said.

Meaning one or both of them would be dead. "Then I'm glad he wasn't," Hetty said heatedly. "This was bad enough."

Reynolds looked at her as if to go on, but hesitated.

"She can take it," Spence said.

That got him a flashing smile from Hetty. But the smile died when Reynolds said, "He knows that you saw him."

Spence had figured that out early on, because there'd been no other reason for the shooter to go after them so strongly once he'd discovered his true targets had not kept their part of his evil bargain.

"He knows Hetty did. I think I was just insurance."

Reynolds nodded. "Maybe, but I kind of doubt he'd risk that you didn't see him. A hired gun isn't usually the type to leave loose ends."

Spence's brow creased. "But he's not from here. Maybe he'd just head back to wherever home is and figure we're far enough away we'd never find him."

"Could be." Reynolds's mouth twisted wryly. "Lots of people from down there think we're a different country anyway. So maybe he's gone and will never come back. But do you want to pin your lives on a maybe?"

"But he doesn't know who we are," Hetty said. "I mean other than we're from RTA."

Reynolds grimaced. "You're all over the RTA website. Named and labeled as locals. In a town of less than four thousand, that narrows his search a lot already. And it's clear that you're the one who flies the floatplane, and Spence is the premier guide in the area, if not the entire state. And in case you haven't looked lately, there are a ton of photos of the two of you with various guests. It's easy to extrapolate that you're usually together."

Spence knew that, in light of the subject matter, it was silly to feel a pleasant little jolt at those last three words, but he couldn't seem to help it.

...you're usually together.

He wanted that to be the mantra for the rest of their lives. He wanted it to be just as true fifty years from now as it was today. He wanted them to be like his parents were, still in love after all these years and all they'd been through.

And he'd do whatever it took to make that happen.

The first thing he had to do was keep Hetty safe, because Reynolds was right, they were all over the website, with pictures clear enough to make them recognizable to anyone who took the time to look. And while the hired gun might not be the best shot—at least, not out here in the backcountry—they couldn't assume he hadn't done his homework.

"The state troopers are being good about sharing information, and I'll pass along anything that's relevant," Reynolds said. "But until we nail this guy down, watch your back."

When Reynolds left them, with assurances they were doing all they could, Spence sat for a moment longer before he could bring himself to meet Hetty's eyes. The incident at the camp was one thing, knowing a hired killer was afraid you'd seen and could identify him was something else altogether.

When he finally shifted his gaze, he saw that she looked troubled but not panicked. But then, Hetty never panicked. She was a lot more likely to get angry about a threat than scared.

He mentally abandoned his wishful thinking about her moving into his place with him. She was better off at the big house, with more people around to keep an eye out. In fact, he'd best stop by his place, grab some things and stay there himself until this was resolved. Better to have three people there looking out for her. He needed to tell his folks about this anyway, so they could be on guard.

So much for that grand seduction scene I was imagining.

"What was that face for?" Hetty asked.

"You don't want to know," he muttered. "Come on, let's go. I need to tell Mom and Dad about this."

She didn't resist. In fact, she nodded quickly when he mentioned his folks. But once he'd gotten up and helped her—which she did try to refuse, but relented when he mentioned that speed was kind of important at the moment—to her feet, she slanted him a troubled look.

"Maybe I shouldn't stay there," she said. "It might put them in danger, too."

"The more eyes watching out, the better," he said shortly as he folded up the tarp they'd been sitting on. "I'll stay there, too. And I have to let Kansas and Parker know about this, too."

"But if I went somewhere else, they wouldn't need to worry."

"Fine," he said shortly, finishing with the tarp and looking at her. "You can move into my place and I'll cancel all my upcoming jobs—"

"You can't do that!"

"I can if you're going to let this clown decide what you do. Which," he added when she glared at him, "is totally unlike you, so I'm going to assume you're just worried about everybody else instead of yourself."

Her expression changed completely. The distress faded away, to be replaced by something else, something warmer, gentler, something almost…pleased? As if he'd somehow, despite the worry that wanted to swamp him, managed to find the right thing to say to her.

"What?" he finally asked when she continued to just look at him.

"You really do know me," she said softly.

All traces of anger faded away, as if she had the power to erase them with those simple words. Or the way she said them. Or the way she looked at him when she did. He didn't know. And right now he didn't care.

"That's because I love you."

He said it, knowing this could easily be the worst possible time, knowing this wasn't at all the kind of romantic setting he would have preferred, knowing he'd intended to play it safe and wait until she said it first. But none of that mattered now. It was the truth, and he'd had to say it now in case things went bad and he didn't get the chance later.

She was staring at him, looking a little shocked. She couldn't be surprised, could she? Or was her reaction because he'd actually said the words? He didn't know. The only thing he knew for sure was that he didn't want her to say the words back at him—not now, not as a reflex kind of reaction. He wanted them from her in the same way he'd given them—because he hadn't been able to stop them.

"Let's go," he said abruptly, bending to pick up her crutches and hand them to her. He tucked the folded tarp under his left arm, then grabbed up the cooler and shifted it to his left hand so his right was free to help her if she needed it. The ground was uneven up here, and better safe than sorry.

She took the crutches and began to make her way back to the vehicle. She didn't say another word.

But she was smiling.

Chapter Thirty

Because I love you.

The words Hetty had never, ever, expected to hear played on a seemingly endless loop in her head. And all the while as she made her way rather laboriously back to the car, she was aware that Spence was right there. Not forcing his help on her, but right there just in case.

A bit of rueful self-understanding went through her mind. Nobody knew better than Spence how irritated she got when people insisted she needed help she didn't need. She'd certainly snapped at him more than once for his assumptions she couldn't handle something herself. But after how attentive he'd been since she'd been hurt, how—*face it, girl*—how sweet he'd been, she realized it was just who he was underneath the carefree exterior she now knew was a shield of sorts between himself and those who might judge him for that brain quirk he'd been born with.

Despite the effort with the crutches on this uneven ground, she kept smiling. She couldn't seem to help it.

Because I love you.

Why wouldn't she be smiling, after that?

She was a little puzzled by his demeanor after the words had come out. He'd seemed to be...she wasn't sure what to call it. She was only sure that, unlike most people would be, he wasn't waiting to hear her say the words back to him. In fact, he'd acted almost as if he didn't want her to say it. As if what he'd said didn't change…well, everything.

Hetty gave herself a mental shake. She needed to remember the news Officer Reynolds had just dropped on them; that not only had that man been a hired killer, he could now be after them. She wanted desperately to believe he truly had gone back to where he'd come from, never to darken Alaska's door again, but as Reynolds had said, Did they want to risk their lives on a maybe?

Spence was so quiet on the drive back toward his folks' house she couldn't help wondering if he was regretting what he'd blurted out. Was that why he hadn't pushed her to say it back to him? Had it come out of some emotion, some weak spot in his armor that he now regretted?

"Are you okay for a bit longer?" he suddenly asked. "I need to stop by the office."

"Fine," she said. "I'd like to see Lakin, if she's there."

"She'll be there. Place would fall apart without her."

She hesitated then said, "I'm going back to your parents' place. You're not really going to cancel all your upcoming jobs, are you?"

He gave her a sideways glance. "No. I can't really. Parker's covering, but he can only do so much alone."

"I know." She sighed. "Even your dad and uncle are having to come back to work."

She heard him chuckle and looked up, startled. "How's it feel to know it takes two grown men to replace you?"

She couldn't help it, she burst out laughing. "Hey, and you," she said. "You've been too busy taking care of me."

He shifted his gaze back to the road as they neared the turn to RTA. "Mutually exclusive," he said.

"What?"

"I can't be too busy if I'm taking care of you." His voice sounded a little gruff, as if he were trying to be his usual smart-mouthed self and failing.

Hetty felt a stinging in her eyes and blinked rapidly to hold back the welling tears. She swallowed past the tightness in her throat, thinking oddly that while she'd been brought to tears by pain a couple of times in therapy, the difference was unmistakable.

When they arrived, Spence was right behind her as she maneuvered up the three steps to the entrance to RTA. Not beside her, as he'd been before, but behind her, no doubt figuring if she fell, it would be backward. But he didn't, as he once had, offer to just lift her up, nor did he take her arm to steady her; he let her make the short ascent herself.

"Liz said I wasn't helping you by…well, helping you all the time," he said when they were on the porch, as if he felt an explanation was required.

"I know. I have to do as much as I can by myself, even if having to go so slow drives me nuts."

He did open the door for her and hold it, but she quickly decided that wrestling with a big, heavy, wooden door while hanging on to her crutches and keeping her balance was a three-way battle she wasn't quite ready for. Besides, he'd do that for anyone. He was just…polite. She'd seen him do it recently, when he'd held the door to Roaster's open for Mr. Harper from the hardware store, who'd had his hands full. That had been—was it really only two weeks ago today, on the Fourth of July? It seemed like it should be much longer ago, so much had happened since.

And he was kind. Like when he'd comforted that little boy whose dog had been lost, and in fact had found the critter a couple of blocks away.

And thoughtful, as he'd proved when all her favorite foods had showed up in his mother's kitchen.

And she had been too wrapped up in sniping at him for flirting with clients to notice. Too busy doing that to realize that it was all a cover. A protective front. She had the feeling she'd underestimated the amount of mockery and teasing he'd likely undergone in school before they'd had that breakthrough.

She'd always thought he hadn't wanted to go to college because he'd already known his future was with RTA. But maybe part of it had also been that he'd had enough school to choke on. And she couldn't really blame him. After all, she'd chosen her own path, too, forgoing college for flight training.

The thought made her smile. Maybe they were more alike than she had ever realized. She'd had her own kind of protections in place in school. She'd always known she got second glances because of her mixed heritage. More even than Lakin because, as an Inuit, her ancestors were at least native to the area. But Hetty's grandfather had been the first of her family born here, a few years before Alaska had become a state in 1959, and the fact that she was a third-generation Alaskan had always been her armor against anyone who made unwise comments. Honest questions were fine, it was the smart-mouths she took off at the knees.

Spence had just closed the door behind them when Lakin came out of the back office into the lobby area. She spotted them immediately.

"Hetty!"

Lakin ran toward them with her arms extended, as if she were going to throw them around her. Hetty saw the moment when she realized that might not be a good idea—Had that been Spence making that low "ahem" kind of sound?—and she slowed down. When she was close enough, Lakin reached out and gave her a gentle hug, quite a difference from the high-speed collision it could have been. Which could have been disastrous for Hetty.

"It's so good to see you here," Lakin exclaimed. "We've all been so worried, and we've missed you so much."

Hetty smiled widely. She'd missed the long talks she and Lakin always had. And she sent out a mental jab to her brother to quit taking this wonderful person for granted and put a little—no, a lot—more effort into the relationship. Because she wanted this sister of the heart to become one for real.

"I'll just be in the office while you two catch up," Spence said rather diplomatically. And he looked a little stunned when his cousin spun around and gave him the more enthusiastic hug she'd almost knocked Hetty over with.

"Thank you for taking such good care of her, Spence."

"I'm not—"

"Hush," Hetty said to him, startling him anew. "You are and you have."

And she thought the combination of his embarrassed expression and the heat that flashed in those gorgeous blue eyes of his was the most wonderful thing she'd ever seen.

When they were alone, Lakin ushered her to the seating area in the lobby. Hetty took one of the armchairs across from the sofa, since the seat was higher and it would be easier for her to get up. Lakin sat on the edge of the coffee table, as if she needed to be closer to her. Hetty noticed, and felt a renewed rush of the warmth she always felt toward this friend she so much wanted to be family. Yes, Troy better get his act together.

They talked about that for a bit, but not long since it was old ground they'd been over many times. Then Lakin caught her up on the doings at RTA, including how they'd rented a floatplane temporarily until the one she normally flew was fully repaired, and how her dad was saying after only two weeks of filling in that they needed to give Hetty a raise.

Hetty laughed at that. "They just gave me one six months ago. A healthy one, too."

"They want you happy and staying," Lakin said fervently. "Even more now that we're limping along without you." A grin flashed across her face. "And with you."

"I'll be back soon, I swear." *And that's to myself as much as anyone. No matter how much it hurts, I'll push through.*

Lakin glanced at the closed office door then back to Hetty. "Maybe, in the end, this will have been a good thing." Hetty blinked and Lakin went on hastily. "I mean you and Spence... I'm not imagining things have changed between you, am I?"

"I...no. Not, you're not." Somehow admitting it out loud to Lakin made it even more real to her.

Her friend hesitated, but Hetty could tell by her wrinkled brow she was on the verge of saying more.

"Out with it, girlfriend," she said.

"I just... I know it's none of my business, but you've always been there for me about Troy and..." Hetty stayed silent, knowing Lakin would get there. And when she did, it came out in a rush. "You're sure it's not just...what happened? I know crazy feelings can happen when you go through something like that together. And my brother Eli has talked about how all that danger, and tension, and the rush of relief when you survive can skew your thinking and your emotions."

Hetty stared at her friend. "You think…it's not real?"

"Oh, no, and I hope it is!" Lakin took a deep breath. "I've always thought there was something else behind all the annoyance and the little jabs you fired at him. I just don't want either you or my cousin hurt."

Hetty leaned forward, ignoring the tug from her leg, until she could take Lakin's hand in hers. "My brother is a very lucky man. And he'd better wake up darn soon or my next therapy exercise is going to be to kick his butt."

Lakin laughed and could barely stop to say, "I want to watch that."

"I'll be selling tickets," Hetty promised.

Yes, she was going to be having a long talk with Troy when he finally got that butt she was going to kick off that oil rig.

Chapter Thirty-One

It had been a bit of a rough ride on the ATV, but Hetty gauged the slightly increased ache in her leg and labeled it worth it.

But then, this spot would be worth almost anything. And Spence had said it wasn't even in the top three on his list, so she couldn't even imagine what incredible place held that number-one spot.

He'd arranged his work schedule so that he had time to make this trek. Changed everything for her, as he had for days on end now. She knew he had made a run to take some regulars up to one of the family-style camps they had set up this Friday morning, but didn't have to go back for them until Sunday afternoon. And so here they were, in this place she'd never been and that he apparently never shared.

Until now.

It was strange, she'd always thought she had the best views possible of this beautiful land she lived in. Because what could be better than flying high above it, able to see for miles and miles in all directions? What could be better than truly realizing the size and scope of this state she loved, which was bigger than the next three largest states combined?

But she had overlooked the things she didn't get from

altitude, from her plane. The caress of a summer breeze, the scent of things growing so madly fast since they had so little time, the vibrant life of the birds and animals making the most of this short season.

The distinctive calls of a pair of bald eagles, talking to each other, cut through the silence that she'd realized wasn't really silent at all. It had been Spence who had told her to just sit there, quietly.

"Wait and listen," he'd said when they'd reached the top of the rise that overlooked their hometown in one direction and a small verdant hillside in the other. She had, and soon had realized she could hear the rustle of leaves and branches where there was no wind, the differing calls of so many birds and, as they'd waited, eventually the chatter of other, grounded creatures also making the most of the sunshine and warmth.

Things she was never aware of from the cockpit of an airplane. She'd been so busy flying over this land, she'd forgotten the wonder of walking it. She wouldn't let that happen again.

Hetty smiled inwardly as she thought that Spence would see to that.

"Thank you," she said softly, not wanting to disturb their temporary neighbors. "I'd forgotten how different it is… down here."

"If you only see the big picture all the time, you can miss the little details that make it worth it." Spence spoke as quietly as she had, barely above a whisper, but with the rough edge that made her skin tingle.

"I'm realizing that," she answered. Then, with a smile, she added, "They must be used to you, the locals up here. They barely turned a hair—or a feather—when we motored up to this spot."

He gave her a smile. That slightly crooked one she treasured. "They are, I think. This is my closest secret spot, so it's the one I come to when I need the break but don't have time for one of the others."

"Will you show me those, too? When I can make it that far?"

"Everything," he said in the tone of a vow. "No secrets, not from you."

Her throat tightened. When Spence Colton made up his mind, he obviously didn't do it halfway.

"Well," she said, turning in the ATV's surprisingly comfortable seat to look straight at him, "in that same vein of no secrets, I had a little chat with my doctor this morning."

Spence went very still. He of course knew she'd been for a follow-up, since he'd been the one to take her there.

"Not bad news?" he asked, sounding rather endearingly anxious.

"The opposite. She said I'm healing well, and that if I'm careful, I can do anything I feel up to, short of climbing Denali."

"Well, darn," Spence said, grinning with obvious relief now, "there go my plans for us for the weekend."

She took a deep breath. She wasn't sure why this was so difficult. The man had been taking care of her for three weeks straight, and once how he felt about her was out in the open, he'd apparently had no qualms about admitting it. And she'd confronted her feelings for him while she was still lying in that hospital, watching him sleep restlessly in the chair beside her bed.

"I was hoping we could make other plans for the weekend," she managed to get out, feeling heat rising up to her cheeks.

"Sure," he said cheerfully. "Where do you want to go?"

She needed another deep breath. Wondered if she was jumping the gun, if it was too soon, if she had misinter-preted—

"Hetty?"

She met his gaze, stared into those eyes she knew so well. "I've never been to your place."

"I know, you never wanted to—" He broke off and she saw his eyes widen. He swallowed visibly. "Hetty?"

"You've been in and out of my place picking things up for me for three weeks now. Don't you think it's time I saw yours?"

"I…sure."

He looked a little nervous and she wondered if it was be-cause he was a guy nervous about what mess he might have left behind, or if he'd read her intent. Her intent that the tour would end in his bedroom. She'd waited long enough, and the doctor had indeed said, if she was careful, it would be all right.

"Just let him do all the work," she'd said in a teasing tone that made Hetty like her even more. She'd even dug into a supply drawer and come up with a box of condoms, which she'd tossed to Hetty with a grin. That box was now tucked away in her purse, which was locked in his SUV back at RTA where they'd picked up their ride.

Spence's home was nothing like she'd imagined. The cabin-like two-bedroom place not far from the RTA office had large windows facing downhill toward the sound. To the rear, it was tucked into a stand of trees, and knowing Spen-ce's penchant for being outside whenever possible, she'd bet there was a deck out there.

The inside was…cozy. Warm. Welcoming. She thought

she recognized Abby Colton's fine hand in the décor, but the color scheme was pure Spence: evergreen, blue, and the gray of a young Sitka spruce. Like the one masking the cave.

And it was tidy. Tidier than her own place sometimes got. Sure, there were some boots by the door, but that was typical of just about anyone up here. There was a jacket tossed over the back of a chair, and an empty coffee mug on the counter between the kitchen and the living room, but other than that, if there was a mess, it was hidden.

In the bedroom?

She wondered when Spence Colton's bedroom had become the focus of her existence. That night in the cave? Or when he'd kissed her in his parents' house? Or when Dr. Masters had given her the okay to…what? Jump him? No, she was supposed to let him do all the work.

Her pulse kicked up at the images that brought to mind. Trying to slow herself down, she looked around the living room. Her gaze stopped dead at the unexpected item on the wall above the couch. A large, framed photograph of, of all things, a big city. She scanned for any landmarks she'd recognize that would tell her what megametropolis it was, but found nothing.

Finally, she looked at Spence. "Well, that was the last thing I would have expected to see on your wall."

He started to respond but stopped. Then the words finally came. "You want to know why?"

She went very still inside, sensing there was much more to this than the surface question. "I want to know everything," she said quietly.

She saw him swallow, as if her words had reached him

beyond their mere definition. It was a moment before he said, "It's all about the sequence."

She blinked, not understanding. Instead of explaining in more words, he walked toward the couch. She made herself look at more than just the way he moved, and saw he was looking at the picture. When he reached the couch, he turned around and sat down. And was, she realized, facing the large windows with the spectacular view down to the sound, with the mountains on the other side sharp and clear on this cloudless day. If anything, an image of that panorama was what she would have expected to see on his wall.

It's all about the sequence.

It hit her then. He'd walked over facing the city and then...turned his back on it. Turned to face the reality outside. His reality, the place and the life he loved.

"It's there to remind you how glad you are to live here," she said.

"And not there," he said. "I knew you'd get it. Because you get me."

"More now," she admitted.

To her surprise, he shook his head. "You got me back when I needed it most."

She knew he meant back in school. "I always knew how smart you were, you just had this glitch. It took until I realized how brilliant you were at math, unless it was a word problem, to put it together."

"But you did. I thought I was just stupid, like everybody said."

"Surely your parents didn't."

He shrugged and looked a little sheepish. "No, they didn't. They told me just the opposite. But at that age, what do your parents know?"

She laughed. "I was always amazed at how smart Mom got after I turned twenty-five."

"Yes. Mine, too."

"They are very smart," she confirmed.

"But they think…" He shifted his gaze back to the window.

"They think what?"

"That we…belong." He looked back at her, took a deep breath and added, "Together."

And there it was. The opening she'd wanted. And, for the first time, she didn't hesitate. "Told you they were smart."

"Hetty…"

"I'd run to you, like in the movies, if I could."

He was on his feet in an instant. He didn't quite run, but only because the room wasn't that big. Still, he was with her in mere seconds, close, warm, his arms around her as he looked down at her.

"You're sure, Hetty? Because if you change your mind, I'll stop, but it may kill me."

She smiled up at him, letting all the feelings that had been swirling between them show. "When do I get to see the bedroom?"

He swore under his breath, low, harsh, and so hungry, it made her flush with heat.

"By the way," she added, feeling a little giddy, "the doctor says you have to do all the work."

"My pleasure," he said, and he sounded every bit as hot and eager as she felt.

The promise of that night in the cave was about to be kept.

Chapter Thirty-Two

Spence wasn't a slob, something he was thankful for at the moment. He might have tossed a shirt over the back of that chair by the window and hung the towel to dry from the bathroom doorknob this morning, but other than that, the bedroom was tidy enough. Besides, to him, the big window that looked down at the sound, and the fact that he could see just the edge of the RTA building in the distance, made him not care so much what the inside looked like. Of course, it made life a little interesting this time of year when the sun never really set, but a good pair of blackout curtains helped.

But right now, absolutely nothing mattered other than the woman he held in his arms. He'd never dreamed, never dared even hoped, that they might end up here like this someday. He'd always thought she'd disliked him so much it could never, ever, happen. He'd always thought she still remembered him as that kid everyone wrote off as stupid, or whose brain was weird.

And then he couldn't think at all because Hetty, his Hetty, the woman he'd always assumed was far beyond his reach, was kissing him. Hotly, fiercely, until he was breathless. He had the crazy thought his muscles had melted from it, because he felt as if they couldn't hold him up any longer.

It was all he could do to control how they fell onto his bed, making sure he took the brunt, with Hetty deliciously on top of him. She was so lithe, energetic and strong, he almost forgot about her leg. And the doctor's orders.

He tore his mouth from hers long enough to say, "I'm supposed to be doing all the work, remember?"

"Then stop being so hot," she whispered.

Spence didn't know whether to laugh or yell with joy, and what came out was a tangle of both. Clothes disappeared in a rush and it was all he could do to handle hers gently, although when she was fully healed and well, all bets would be off. He fumbled with the condom. He would have written it off to it having been a while, but he had the feeling it was just Hetty.

His imaginings of how this might be, if it ever came to pass, were nothing compared to the living, breathing reality. Fiery was the only word he could think of. Every time he touched her, heat leapt along his nerves, and when she touched him, it roared to life so fiercely he was surprised he couldn't hear the crackle of the flames.

What he did hear were the small sounds she made. A moan here, a gasp there, to a cry out loud when he found one of those places on her body that did the same thing to her that she was doing to him. He memorized every single one. Because he planned to visit them again and again and again.

But then she slid her hands down his back, cupping his backside and pushing, as if she wanted him even closer.

"Can we hurry this time and go slower next time?" he

asked hoarsely, not sure how he was going to stand it if she said no.

"I think…" she began, stopping for another little gasp as he gave a nipple a gentle squeeze. "We'd better hurry two or three times. Then maybe I can slow down."

With that, she shifted a hand to reach between them, wrapping her fingers around that part of him that had paid attention to her since they were sixteen. He groaned, low and harsh, gritting his teeth to keep from exploding. She guided him and he let her, but when he felt the slick heat of her, he couldn't wait. He slid into her with a muttered oath, and at her cry of pleasure at the invasion, he nearly lost it right then.

On some level, he knew there would never be another time like this first time. And in a way he was glad, because this was going to be embarrassingly quick. But any embarrassment vanished as, on his fifth, long, driving stroke, she cried out his name and bucked beneath him, her body clenching around him until he cried out as it engulfed him and he spiraled upward with her.

In the quiet aftermath, as he shifted so he could hold her gently, even now aware of her injury, he realized none of his teenage imaginings had even come close.

SPENCE HAD ALWAYS liked this little home of his. He was grateful for the amount of space, which was enough but not too much, appreciated the pieces Mom had helped him pick out, and the colors that, for him anyway, brought the outside in. Because the outside was what he loved the most. Half hidden in the trees, with the secluded feel, while keeping that glorious view, yet he was just a short distance from work. For him, the best of both worlds.

At least, he'd thought it the best. He realized it had only been good. Now that Hetty was here, it had moved up to the best.

It had moved up to more than he had ever imagined. He supposed a week of heaven would do that to you. A week of realizing that his imagination had fallen far short of reality. Because being with Hetty, touching her, making love to her, had made him feel things he'd never realized were possible.

And he had the sneaking suspicion, awkward as it was, that he understood his parents a little better now. The fact that he could think of himself and Hetty together in the same way he thought of that rock-solid couple who had built this life after tragedy only confirmed what he was feeling.

This was it.

This was his forever.

He was smiling as they sat out on his front porch, sipping hot chocolate while watching a pair of eagles atop a tall cedar tree to the west. They'd alternated between sitting out here with the view down to the water and the back deck that looked out to the thick trees. The fact that it had been Hetty's idea only proved his feelings right. She got it; she understood the appeal of both the expansive view and the secluded ambience of the tall trees.

The eagles took off, one after the other, their calls to each other loud and clear and as distinctive as the striking white head and tail against the dark brown body.

"They're unmistakable not just in looks, aren't they?" Hetty said.

He looked at her then, as once more she'd mirrored his own thoughts. He wondered if it had always been like that, if she'd always been thinking what he was thinking and they'd just never known it because of that wall they'd built between them.

That wall that had been utterly and thoroughly destroyed in the last week. The wall he wanted to make sure was never, ever, rebuilt.

"Yes. And appropriately regal."

She smiled. "That, too."

"And noble. They mate for life, you know."

She gave him a look he couldn't read. But all she said was, "I did know."

For a moment, he was worried, but then she let out a sigh that sounded utterly relaxed. And she wasn't, as she had once been after her therapy sessions, rubbing at her healing leg. She was merely sitting, enjoying.

"So, therapy went well today? You don't seem as sore."

"I'm not. Enough that Liz said I could do whatever I felt up to, as long as I went slow and careful."

He couldn't help the satisfied smile that curved his mouth. "I think we've accomplished that this week."

Hetty laughed, and it was that light, lovely sound he'd rarely heard in his presence before. "I'd tell you to quit grinning like a Cheshire cat if I wasn't pretty sure I'm wearing the same expression."

"You are," he said, not even trying to hide his delight.

He reached out and grabbed her hand, held it, suddenly needing the contact. Visions of this last week rolled through his mind until he had to consciously divert his thoughts, because he was about ready to cart her back to the bedroom to start all over again, even though after that early morning wake-up call she'd given him, he'd felt so sated he could barely move.

"It's so peaceful here," she murmured. Then, with a look

at him and a squeeze of her fingers around his, she quickly added, "Not that I mind your folks. They've been wonderful, taking such good care of me, but..."

"They hover. And fuss," he said, his mouth quirking upward at one corner.

She gave him a relieved smile. "Yes. It's a bit overwhelming sometimes."

"You need this kind of peace."

"I never realized how good it could feel to just...be. To just sit like this and soak it all in."

He had to steady himself before he took the plunge. "So...why don't you stay?"

That stopped her. She'd stared at him a long, silent moment, during which he held his breath, waiting.

"Stay?"

"Here. Where you can have this all the time." When she just kept staring at him, he felt a burst of panic. And turned to the cover he'd used for a lifetime: joking. "I promise not to fuss."

She finally spoke. "Careful, boyo, or you'll wind up with a permanent roommate."

There was no denying the emotion in her voice, even for him, who had a bit left to learn about female emotions. But he risked giving his gut-level response to those glorious words anyway, because, in this moment, the rest of his life seemed to depend on it.

"Exactly," he said.

Chapter Thirty-Three

Spence handed Hetty the glass he'd poured for her before he sat down beside her on the back deck. Then he held up his own glass full of the sparkling champagne for a toast.

"Here's to progress," he said.

She grinned at him as she clinked her glass against his, and he had the thought that he'd never seen so many smiles from Hetty Amos as he had since she'd essentially moved in here. He took a certain pride in that, even as he was aware that sometimes his face ached from all the unaccustomed smiling he himself was doing all the time.

But her glee today was because she was off not only the loathed crutches, but all pain medications, which would allow her to fly again. Hence the champagne celebration.

The sun was dropping, setting as much as it ever did here this time of year. But soon it would be below the tops of the old, tall trees and they would have at least the appearance of deep twilight, especially with no moon present. He liked the look of it, from this spot.

They sat in silence for a while, soaking up the quiet as they sipped at the bubbly he'd picked up while she'd been in her rehab session. It had been a little embarrassing when the clerk, the rather nosy wife of one of the local town council members, had teased him about having something romantic to celebrate, but he'd just smiled and let her think whatever she'd wanted.

Because it's true.

And the fact that he was drinking this with Hetty still made his pulse rate kick up a notch. He'd been so convinced it would never happen, and if it had taken a near tragedy to do it, then so be it. She'd survived, there'd been no further attacks, and the circumstances had forced them to face what they'd hidden all these years. What was now a living, growing thing between them.

Spence could practically feel the energy radiating from her as she sipped her champagne. She was recovering rapidly now, and he knew she was chomping at the bit to get back in the air. So he made sure he was watching her face when he gave her the last bit of news.

"The replacement glass came in."

She lit up, just as he'd expected. "Finally!"

He shrugged. "Alaska. Nothing gets here fast." Especially not commonly needed airplane parts.

"How long will it take Chuck to—"

"He promised he'd have it installed by this afternoon," he interrupted with a grin.

Hetty let out a whoop. "Then all I need is the doctor's okay."

He clinked his glass against hers again. "Then we'll take it for a ride, just to do it."

"*Yes,*" she said, lingering on the word in a way that warmed him. And he liked even more that she didn't question the "we" part of his statement. Like she assumed, of course they would do it together.

"I'll check with Lakin to get a time that won't interfere with anything."

Her joy seemed to ebb a little. "I know this must have really messed up the scheduling—"

"Everybody at RTA is so glad you're okay, nobody cares about a little juggling," he said firmly. "Dad and Uncle Will jumped in, and got almost everything covered. Oh, and when we had to change the Freemont trip, the only thing they wanted to know was if you were going to be all right."

She smiled, and blinked a couple of times, as if tearing up a little. "They're sweet." She swallowed visibly. "You're sweet, too."

"Took you long enough," he said with a wide grin.

"Look who's talking," she shot back, and then they were both laughing.

They sat enjoying the quiet. He loved that about her, too, that she had no problem just sitting and soaking it in. The sight of the various creatures, the scents of summer, the lack of human-generated noise, created the essence of this very special place that was in their blood, their bones.

It was a while before she spoke. "Do you have any close neighbors up the hill through the trees?" She was gesturing toward the thick forest just past the small clearing behind the house.

"Nope. Nearest one's nearly a mile away, and he's at about the same level, just further west."

"But you get hikers and climbers going through?"

His brow furrowed. "Not usually. Nothing up here to draw them, not when there are so many other destination-type trails."

She went silent then, and as he looked at her, she bit the luscious lower lip of hers, making him want to kiss away whatever had her thinking…whatever she was thinking. Then, belatedly, a possible reason for her questions hit him and his mood shifted like an iceberg breaking off a glacier. But he kept his question simple, not wanting to unnecessarily plant an idea that might destroy this mood.

"Why do you ask?"

"I…saw someone up there—" she nodded toward the trees "—when I first came out here. But he—or she, I couldn't tell—vanished behind that big tree the eagles like to use as a lookout."

Spence felt a chill as cold as an Alaska winter sweep through him. It took everything he had in him not to snap at her to get inside, out of sight. Instead, he asked casually, "So you didn't get a look at whoever it was? Maybe it was the guy from what passes for 'next door' up here."

"No," she said. "It was just a flicker of movement. I could only tell that it was a person, not an animal."

He tried to rein in his gut reaction. "So it wasn't Sasquatch, huh?"

She laughed and suddenly sounded relaxed. "No. Not nearly tall enough."

He held out a hand to her. "Come on. I need to do something."

She looked puzzled, but took his hand. She didn't really need it anymore, her leg was cooperating, but he wanted to be sure he got her inside. Once they were in, he closed and locked the door to the deck. When he turned around, Hetty was staring at him and he knew what he'd done had registered. And he saw the moment in her alert green eyes when she understood.

"You think it's him," she said.

"I don't know. But I'm not taking the chance it is." He

walked over to the rack on the wall and took down his Kimber rifle.

"Spence, no!"

He checked the load and grabbed a box of extra rounds from the lower cabinet—for the first time really wishing he'd gone with the .300 Winchester Magnum instead of the standard .308—before he turned around to face her. This was Hetty. He loved her, and he would not lie to her. She wouldn't tolerate it anyway, and he wasn't about to risk this new precious thing in his life.

"I need you to stay inside, Hetty. I'm just going to go look around."

"You can't go out there alone, what if it is him?" She nearly yelped it.

"I'll be fine."

"Like I was?" The difference was that he was on guard now, and armed, but before he could say anything, she was reaching for her jacket. "I'm not some helpless female who can't—"

"I know you're not," he said. "And you're doing great, better every day, but you're not to the point where you can deal with creeping around out there without giving yourself away."

She opened her mouth as if to argue with him. But then she stopped, and he saw the reality, the truth, of what he'd said register. She let out a disgusted sigh. And Spence had the feeling this would not be the last time he'd be glad that reality beat out emotion in her mind. She was special, his Hetty was.

"I hate it that you're right," she muttered. "But I'd only be a hindrance out there."

"Call my folks," he said, more to give her something to

do than because he thought this might really be something. "Just tell them you saw something and I'm checking on it, so Dad will be on standby."

She rolled her eyes at him. "If I know your father, he'll be on his way here by the time I get the second sentence out."

In an instant, the atmosphere shifted as he laughed at the pure truth in her words. "You obviously do know him." He leaned in and kissed her cheek before saying, "Which is a good thing. It'll make our life easier."

He saw in her eyes that she'd registered what he'd meant. Definitely our life, together.

She walked, still noticeably favoring her left leg, which reinforced his certainty that he was right to make her stay here, over to the counter and grabbed up the two RTA walkie-talkies that sat there.

"Every five minutes," she said in a flat, no-compromising tone.

"Make it ten," he bartered back. "And no voice, if possible. I might need the silence. Two clicks is 'all's okay.' Three is 'tell Dad to hurry.'"

He said the last words jokingly, but Hetty didn't take them that way. He'd never seen a more solemn gaze from her, even when she'd been so hurt. He registered the magnitude of that, wanted to kiss her for it, but there was no time.

"Be careful," she said, and it sounded as if she'd had to force the words out past a lump like the one he felt in his own throat.

"More now than ever," he promised. And meant it. But the bigger promise, made only to himself, but the one he had to keep right now, was that he would do whatever it took to keep her safe.

Still, as he went quietly out the door, he found himself hoping to run into Sasquatch instead of a hitman.

Chapter Thirty-Four

Spence left out the front door, thinking his quarry might be watching the back of the house, where he must have seen them standing. He walked downhill, quickly, away from where Hetty had seen the man, but only because he knew the edge of the thickest part of the forest curved around the west side of the house and he'd be able to work his way back under cover. He entered the trees there and, once under their cover, started up the hill toward that big tree. Another Sitka spruce, he'd noted when she'd pointed it out. The big evergreen with the very Alaskan name seemed to figure large in their story. Which seemed appropriate, somehow.

It was up to him to see to it their story had a happy ending. Because in all the time he'd lived here, there had never been a trace of another human skulking through those trees. That one would show up now was just too much of a coincidence. Sure, it could be just some lost hiker, but Spence wasn't going to assume that.

He wasn't going to assume anything, not when Hetty's safety could be at stake.

Yet even as he moved through the woods, as quietly as any native to these parts could, he found himself smiling. She was one of a kind, his Hetty. When it came to the crunch, she'd weigh the options and make the right decisions. Just as she had when that engine had quit on them.

For just a few seconds, he let himself think of their life ahead, what it would be like to have her with him all the time. To have her loving him as much as he loved her. To maybe starting a family of their own, with the best examples of their parents to guide them.

He felt a weird sensation he'd never known, because, despite Dad's enthusiasm for grandkids—and the glint in his eye when Spence had told him they were losing their houseguest—he'd never thought about it seriously before. Never imagined what it would be like, to be a father. And now, here he was, heading out to maybe face down a killer, and wondering if their kids would have her green eyes or his blue.

He shook it off and focused on the feeling he'd been lugging around ever since that day she'd been shot. The feeling that it wasn't over yet, that the hired killer wasn't about to leave witnesses behind. He might be a city guy out of his element here, but sooner or later, he could get lucky. And Spence damned well wasn't about to lose what he and Hetty had finally found together. Neither was he willing to spend time that should be spent building the new life he wanted with her in constantly watching their backs.

This needed to end, and now.

He put himself in stealth mode; that way of thinking and moving that he used when he wanted to get closer to some wild, wary creature he wanted to watch. He played it like the very first time he'd come across the lynx family, among the wariest of animals, especially when there were kits to be protected.

I know the feeling now. That need to protect above all else.

And he knew it would apply tenfold to those kids he'd never thought about until now.

He knelt behind a thick cluster of prickly wild rose. He stayed there for several minutes, rifle at the ready but motionless, listening. He closed his eyes for a moment, concentrating on his other senses, a lesson he'd learned early when his father had taught him that even a human's pitifully weak sense of smell could be useful, and how to focus on things other than what he could see.

Spence was about to start moving again when he heard it. A slight rustle then a distinctive snap. Something—or someone—had just stepped on a downed branch, up the hillside.

He knew what his vote was.

Everything changed in that moment. His question had been answered and he was no longer just checking, he was sure. Hetty had been right; she had seen someone out here. And as far as Spence was concerned, the way that person was acting put them in the enemy category. And right now he had only one: the man who had nearly killed Hetty.

He moved slowly, silently, careful about where he made every step. This was like stalking an already-spooked wild thing. It was going to take some time, but the ending— peace and safety—would be worth it. And he had one thing going for him the intruder did not…he knew this ground. This was his own backyard, in essence, and he wasn't about to cede it to some city guy who thought he could just come here and start killing people.

Welcome to Alaska, chump.

He skirted the rocky slope that was far too clear of cover for his comfort. He stayed, as Uncle Will put it, a couple of trees back from the open terrain. He wouldn't assume his quarry hadn't at least glimpsed him, but he would make it as difficult as he could for the guy to find him. Enough to get a bead on him, anyway.

He zeroed in on the spot the sound had come from. Caught a glimpse of metal. Rifle. A hand gripping it.

A left hand. Confirmation.

Spence double-checked his own rifle even though he knew it was ready; a round in the chamber and four in the magazine available to take its place. He'd be taking no chances with this guy, even if he wasn't backcountry smart. The guy had gotten lucky once and it had nearly cost Hetty her life, and him the reason his own life had suddenly become so much more worth living.

And that thought reminded him that he now had a much larger vested interest in staying alive, so he reached for the walkie-talkie and clicked it. Three times.

Tell Dad to hurry.

Almost in that same moment, he heard another rustling up ahead. Wondered for a moment if his target had heard the radio. Decided he didn't care. He was determined now; he was going to take this guy down. He wasn't a big hunter, he never liked killing living creatures, but this was different. In so many ways, this creature had it coming, more than any wild animal who acted only on instincts it couldn't ignore.

And maybe knowing he was now the pursued instead of the pursuer might rattle the guy enough that he'd make a wrong move, a misstep. And out here, that could be the end of you, in more ways than one.

Spence, knowing where the sound had come from, decided to shift his course slightly westward. If he came at him from that direction, the natural instinct for the hitman would be to change course to get farther away rather than to continue up and get closer by coming in from the side. If Spence could push the guy just far enough, what he knew and the killer likely did not was where he'd end up.

It took a few long, agonizing minutes to be sure it had worked, but then he heard another rustle. And—maybe, he couldn't be sure, could only hope—a low sound that might have been a smothered curse.

Spence headed for his next goal, the large boulder just inside the tree line, the one he often joked would end up in his bathroom if it ever let go and rolled down the mountain. Because they were pretty much on a mountain now. While the formation was nowhere near the towering peaks that surrounded them, it was definitely bigger—and steeper—than just a foothill.

He crouched in the shelter of the rock, again tuning in to his surroundings with every sense. He saw and heard nothing. Smell wasn't helping, either. He waited. And waited. Funny how he usually had all the patience in the word for this kind of thing, but now he was antsy as hell and wanted it over. Over and done, so he could get back to Hetty and they could start that new life.

Finally, driven by an urge he could no longer deny, he reached down and grabbed a piece of rock that had over time broken off the big boulder. He hefted it. It was only a little bigger than a baseball, but it weighed a lot more. It would have to do.

He straightened enough to be able to put some power behind it, then hurled the rock out toward where he would be if he hadn't changed direction. But his attention never wavered from his best guess as to where his prey was; he had the rifle trained and ready. And the instant that rock landed with a thud even he could hear from here, a flash of movement proved him right.

He fired. With the ease and speed of long practice, he sent three rounds in quick succession. One where the intruder was now, one in the direction he thought the guy would jump, and one a step back toward where he'd been hiding.

Selection B.

He thought it with grim satisfaction as the man screamed and went down. Now, finally, the hitman was vulnerable, hit himself. Spence started forward, staying in a low crouch in case the guy was still functional. All he'd need was a trigger finger, after all.

Spence heard the scrambling as he neared the spot where he'd seen him. Obviously, silence was no longer an issue since they both knew the other was there. But concealment was, so he made his way from big tree to big tree, figuring that even if a bullet got through all that wood, it would be so slowed down it would only make a dent. That was his theory, anyway.

He readied himself to make the next move. But a sharp, different kind of scream froze him in place. When it was followed by a distinctive, tumbling sound, he risked a look toward the clearing he'd been edging the guy toward. Just in time to see him disappear downhill, rolling like Spence had always imagined that boulder would.

Toward his house.

Toward Hetty.

Without hesitation, he darted from his cover and headed down, sticking to the path along the edge of the rocks, the trail he knew so well. If the guy could somehow still manage to get a shot off, so be it, but he wasn't about to let him get near Hetty again.

The moment he heard the metallic clatter of the man's rifle—an old-model ArmaLite, he guessed from his brief glimpse as it skidded across the rocky terrain—he discarded all caution and scrambled as fast as he could. He suspected that wasn't the only weapon a hitman would carry, but guessed whatever else he had would likely require closer range than the rifle. And he wasn't about to let this jackass get close to Hetty again.

At the bottom of the slope there was a steep drop and he took it as he had before, down on one knee to slide while catching the bottom with his other foot and using the momentum to launch himself into a run. But a moment later, he was slowing because he'd seen the unmoving shape at the base of the rocks. And Spence breathed again, looking at the out-of-action shape, because he was within a few yards of his house.

The downed hitman groaned, so Spence knew he was still alive. He wasn't sure if he was glad he hadn't killed him, or sorry he hadn't. Time for that later. He crept closer and smiled with satisfaction when he realized he'd hit the man's left leg very close to the same spot as he had shot Hetty.

The man didn't move, but Spence was still cautious as he stepped toward him, heeding his father's long-ago advice to never assume. And then that same father appeared on his back deck, his own rifle at the ready. Spence waved him down.

"You got him," Dad said when he got close.

"I started it, the mountain finished it for me."

Dad grinned at him. "So you didn't really need my help."

"Yeah, I did," Spence said, glancing toward the house where Hetty had now emerged onto the deck, looking wonderful, as she always did, to him.

His father studied him for a moment before saying quietly, "So, your mother was right. As usual. You two finally got it together."

He let out a short laugh. "Finally."

"Then let's wind this up," Dad said briskly, taking out his phone. "So we can start making some plans."

It took Spence a moment to realize what he meant, and when he did, it was as if his entire future had just unrolled before his eyes.

He never in his life figured he'd be grinning while calling for medical help for a wounded hitman.

Chapter Thirty-Five

"He screamed louder than you did, hit in the same place."

Hetty laughed, as much at the happy expression on Spence's face as the words themselves. She was still feeling a little weak, only now it was with relief. The nightmare was over.

They were on the front porch today. She wanted some time to put the memories out of her head. Although she thought she just might hang on to the one of the man who had shot her tumbling down that hillside, and the realization that Spence had done exactly that, shot the hired killer in almost exactly the same place that he had shot her.

"Talked to Officer Reynolds this morning," Spence went on. "He says the guy calling himself Strauss—George Merrick is his real name, by the way, if you want to cross him off your Christmas card list—is singing like the proverbial canary. Reynolds has been on the phone to Portland, and they already have a warrant out for his employer. And our clients are so grateful about how it worked out, they've already rebooked."

"You mean now that you captured the guy who would have killed them?"

Spence didn't speak for a moment. When he did, his

voice was very quiet. "I never thought of him like that. To me, he was always the guy who hurt you. That's all I needed to know."

Hetty couldn't even describe the feelings that welled up inside her when he said things like that. It was as if he'd had all this bottled up inside him all these years, and now that they'd popped the cork, as one of her brothers jokingly said, it just all came bubbling out.

She thought something of those feelings must have showed in her face—in fact, she figured she was probably glowing with them—because he suddenly took on what she'd taken to calling his Serious Spence Look.

"You're walking a lot better..." he began.

"Yes. I still need the cane now and then, but Liz says I'm good to go. Keeping up the exercises and stretching, of course."

"Which you do anyway," Spence pointed out.

"Yes, but I need to focus on it a bit more then I was."

"But...you could do the stairs at the apartment now."

She noticed he'd said "the" and not "your." She thought about all the times when he'd gone there to get something for her, back when the stairs would have been out of the question. Times that had ended with a large portion of her belongings now being here.

Hetty's brain did some figuring and she hoped she was right about where this was going. "I could, if I had to." She met and held his gaze. "Am I going to have to?"

She saw his jaw tense for just a moment and wondered if she was wrong, if she'd misinterpreted where they were in this strangely born relationship.

Then he said, fervently enough that that glow she'd felt

earlier came rushing back, "I hope not. I hope you'll stay. Here. With me. You like the place, don't you?"

She let out a relieved breath. "I like it a lot. I like the setting—minus hired killers tumbling into the backyard, mind you—the view from all sides. I like the way it's laid out. I like the wood, the line of the roof…all of it." She couldn't help herself, she gave him an impish smile before adding, "And I happen to love the owner."

"So…does that mean yes? You'll stay, permanently?"

She wanted to giggle. She hadn't giggled since she was twelve. To cover the silly urge, she put on her most serious expression.

"Well…there would have to be a big change first."

He blinked and she saw that jaw muscle twitch again. She wasn't normally a tease, but it did her heart good to see how nervous he was about this. Because she knew him well enough to know he only got nervous when genuine emotion was involved. Being angry and determined when hunting a killer was one thing, but laying himself open like this was something new to her. And she had to admit, she liked it. And liked even more that it appeared new to him, too.

"What? Tell me, and I'll get it done." His mouth twisted. "Unless the change you want is me moving out."

"Well, that would defeat the purpose, wouldn't it?" she said with a laugh. And decided to quit teasing him. "No, the big change I want is…a bathtub."

He blinked. "A…bathtub?"

"Not that that big shower of yours isn't nice," she said, remembering a certain close encounter that had ended with them both on the tiled floor, wet, slippery and breathless. "But sometimes I like to have a long soak after a rough day."

He was smiling now. "I think we can arrange that," he said. "Under one condition."

She arched a brow at him. "You're putting conditions on my one request?"

"Yeah. That tub needs to be big enough for two."

Hetty laughed, letting the delight she was feeling spill over. "Oh, yes, it must be."

Luscious images rolled through her mind. What she was thinking must have showed in her face because his expression changed. He wasn't smiling now. He was looking at her as if she were that sunrise over the mountains he loved to watch.

As if he were…awestruck.

She couldn't even find words for how that made her feel. And when he moved toward her, her pulse kicked up, her body went taut, waiting, anticipating, longing for the kiss she knew was coming. She would have thought that by now her physical response might have ebbed a little—they'd certainly been indulging enough—but she was beginning to realize that with Spence it never would.

His lips were just starting to brush hers when a firm knock on the door blew up the mood. She heard Spence swear under his breath, and for some reason—maybe the undercurrent of happiness she was carrying around these days—it made her laugh.

"Could have been worse," she said teasingly. "It could have come ten minutes later and you'd have had to get dressed to go answer."

She'd never heard anyone growl and laugh at the same time, but Spence managed it. Then, clearly reluctantly, he got up and headed for the door.

"Your timing sucks, cuz," he said.

She couldn't see from where she was on the couch, but there was no mistaking the voice that answered, laughing. "Sorry, but I'm not used to having to think about that yet."

She was on her feet, much more easily now although the cane was still close by, before Eli Colton got in the door. He spotted her and crossed the room quickly. He gave her a quick hug.

"It's good to see you back on your feet again. You look great."

"I'm feeling much better."

"And she'll feel perfect when she gets back in the air," Spence said, coming to stand beside her and slip his arm around her.

"The plane's repaired?" Eli asked.

"Ready to go." Spence tightened his arm around Hetty for a moment. "And a good thing, I think she's ready to take off even without a plane."

She laughed at him, but couldn't deny what he'd said. How could she when she was so wound up it really did feel like she would spin out of control if she didn't get back in the air soon?

"Good job taking out the shooter," Eli said, nodding at Spence.

"It had to be done."

And that, Hetty realized, was the distillation of the man she loved in a simple five words. *It had to be done.* And therefore Spence would do it. She knew deep down that that would apply to anything, that she would always be able to count on him to do what had to be done.

"Would you like some coffee?" she asked, still not quite used to playing hostess here in this house, even though she felt so at home. Because it was home, with Spence here.

"No, thanks," Eli said. "I just stopped by to let you know we got an ID on the woman you found."

Hetty tensed, and Spence immediately held her tighter again.

"Who is she?"

For some reason she liked that he'd used the present tense. It felt like he thought that poor woman was still here, still important. Which was how she'd felt from the moment she'd found her.

"We got a DNA match on an old missing person report. Her name's Phoebe Smith. Her family is over in Cordova, near Orca Inlet. Fishermen, mostly."

"Copper River salmon," Spence said. Hetty knew the species well, and that it was the backbone of the economy over there, the incredible-tasting fish selling in limited batches for very high prices.

"Probably," Eli agreed.

"How did she end up here?" Spence asked. "Cordova is an eighty-mile, twelve-hour ferry ride with that stop in Whittier, even though it's only forty miles away as the eagle—" he glanced at Hetty "—or floatplane flies."

That got him a small smile, despite the subject.

"Came for a job," Eli said. "And rented a room near Roaster's. But when she vanished after a couple of weeks, they assumed she hadn't liked the work there and quit without notice."

"But how did it happen? Who here would do such an awful thing?"

"That's the big question, isn't it?" Eli said. "And, of course, that's assuming it was someone from here and not some sick-headed tourist who happened to be here. And don't even ask me about motive, because right now we don't have a clue."

"Except that she was set up with that ring," Spence said.

She saw his cousin give Spence an appreciative look and a nod. "Yes. Except for that."

Hetty hated to think that there were people like that in the world, let alone here in little Shelby. She loved this town and the idea of some killer roaming around loose made her queasy. She hoped they caught him before her mother came back home; she was already worried enough about her.

Eli promised to keep them updated—he felt they'd earned that, having found the body. But before he left, he gave Hetty a steady, clearly approving look.

"Welcome aboard," he said.

When he'd gone, she looked at Spence. "Welcome aboard?"

"Yeah," Spence said but didn't explain. She was about to push when he derailed her. "Why don't we go take a look at your baby? Maybe a little test run, if it's ready?"

Her heart leapt at the idea of getting airborne again, so she filed Eli's comment away for future questioning. She was so excited at the chance to get back in the sky, she barely noticed the slight ache in her leg.

But that Spence knew and understood was the biggest thrill of all.

Chapter Thirty-Six

Hetty didn't even need his help climbing aboard. He knew the leg still bothered her by the way she massaged it now and then, but she clearly wasn't going to let it keep her down. In fact, she was just about flying on her own, sans plane, she was so excited. It made him smile. He wanted to see her this way again and again and again. He wanted fifty years of seeing her like this. Hell, sixty or seventy, as long as he was dreaming big.

"Where are we going?" he asked. He had his own goal in mind but didn't want to push her.

"I don't care. Somewhere. Anywhere, as long as I'm flying," she said as she settled into the pilot's seat.

Chuck had done a stellar job; you never would have known the plane had had a couple of bullet holes in it and every wire of the instrument panel hanging loose. Which was why she'd thrown her arms around the startled mechanic when he'd come to see them off.

And not for anything would Spence have missed the look on her face when the entire Colton/RTA crew showed up to see them off.

She didn't say anything about that until they were up. She didn't have to, because what she was feeling was all over her face. For a while, he just watched her, feeling a warmth inside at how happy she was.

You're going to stay that way, he vowed silently.

"I didn't expect everybody to show up like that," she said when they were leveled off at altitude.

"That," he said with no small amount of satisfaction, "is what Eli meant by 'welcome aboard.' You've always been part of the foundation of RTA, Hetty, but you're part of the family, too."

He almost dived right in then, but made himself wait. The time would be right in just a few minutes. So, for those minutes, he just let her fly and soak up the joy of it. She banked here, dropped and climbed there, did all kinds of maneuvers as if she couldn't quite believe her baby was truly fixed. And the smile on her face widened with every perfect response to the controls.

At the same time, she was as alert as ever, watching for other aircraft in the area. And he realized he'd forgotten to tell her something important.

"It's all yours, Hetty," he said.

She gave him a curious look. "What is?"

"Local air space. Dad and Uncle Will put out the word that today would be your first day back in the air and everybody agreed to clear out for you."

She blinked. "What?"

Spence laughed. "You really don't realize how much respect you have around here, do you? But they could only finagle an hour, after that, it's back to watching your back. And sides. Or backside."

That last had just slipped out, teasingly. The kind of smartass remark he once would have made. But he didn't want to change the mood now, so he was relieved when she just gave him a rather arched look and said, "Well, if you want to talk about backsides..."

Spence felt himself flush. Because more than once she'd complimented his, and he'd found there was nothing that made him hotter than her hands on that particular body part as they made love. It took him a few minutes to get his focus back. He tried to ease his tension by jokingly thanking her.

"For what?" she asked with a curious glance.

"For saving me from ever having to fraternize with a customer again. Now I can just tell them to back off because the pilot's my girlfriend."

It got a laugh out of her. "And you can bet I'll be watching," she said, her tone full of teasing warning.

When they reached the point where she'd need to make a direction change, he took the plunge.

"How about we fly back to the lake," he suggested a little cautiously. She gave him a startled glance. "It's always been a favorite place for both of us. I don't want what happened last time to ruin that for us."

The look she gave him then made the caution fade away. Because it was the look that told him he'd said the right thing at the right moment.

"Yes. Oh, yes."

A few minutes later, he caught the reflected shine of the summer sun on the lake, the place where this had begun as a nightmare. He knew they could never erase the memories of what had happened there, but they could make newer, better memories. And he wanted to start that right now.

"Hetty?"

She turned her head to look at him. "I'm glad you wanted

to come here. You're right, we can't let what happened ruin this place for us."

"Then let's make something new happen." He took a deep breath. "I wanted to do this while you're doing what you love, in a place you love, because… I love you, Hetty. And I want us to build a life together, one that is so good that the bad stuff doesn't matter anymore. A forever life."

For a moment, she just stared at him. He was afraid he'd somehow blown it, this most important moment of his life. That he'd said it wrong, or that he'd been wrong all along, that this wasn't for her what it was for him.

But then, sounding almost breathless, Hetty said, "We need to set down."

Fear jabbed at him and he looked at the control panel for any sign of a problem. Had Chuck missed something? Were they going to go through it again, was there—

"Not that, silly," Hetty said, cutting off his careening thoughts. "We need to set down so I can kiss you before I say yes, yes, *yes*!"

Spence breathed again. And didn't even care that he probably had the dopiest expression ever seen on his face.

When they were down safely, she did kiss him, her mouth fierce and possessive. And there, in the precious Alaska summer sun, they put the seal on the deal, hotly, passionately.

Spence knew they were going to build that life. And it wasn't going to be just good.

It was going to be great.

* * * * *

COMING SOON!

We really hope you enjoyed reading this book.
If you're looking for more romance
be sure to head to the shops when
new books are available on

Thursday 28th August

FOUR BRAND NEW BOOKS FROM
MILLS & BOON MODERN

The same great stories you love, a stylish new look!

OUT NOW

Eight Modern stories published every month, find them all at:

millsandboon.co.uk

Afterglow Books is a trend-led, trope-filled list of books with diverse, authentic and relatable characters, a wide array of voices and representations, plus real world trials and tribulations. Featuring all the tropes you could possibly want (think small-town settings, fake relationships, grumpy vs sunshine, enemies to lovers) and all with a generous dose of spice in every story.

♪ @millsandboonuk
📷 @millsandboonuk
afterglowbooks.co.uk

#AfterglowBooks

For all the latest book news, exclusive content and giveaways scan the QR code below to sign up to the Afterglow newsletter:

SCAN ME

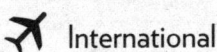
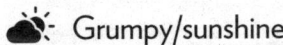
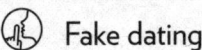

LET'S TALK

Romance

For exclusive extracts, competitions and special offers, find us online:

f MillsandBoon

X @MillsandBoon

◎ @MillsandBoonUK

♪ @MillsandBoonUK

Get in touch on 01413 063 232